Sandringham Rose

Mary Mackie is an English writer of over 70 fiction and non-fiction books since 1971. Work of hers has been translated into 20 languages. She is known especially for light-hearted accounts of life looking after a country house for the National Trust.

Also by Mary Mackie

Sandringham Rose
The Clouded Land
A Child of Secrets

MARY MACKIE
Sandringham Rose

CANELO

First published in the United Kingdom in 1999 by Knight, an imprint of Brockhampton Press

This edition published in the United Kingdom in 2022 by

Canelo
Unit 9, 5th Floor
Cargo Works, 1-2 Hatfields
London, SE1 9PG
United Kingdom

A CIP catalogue record for this book is available from the British Library.

Print ISBN 978 1 80032 808 2
Ebook ISBN 978 1 80032 496 1

Look for more great books at www.canelo.co

Printed and bound in Great Britain by Clays Ltd, Elcograf S.p.A.

1

For my husband, Chris, who discovered the story of the Lady Farmer and visualised most of the major scenes. With love, as always, and with thanks – for moral (and financial) support, and for the loan of your imagination!

And in memory of Louisa Mary Cresswell (1830–1916), the redoubtable real-life 'Lady Farmer', whose pamphlets on farming and whose book Eighteen Years on the Sandringham Estate *provided the genesis material for this novel.*

Part One

Will Hamilton

22 January 1844

Farmer George Pooley hummed to himself as he stropped his razor to an even keener edge. He had just come in from the freezing yard, having given his men their orders for the day and set them barrowing dung. Now he was looking forward to joining his family in the kitchen where, to judge by the hints of frying bacon and potato that drifted up the stairs, his wife was preparing the usual hearty breakfast. His stomach rumbled in anticipatory delight.

As he applied warm lather to his whiskers, a dog outside began to bark. Pooley sent a cursory glance at the window, but it was set low under thatched eaves, the corners of the glass hazed with a coating of ice; he could see nothing but the frosted front garden and the beech hedge stiff with dead brown leaves. He finished his shave, carefully wiped his razor dry, greased its blade and fastened his shirt. All the time the dog kept up its sharp warning.

Grabbing up his coat, Pooley went to the window, wincing as his arthritic hip twinged and pain shot pins and needles down his leg. He threw up the window, bellowing, 'Blast your eyes, bor! Quiet, for—!'

The curse bit off as he saw what was alarming the dog: beyond the brown hedge a mist-wreathed figure, clad in clothes more fitted for drawing-room than saddle, sat slumped on an exhausted horse, too weary to move. Pooley caught his breath as he recognised the man.

'Mr Will?' he called. 'Mr Will, is that you?'

Very slowly, as if the effort were almost too much for him, Will Hamilton turned his head. In the cold light from the sky his face was deathly, his eyes hollowed with shadow.

'Good morning, Pooley.'

'Wait there,' Pooley replied. 'Just wait, Mr Will.' Something was terribly wrong. He hurried down through his house, hearing his wife call to him from the kitchen. Her 'Hurry up, Pooley, your breakfast's ready,' turned into an exclamation of astonishment when he opened the seldom-used front door and went out.

As Pooley reached the garden gate and stepped into the lane, the dog came leaping round him, excited and noisy. He quieted it with a word and it fell to watching, tongue lolling, its breath visible in the cold air, while its master looked worriedly up at the young man astride the horse.

'Forgive me,' Will Hamilton said with a pale smile. 'It's a devil of a time to come calling, I know. To tell the truth, I don't rightly recall how I got here. I suppose instinct drove me to your door. You seem to be the only friend I have.'

'I don't suppose that's true, not for a minute.' Pooley's florid face was blotched with concern. 'Mr Will… What's happened that could bring you here at this hour – and in this state? Why, you've beaten this horse half to death! Such a fine animal, too, and you so fond of it. Whatever—'

'Hester's dead.'

The blunt words stopped Pooley. He stared at his young friend, too shocked to respond.

Will's eyes were swollen, but they were dry now. 'She died this morning. As dawn was breaking. Haemorrhage. They couldn't…'

'And the child?'

'It's a girl,' the answer came flat, then: 'I couldn't bear the house, or the pity. My mother…' He gritted his teeth but the words burst from him. 'Dear God, Hester should never have had the child! That cursed child…'

'Hush now!' the voice of Eliza Pooley broke in sternly from the gateway as she came bustling out. 'We'll have no talk like that, not on *my* doorstep. Come along, Mr Hamilton, get down from there and come inside. Pooley, you take charge of the horse.'

Glad to escape a scene that was becoming too emotional for his liking, Pooley did as he was bid, leading the horse round to the yard where he charged his stableman with the care of it: 'Proper care, mind, that's a valuable animal. It belongs to a friend of mine – a gentleman.'

'That's a pity he don't take better care of his hosses, then,' the stableman grunted. 'Look at it – it en't fit for nuthin'.'

'Just tend it,' Pooley said shortly.

–

Will sat at the scrubbed kitchen table confronting a plate piled with smoked ham sliced from the haunch that hung from the ceiling, eggs fresh from the yard, and fried potatoes left over from yesterday's dinner. Eliza Pooley carved wedges of fresh bread and spread it with yellow butter, leaving the plate near a fat pot of her own bees' honey. She had sent her daughters, her maid, and the two farm apprentices out of the room to find chores to do elsewhere while she fed her husband and their visitor.

'Eat, Mr Will,' she bade him. 'Starving yourself won't do no good to nobody, least of all your dear wife, may Heaven bless her. Or your two poor motherless little 'uns. You'll need your strength.'

The sight and the smell of the food had made Will's stomach churn. He stared at the plate, feeling detached from the scene about him. 'I have no strength, not any more. Hester was my strength. Without her I've got nothing.'

'There's your children! *They* need you! Now, eat.'

Like an automaton without will of its own, he picked up the two-pronged fork and the knife whose blade was concave from years of sharpening. Their buckthorn handles fitted nicely into his palms, comforting in their sturdy normality. Slowly, forcing down each mouthful, he began to eat.

The Pooleys offered companionship without intrusion, the farmer busy with his breakfast while his wife waited on both of them. For a big woman she moved gracefully and softly, expressing her concern for Will by anticipating and supplying his basic needs. Food in his stomach sent tendrils of comfort through his cold body. He was grateful for the respite, and for the silence.

Back at Weal House, in Lynn, it had been all words, all clamour of advice, crying clichés. His scalp pricked with horror as he remembered the nightmare of voices all wanting their say. They had meant to comfort, but their cant had sickened him. *God takes the good ones first, Will. Have faith. Trust in Him.*

God! God had little to do with this. This was his – Will's – fault. His, and the child – the cursed, cursed child. What use was a mewling girl? She could never take Hester's place, never!

When he had escaped the house he hadn't known where he was going. Instinct had guided him through the town and out into the frozen countryside. Where else should he go in extremity but to his old friends the Pooleys? They expected nothing from him, made no demands, forbore to judge; they offered only unquestioning friendship and support. With them, as with no other people in his life, Will was able to be himself.

How long was it since he had first come, as a boy, to Pooley's farm and fallen under the spell that had brought him back at every opportunity? Amazingly, it must be at least fifteen years. He had known and loved this farm, these people, for more than half his life.

Sitting there in the Pooleys' kitchen, a great truth came to Will with a clarity and sureness that sent awe rippling down his spine: this was the life he had always wanted.

He stared across the table at the fire, seeing visions of corn waving gold under an August sun, of cattle growing fat, and of himself walking the coverts with a shot-gun in the crook of his arm, after rabbits. He said aloud, 'I'm going to need your help, Pooley.'

'My help?' The farmer paused in his eating, a forkful of potato dripping egg yolk on to his plate. 'Of course, Mr Will. Anything. You know that. Anything.'

Will looked at the honest, florid face, knowing he could count on Pooley come storm or sleet. 'I'm going to take up farming.'

The fork dipped, and was laid down. Pooley pulled a spotted kerchief from his pocket by one corner, roughly balled it and wiped his mouth with it, his eyes darting about Will's face. 'Take up farming, Mr Will? Why, what put that idea into your head?'

'It's been in my head a long time. You know that.'

'A boy's dream. That's all that was. You're a banker, Mr Will. It's in your blood. Your father, your grandfather, your uncles…'

'Not to mention my two older brothers, and my nephews to follow them!' He slapped his hand down on the table, savouring the rough surface weathered by chopping and baking and scrubbing. It was real, solid, dependable, evincing a life of honest toil with the wind in his face, the sun on his shoulders, the frost breaking up the clods. 'The bank doesn't need another Hamilton. It's already stuffed with them. Stuffed to stupidity.'

Pooley pulled at his upper lip, frowning. 'That still don't seem right to me, Mr Will. You're a professional gentleman.'

'I was. I have been. Now I shall become a farmer. Others have done it before me, and most successfully. "Turnip" Townshend came of the nobility. So did Coke at Holkham. Jethro Tull himself was a lawyer by profession. And Marshall... Marshall believed that "attendance and attention will make *any* man a farmer". You see – I've been reading up on it! Pooley, dear old friend, will you help?'

As Pooley opened his mouth to protest, his wife's hand on his shoulder stopped him. ''Course he will,' she answered. 'We'll both do whatever we can for you, Mr Will.'

Behind her kindly smiles Will saw that she was humouring him. She believed he was crazed by grief and voicing mad schemes in an effort to evade the bitter truth. She believed the madness would pass.

Well, he would not argue. Time would prove his mettle.

Bluff old Pooley, failing to divine the undercurrents, took his cue from his wife and said, 'Well, if you're serious, Mr Will, it so happens that Orchards Farm, on the Sandringham estate, is up for—'

Will grasped eagerly at the name. 'Orchards Farm? The old Motteux place?'

'That's right, Mr Will.'

Fate was opening the way. Only the previous year, Sandringham estate had been left to Mr Charles Spencer Cowper, a diplomat currently based in Sweden. He was not expected to spend much time in Norfolk or to take a close interest in his new estates. Anyone leasing a farm from him would have a free hand, so long as the rent was paid on time.

'How soon will it come available?' he asked.

'The usual time. Michaelmas.'

'Michaelmas?' It seemed an inordinately long time to wait.

'That's when Norfolk farms change hands, Mr Will,' Pooley said. 'When the accounts are reckoned and the audits fall due.'

'Yes, of course.' In his eagerness he had forgotten the tradition.

Eliza Pooley said, 'That's only eight months, Mr Will. Time enough to think about it and be sure you're doing the right thing.'

He stabbed a piece of potato with his fork, his mind working. He didn't want to wait eight months. He didn't want to wait eight days. The decision made, he was impatient to make a start.

'Will you come with me, to see the agent?' he asked of Pooley. 'Might as well get my bid in right away. Can we go today?'

'Today? Why… Well, yes, if you're sure. Why not? I have to call and see Mr Ferrers, at Esham Hall, and then we can go on to Lynn.'

Muttering to herself, Mrs Pooley began to clear the dishes with a deal of clatter and scraping. She evidently considered the whole thing to be a foolhardy venture, and under her breath she condemned her husband as an 'Old fool!' Pooley ignored her, except to wink at Will behind her back.

The interplay made Will smile to himself. How he loved this open, honest, down-to-earth pair. He, too, would find a similar content-ment, among craftsmen and labourers, with horses and farm-stock to tend, crops to grow, living life to the rhythm of the sun and the seasons. In time, he would have a thriving livelihood to pass on to young Victor, his son and heir. He could hardly wait.

Feeling elated, he got to his feet. 'Let's go at once. Let's go right this minute.' A shaky laugh escaped him. 'Strike while the iron is hot, eh? Your business with Mr Ferrers won't take long, will it?'

'Oh, Mr Will!' Mrs Pooley could no longer contain her agitation. 'Mr Will, do think what you're doing! This is no day to go dashing headlong into anything. You're not in your right mind. What will your family say? And what about your children? Will you take them to live on a farm? Who'll take care of them? You can't do it alone.'

Will stretched his mouth in what was meant to be a reassuring smile. 'They'll do well enough at Weal House with my mother. Victor is almost five years old, you know. In a couple of years' time he'll be attending school.'

'And the baby? What about your daughter?'

'Pray don't concern yourself for her, my dear Mrs Pooley. There are nursemaids to be found in plenty. The child will be well cared for, I assure you.' Avoiding the censure in her eyes, he turned away. 'Well, Pooley, shall we go?'

—

At a great desk set centrally in the library of East Esham Hall, Squire Bartram Ferrers sat staring into space, chewing the shredded end of his pen while he considered the exact phrase that would express his feelings without giving offence. How did one tell a beloved son that one's fortunes were not endless, that many more requests for help would lead to ruin for both? If Gervaise did not mend his ways, there would be precious little left for him to inherit.

As for Flora… The thought of his daughter, left penniless and friendless, caused a sick chill in the pit of his stomach. He felt his heart pound, a sensation like a squeezing hand reaching inside his chest. Sweat broke out on his upper lip as he clawed in his waistcoat pocket for the small enamelled box that contained his pills.

Forcing himself to breathe slowly and deeply, he waited for the pain to subside before taking off his spectacles to rub his aching eyes. Then he pushed back his chair and went to lean on the broad window-sill, squinting against the low, pale sun. How he loved this view. Oaks and elms were placed in pleasing asymmetry across the park, and the distant lake was shrouded by a veil of mist. In a ploughed field beyond the double row of oaks that marked the driveway, sheep were penned behind hurdles, with the shepherd's wheeled hut not far away. A thin spiral of smoke lifted from its tin chimney.

Lambing had begun. Another year was under way. Ferrers caught himself wondering how much of it he would see. His doctors had assured him that, with care, he could live for years. What they hadn't said, not out loud, was that he could just as easily die at any moment.

And with him would end generations of his family's tenure of East Esham. On inheriting from an uncle, Bartram's father had overspent on extending the house, purely for his own aggrandisement; Bartram himself had been badly served by various advisers; his son's vices had hastened the decline, and now the estate hovered on the brink of bankruptcy. It was a question of time; which would come first – financial ruin or death?

Hearing the click of the door knob, he turned to see his daughter coming in, a warm shawl wrapped about her shoulders and slender throat. Her shy smile caused him a pang that mingled affection and concern. Dear child! So like her mother, pale and frail with huge dark eyes set in a flower-pretty face. But where his wife had been animated, her eyes sparkling with intelligence and humour, Flora had inherited his own withdrawn nature. Now twenty-five, she was still in many ways an innocent, a timid creature whose wide eyes constantly begged approval and feared reproof. Was that his fault? Had he kept her too close, too sheltered, in his efforts to protect her? If only her fiancé had lived, she might by now be safely married, but the young man had drowned in a boating accident some three years before. No one else had offered for her: her father's penurious state was widely suspected, and few gentlemen would take a girl without hope of a marriage settlement.

7

'Papa?' Flora's voice was small and breathy in the big room. 'Forgive me, I didn't mean to disturb you.'

'You're not disturbing me, my love.' Gathering his forces, he straightened and walked across to take her hands, finding them cold and fragile. 'You're perished. Come to the fire. What have you been doing?'

Flora allowed herself to be drawn nearer to the blaze in the hearth. 'You'll think me silly. I've been searching the closets for my ivory counters. Do you remember, you gave them to me one Christmas, long ago? Narnie and I wanted to play a game and I suddenly thought of those counters and nothing would do but we find them at once. They are so pretty and I haven't seen them in such a long time. I left Narnie searching. I suddenly thought… Do *you* know where they might be?'

'I'm afraid not, my love.' He didn't even recall giving her a set of ivory counters.

'Then I'm sorry to have troubled you, Papa. It's really of no consequence. But you know how it is – you remember an old treasure and suddenly you can't rest until you find it.'

'Indeed, my love. Indeed.'

He watched her indulgently as she bent and stretched her hands to the fire. The glow from the flames drew mahogany lights from her dark ringlets while her wide skirts spread about her like the petals of a flower. Flora always made him think of flowers, soft and delicate, so easily scorched by heat and wind, so soon withered by frosts.

He didn't fear death. What terrified him was the uncertainty of his daughter's future without him.

A sound outside drew his attention and, glad of the distraction, he returned to the window. A dogcart bowled up the drive, bearing two men to his front door. The driver was a burly man wearing a caped greatcoat, a battered beaver hat jammed on to his head. Beside him a younger man sat wrapped in a heavy cloak. Sunlight gilded the brown curls that clustered about his ears.

Ferrers peered down at them, recognising the driver, whom he had been expecting, but too short-sighted to make out the identity of the other man.

'Callers?' Flora's padded petticoats flapped heavily against her father's calf as she joined him at the window.

'It's Farmer Pooley,' he said. 'I was expecting him to call about that foal he's thinking of buying from us. I can't quite see who the other man might be.'

'Why, it's young Mr Hamilton,' she informed him, her voice soft with pleasure, her cheeks pinkening a little. 'Will Hamilton. From the bank in King's Lynn.'

'Hamilton?' His voice sharpened as he leaned on the sill and squinted at the pair below, feeling the tightness return behind his breastbone. What was Will Hamilton doing here? Had the bank decided not to extend credit, after all? Had they warned Pooley off from buying the foal? Dear Heaven, was the end upon him so suddenly?

'What is it, Papa?' Flora touched his arm, her face full of concern. 'Aren't you well?'

'I'm perfectly well, my love,' he lied. 'You run along, now. Go and see if Narnie has found your counters yet. Later, we'll take a cup of chocolate together.'

She reached to kiss his cheek, drawing back to give him a troubled look before obediently leaving the room. He would have to be more careful, he thought. Flora might be an innocent but she was not stupid. She must not guess how ill he was. He must protect her from that knowledge at all costs.

—

Flora paused on the gallery outside the library, removing the small statue and a velvet cloth which covered an oak chest. She lifted the heavy lid and knelt down, ostensibly searching among the bric-à-brac in the chest for her ivory counters while actually keeping half an eye on the stairs. She was anxious about her father, anxious to know what Will Hamilton's unexpected visit might mean. And, though she hardly dared admit it even in her own thoughts, she was not averse to another brief meeting, in the flesh, with the young man whose apparition often walked unbidden through her dreams.

After a few minutes the butler appeared, ascending the broad stairs with George Pooley a few steps behind and Will Hamilton bringing up the rear.

He was so handsome! Unobserved, still kneeling by the chest, Flora allowed her eyes to feast on the young man. But how pale he was, pale and strained. Something *was* wrong! Her heart contracted with fear for her father. She had long suspected that all was not well, but he would never confide in her; besides, she could be of no practical help to him, having not brains enough to understand business matters.

Then through the slats of the banisters she caught Will Hamilton's eye and reality drenched her in mortification. He looked through her rather than at her, clearly signalling that he had not the least interest in her as a person. Indeed, he scarcely seemed aware that she was a woman. His lack of interest confirmed her fears that she was plain and unattractive. Kingsley Doyle, her fiancé, had been the only man who had ever shown any interest in her. Now that he was dead, she knew she was destined to become an old maid. Besides which, Will Hamilton was a married man, and loyal to his wife. She was a fool to think of him.

A flush suffused her throat and face with unlovely blotches as she sprang to her feet and stood poised, hands locked in her skirts as she prepared to lift them and run. But the memory of her father's strange unease held her there, blinking convulsively.

'Mornin', Miss Ferrers,' Pooley greeted as he reached the gallery, his big beaver hat clutched to his chest as he nodded a bow.

'Good morning, Mr Pooley,' she replied.

'Do you know Mr Hamilton, from King's Lynn?'

'Yes, I do. Good day to you, Mr Hamilton. We hadn't expected to see you here today. Is… is something wrong?'

Will smiled thinly, his eyes bleak. 'Wrong, Miss Ferrers? No, indeed. Unless you call it a wrong that I lost my wife last night.'

'Oh!' Feeling as if she had been hit in the ribs, she stared at him, colour ebbing and flowing in her face.

'Lost a wife and gained a daughter,' he added. 'Would you call that fair exchange, Miss Ferrers?'

'Now, Mr Will…' Pooley took his arm, saying to Flora, 'You must excuse him, Miss Ferrers, ma'am. He's not himself. You'll understand that he's had a bad shock and—'

A step in the corridor presaged the arrival of a stern-faced woman in grey, who glowered at Will and Pooley. 'Miss Flora, what are you doing here? Come away at once. Come away. And you two… Be about your business. Todd! Don't just stand there like a lump on a log. If these gentlemen are here to see the master, announce them and be off.'

'Yes, Miss Narborough,' the butler replied, and made for the door of the library.

Behind him, Will sketched a bow in Flora's direction, his expression begging her pardon for his ill manners. Her heart skipped and began to pound, so fast it made her breathless.

'Miss Flora!' her nurse exclaimed in outrage.

She flushed, turning away. 'Coming, Narnie, dear.'

–

On Wednesday 31 January 1844, nine days after she died in childbed, Hester Mary Louise Colworth Hamilton left Weal House, in King's Lynn, for the last time. The local newspaper reported how six sable horses, plumed and caparisoned in black, drew the hearse, and a long line of carriages followed, bearing the chief mourners, the family and close friends, and domestic servants. Along the route, many houses had their blinds drawn out of respect. Flags hung at half mast, flipping wetly in a wind that drove flurries of iced rain into the unprotected faces of people who paused to pay respects as the cortège went by.

Hooves clopping, wheels trundling on cobbled streets, the funeral procession passed out of the town by the ancient Roman South Gate, making its way the seven frost-hardened miles to Morsford, where the funeral service was held in the little country church. Afterwards, Hester was buried beside other lost Hamiltons, under the shelter of dark yews.

Standing bare-headed in a flurry of sleet, Will stared at the obscene slot, freshly dug to receive the coffin. About him his family and friends clustered, all clad in deep mourning, his mother and sister veiled like widows, his aged grandmother thin as a hawk and leaning on her stick, his older brothers and their wives nearby and, beside him, hand clutched in his, his son, Victor. His daughter had been left at home with her nursemaid; less than two weeks old, she was vulnerable to the cold. Besides, he couldn't have borne her wailing. At Weal House it was irritating; here at Morsford it would have been intolerable.

He had himself under hard control, so hard that retaining it took all his concentration. He was unaware of his son's growing discomfort until the small hand tried to tug out of his. Will looked down at the child, not seeing Victor himself but thinking of the hopes and dreams that he and Hester had had for the boy. She would never know what kind of man her son would turn out to be. Victor would grow up without his mother's love and care, without her common sense, her gentleness, her laughter... He sought for her face in his memory but found only her death-mask, as she had lain in her coffin. He couldn't find the real, warm, laughing Hester whom he had loved so well. He had lost her. Lost even her memory. Lost her for ever.

His hand tightened convulsively. The small freckled face contorted and Victor squirmed, trying to pull away, starting to cry.

'Will!' his mother hissed from beside him. 'Will!' She bent and unlocked the two hands, passing Victor to one of the nursemaids who came wet-eyed and sniffing to take charge of the child. From behind her veil, Anne Hamilton glared at her son. 'You were hurting him!'

He almost laughed. Wasn't everyone hurting on this awful day? Why should Victor escape just because he was so young? The boy's own sweet mother was even now being lowered into icy ground while the rector intoned words that sounded thin as the sleet and just as cheerless.

Suddenly Will couldn't stand any more. He turned on his heel and pushed roughly through the crow-black crowd behind him, ignoring their gasps and exclamations of dismay. His sister Agnes would have detained him but, when he looked at her and she read his eyes, she let him go. Agnes had always understood him. The others would see his behaviour as further proof that he was mad, deranged by his grief. Perhaps he was.

He escaped the churchyard and headed through the village, out to open country lanes where hedged fields lay bare, combed into straight furrows by skilled ploughmen, and where rooks tossed noisily against heavy, snow-laden clouds. Without Hester he had nothing. She had been both his anchor and his guiding star. Now he was adrift, directionless. Except for a dream.

Climbing a five-bar gate, he walked out on to the freshly turned earth and sank to his knees, careless of his clothes and polished boots. The land was the thing. The land would endure, when everything else was done. He threw off his gloves, digging with his hands into cold, muddy loam, bringing out a clod of clay. Within a few short months, nature's alchemy would produce good things from this bare soil. Perhaps the same miracle might work for him. Perhaps, by giving himself to the land, he might find a new purpose.

The wind breathed with Hester's voice. 'Yes, Will. Yes, this is the way. A new direction. You must go on. For me. For Victor.' If he looked up he would see her. She was there, on the edge of his senses, wavering against the grey sky and the whirling rooks, her eyes soft, her arms held out to him. Hester...

He didn't look up. He stared at the muddy clod he held in his hands until its image splintered and dissolved. A great sob dredged up from the depths of his being, a cry of anguish hurled at the uncaring gods. And then at last the tears came.

—

After the interment, the mourners repaired for refreshment to Morsford Hall, ancestral home of Lady Mary Seward Hamilton, matriarch of the family. Relatives and friends gathered in groups in the panelled hall with its tall-backed chairs, its plump sofas and its potted plants. Its chill recesses remained unmoved by the heat thrown out by a log fire blazing in the vast medieval hearth.

Only the most insensitive of persons so much as alluded to the odd behaviour of the chief mourner, though later in private many opinions would be voiced. Where could Will Hamilton be? Everyone covertly watched the entrance for his return.

Having done her duty in welcoming her guests, the aged hostess withdrew, making her slow way up the stairs on the arm of her personal maid. Lady Mary was in her eighty-sixth year, too old to be standing in damp churchyards on freezing winter days, or so the doctors had told her. Little they knew!

Funerals always depressed her, though she was no stranger to death. It was all part of God's Great Plan. One lived, and one died, at His behest. His purpose was not to be fathomed by man's enfettered understanding.

In the first-floor drawing-room, where family portraits stared out from walls clad in crimson brocade, her favourite chair stood beside the fire. Sighing, Lady Mary eased her aching back down among piled cushions and sat for a while recouping her strength. Her hand lay pale and thin against the black crape of her skirts. It reminded her of a claw, dotted with liver spots, twisted with arthritis. Impossible to believe that this ancient hand belonged to her. In her head – and in her heart – she was still a young girl. Yet her body was tired. If God called, He would find her not unwilling to go to her rest.

Lady Mary's reverie was invaded by the arrival of her two oldest grandsons. Jonathan and Seward were both in their thirties, the older one thin and restless, the other growing broader every year. Jonathan stalked the carpet with long-legged, jerky strides, reminding his grandmother of a mantis, while Seward took up his favourite position by the hearth, back to the fire, glass in one hand. A gold watch chain gleamed across the black silk waistcoat that swathed his paunch.

It amused Lady Mary that her grandchildren resembled the cattle of Pharaoh's dream – some were lean kine and some were fat kine. The lean ones took after their late father – her son, James; the fat ones were more like their mother.

Anne Hamilton came sailing in behind her sons, skirts swaying, corsets struggling to contain her ample waist. Her grey hair was tortured into fashionable ringlets that dangled either side of a face moulded into lines of disapproval by years of practice.

'We thought we'd find you here,' she said, settling in the middle of a settee. 'Mama, we want to talk to you. About Will.'

Lady Mary took a sip of port and carefully replaced the glass on the table beside her. She dabbed a lace handkerchief to her lips. 'What about Will?'

'My reply exactly!' Seward exclaimed. 'I knew you'd understand, Grandmama. Grief takes people in different ways. He'll come to his senses. But he needs time.'

'Time to make a complete fool of himself,' his brother Jonathan snorted. 'I hardly care to imagine what everyone must be saying after today's performance. I agree it's hard to lose a wife, but does one have to lose one's head as well?'

Seward slanted him a gleaming look. 'Perhaps one does. How would you know? Will isn't like the rest of us. Never has been, never will be. A changeling, I shouldn't wonder.'

His mother quelled him with a look, her face pinched. 'I find your humour in very poor taste.'

'You should know by now, Mama,' Jonathan said, 'that to include Seward in a discussion of any gravity is like asking a crow to sing like a nightingale. The question is, what are we, as his family – as Hamiltons – to do about this?'

Seward threw out his hands. 'Why should we do anything? Will's a grown man. Let him plan his own life.'

'But a tenant farmer!' Anne Hamilton exclaimed. 'It's not the thing. It's really not.'

'*I* say we confront him,' Jonathan said. 'Give him an ultimatum. *Force* him to come to his senses. The scheme is madness. I certainly don't intend to keep his position open while he plays farmer.'

Lady Mary, sitting erect on her high chair with one hand resting on her cane, said gruffly, 'You can't dismiss a shareholder.'

'No, but I can dismiss a managing clerk. And, if necessary, I'll call a meeting of the board and demand that he sell his shares. I'll have him declared incompetent.'

'Do that and you'll lose him,' she argued. 'Will's stubborn, and proud. Try coercion and it will rebound on you. On this occasion I agree with Seward. The best action is no action. Stand neutral. That's my advice.'

Jonathan grimaced. 'You always were too lenient with him, Grandmama.'

Ignoring that, for she had heard the charge many times and was bored with it, especially since it was true, she looked at her daughter-in-law. 'And the children? What does he propose to do with the children?'

'Leave them where they are, at Weal House,' Anne said, her mouth thinning so that a sunburst of deep lines formed around her lips. 'He can't take them to that farmhouse. It would hardly be seemly for him to hire a nursemaid to live in. A man on his own... No, I shall have to keep Victor and Rose with me, though at my time of life I had hoped to have done with raising children once Henry was away at school.'

'Beatrice will help,' Jonathan said. 'And Agnes.'

'Indeed?' his mother scoffed. 'Agnes has little enough time for family as it is, what with her charity nursing, her arts societies, and her visits to friends. And what does Beatrice know about children? She shows precious few signs of producing any herself. Too busy visiting that common little tin-roofed chapel and ranting with the rest of those ridiculous Methodists.'

Sighing to herself, Lady Mary closed her eyes. She had heard it all before and she was very tired. In the midst of death we are in life, she thought, her lips quirking at the inversion. Families were strange things, bound by blood but not necessarily by affection. The Hamiltons – *her* Hamiltons – were no better and no worse than any other family. They maddened her, but she loved them.

Just before she fell asleep she wondered what fate held for the motherless scrap left alone with her wet-nurse at Weal House. Lady

Mary decided she would take the child under her wing, give her special attention. The oldest of the Hamiltons, and the youngest. For Hester's sake, and Will's.

Perhaps she wasn't ready to die, not quite yet. She was intrigued to know what lay ahead for Rose Mary Hester Hamilton.

Part Two

Rose Mary Hester Hamilton

One

At King's Lynn, I climbed wearily aboard yet another train, bound on the final leg of my journey. Friday 3 November 1865 – the date is etched indelibly on my memory. After three long years of exile and disgrace, I was coming home.

The train chuffed and strained and clanked as it drew away from the station, heading out on the new Hunstanton branch line. Through heavy eyes I watched flights of birds scatter, like chaff on the wind, over ragged woods and fields of ploughed stubble. Clouds edged with cold crimson streaked the sky, and the evening star was brightening above the dark outline of the ridge. Despite my tension, exhaustion tempted me to close my eyes and drift.

The scream of the train's whistle startled me and I saw a group of bullocks lumber away from the line, ungainly shapes blurred by a rising mist. Condensation on the window haloed a glow of light ahead. Steam billowed by like a phantasm in the dusk and a judder ran through the carriages as the train slowed, its whistle announcing our imminent arrival at Wolferton.

The last time I had seen the place it had been a quiet hamlet invaded by gangs of men driving the railway along the edge of the Wash. Now, amid a cloud of steam and wind-blown ashes, we slid into a cave of light. The brilliant blaze from a score of lanterns showed up fresh cream paint and polished brasswork. Someone had contrived to have chrysanthemums in pots hanging from iron brackets; flags hung limply in the damp evening, and the railway staff were spruced up like soldiers on parade.

In my absence, sleepy Wolferton had become an important place; it was now the gateway to royal Sandringham, home of the Prince and Princess of Wales.

Struggling with bag, umbrella and cumbersome black skirts, I gained the platform. Men unloaded goods from the guard's van with a deal of shouting and clatter, and from an open third-class carriage a man in working clothes emerged to hurry off towards the village.

'Carry yore bag, miss?' A porter touched his cap beside me, bending to relieve me of the weight of my valise. 'Is this all yore luggage?'

'No. No, there's a trunk…' I glanced at the rear of the train, where a portmanteau was being manhandled on to the platform. 'Yes, that one, with the black strapping.'

'Someone meeting you, is there?'

'I'm not sure.' My thoughts were sluggish with exhaustion. 'If no one comes, I'll leave the trunk to be collected later.'

As I followed him towards the exit, doors slammed and a whistle blew. The train exhaled, panting slowly at first as it gathered strength to take the weight of its carriages and draw them off into the night.

In the station yard, a man was hefting boxes into a wagon already laden with rough-cut timber. The wind came keen, and the first spots of rain dashed silver across the light. I raised my umbrella, angling it against the wind to peer into the darkness by the gate. There was no sign of anyone waiting.

'Did they know what train you was a-takin'?' the porter asked.

'I didn't tell them the exact time, but they knew—' Looking at him fully for the first time, I saw his shattered face. His whole left cheek was sunken beneath scar tissue, as if the bone had been blasted away, taking most of his ear with it. 'They knew I'd be coming today,' I went on, aware that the pause must have betrayed my horror. 'I'll wait a while. If no one comes, I'll walk.'

'Walk, miss? But that'll soon be dark.'

'It's not far. I can manage.'

As he bent to put my bag on the ground, I dug in my reticule for some change, torn by pity and guilt.

He accepted the coin, touching the peak of his cap in salute. 'Thank you, Miss Rose.'

Surprised, I looked again into his ravaged face and saw beyond the scars to a steady stare that stirred echoes in my memory and set ants of horror crawling in my scalp.

'Davy Timms, miss,' he answered my unspoken question.

I stared at him, my mind working, picturing him as I had known him, how long ago? – ten years, perhaps, when I was a child and he a carter's boy going off to find glory with the army, in India. His sister Pam, our housemaid, had been thrilled with her handsome brother in his uniform, then worried to tears when the mutiny erupted, filling the newspapers with accounts of atrocities. Davy Timms had been declared missing, presumed dead.

'Timms!' I managed. 'Forgive me. I hadn't expected... I'm glad to see you came home safely, after all.'

'Yes, miss,' was all he said, his disfigured face unreadable.

I wished I could express my sympathy, but the only words I could find at that moment were: 'And how is your sister?'

'Pretty well, miss. Two young 'uns round her skirts now and another on the way. And you, miss?' A glance swept me, from eyes that seemed to glitter with speculation.

The chill that washed over me had little to do with the weather. What gossip had spread, whispered and tittered around the villages by courtesy of the boy, Finch? Would it start again, now that I was home? I had forgotten there would be that to face, too.

'I'm well,' I said. 'Are you, er, always this spick and span, or are you expecting important travellers?'

'The Prince of Wales is due in this evening. If you wait long enough, you'll see 'im. 'Course, I shan't be around then. They alluss send me off afore any important people come through. I was good enough to fight their fights for 'em, but they don't want to have to look at what it done to me.'

As I struggled for a reply, a voice from the station building bawled, 'Timms! Get back in 'ere, bor, there's work to do afore you slope off!'

Davy Timms touched the peak of his cap again, though his eyes remained hard and bold as he backed away.

Making my way to the gate, I stared out through fading light, my head throbbing. Distress pressed at the base of my throat like a lead ingot. There was no sign of a cart. Oh, I hadn't really expected anyone to meet me, but still I had hoped... Foolish hope. Convention had summoned me back, not forgiveness. I had had to come home. I had to be with my family. Because...

Victor.

My brother's name lay like an uneven flagstone across the path of my thoughts. Every time I came to it, I baulked and tripped, every encounter bringing fresh pain. But I must be strong. The others would need my strength: Mama, Grace, young Johnny, and... and, yes, perhaps even my father. He would be devastated by his loss; that much I knew. Perhaps this dreadful tragedy would bring us closer at last.

Taking a deep breath, umbrella and crinoline buffeted by the breeze, I strode out of the lamplit yard into deceptive half-light that crowded beyond the gate. If someone from Orchards was on the way to meet me, I would be bound to encounter him on the road. If not, there were only four miles or so to walk.

An intermittent drizzle seeped from moving clouds behind which the sky was streaked with cold light. The road was a grey ribbon winding away up across the scrubby heath. After weeks of damp autumn weather it was churned into sticky ruts, mute evidence of the traffic that plied to and from the station, though most of the worst hollows had recently been filled with stones; evidently the Prince of Wales's agent saw that his roads were well kept. I trudged on, keeping to the verges where there was grass and the going was less treacherous beneath the soles of my buttoned boots. My skirts brushed the grass, getting wetter and heavier with every step.

Off to one side, a gleam like a will-o'-the-wisp caught my eye, making me peer at the dark rise of the heath, where copses of stunted trees showed as irregular bulges. On a side track in the lee of a stand of thorn, twin lights glowed faintly.

I peered towards the spot with aching eyes. Was that the shape of a gig I could make out? Yes, a light, two-wheeled, one-horse vehicle was poised there. Faint light slanted across its wet hood and its lamps flickered. Though I could see nothing of the driver, instinct said I was being observed. The hairs on my nape prickled. Who could be out on the heath at this hour, sitting in a motionless conveyance and watching a lonely road?

Unsought, an answer occurred to me, an answer so shocking that a hot flush swept from the base of my spine to flood my face and make my scalp tingle. How pitiful – how shameful – to entertain such thoughts even for an instant. Where was my pride? I had promised myself never to think of him again.

Nevertheless, all the long way from Brighton, behind my grief, I had been aware that every turn of the wheels brought me closer to Geoffrey Devlin.

My heart lurched as the vehicle moved. Its lamps danced, the sheen on the hood advancing towards me, the horse stepping lightly. Fright seared through me – fright mingled with anger, and a curious sick despair. No. No, he mustn't come. I wanted never to see him again. I hated him. But oh... oh, if it were really he...

Torn by a bewilderment of emotions, I stood helpless, staring into rain-washed shadows.

Then a whip cracked behind me. A wagon was lumbering up from the station, pulled by two horses and flanked by four swinging lanterns, two at the ends of the shafts, two more suspended from the high corners of the vehicle. Their yellow light flitted back and forth across the road like tamed lightning, shining in rivulets of water. Glinting brass ornaments jingled as a counterpoint to the bump and crunch of wheels on sandy, stony ground.

On the heath, the gig, or whatever vehicle it was, had stopped again, becoming all but invisible as the clouds closed down and the rain fell ever more wetly.

Drawing alongside me, the wagon driver eased his horses to a stop with a soft, 'Whooah!' and sat looking down from his high perch. He said, 'D'you need a ride to Orchards, Miss Hamilton, ma'am?'

With the light of a heavy-duty lantern slanting into my eyes, the man was no more than a bulky shape in a floppy broad-brimmed hat and voluminous leather cape from which water dripped. But I knew his voice – that quiet, caressing bass with its Norfolk inflection.

Shielding my eyes with the umbrella, I peered up at him.

'Ben?' I queried softly. 'Ben Chilvers?'

'Aye, Miss Rose, that's me. I seen you in the station yard, a-talkin' to Davy Timms. You didn't notice me.'

Had it been he, loading up his wagon? 'I don't think I wanted to see anyone,' I confessed. 'Not tonight. I've come home because...'

'Because of Mr Victor,' he supplied when the silence lengthened. 'Aye, I know. That's a terrible thing, Miss Rose. He was a good man. Some of us in the village was proud to call him friend. We'll all miss him sore.'

It was true, then. If Ben Chilvers said it, I must believe it: my brother was gone. It seemed like a bad dream, to be standing in the wet, windy night, calmly discussing Victor's death with the village carpenter. The presence of an invisible witness, in the shape of the driver of the gig – who might be Geoffrey Devlin – made it all the more unreal.

'Let me tek that there bag,' the carpenter said, and, with an agility that was surprising in a man of his bulk, he leapt down from the wagon

23

and relieved me of my case, setting it on the wagon before helping me after it with his usual courtesy.

Safe on the high seat, I rearranged my damp skirts over the awkward crinoline frame, slanting my umbrella against the downpour. My rescuer climbed back to his reins, unhitched them and let off the brake. With a few gentle slaps of wet leather, he clucked his horses into motion.

Beyond the haze of light from our lanterns, not even a twinkle of lamps was visible now in the darkness across the heath. I would never know who was in that gig.

Perhaps it was as well.

'I didn't expect to see Davy Timms,' I said, making conversation to fill the silence. 'Your wife must have been delighted to find her brother alive after all. But he didn't point you out. Didn't he know you were there in the yard?'

'Oh, he knew, all right.' He slanted me a look. 'Truth is, Miss Rose, Davy Timms and me... well, he don't think as I'm good enough for his sister.'

'Not good enough? You're the village carpenter!'

'It's 'cos I'm lame. One of the little 'uns... she's got the club foot, too. When Davy saw that, he went wild. We've not spoken since.'

'I'm sorry.' Sincerely as I meant it, it sounded inadequate.

'Aye, me too,' he said, and clucked at the horses. 'Gooa-on, you lazy dickies.'

The wagon jolted over the uneven road, its lamps revealing the few yards ahead of the plodding horses. Everything else was wet darkness. The man beside me maintained his silence, only murmuring now and then to encourage the horses. In his big hands the reins looked slender as silk ribbons.

Of all people in the world, if I had had to meet someone on this ghastly night, Ben Chilvers was more welcome than most. His calm, solid presence was like an anchor, holding me fast against the storm. Whatever else might have changed, I could surely still rely on my old friend Ben.

He had worked at Orchards Farm when he was a boy. They had called him 'Limpy' and he had been the butt of much unkind teasing. It had given us a bond; I too had felt outcast among my own kind, a changeling child unwanted and unloved, even by my own father.

Ben's father, Amos, had been our head horseman, but he was always at odds with my father; some old grievance rankled between them. One morning, I had gone to the stable very early and had found the horses loose and agitated; I had nearly been trampled. Ben had rescued me, but despite my protests that he wasn't to blame both he and his father had been dismissed. I still didn't understand why.

It occurred to me that Ben, too, must have heard the gossip when I left, whatever the gossip had been. What had he made of it? Did he believe it? One thing was certain: if I didn't allude to my long absence neither would he, not ever. Uncultured and unlettered as he was, Ben Chilvers was nonetheless a gentleman.

'What were you collecting from the train?' I asked.

'Oh, a few bits and pieces as I ordered. I've been over to Snet's'am – that's where the wood come from.' He jerked a thumb at his load. 'That wind two week ago brung down some old trees on Mr Pooley's place. He said as I could have the wood cheap if I collected it. There's ellum, and ash, and some oak. Good English oak. That's all split, but I'll find enough to make handles and small things.' He flipped the reins, saying, 'Gooa-on, Goliath!' before adding in an undertone: 'Mr Hamilton wanted oak for Mr Victor. That was beautiful wood. The best I could find. That polished like velvet. I worked all night to get that finished, so he'd lie easy.'

Clearing a cobweb of distress from my throat, I said, 'Do you know what happened?'

'It was that threshin' engine.'

'The engine?' My thoughts flew back to Brighton, to the last time I had seen Victor, only two weeks ago, when he had come to see me and told me about the trial he and his partner William Turnbull were planning to hold. 'I don't understand.'

'Well, now, Miss Rose...' He hesitated, regarding me with grave eyes. 'Are you sure you want to know?'

I inhaled deeply, stiffening myself. 'Tell me, please.'

He continued to watch me for a moment as if wondering how much to say; then he said simply, 'The boiler exploded.'

Dear God.

'The engine come by rail,' he added, 'to Wolferton, where Mr Victor met it. I don't know who the driver was. They come through the night, wi' a red flag bein' walked in front, you know.'

'It was a *mobile* engine?' I said in disbelief.

25

'That's right. In the village it wholly scared 'em to death, and set all the dogs a-barkin', goin' through in the dead o' night, a-rumblin' and a-hissin' like some old dragon. They were nearly home when that blew. Killed 'em both. Instant, so they say. The flagman was hurt, too – got a piece of metal in his shoulder. Mr Turnbull got here the next morning. But the trial was cancelled, of course.'

Through the agency of one of his beloved steam-engines, Victor was dead. I would never walk arm-in-arm with him again, never listen to him enthuse about his plans, never watch the sun catch in the unruly tangle of his auburn hair or hear him laugh aloud…

Had I ever told him how much I loved him?

Wordlessly, the big man beside me pressed a large blue kerchief into my hand. I shook myself and cleared my throat, carefully removing moisture from the corners of my eyes. The wagon rumbled on. Ben Chilvers attended to his driving. For that, I blessed him.

The rain had stopped. The wind shredded the clouds so that ghosts of moonlight drifted over a landscape of slopes and hollows, copses and coverts, mangold fields, cow pastures, bare acres combed into neatness by the plough. In the hamlet of West Newton, lamplight glowed through curtains at the windows of a new row of cottages. The scent of smoke from a dozen chimneys tinged the night with hints of warmth and companionship around turf fires.

Guiding the wagon past a pile of rusty-coloured carrstone from the local quarry, waiting to make another new wall, Ben Chilvers said, 'There's been all sorts o' buildin' a-goin' on here lately.'

'So I've been told.' I grasped with relief at a topic that avoided emotional hurdles. 'I'm looking forward to seeing the changes His Royal Highness has made at Orchards. I gather he's coming home this evening.'

'Be his birthday next week. Alluss big doin's then – shoots and hunts and parties and all.'

The royal pair had formed the habit of spending most of November and December, and part of January, a period which included both of their birthdays, in their Norfolk home. The prince enjoyed the shooting. My stepmother had written about the graciousness they displayed in their dealings with local folk, and Grace, my half-sister, had expounded on the subject of Princess Alexandra and the clothes she wore.

'Have you met His Royal Highness?' I asked.

'I've seen him about. When he's up at the big house he do often ride about the villages, takin' an interest. He seem a very pleasant gentleman. As for the princess... ah, well, everybody love our little missus.'

Coming out of the village, we clopped over a crossroads and travelled on under the lee of a low hill to our left. After about a mile, hedged fields gave way to a stretch of woodland that whispered in the rainy darkness. Poacher's Wood. I was nearly home.

As the wagon slowed, approaching the gap where a lane led through the wood to the farm, a hooded conveyance came bowling out of the darkness from behind us. Ben Chilvers hauled his startled horses to a stop, shouting a protest as the lighter vehicle skittered by with inches to spare. It hit a clump of grass on the verge, teetering on one wheel. Then its driver skilfully shifted his weight and saved himself from disaster. He yelled some epithet that was swallowed in the whirl of wheels and wind, and then he was gone, merging with the night along the lane that led to Ambleford.

'Gracious!' I breathed, with a choked laugh. 'He's in a hurry.'

'Some gentlemen hen't got nothin' better to do than career around makin' life difficult for ordinary folk,' Ben Chilvers said darkly.

'Did you... did you see who it was?'

'No, but I could make a fair guess. I replaced them springs on that there cabriolet, and chamfered the spokes to make that lighter, only a week or so back. That's Mr Geoffrey Devlin's rig.'

I had thought – hoped – feared – that it was so. Was it the same vehicle that had been waiting in the darkness off the road at Wolferton? Had Geoffrey been waiting for me, knowing I must come home today? I was trembling, my heart unsteady inside me at the absurdity of such imaginings. Why on earth would Geoffrey Devlin trouble to watch for my return?

'On his way back from Dersen'am, I 'spect,' Chilvers added. 'Spend many an evening in the inn there, he do.'

We turned down the farm lane. Where the wood ended, fitful moonlight showed the gap where the old farmhouse had stood to the right of the lane. Behind it, familiar barns and outhouses still clustered round their yards. The new house had been built opposite, back from the lane, on rising ground where apple orchards clustered. Some of the trees had been cut to make way for the house and its sweeping driveway. Twin gables showed against a cloud-torn skyline.

And, fronting the lane, a part-built wall led away either side from a wide gap where gates would hang one day.

Ben Chilvers stopped the horses, looped the reins and climbed down to assist me. 'Good night, then, Miss Rose.'

'Good night, and… thank you. Give my regards to your wife.'

'She'll be pleased to know you're back.' Twisting his sodden hat in his hands, he added diffidently, 'You've been sadly missed, Miss Rose.' Then, as if embarrassed by his own speech, he jammed the hat back on to his head, tugged it low on his brow, and climbed back to his wagon, circling it to go back the way we had come, back towards his home in Dersingham.

I waited, watching until the manoeuvre was safely accomplished and the wagon on its way, swinging lamps showing red from behind. The trees whipped wetly as the wind rushed by, bringing a fresh mist of drizzle, but I was too weary to raise my umbrella and battle the bluster. Soon I would be inside, warm and dry.

As I passed through the opening and started up the unfamiliar driveway, a dog began to bark from somewhere in the outhouses. No chink of light showed from the new Orchards House. No one looked out to see what was alarming the dog. The place might have been deserted.

Gaining the shelter of the porch, I made out the gleam of a brass bell-push, use of which resulted in a faint jangling from within. I set down my bag and waited, staring numbly at the garland of black crape that adorned the door.

What seemed like long minutes went by before I heard the patter of feet, heavy bolts being drawn, and then a key turning. The door opened just enough for me to see a young maid holding up a lamp by whose light she peered blindly out into the night.

'Mr and Mrs 'amilton en't receivin' callers,' the girl announced in a sing-song voice, as if she had learned the message by rote. 'There've been a b'reavement in the family, but if you'll leave your name…'

I was tired and wet, my shoulders cold, my skirts dripping. I hadn't expected a warm welcome – not for me the fatted calf – but to be greeted like a stranger, by a maid I had never seen before, was one humiliation too many.

Containing my feelings behind clenched teeth, I said, 'I'm not a caller, I'm a member of the family. This happens to be my home. Let me in, girl, and go and tell Mr Hamilton that Miss Rose is home.'

'Miss Rose? Oh… Miss Rose! Oh, I'm that sorry. I didn't know as you was… Oh, come you in, miss. Come you on in out of that there weather.' Stepping back, she flung the door wide and hurried away into the house, shrieking, 'Miss Narbro'! Miss Narbro'!' She took the lamp with her, leaving me in the dark.

As I stepped into the hall, a door to my left flew open. Pale candle-light seeped out. Against it, my father's tall, lean figure loomed in the doorway.

'Silence!' he rasped. 'I shall have silence! I shall have respect for the dead in this house!'

The ragged edge to his voice made me flinch. I took a half-step forward and hung there uncertainly, saying, 'Father?'

His head jerked, seeking me out among the shadows. 'Who's that? Grace?'

'It's I, Father. Rose. It's Rose.'

He became still. I wished I could see his face, but the flicker of light behind him wasn't strong enough.

His voice, when it came again, was ragged with accusation. 'What are you doing here?'

'Why… you sent for me. Didn't you?'

His only answer was a snort of disgust in his throat.

Beyond his shoulder, inside what appeared to be a large room, three candle flames fluttered in the draught from the open doorway. The room was silent, with no stir of movement, no hint of life. And yet in the hushed stillness I sensed another presence. The tightness in my throat increased to pain and I became aware of a clock ticking behind me, ponderous in contrast with the suffocating beat of heart against breastbone as I guessed what waited inside that room.

'So… Rose…' He spaced the words slowly. 'Well… since you're here…' He stood aside, holding the door for me to enter the candle-lit room, 'You'd best come in.'

A chill rippled through me and I hung back, keeping the friendly shadows about me. I could hardly breathe. Ever since Great-grandmama died, when I had been forced to kiss the corpse, I had had a horror of dead bodies. The memory came back now in full force – the square of cloth lifting to disclose the white, wrinkled face with its sunken eyelids and a bandage tied round its head to support its chin; the scent of lilies and lavender, the flicker of candles, the sickly-sweet odour emanating from the coffin. I had a mental picture of Victor lying in the same waxen pose. My soul recoiled from it.

'You'd best come in,' my father repeated, his voice hard-edged. It was an order, not an invitation.

'Father…' Knowing how deeply he must be hurting, I stretched out a tentative hand, wanting to comfort him. But he stiffened, withdrawing himself. A brusque gesture bade me do as I was bid. I let my hand fall, fastening it in the damp folds of my skirts as, with my gaze on the floor, I stepped into the room where Victor lay.

Mother's portrait, curtained in black crape, still hung in the place of honour above the fire. Swathes of black material draped every surface, mantelpiece, picture-frames, furniture. A silver candelabrum stood on a table by the head of the coffin, which was raised on trestles covered in black velvet cloth. Light glanced across the polished lid, showing up the pattern of the grain. 'Good English oak,' Ben Chilvers's voice echoed in my head. 'That polished like velvet.'

Though I had feared seeing Victor dead, finding the coffin already closed made me feel excluded. Was I not even to have one last glimpse of my brother's dear face? No chance to say goodbye, living lips on dead brow?

'It's closed,' I managed. 'Why is it closed?'

'Because I ordered it so,' Father said from behind me.

Grief dragged at my stomach, welling up with an insupportable sense of loss and hopelessness. Why had he done that – to shut me out yet again, to punish me for not being here when this dreadful thing happened? If it hadn't been for him, forbidding me my own home, I would have been here long ago. Frightened of the emotion that raged through me, I stifled my mouth with Ben Chilvers's handkerchief.

'I closed it myself,' the low, harsh voice came. 'Screwed it down securely. I didn't want anyone seeing him like that. Not anyone.'

I glanced over my shoulder, seeing him through aching eyes. 'Like what?'

But he was unaware of me, looking into his own particular pit of hell and speaking as if to himself. 'Cursed steam-engines. Devil's invention. I should never have let him get involved… The thing exploded. I heard it. I knew what it was. Too late. He was dead the instant it hit. The steam, scalding, and the metal… Sheared off in great, jagged chunks, thrown with the force of the devil… He hung there, in the tree. Caught up in the branches. His body torn nearly in two, his entrails slithering out in a welter of blood and slime... Wounds in his chest, his limbs...'

The words beat at me like physical blows. Under their battering I sagged to my knees, my hands to my head as if to hold my shrieking brain in place.

Behind me, the brutal words went on, forcing me to share it all. 'He had no face left. No face. Only a bloody mess.' Quiet as it was, his voice shook with raw passion: 'Do you think I'd let anybody see Hester's son like that?'

There came a patter of feet, a bloom of more light. A swish of satin petticoats preceded the voice which breathed in horror: 'Mr Hamilton! Oh, no. You mustn't... Rose... Rose, my lamb...'

Narnie. Thank God for Narnie. Hands came on my shoulders, warm arms encircled me, helping me up. Tears burst from me, dredged up by ugly sobs. Giving way to my grief and pain, I wept helplessly on the shoulder of the old woman who had been nurse, nanny and confidante for so long.

'You come along with Narnie,' she crooned, guiding me towards the door and into the hallway where the young maid was waiting, her pale face lit from beneath by the two lamps she was carrying. 'Bring some hot water,' Narnie said, taking one of the lamps. 'And hurry about it, girl!' Then she was moving for the stairs, saying to me, 'She's not very clever, but she's willing. Come, come, my lamb. Stop these tears now. Narnie will take care of you.'

By the time we reached the top of the stairs, I had myself more under control. I stopped to take a deep breath and calm myself, aware of familiar furniture and ornaments set in the different surroundings of the new house. The circle of light from Narnie lamp illumined the upper hallway where I discerned a female figure hovering uncertainly.

'Grace?' I queried.

My half-sister came closer, further into the light, showing me her pale face and swollen eyes. Her mouth trembled, her lips forming the shape of my name as she opened her arms and flew to hug me. 'Oh... Rose. Oh, Rose, Rose! Rose!'

We clung together, both overcome by emotion. I remember thinking that here was one barrier torn down at last. Then Grace came to her senses, noticed my state and withdrew with delicate distaste, saying, 'You're soaked! Oh – you've wet my gown. I must change it at once before I catch a chill. Excuse me.'

I had been wrong: with Grace, nothing had changed.

'Where's Mama?' I asked.

'She's in her room,' Narnie said, the tone of her voice making me look at her.

'She's not ill, is she?'

'No, no, Miss Rose, she's not ill, not "ill", as such. But she's very troubled. Of course she is. She was very fond of Mr Victor, you know. She's sleeping now. I gave her some laudanum and if the Lord be kind she'll sleep till morning. It's the best thing. Weeping like she's been she'll make herself ill if she doesn't rest. Don't you fret about your mama now.'

'What about Johnny? Is he home?'

'Yes, yes, and you can see him later. For now, let's worry about you. Your room's this way. Come and let me help you out of these wet things.'

She spoke to me as if I were a child, but at that moment I was only too happy to let her take charge. I seemed to have no reserves left.

—

The room which had been allotted for my use lay at the side of the house. It could hardly be called 'my' room, devoid as it was of any personal touches. I discovered later that my belongings had been stored away in the attics, and when I eventually had them brought down I found that most of my precious books, my toys and childhood mementoes had gone, given for charity or simply thrown away.

A fire had been laid in readiness, but lit only after my arrival. Its pale warmth nibbled the chill from a few square feet near the hearth as Narnie helped to free me from the constrictions of bonnet, boots, crinoline and corsets, and enveloped me in the embrace of a warm wrap. From her gossip I gathered that nobody had been entirely certain that I would come home, or at what time I might arrive. It would have been wasteful to light a fire that might not be needed, and to send someone to meet every train. They had known I would find my way, if and when I came.

This was obviously my father's reasoning. He was determined not to bend in any way to welcome home his prodigal daughter, and no one had dared to go against his decision.

'He's not himself,' Narnie said. 'This has turned his mind. You know what store he set by Mr Victor. He's taken it into his head that he's going to stay in that room, guarding the coffin, until the funeral. All of us have tried, but he won't come away, nor let one of us sit with him. Won't eat. Won't drink; only a drop of brandy and water now and then. "Leave me alone. Let me be with my son." That's what he keeps saying. As if he only had one son.'

'Victor was the eldest. The heir. Father had all his hopes pinned on him.'

'I know that. But it's hurtful for Master Johnny, and for my poor Miss Flora. Cut to the quick, she is. Not allowed near her own husband. He's shut everybody out, even her.'

'And Johnny?'

'Keeping to his room, poor boy. Sobbing his heart out. He thought the world of Mr Victor. White as a sheet he looked when he came home yesterday.'

I had not realised that Johnny had been so attached to Victor, nor that he too might feel excluded from Father's affections. Mama adored her own two children, naturally, but Father, now that I thought of it, had never been as close to them as he had been to Victor. Victor had been special. *Hester's son*, Father had said.

But I was Hester's daughter! Didn't that mean anything?

As Narnie was leaving, my wet clothes draped over her arm, I asked her which was Johnny's room.

'Maybe you'd best leave it 'til morning,' she advised. 'You're tired now. I'll send Howlett up with a tray, shall I? You won't want to come down for supper.'

'I must see Johnny first.'

Narnie started to argue but before she had done more than take breath I added, 'I intend to see him, Narnie,' and she subsided with a sidelong glower, seeming disconcerted by my firmness.

'His room's at the front,' she said, leading the way along the hall where she pointed out the door I wanted. Then she went away, muttering, 'On your own head be it.'

A gentle tapping on the door received no reply. I tried again, and called softly, 'Johnny! Johnny, it's Rose.'

After a long moment, his voice came low, saying, 'Go away.'

I rapped harder. 'Let me in, Johnny. I want to see you.'

Silent seconds ticked away; then the key turned and the door opened a few inches. I laid my hand on it, pushing it slowly wider.

Johnny had retreated to the far side of the room. Back turned to me, he leaned on a tallboy seemingly intent on rearranging the lead soldiers which paraded there. Lamplight shone softly on his lank, pale brown hair, so like Father's in colour and texture. Since last I had seen him, he had grown like a reed, adding several inches to his height without increasing his breadth. Though I couldn't see his face, the set of his thin shoulders expressed stubborn misery. Thirteen is a dreadful age to be.

Closing the door, I moved slowly across the room saying, 'I know how you're feeling. I loved Victor, too. Johnny...' I put out my hand, but had hardly touched him before he pulled away and went to sit in a chair. He had one of his soldiers in his hand and pretended to study it, his head bent over it.

Watching him, I hurt for him. 'It doesn't make sense that this should happen, does it? But life often doesn't make sense. We have to trust that God has a purpose, even if we can't see it. We have to lean on each other and—'

As I reached to touch his hair, he ducked under my arm and ran to place himself with his back to the wall, regarding me with a set face. 'Why did you have to come back?'

'What?' The attack astounded me. 'This is my home!'

'No, it's not. Nobody wants you here.'

Distress bit behind my eyes, as if I had breathed pepper. 'Don't speak to me like that.'

'It's the truth!'

What had he been told about me? What had he heard, surmised, imagined? I couldn't blame the child for being confused. 'If you're trying to hurt me, Johnny, you're succeeding. Does it make you feel any better to know that?'

His expression remained sullen, but I saw his eyes flicker with uncertainty.

'You're not the only one who's grieving,' I said. 'I know how unhappy you must be, so I'll make allowances, for tonight. But tomorrow... tomorrow we must talk about this. We should all try to help one other.'

He said nothing, only looked at me with hard bright eyes, so that I thought again how like Father he was, more like him than Victor, or I, had ever been. Thinking that we should both feel better in the morning, I left him and returned to my own room.

The new maid, Howlett, brought me a supper tray, but I only toyed with the food and left most of it, having no appetite. Eventually I pushed the tray aside and went to sit near the fire, trying to soak up some of its warmth.

Everything had changed. And yet, depressingly, everything was very much the same.

Narnie appeared again, ostensibly in order to help me with my hair but actually, I felt certain, because she too was in turmoil and needing reassurance. The tragedy had touched everyone.

I sat with eyes closed, hands folded in my lap, my mind drifting inside my aching head, while Narnie tended me. As she unfastened pins and loosened the knot at my nape, so the tension eased out of me. How soothing the slow rhythm of the brush in her expert hands, beginning at the ends, smoothing every knot and tangle, sweeping and stroking. I felt drained, welcoming the thought of a warm bed.

'Rose?' Grace said from the doorway. 'May I come in?'

Though I could have wished to delay any more confrontations, I opened heavy eyelids to smile at her and held out my hand. 'Yes, come and join us. Come and tell me how you are.'

She came closer, though she ignored my outstretched hand. She settled on the hearthrug with her arms wrapped about her knees, shivering as she frowned at the fire. 'It's cold in here.'

'It feels warm to me,' I said. 'Warmer than riding the train, or walking across the heath in the rain. It was lucky that Ben Chilvers was at the station. He gave me a lift in his wagon.'

'Ben…?' Her puckered brow cleared. 'Oh, you mean Chilvers, the carpenter. You shouldn't be so familiar with people like that, Rose. They only take advantage.'

'Ben Chilvers has been a good friend to me.'

'That's more than his father was to Papa, by all accounts.'

'Papa?' I queried.

She flushed. 'That's what my friend Maria Kinnersley calls *her* father. It sounds more elegant.'

My half-sister was almost eighteen. She had blossomed into a beauty, brown eyes wide as pansies set in a pale oval face framed by shining dark tresses. She was small in stature, with a slender but generously rounded figure. The only thing that marred her looks was a habitual expression of petulance, with excursions into frowns, sulks and tantrums. Grace had yet to learn that the most effective aid to beauty could be a smile. She remained a child at heart – a silly, selfish, yet uncertain child.

'Dear Grace!' I murmured. 'I'm only just beginning to realise how much I've missed you.'

The confession brought no response, no 'We've missed you, too,' nor – what I most feared – any question about the reasons for my absence. Instead, my sister slid me a glance through luxuriant lashes.

'Now that you're home, shall you be staying?'

A sigh breathed out of me. 'I don't know. I have to decide what to do with my life. I shall probably apply for a position as a teacher, or a governess. But I can't think about that yet.'

'I see.' Grace's expression was eloquent: she was pleased to hear that I was not intending to remain on a permanent basis.

I closed my eyes again, wishing she were not so transparent.

'Your hair doesn't get any easier, Miss Rose,' Narnie remarked.

'It still looks like rusty wire,' Grace said. 'It sticks out in all directions. And all that brushing's only making it worse. Narnie, you must have given it over a hundred strokes. Do mine now. Do mine.'

She had leapt to her feet and was pulling at the old woman's arm. Narnie resisted, counting aloud, 'Ninety-seven, ninety-eight, ninety-nine, one hundred! There, Miss Rose. You braid it while I attend to Miss Grace.'

'Where shall I sit?' Grace glanced about the room but saw no suitable chair near enough to the fire. 'You'll have to move, Rose. That stool's just the right height.'

Too weary to argue, I went to sit on the bed, watching the ritual. The old woman's hands, gnarled with arthritis, stroked the wavy, silken strands of my sister's hair with obvious pleasure and affection. I have to admit to a twinge of the old envy. Grace was still the favourite.

'I suppose you had that black travelling outfit made when Miss Frazer died,' she said.

'Oh… yes.' I could hardly reveal that I had worn widow's weeds most of the time I was in Brighton. Aunt Agnes had decreed that I should play a widow's part to cover my disgrace.

Nostrils and mouth pinched, Grace said, 'Father's not letting *me* have crape. He made Mama order bombazine. Mrs Tubbs came yesterday to measure me for it and take Mama's best black for alteration. It's not fair, Rose. I'm to be allowed only one new gown this

36

winter, and now it has to be mourning. I look perfectly *hideous* in black.'

'Now, child,' Narnie put in. 'You wouldn't want to be wearing bright colours with your brother lying cold in the ground. Would you?'

A guilty look flicked in my direction as Grace said sullenly, 'No. No, of course I wouldn't. Anyway, it's winter, so we shan't be going far from home. There'll be no birthday party – or Christmas party – for *me* this year. *And* Mama has had to refuse her very first invitation to Sandringham Hall. It's the Birthday Ball next week. His Royal Highness had asked Mama and Papa to go.' She pouted over that thought for a while. 'Still, next year he'll probably invite me, too. I shall be almost nineteen then. Oh, Narnie, I shan't be expected to go on wearing mourning when spring comes, shall I? How long does one have to wear mourning for a half-brother?'

Unable to sit still and listen to her prattling, I got up and adjusted the swathe of black crape at the mirror, draping it to cover the glass more fully, then went to the window to ease an edge of the curtain aside. All was darkness, with worms of rain oozing down the pane, touched golden in the edge of lamplight from the room. I thought of the coffin lying below, and of Father keeping vigil beside his son. My heart ached for both of them as I leaned my forehead against the cold glass and stared out into the night, tears hot behind my eyes.

Behind me the voices went on, Grace's strident and complaining, Narnie soothing. I was home, but I had never felt so lonely in my life.

Without my willing it, I saw again the shape of the gig that had been waiting in the twilight off the station road. Geoffrey's gig. Would he have approached me if Ben Chilvers had not come along? And said what? What was there left to say? His letter had said it all – he regretted having become involved with me, and he hoped I would be civilised enough not to cause him trouble because of it. That was the impression that remained with me – that he was afraid I might cause him trouble in the future.

Then why had he been waiting for me tonight? Had he changed his mind? The hope that soared through me made me clutch at the curtain and tremble, afraid of my own weakness.

To counter it, I made myself remember a humid night in June, over two years ago, when the agony of labour had made me will curses on Geoffrey Devlin's head. Again and again I had striven to bear down, wanting only to expel the thing that pained me.

Then at last the midwife had shown more interest. 'I can see the head. Push now, Mrs Jones. Push hard.'

My daughter was born at seven-thirty on the morning of 23 June. I saw her, all wrinkled and purplish, with a mass of dark hair, her little body swinging by the ankles from the midwife's fist. I heard her first gargling cry.

I lay weeping, laughing, drenched with exhaustion, waiting to hold my child for the first time. The women muttered, wrapping the crying baby. 'Take her,' the midwife said, and I saw her companion glance at me as she sidled swiftly to the door and away.

The carriage must have been waiting. Moments later, I heard the clop of hooves, the drum of wheels, and only then did I realise what it all meant.

They stilled my weeping with ether.

Now, left even more alone by a cheerless homecoming, I ached for my lost daughter. I longed to hold her, to seek comfort from her small warmth. I could only pray that the home they had found for her was a happy one, where the child would grow up in safety, never knowing her shameful origins.

I seemed to have lost everyone I had loved. Mother, Geoffrey, my baby, and now my brother… With my forehead still resting against the cold pane, I closed my eyes and let the tears seep out.

Eventually, the hundred brush-strokes completed, Grace stood up, stretching and yawning. 'I think I shall sleep now. I'll see you in the morning, Rose.' She came to kiss me lightly, avoiding the wetness on my cheeks, and spun away to the door, where she paused to look back and add, 'Narnie, don't forget my hot milk. And make it sweeter this time. *Two* spoonsful of honey.'

In her wake, after the door closed, I found Narnie watching me as I dried my face. She turned away at once to begin tidying the room, replacing the stool and laying the hairbrush in its tray on the dressing-table. The silence between us was eloquent.

'I expected questions,' I said, my voice thick. 'I've been away for three long years, yet my sister isn't even curious.'

'Nobody in this house will ask questions. You'd been unsettled, growing up, needing a change. Everybody could see that. So your aunt took you with her on one of her trips, you met Miss Frazer and decided to stay in Brighton and be her companion. That's an end to it. It's over and done. Least said soonest mended.'

The truth had been locked away, the proverbial skeleton in a closet. Even so, I wondered how much more Grace guessed, or suspected.

'It's all in the past,' said Narnie, grunting and blowing with the effort of going down on one knee to settle the fire for the night. 'Let it stay there.'

When I made no reply, she looked round at me, saying, 'You've forgotten it, haven't you? Like a sensible girl. Learned a hard lesson. Paid the price.' She paused, the poker deep in hot coals, her eyes on me as she waited for some response. 'Tell me the truth, child. That young gentleman's of no interest to you. Not any more. Is he?'

But which 'young gentleman' did she mean? A pang of disquiet shivered through me as I wondered if she had guessed his identity. But no – no, that couldn't be so. No one suspected that it was Geoffrey Devlin I had been meeting. That was my secret, and his. It was a small consolation.

'Not of the least concern,' I said levelly, the pain an icy core buried deep inside me. 'You may rest assured, Narnie, that foolishness was ended long ago.'

Two

After three years of being soothed by the constant moving of the sea, and being wakened by gulls scrawking, I found the silence of Orchards oppressive. Once or twice I heard a barn owl cry, and then a fox barked distantly. But inside the house all was still. I lay awake thinking of the candle-lit room downstairs, where my father kept his vigil beside my brother's coffin. The image lay like a weight on me, making breathing difficult, until I imagined that I was dying too, of asphyxiation, and I threw back the blankets and fumbled for matches to light my lamp. Seeing that it was after five in the morning, I set about dressing myself.

I made my way downstairs, lamp in hand, and paused at the door of the room of mourning, wanting to knock and go in, to share the watching with my father. But his bitterness seemed to reach out and ward me off, and so I turned aside and went through the baize-covered door at the rear of the hall, looking for the kitchen.

Instead, I found a side passage, and an outer door beyond which cold air caressed my face, bringing the scent of wet earth and old bonfires. Somewhere a gate closed with a clash of wood, then a dog's yapping began. Drawn by the familiar sounds of a farm's stirrings, I stepped out of the house and let my lamp guide me round by a side path to the carriage drive, down to the gateless wall and across the lane into familiar territory – except that the old house had gone. And, when I looked, the shape of the buildings was altered, renovations here, a new arcade with boxes for bullocks, new houses for turnips, chaff and meal…

But the old deep-littered yard where the carthorses spent their winter nights was the same. Four of them stamped there, their breath steaming in the yellow light that glowed from a doorway. The dog – a cross-breed bitch of tan and white – appeared in front of me, standing splay-footed, barking a challenge. It was scarcely more than a pup, probably one of old Nell's.

'Hush up, gel.' Ned Plant, the teamsman, came to see what was disturbing the dog, and stood for a moment peering out at me, until I came close enough for him to see me as I lifted my lamp. 'Oh, good mornin', Miss Rose. We heard as you was back. Somethin' I can do for you?'

'I couldn't sleep, so I came to...' But my motives were hard to articulate.

Plant nodded as if I had made sense, and turned away to get on with his chores. I wandered about the stable, noting the new wooden stalls and mangers, the high windows where cobwebs curtained the corners, the old familiar tackle that Plant took out to the yard, the worn collars that went round the patient necks. Not least, I slapped and petted the bay cob, Harry – Father always called his horses Harry – and white-stockinged Dandy, who seemed restless, as if he knew his master would never be coming to him again, and a pony whose name-plate above his stall read 'Copenhagen'. There was a boy about the place, too, sweeping out the soiled straw with industrious concentration and ignoring me. The familiar stench of ammonia, the chomping of strong teeth in hay, the clap of hoof on paving, all swept me back to where I belonged. Welcome or not, the farm was where I felt most at home.

Exploring, I found more reminders of the past. Here was the broken paving where Grace had tripped and torn her knee; here the pump with its curling handle, where the men would sluice themselves down in summertime. As I passed the sty, fat pigs thrust their snouts at its creaking gate, grunting, anxious for their morning mash. I paused to scratch their rough heads, aware of the looming bulk of stacks of corn fortressing the rickyards. Familiar scents assailed me – odours of pigs, horses and cattle, crushed grass, mud mingled with ordure, and wet thatch. And from high on the roof of the wagon shed, a cockerel started crowing to celebrate the growing light in the sky.

The glow from my lamp fell on a broad, iron-shod wheel, larger and heavier than any wagon wheel I had ever seen. It lay in a corner behind the barn, leaning against a great shard of metal, and as I went closer I realised, with a shock of horror, what it was. I let my light play over the heap, seeing the twisted ironwork, the sharp fresh edges where the boiler had split as if torn apart by giant hands, and the driver's seat, all misshapen, smeared and spattered with some dark dried... Oh, dear God. Stomach heaving, I stood there, staring at it, imagining the full horror, remembering how Father had so graphically described it.

Then, tears splintering my sight, I turned away, leaving the wreckage hidden by shadows as I fought with waves of nausea.

From behind me, Plant said, 'Begging your pardon, Miss Rose…'

Pushing my distress to one side with an effort, I tried to make sense of what he was saying.

Apparently Victor's death had so unsettled my father that since it happened he had failed to appear to give his orders for the day. Such an eventuality was unknown at Orchards. The men were getting restive, especially Benstead, our old yardman, who wanted to know if he should bring the bullocks back from the marshes to the yard for the winter. He had also been asking about his cash prize for preparing the Best of Breed at the county show; my father should have had it through the post by now, but Benstead had heard nothing.

'That's typical Benstead,' I said, glad to know that some things hadn't changed. 'Always complaining about something. He doesn't mean anything by it. Mrs Benstead says he's just "exercising his jaw".'

'She en't the one what has to spend half the day listenin' to him,' Plant grunted. 'That's makin' the others start to grumble, too. And there's another thing…' He was in a quandary over what to do about the threshing. Mr Victor had been confident that his steam engine would soon deal with it all; now it looked as though they'd have to make shift to catch up.

Benstead wasn't the only one to be in a complaining mood. Even the stolid Plant was disturbed by Father's strange behaviour.

'You must know what needs doing,' I replied. 'You've been with my father for years now, Plant. You know how he works.'

'I know what *I'd* do,' he replied, rough hands fastening on the lapels of his shapeless jacket. 'But it don't alluss tally with what Mr Hamilton want. If I guess wrong…'

I had no energy for worrying about it, so I placated Plant: 'You won't get it wrong. And, if you do, I shall say that I gave you leave to use your own judgement.'

He looked at me askance, but he said, 'Yes, Miss Rose.'

—

When I returned to the house the servants were stirring, raking ashes and shaking coals. In the lamplit kitchen, a lad was breakfasting on bread and cheese under the eye of the placid maid, Swift. She bobbed a curtsey in greeting to me, and made the backus boy get down from his stool to be introduced.

The backus boy was king of the 'backhouse', that is to say he did the most menial jobs, cleaned the knives and brought the coals, swept the yards and ran errands – generally, anything that no one else wished to do, which gave him ample opportunity for loafing about, or pretending to be off about a job for someone else when actually he'd sneaked off after rabbits, or gone fishing. This lad's name was Jarvis, I seem to recall, though our backus boys changed so many times over the years I can't be sure. With one or two exceptions, they blend into a single image of miscreance.

Learning that my father was still keeping his grim watch, I had Swift prepare a breakfast tray, which I took to him myself. In the hallway the young maid Howlett, emerging from the candle-lit drawing-room with an empty coal bucket in her hand, jumped as if I were a ghost. Eyes wide in her dirt-streaked face, she sidled around me in a wide circle.

'Door!' my father's hoarse voice rasped. 'Close the door, girl!'

Evidently frightened half to death by what lay inside the room, Howlett glanced back at the door, and then at me. She seemed relieved when I gestured her on and she scuttled past me into the shadows.

I found Father slumped in an armchair, an empty brandy bottle on the table beside him, his head supported on one hand. As I bent to set the tray down and remove the bottle, he grated, 'Take it away.'

'You have to eat,' I replied.

He looked at me as if he hated me, eyes bright and hard in deep bruised sockets. His face was haggard, cheeks shadowed by a growth of beard. He had neither washed nor changed his linen since Victor died.

But his piteous state failed to move me. I felt nothing. Nothing but a cool, bleak emptiness. For that I was fiercely glad. At that moment I believed he had lost the power to hurt me.

'Take it away!' His voice rose in a familiar way – a way that usually made me argue, that usually led to an escalation of our differences. This time, though, I no longer cared. If he wished to torment himself then so be it.

I picked up the tray with the empty brandy bottle on it and, conscious of his animosity boring at my back, made for the door.

'Bring me another bottle,' he ordered. 'And close the door!'

Without a backward glance, I left him. I told Swift that when Narnie came down, with the key to the cupboard, another bottle of brandy was to be taken to my father.

'He'll kill himself, Miss Rose,' Mrs Benstead fretted.

'Yes, he probably will. But if that's what he wants why should we stop him? He's a grown man.'

As I turned away I saw her gape at me in disbelief.

Hearing Narnie go into Mama's room, I went to the door and saw my stepmother being helped to sit up in bed so that she might be given her morning tray. Narnie's bulk blocked my view as she bent over the bed, so I had time to see the tray, which lay on the dressing-table, set with a pretty cloth, a dish of oatmeal porridge, dainty slices of bread, boiled egg under a knitted cosy, and a thin china cup with its matching tea-pot and milk jug. Narnie had always taken special care of Mama, but that tray looked as if it had been prepared to tempt the appetite of an invalid.

'Mama…' I began, and as Narnie turned, startled to find me there, I saw my stepmother for the first time in three years. The sight drove all other thought from my mind.

She had lost at least three stones in weight, and her face was pallid, shadowed with grey beneath her eyes and in the hollows of her cheeks. Even the turning of her head seemed to cause her an immense effort and her eyes, as she looked at me, seemed lifeless. Such a change had not been effected in the few days since Victor died. She must have been sick for months.

'Mama!' Concern threw me across the room to kneel beside the bed. 'Mama, are you ill?' I turned on Narnie, blaming her for this. 'Why didn't you tell me? You said she wasn't ill! Oh, Mama, why didn't you let me know…?'

She stared at me with a slight pucker to her brow, as if she couldn't quite place who I was. She said vaguely, 'Why, Rose! My dear, you're home. Oh…' Her mouth sagged open as her eyes welled with tears and she threw a hand to stifle a moan. 'Victor! Victor is dead! Oh, Rose, how can we bear it? How will your father ever do without him? Poor Will. Poor Will!'

'Hush, my lamb.' Narnie pushed me out of the way as she bent to offer comfort and a clean handkerchief, crooning softly as was ever her way.

I backed away, feeling as if I were trapped in one of my nightmares.

After a while, having calmed Mama, Narnie turned and took my arm, easing me towards the door. 'She'll be all right. Don't worry. She's not really sick, she's just not herself in the mornings. It's the laudanum. But she needs it if she's to sleep at all. Wait until later. You'll see, she'll be more her normal self later.'

Too shocked to do other than obey, I allowed myself to be persuaded out of the room. The door closed in my face.

–

I found myself in the dogcart, driving along a lane. I don't recall how I got there, only that I snapped back into awareness to find myself at the reins, the cart bowling along. Overhead the clouds were breaking, allowing glints of sunlight to break through. For a frantic, panicky moment I didn't know where I was. The woods and fields were unfamiliar, the lane like so many others. Then I recognised a gateway, whose gate had a broken middle bar, and all at once I knew that the road would lead me to Feltham Grange. Like a homing pigeon, with nothing but instinct to guide me, I was on my way to see Cassie Wyatt. She was my oldest, dearest friend. Nothing would ever come between Cassie and me; we had always sworn it.

We had been friends since childhood. Cassie's mother, Mrs Lydia Wyatt, was actually a cousin of Mama's, though there was some estrangement between them because of a reversal of fortunes. It had always galled Mama that her low-born cousin, now married to a wealthy merchant, could live in luxury while she, though daughter to the squire of Esham, was reduced to counting pennies.

When Squire Bartram Ferrers died a bankrupt, the Wyatts offered his daughter a home with them, but Flora had no intention of becoming an object of charity to her despised cousin. Another answer presented itself and she accepted gladly when my father, needing a mother for his two small children, asked for her hand in marriage.

Since Orchards Farm lay only a few miles from Feltham Grange, the irrepressible Lydia Wyatt had begun to visit. Mother of eight children, she was a lady of large presence and larger personality, not to be deflected from her purpose. Thanks to her generosity, her unselfish sympathy for her dispossessed cousin, and not least her middle-class awe of the noble blood among my own ancestors, I had enjoyed lessons with the Wyatt girls and their governess.

Those years gave me a good grounding for what came later; my aged great-grandmother, Lady Mary Seward, left money in her will for my education 'as a lady', so at the age of fourteen, at the suggestion of Aunt Agnes, I was sent to Miss Waterburn's Academy for Young Ladies, in Cambridge. But I kept my close ties with the Wyatts, corresponding regularly with Cassie, and for Mrs Wyatt I held a warm regard. She had allowed me to feel almost a part of her family.

Nevertheless, on this first visit in three years, something caused me to eschew the familiarity of the side door. I approached the Grange by its main entrance, where I tethered my horse by the porch and pulled the bell.

After a short while the door opened and the butler stood there, his look of astonishment smothered at birth by polite, professional detachment.

'Won't you come in, Miss Hamilton?'

As I stepped past him, a voice enquired, 'Who is it, Reed?' and Mrs Wyatt appeared in the inner doorway of the lobby, draped in a light, flounced, morning gown of puce and magenta. At first, with the brightness of the day behind me, she didn't recognise me, and when she did she didn't believe her senses. 'Rose Hamilton?' she stared at me as I stepped further into the lobby. 'It *is* you. But… whatever do you mean by coming here?'

Her words came like a slap. 'I'm sorry, Mrs Wyatt. If I'm not welcome—'

She took my arm, her brow clouded with sympathy as she drew me into the inner hallway. 'My dear, I didn't mean to turn you away. You will always be welcome in this house, never doubt that. But, my dear child, with your brother lying unburied… You should stay within doors until after the funeral. Don't you know that? What is your mama thinking of?'

Relief made me weak. I had feared that she was rejecting me because of my shameful past. 'I'm afraid… I never thought—'

But Mrs Wyatt, dear soul, was always ready to make allowances – to be over-indulgent, according to my stepmother. 'Stuff and nonsense!' she cut me off. 'You were anxious to see Cassie as soon as you could. That's why you came. I'm sure no one will think any the worse of you for that. We've missed you, my dear. The house hasn't been the same without your visits. Come…'

In the staircase hall, lined with portraits and lit from high above by the domed glass lantern, she paused to give me a long, assessing look. 'How *are* you, Rose? You look… older.'

'How should I look, with my brother lying dead and my parents half mad with grief?'

Her eyes flickered and softened. 'Of course. Yes. Victor was a fine young man. So much promise. It's a great sorrow to us all. Please accept my deepest sympathies, my dear. My poor Felicity is distraught because of it. You know what a soft heart she has.'

'Yes, indeed,' I said.

'And… Forgive me. It's hardly the time to rake over the past, I know, but I very much need to know… Your going away. It didn't have anything to do with my son, did it?'

I held my breath as my thoughts scattered wildly. 'Your son?'

Her eyes met mine, anxious and probing. 'It wasn't because of Hal that—'

'No, Mrs Wyatt, it was not Hal's fault.'

I saw her relax and her fingers pressed my arm confidingly. 'That's what he told me, of course. Hal is far from an angel, but not even he… But there was some talk – wicked gossip, so it seems. I heard a little of it. And then your father implied…'

'My father?' I prompted. 'What did he say?'

'He heard me discussing your absence with your mama,' she confessed. 'He all but threw me out of the house. And… he made veiled accusations about Hal.'

He would! I thought. Couldn't he leave well alone? Did he have to spoil my relationship with the Wyatts, too?

She waited, watching me, wanting explanations – deserving them, it seemed to me.

'I did have an argument with Hal,' I replied. 'That's all it was. We quarrelled, and we were seen by our backus boy – a stupid, lazy boy named Finch. He thought I was in danger, and went running for help. My father… misunderstood what had happened.'

'You mean he thought it prudent for you to go away for a while – before my wicked son could ruin your reputation,' she guessed sadly. 'Yes, that would be like Will Hamilton. Thank you for your frankness, Rose. I must confess it has been troubling me. I'm truly sorry for Hal's part in it. I hope you will be good enough not to hold it against the rest of us.'

'I could never think ill of any of you,' I assured her.

'Bless you!' With tears in her eyes, she reached to kiss my cheek and hug me. 'You've set my mind at rest. I tried to talk to Flora, but she wouldn't listen. She prefers to sweep all hint of unpleasantness under the carpet. I fear, my dear, that I don't call at Orchards as frequently as I used to do. I cannot tolerate your father's rudeness. I pity my cousin, married to such a man.'

I opened my mouth, about to make excuses for my father, but Mrs Wyatt stopped me with a gesture.

'Forgive me, my dear. He's your father, I know. It's inexcusable of me to complain of him to you.'

'I know he's not an easy man.'

Her wry expression appreciated the understatement. 'No, indeed.'

'But he does care for Mama.'

'Yes,' she sighed. 'Yes, I'm sure you're right. As for Hal, my dear… I have a feeling… I fear we may never see Hal again.'

'Is he ill?' I asked in concern. 'I thought he was planning to come home very soon.'

'He was. Yes, he was. But his plans have changed. He and Melinda – his wife, you know – have decided to go west, to seek their fortune in California.'

'He's married?' I asked, surprised and somehow relieved. I had not looked forward to encountering Hal again.

'Yes, didn't you know? The wedding took place… why, it must be four months ago. Now that the war's ended over there, everyone is anxious to make fresh starts, and Hal, he was always too… too energetic, to be confined in our small, provincial England. America… they call it the New World, don't they? Land of opportunity, for those who have the courage to take it. And now Robert's gone, too. Did you know? To New Zealand. I've lost both my sons.'

She still had six daughters, I thought, but as I knew to my cost girls didn't really count. 'Who knows,' I comforted, 'they may make their fortunes, and come home rich men – or send for you to visit them.'

'That's what I told Mr Wyatt!' she smiled, clasping my arm. 'Oh, thank you, Rose. I knew you would understand. But why are we standing in the hall? Cassie has missed you. Come up and see her.'

She led the way up the stairs, puffing a little as if the effort tired her, and paused on the gallery to say, 'Did you know your aunt Agnes is here? She's such a comfort to us all, especially Cassie. But, my dear,

I must ask you to excuse me. I must go and get dressed. You know your way.'

Indeed I did. Over the years I had come many times to Cassie's room. She was my best friend, the gentlest of souls. Like me, she rejoiced in the turn of the seasons and the beauties of nature, but she also possessed many qualities that I lacked; she was obedient, clever, tidy, patient... I could never understand why it had pleased God to make her fall under the wheels of a laden hay wagon, so that at the age of eleven she lost the use of her legs and was confined to bed for the rest of her life.

But after three years I stood uncertainly before the door, my hand raised to knock. I could hear female voices inside. If Aunt Agnes was here, how would she greet me? And what of Cassie? She had always been so perceptive; she would see through any prevarications.

My knuckles rapped on the panel, bringing a silence to the room beyond, then my aunt's voice called, 'Come in, Sarah.'

The blue and white room had not changed. A fire burned in the grate; Chinese screens shielded the bed from draughts; a faint sick-room odour of mingled liniment, perfume and carbolic soap swept me back to memories garnered over many years.

Against that setting, the occupants of the bed formed a tableau that burned itself into my mind. Framed in swathes of blue bed-curtain, Cassie sat propped in a nest of pillows; and, nestling close beside her, brush raised in the act of grooming my dearest friend's hair, was my aunt Agnes. They were both wearing loose wraps of complementary blues, their hair flowing loose, Cassie's softly fair, wispy with curls, Agnes's a rough, stringy grey, as it had grown after her experiences of nursing in the Crimea. They stared at me, both caught in a moment of surprise – of guilt? – that seemed to last for ever.

I felt like an interloper, embarrassed for no reason I could have put into words. Then other emotions tumbled over me in waves – hurt, resentment, jealousy... In all my life I had had only two real friends – Cassie and my aunt. Agnes had deserted me three bitter years ago, but Cassie... Cassie had been there still, a calm anchorage for me to return to in need. Or so I had believed. Her intimacy with my aunt made it seem as though a door were being slammed in my face, being bolted, locked and chained against me, never to reopen.

'Forgive me...' I began uncertainly.

'What are you doing here?' Agnes climbed from the bed, away from me, hampered by a certain stiffness in her joints. She stood there with the hairbrush clasped in her hand, arms crossed in a gesture that warded me off. 'We thought you were the maid.'

Our eyes met and I saw that she remained implacably hostile towards me. I also saw a flicker of something else that darted away like a rabbit down a hole. Fear, perhaps? Self-reproach? It was gone before I could identify it.

'Rose!' Cassie's vibrant voice drew my attention to her soft, sad expression as she held out her arms in welcome. 'Oh, my poor Rose! I grieve for you. I am so very sorry about Victor. I know how much you will miss him. But he's safe now, beyond further hurt. Think of that, Rose. Try not to grieve too much, my dear friend. Oh… I am so very glad to see you. If only it were not such sadness that had brought you, how happy I should be.'

'And I.' I walked to the bed and took the hand she stretched out to me. Once I would have flown to hug her, but that time was past. 'You look well.' It was as near the truth as it could ever be.

'So do you,' she lied.

Into the lengthening silence, Agnes said irritably, 'I can't believe you would be so irresponsible as to show yourself in public at this time, Rose. Does your father know you're here?'

'I didn't ask his permission, if that's what you mean, Aunt Agnes.' Letting go of Cassie's hand, I faced my aunt across the expanse of the bed, keeping my voice low and as polite as could be. 'You always bade me think for myself, did you not? You exhorted me to break the mould of convention – to follow your example.'

Unable to deny this charge, she caught her breath and narrowed her eyes. 'And is this how you intend to repay me – by making a spectacle of yourself? By becoming the object of more gossip, from the moment you return? Before your brother is even decently in his grave? I may have broken a few rules in my youth, but at least I knew when to show respect. I didn't try to drag my whole family to shame!'

Blood burned in my cheeks as we stared at each other across the bed, she, coldly hostile and I wishing all this scene unplayed. I had come here to find solace, not to add to my tally of sins. But I could find no repentance in me. At that moment I hated my aunt.

'I'm of age now,' I said. 'No one is obliged to feel responsible for my actions except myself.'

'Don't quarrel,' Cassie said anxiously, looking from one to the other of us. '*Please* don't quarrel. You must think of Victor. He wouldn't have wanted bitter words to be exchanged, not at this time.'

'I don't believe Rose cares about Victor,' Agnes replied. 'I don't believe she cares, or ever cared, for anyone but herself.'

The cruelty was calculated. I knew it, but still it hurt me like a knife in my ribs. That she, who had always defended me, could turn and inflict such pain, was a bitter discovery. I wanted to be gone from that place.

'Don't go!' Cassie called after me as I turned for the door. 'Oh, Agnes, go after her. Tell her you didn't mean it. Of course she cares about Victor. Rose, please—'

The door closed behind me. In the hallway I stood a moment, fighting my distress, forcing the tears to recede. I could hear Cassie and Agnes arguing beyond the closed door and though I couldn't distinguish any words the tone of their voices made me feel like an eavesdropper. Taking a breath, I lifted my head high, straightened my back, and departed.

Later that day I went into the candle-lit room where the coffin rested on its trestles. The room was silent, the shutters closed, the window drapes drawn to exclude all light and sound: even the clock had been stopped lest it disturb the departed. And, slumped in an armchair, Father was sleeping.

Beside him a tray lay on the floor, a cup with dregs of tea, a plate with a few crumbs. There was also a brandy bottle, but it was still full. So, he had eaten some food, and he had resisted the temptation to open the brandy. Drained as I felt after my visit to the Grange, I was relieved to know that some gleam of sanity had broken through the dark clouds of his grief. Perhaps I had reached him, however briefly.

As I had done so many times over the years, I stood before the hearth looking up at my dead mother's portrait. Between her drapes of black crape she smiled out dispassionately, the candle-light giving her a semblance of life. Like me, she had curling red hair and blue eyes; her demeanour was calm, elegant and assured. My imagination, and the stories I had been told about her, had dreamed her into the sort of woman I tried to be – independent, strong, unafraid. She too had been a rebel: only daughter of Viscount Colworth, she had married Will Hamilton, the banker's younger son, much against the wishes of her family. They had disowned her as a result. Had she cared about that? Somehow I thought not. She had loved my father, and he her. He had never stopped loving her, never stopped grieving for her.

Would she have loved me, if she had lived? Would she have approved of a daughter who was stubborn, rebellious, wilful? Try as I would, I was not the Curly-locks type. To sit on a cushion and sew a fine seam was to me the epitome of boredom; reading I enjoyed, but otherwise I was hopeless at feminine pastimes. I would have liked to paint a wagon, or thatch a stack, or muck out the pig, but none of those things was 'seemly'.

The candle-lit twinkle in Mother's eye seemed to sympathise. But what would she have thought of my disgrace, and now our losing Victor? She wouldn't tell me. She smiled into space, over my head.

Perhaps that was answer enough.

—

During the next few days I stayed within doors as convention demanded, accustoming myself to my new home. The villa was grander than the old farmhouse, crammed with heavy furniture, clothed in bobbled velvet, with ornaments and framed photographs in every space and aspidistras growing in big pots. It even had a separate bathroom, with a claw-foot bath and a water tap, and next to it the latest style of water-closet. Outside, gardens were taking shape. Grass had been sown, and in spare moments Benstead and his lad were making flower beds, planting shrubs and preparing the conservatory. With bricks still lying in piles, the drive needing shingle, and a gap in the unfinished wall, the place had a raw, cold appearance.

Mama remained in her room, too distraught to face what lay below. Johnny kept sullenly to himself, somewhere about the farm or in his room, appearing at meals to toy with his food. And Grace went about with a long face, picking arguments over every trifle.

Father, as he had sworn he would, stayed beside the coffin with scarcely a break. Each night he drank himself into a snoring stupor, but during the day he kept his wits, needing them to receive the stream of callers who came to offer their respects. Not that he had much to say to them, or to any of us. He kept his feelings locked tight away, as if to deny us the right to share his grief.

I made it my business to keep a watch for callers and to be on hand when one of the maids answered the door, so that Victor's lying-in should be conducted with dignity. By thus confronting most of our friends and neighbours directly, I was able to assess their reactions to my long absence.

They were mostly polite, anxious to express their sorrow at our loss, but behind their outer sanguinity curiosity simmered. Naturally there had been gossip when I left so suddenly; now, I gave it the lie, telling half-truths with a composure that disguised a maelstrom of unease. Yes, I had been away a long time. In Brighton, yes, that was so. Companion to a friend of Aunt Agnes's. A dear old lady, Henrietta Frazer. Dead now, much to my sorrow. As for the future? – I had had no time to think of that yet. Not yet… Most of them appeared to accept what I said. Why should they not, when most of it was true?

Nevertheless, I was no longer entirely accepted among the ranks of the respectable majority. Questions remained unanswered; I was under observation.

My warmest welcome came from our old friends the Pooleys, who both embraced me with love and concern. Their nephew Basil was with them, more subdued than I had ever seen him, and it was with a shock that I realised how deeply my brother's death had affected him. They had been business partners as well as good friends. He shook my hand and held it tightly as he tried to articulate his feelings, eventually turning away, a glaze of tears in his blue eyes.

None of it seemed real. I kept thinking I would soon wake to find everything as it had been before I left home. I would have given anything for such a miracle.

But cold reality ground on.

One afternoon, hearing the doorbell ring, I left the patchwork sewing which gave me something to do with my hands and went into the hall in time to see young Howlett opening the front door.

'Well, my girl,' a male voice greeted in an energetic way. 'Is your master at home?'

Howlett stood there, holding on to the door, gaping at the man in stupefied silence. Curious, I moved further into the hallway, and when he saw me he brushed past the maid and strode into the house towards me, holding out his hand. 'My dear Miss Hamilton, I simply had to come and say how devastated we all are by the terrible accident that…'

I don't recall his words in detail. Like the maid, I was too mesmerised by surprise as I sank into a deep curtsey.

Albert Edward, Prince of Wales, known to his intimates as Bertie, was then twenty-four years old. Personable, charming and lively, he had already acquired the air of easy camaraderie which was to endear him to so many people, of all classes, throughout his long life. He wore a moustache and short beard which gave him a certain *gravitas*, but the alert brightness of his blue eyes made one feel that he noted every nuance of what happened about him.

'Up with you,' he murmured, tugging at the hand I had given him, lifting me back to my feet. Our eyes met on a level and I saw the concern, and the genuine interest, with which he regarded me.

Then a movement in the doorway drew my attention beyond the prince, to where a young woman was coming in, with another man silhouetted by the light from outside.

'Alix—' the prince began.

'Oh, yes, yes, Bertie, my dear,' the young woman broke in sweetly. 'I know you told me to stay outside, but I, also, wish to pay my respects to our tenants in their grief. As your wife, it is my place, is it not?'

Even before I heard the softly-accented English, I had known her from the many likenesses which had been printed in newspapers and magazines ever since she arrived in England for her marriage to the prince, more than two years before. The lovely Alexandra, daughter of the King of Denmark, had already provided her young husband with two small sons, but her figure remained girlishly slender in her velvet riding outfit, with a little veiled hat on her piled hair. Her look was soft and sad as she approached me and, when I made to curtsey, she prevented me and instead embraced me, her cheek to mine. 'I do so understand,' she murmured, her eyes misted as she looked at me. 'We are so sorry. My poor child.'

'Child' she called me on that first meeting. Yet she was nearly eleven months younger than I. Her twenty-first birthday fell on the first of December that year.

As I struggled for a reply, she made a little graceful gesture, drawing my attention to the man who had followed her. 'You are acquainted, I believe, with Mr Devlin.'

Geoffrey.

The rest of the world grew dim about us. He looked older, more mature, more sombre. Otherwise unchanged. Every line of him still achingly familiar – the broad shoulders, the lean, elegant body, the soft dark hair and slate-blue eyes... Waves of heat and cold rolled over me, and pain that said I still cared too much despite the hurt he had caused me. Nor was he unmoved by our meeting. In his searching gaze I read many things – including hope.

I couldn't cope with it, not then. My eyes unfocused, I held out my hand as convention demanded. 'Mr Devlin.'

'You must know how sorry I was to hear the news,' he said, his cold hand folding round mine.

His touch set my blood alight, sending disturbing waves of awareness coursing through me, bringing fever to my cheeks. It made me angry, both with him and myself. He should have known better than to come at such a time! How dared he intrude on my grief? How *dared* he?! Extricating my hand from his grasp, I turned my shoulder to him, giving my whole attention to my royal visitors.

I showed them into the drawing-room, where I hovered by the door as they greeted my father and said more gracious and comforting things, all sincerely expressed. Father was gruff, but gratified that his royal landlord had bothered to interrupt a day's hunting in order to call. He was equally polite to Geoffrey, who said he had called on his father's behalf as well as his own; Sir Arthur wished to convey his condolences.

I fancied a certain constraint between them, and a glint in Father's eye when Sir Arthur's name was mentioned, but it was no more than a fleeting impression.

'We must not intrude any longer, Bertie,' the princess said after a while, holding out her hand to my father. 'Good day, Mr Hamilton.'

He bowed over her hand. 'Goodbye, ma'am. Thank you.'

While the prince and Geoffrey made their farewells, Princess Alexandra turned to the door and I followed her out into the hallway where she again offered her hand, stopping me when I would have made another curtsey.

'No, my dear, it's not necessary. Here at Sandringham we are not royalty. We are your friends.' Her blue eyes shone with sincerity as her fingers pressed mine. 'I hope we shall be good friends, Miss Hamilton. I, too, grew up in a place like this. That is why I love it so much, because it reminds me of my home.' Her gaze grew wistful as she thought of it, then she gave me a sweet smile. 'We have much in common, I think. Shall we be friends?'

'I hope so, ma'am,' I said.

'I hope so, too,' she assured me, and swept out, holding the long skirts of her riding habit clear of the damp gravel. Outside, a group of other riders waited. One of them helped the princess to remount.

A slight clearing of the prince's throat alerted me to his presence in the hall and I stepped back from the door, dipping a curtsey, saying, 'Your Royal Highness, it was kind of you to—'

'It was the least I could do, to offer what small comfort is in my power.' He bent and took my arm, raising me to my feet, his gaze warm and full of understanding. Smiling a little, he lifted my hand to his lips and lightly kissed my knuckles. 'I trust we shall soon meet again in happier circumstances. Such a beautiful lady will be an asset to the company at Sandringham Hall. What do you say, Devlin?'

'I couldn't agree more, sir,' Geoffrey said.

I don't remember speaking. Perhaps I was incapable of coherent speech. I only know I was shockingly aware that the prince was sending me subtle signals of personal interest, disconcerting enough in themselves, but especially inappropriate at such a time.

And then he was gone, striding for the door. Behind him, Geoffrey hovered.

'Thank you for calling,' I said, unable to look at him, gesturing him to leave. 'If you will excuse me…'

'Of course. Goodbye, Rose.'

He was waiting for me to hold out my hand in farewell, but I could not touch him again. Once had been enough.

'Well…' he said. 'G-goodbye.'

I watched him walk from the house, his long, loping stride so familiar it made me weep inside. With agile grace he swung up to the saddle, the prince made some remark to his companions, and then they were off down the drive, making for the gateless entrance. Geoffrey glanced towards the house one last time, adjusting his hat in a way that became a salutation of farewell.

It was not over between us. It was very far from over.

Slowly, I closed the door and leaned on it, seeing Howlett regarding me with wonder, the whites of her eyes showing all round the irises. Fortunately, she had been so amazed by the presence of royalty that she had failed to notice any other nuances.

'Oh, miss!' was all she seemed able to say. 'Oh, miss!!'

Feeling wretched, I lashed out at the nearest target. 'Don't stand there gaping, Howlett. Haven't you any work to do?'

Poor Howlett had me marked down as a termagant.

—

Because Father had decreed that Victor must be buried beside Mother, at Morsford, two services were held. The first took place at the neat carrstone church of St Mary Magdalene, at Sandringham.

Eschewing the luxury of a hearse for this part of the ceremonies, Father had ordered one of our own farm wagons painted black, with a bier set up on it, all draped with black cloth. On it, the coffin was wreathed in winter foliage and chrysanthemums. The cortège moved down the lane, through West Newton, and across the undulating ground of Sandringham Park, skirting the ornamental lake, where the big house dominated the rise beyond.

The church was full and overflowing. Afterwards, stepping out into a cutting wind, I realised how well-loved my brother must have been; farmers, labourers, villagers, craftsmen and shopkeepers, folk from Feltham, West Newton, Dersingham and elsewhere, lined the path to offer their respects as we passed by.

Father walked first, bare-headed in the wind, stone-faced, erect. And beside him came Johnny, thin and pale, knuckling an unmanly tear from his eye with an impatient hand. Father took no notice of him, neither touching him nor speaking to him. Grace and I followed, both of us heavily veiled, my sister hanging on my arm weeping quietly and constantly – weeping enough for both of us. For myself, I felt too much to weep. I felt dead inside, too numbed to accept what was happening. It was as if I were acting a part in a play. Behind me, I heard Mama moan now and then, as she had throughout the service, a wet handkerchief to her mouth and her eyes brimming over it. 'Bear up,' Narnie kept saying. 'Bear up, my lamb, it will soon be over.'

All of our own men, their families, and the household servants, were there beside the path – their work had been suspended for the day. I saw Ben Chilvers and his wife; and, among the crowd, anxious not to intrude, Mr and Mrs Wyatt and their oldest daughter, Felicity, who was sobbing so bitterly that, though she hid her face in a handkerchief, she could not disguise the despair that racked her.

Felicity had always been emotional, but such empathy with our sorrow was extraordinary.

As the undertaker's men fixed the coffin back on the wagon, I saw two well-dressed gentlemen standing nearby; they were equerries from Sandringham, there to represent the Prince of Wales. And with them, his dark head bared to the cold wind, was Geoffrey Devlin. I was glad of the veil that covered my face in moving swathes of black silk gauze as our glances locked. Beneath tight corsets and layers of black crape and wool my skin broke out in a sweat as I read the concern in his eyes – the wish to be able to speak with me and offer comfort.

No! I turned my face away, denying the answering call in my blood. He had no right to come seeking me with that disturbing look in his eyes, not now. Not ever! But especially not on this day when my only thoughts must be of my brother and my grieving family. Did he really think we could go on as if nothing had happened?

Many of the congregation followed in silence, some on horseback, some crowding on wagons, a few on foot, as my brother was taken on his last journey along familiar lanes, to the railway station at Wolferton, where we boarded the train for Lynn. Only as the train drew away, to the accompaniment of the Dersingham band playing 'Nearer my God to Thee', with the crowd of mourners standing bare-headed in a flurry of rain, did a tear trickle down my cheek.

I did not see Geoffrey among the crowd at the station. I guessed that, having done his neighbourly duty, he had gone home. Neighbourly duty, of course – I was a fool to read more into it, but then where he was concerned I had always let wishful thinking override logic. The fact was the same now as it had been three long years ago – his plans for the future could never include a licit place for me.

From King's Lynn we travelled by carriage to Morsford Hall, where we stayed overnight with Uncle Seward and his family before the second service, and the interment, took place. In the yew-shaded churchyard at Morsford, with rooks calling above, Victor was laid beside Mother.

–

Family and friends gathered at Morsford Hall for the funeral repast, a vast buffet laid out in the Great Hall. A log fire spat and sparked in the medieval hearth, sending shadows dancing about the tapestried walls, while draughts stirred and eddied, keeping everyone on the move in an effort to stay warm.

Among the throng of relatives and close friends, Aunt Agnes made play of normality; we were polite, but we were strangers. My uncles, Jonathan and Seward, found themselves a corner where they discussed banking business; my cousin Annette, Seward's daughter, showed off her lawyer husband, her expensive clothes, and her heavily-draped third pregnancy; and Aunt Beatrice, Jonathan's wife, went about, as ever, dispensing words of Christian comfort. The Pooleys were there, with Basil, who kept hovering at my elbow paying attentions that I didn't want. I'm afraid I was sharp with him, wishing he would leave me alone, glad when William Turnbull, the burly engineer, engaged me in conversation. Basil retreated, but watched us from a distance like a kestrel waiting to pounce.

'I blame myself for Victor's death,' Turnbull said, his eyes melancholy in his bearded face. 'The engine must have had some fault. Some hair-line imperfection in the casting, or the welding. I shall send a wagon to collect the pieces for examination at the beginning of next week. I shall work upon it myself, with all the technical skills at my command. Be assured that we shall make doubly certain of our safety checks from now on, Miss Hamilton.'

'That won't bring my brother back,' I replied.

'But it will mean that his death may help to save someone else.'

'It was an accident. No one could have foreseen it.' I wished he would not talk about it; I had almost managed to shut out thoughts of our reason for being here.

'Nevertheless, I feel responsible. I designed that engine.'

'Such things do happen. One reads of them in the newspapers.'

'Not with Turnbull engines, you don't!' His eyes flashed and his full red lips stuck out belligerently.

Tired of his obsession, I snapped, 'Then I must conclude that it's your business you're most concerned about – not my brother.'

His look reproached me as he blinked slowly, owlishly. 'That's a harsh judgement, Miss Hamilton. I'd be a fool not to take into account that customers might think twice about our engines after such an accident. Of course I'm concerned. The business is important to me – and to the men we employ, and their families. That's one matter. My personal feelings about Victor are another. Quite another. I loved him like a brother.'

As he made this speech, I was conscious that Basil Pooley had noted my agitation and was making his way towards me.

'And to me he *was* my brother,' I said. 'My dearest brother. My dearest friend.'

'Then we have a good deal in common,' Turnbull replied.

For a moment our eyes locked and I saw that I had wounded him. Though he was a solemn, humourless sort of man, his regard for Victor had been genuine. His earnest wish to atone for the accident, to make something good from it, made me warm to him despite myself.

'Do you need some air, Miss Rose?' Basil Pooley was beside me, his hand lightly under my arm.

'No, thank you.'

'Are you sure? You look a bit pale. If this here chap's disturbing you—'

'He's not disturbing me!' I denied, and shook the unwelcome hand from my arm with a glance that made him narrow his eyes as I turned again to the engineer, saying, 'Mr Turnbull, forgive me if I spoke in haste. It has not been an easy day for me.'

'I entirely understand,' he assured me. 'My dear Miss Hamilton, please believe that I am not a man to take offence at the expression of genuine feeling – not from you. I was exceedingly fond of your brother, though he too had a swift temper. I enjoyed sharpening my wits in discussion with him. I shall miss that. Perhaps you and I might share the same pleasure, on occasion.'

'Perhaps,' I murmured, and found reason to move away.

I hoped to leave Basil Pooley behind, too. Trying to elude him, I made my way among the company and sought the comparative quietness of the library, where a few gentlemen were gathered by the fire, smoking cigarettes and laughing – laughter that died abruptly as I went in. One by one, they threw their smokes into the fire and moved towards the door, nodding politely in my direction.

I made for the farther of two big windows which looked out across a herb garden set out in squares delineated by box hedges, with beyond it a line of weeping willows marking the progress of the stream. The scene was desolate with damp winter.

Behind me the door opened and closed again. Basil Pooley had followed me. Wishing that he would leave me in peace, I sat down in the window-seat, spreading my crinolined skirts about me, my face turned to the view.

'You owe me an apology, too,' my pursuer said as he paused beside me. '*I* loved Victor, you know. *I* was his friend – and his business partner, just like Turnbull.'

'I know.'

'Then why aren't I good enough to be allowed to look after you?' He slid into the window-seat opposite me. 'That's all I was trying to do – look after you, the way Victor would have wanted.'

From my eye corner, I considered him as he leaned towards me, hands on his knees, his dusty fair hair and fresh complexion vivid against the stark black and white of his clothes. Now thirty, he had learned to curb the worst excesses of showiness, his only item of jewellery that day being a thick signet-ring on his little finger. Despite the slight misalignment of a broken nose, he was a good-looking man, and there was true appeal in eyes like summer skies; they entreated me to be kinder.

'I know,' I said again, sighing. 'And I'm sorry.'

'No need for that,' he replied softly, reaching as if to touch my hand. 'Not between you and me, eh?'

He seemed to have read more into my answer than I had intended, so it was with relief that I saw him draw back as a voice said, 'Excuse me, miss – sir. Would you be Mr Pooley? Mr Hamilton asks that you join him, and the other gentlemen, in the drawing-room.'

'Did he say why?' Basil asked.

The butler lifted his brows. 'Mr Baines, the family solicitor, is with them, I believe.'

'Ah. Then I'll come right away.' He rose to his feet, pausing to look down at me and add, 'I'll not be far away, Miss Rose. From now on. You can rely on me, you'll see. I'll be there.'

I did not find this assurance of much comfort.

The 'gentlemen' – my father, my uncles, Victor's two business partners, and the family solicitor – were meeting to discuss the legalities. In the absence of a will, all that my brother owned would pass by law to his next-of-kin – to Father.

–

We returned to the farm, where I went early to bed and fell into a sleep deeper than any I had enjoyed since coming home. That, I presume, is the reason why I failed to hear any commotion until I woke suddenly to see a red glare beyond my curtains. After a moment I identified it as the sway and brightening of leaping flames. I slipped out of bed and, shivering in the chill, ran to look out of my window.

A bonfire was blazing, on rough ground where a flowerbed was partly dug. Its brightness silhouetted a dark figure moving jerkily between the fire and a box that stood on the ground, each journey taking an armful of things from the box to throw on the blaze. Nor was he alone. As my eyes adjusted to the odd light, I saw Mama's night-clad figure standing a few yards away, apparently pleading with him to stop.

I threw up my window, leaned out, heard Mama's plaintive: 'Don't do this, Will. Oh, please don't! You frighten me. Please!'

Father ignored her. He was bent on destroying whatever he had in that box.

Knowing that someone had to intervene, if only to get Mama back into the house, I threw on a wrap and ran from my room.

The door of Victor's room was open, with a brass lamp set on the marble-topped wash-stand. Its light showed clothes spilling from wardrobe and drawers, books scattered on the floor. The glass-fronted cabinet which had contained my brother's collection of hand-carved wooden engines stood open, some of the models missing, some splintered on the floor as if someone had stamped on them, others lying on their sides. In the centre of the chaos, cross-legged on the floor in his nightshirt, Johnny sat with his head bent over something he held in his hands, rocking back and forth, weeping.

'Johnny?' I breathed.

His head snapped round, showing me his tears. 'Father's done it. He's gone mad. He's burning all Victor's things. But he's not having this. Victor promised that I could have it when he got a new one. I know he'd want me to have it. Wouldn't he, Rose?'

'What is it?'

He opened his hands, showing me Victor's big old turnip pocket-watch. Cased in silver, chased and engraved with a family crest, it had once belonged to Great-grandmama's father, Lord Seward.

'What's happening?' Grace's worried voice enquired from the door of her room.

I left her to look after Johnny.

In the garden, Narnie was trying to persuade Mama to, 'Come inside, Miss Flora, before you catch your death', but Mama was weeping, imploring Father to stop what he was doing.

He ignored her. His lean figure strode back and forth against the glare of the bonfire he had made, and with every trip sparks flew as he

added more papers, more shirts, a broken carving of a railway engine…
I felt sick. The heat from the fire seemed to reach out, wanting to
devour me, making my skin break out in clammy sweat.

'You can't do this!' I cried, running to catch his arm. 'Father, you
can't!'

He shook me off as if I were a fly. 'He won't be needing it. It must
all be destroyed. All of it.'

'Someone might be glad of those clothes!' My hands to my throbbing head, I watched him fetch another armful – good underwear, and
a pair of boots. 'Father, it's wicked to burn such things. Someone in
the village could make good use of them. Victor would have wanted
that. He wouldn't have wanted you to throw away all his belongings.
Give them away. Give them to the needy poor. Please!'

He paused in his obsessional pacings to glower at me. 'You always
did argue too much, girl. Always think you know best. All right!' On
the words, he threw his latest burden full in my face and, as I shrugged
free of the shrouding garments he said, '*You* dispose of them. Get rid of
them how you please, but get rid of them. I want that room emptied.
I want no reminders. Do you understand?'

Without waiting for a reply he pushed past me, to where Mama
was weeping, with Narnie supporting her.

'And as for you…' he muttered as he paused in front of her.
'Weep, woman! That's all you know how to do. Work the handle
and out comes the water. Like a mechanical doll. No real feeling in
it, anywhere.'

'Mr Hamilton!' Narnie gasped in outrage.

I doubt he even heard her. 'You never cared for my son.' He spat
the accusation into Mama's flinching face. 'You were never a mother
to him. Never! I curse the day my pity made me take you to my bed.
There, that's the truth at last. Weep on that, woman!'

And he left us, making down the hill for the stables and his horse.

Three

Father did not come home, not that night or the next. Mama kept to her bed, racked with migraine. The household seemed to be holding its breath, waiting.

In the meantime, Johnny and I cleared Victor's room. Grace tried to help, but every few minutes she came across some item that brought back distressful memories and after a while she retreated, to share her tears with Mama. She said we should let the servants do it, but it seemed to me that such a personal task was best accomplished by someone who had loved Victor. I didn't want the maids gossiping about the village with tales of my brother's intimate possessions.

One thing that most assuredly would have shocked the maids was a pack of cards printed with pictures of women in undress. Snatching them from the goggling Johnny, I threw them on to the fire and, as they burned to ashes, I lectured my young half-brother on the dangers of keeping bad company: Victor would not have known such abominations existed if he had not been led astray – most probably by Basil Pooley.

We packed several boxes of clothes to be distributed in the villages, but despite Father's orders we could not dispose of everything: Johnny desired the turnip watch, and a shirt-stud of gold inlaid with mother-of-pearl; Victor's books I kept for myself, to replace those of my own which had vanished during my absence. Other things had sentimental value: a silk cravat I had tied for Victor on more than one occasion, and a dozen other small items, insignificant in themselves but to us redolent with memories of our brother. We shared them between us, keeping one or two mementoes for the others, and for the staff. The penknife I saved for Benstead, who had taught Victor to whittle.

Finally, when all was done, the cupboards emptied and the bed left stripped, Johnny and I stood together in the doorway and looked at the awful emptiness we had created.

'It doesn't matter!' he said fiercely. 'I shan't forget him. I shan't ever forget him, whatever Father says!'

He turned and pressed his face to my shoulder, his young arms bony and painfully tight around me as he wept. I held him, stroking his hair, sharing his grief, my throat thick and my eyes wet, until he broke free. Without looking at me, he whirled and ran into his own room, shutting the door firmly.

Later, unable to sleep, I lit my lamp and took one of Victor's books down from the shelf. I had been surprised to find it among my practical brother's collection, but I had always loved poetry and hoped it might soothe my spirit enough for me to sleep. The book fell open where a card had been left at a page where a pencil line drew attention to a poem beginning, 'My true love hath my heart, and I have his...' Intrigued, I turned the card over; it was a carte-de-visite, a misty sepia photograph of a smiling, rather plain young woman in a summer dress, with a parasol poised behind her bonnet. I squinted at it, trying to make out her face, not believing what I saw.

If I needed confirmation, her name was written on the fly-leaf of the book of poems: 'For Felicity Georgiana Wyatt, 17 July 1861'. Someone had given this book to Felicity as a gift for her twenty-first birthday. What was it doing in Victor's collection?

In my mind's eye I saw again Felicity's acute distress on the day of Victor's funeral. I remembered, too, Victor flushing scarlet over a casual mention of Felicity's name. The conclusions I drew caused me to write a note, enclosing the photograph and saying that I had found it in a book. Would Felicity like to meet, and talk about it?

I had the boy Jarvis take it over to the Grange the next day. He returned with an answer from Felicity, requesting me to meet her in Feltham church.

–

Rooks croaked from dripping trees as I walked under the lychgate; a pigeon took off with a clatter of wings, a pheasant cried from an adjacent copse, and a rabbit's white scut vanished among gravestones. Distantly through November mists came the sound of shooting.

In the dim, cold quietness of the church, a figure stood by the lectern arranging chrysanthemums. She was dressed in unrelieved black – deeper mourning than etiquette required. But, to her, Victor had been more than a second cousin. All at once I was sure of that.

My boots scuffed on the uneven stone slabs down the aisle, but though the sound seemed loud in that hushed place she didn't look round. I paused a few feet behind her, saying softly, 'Felicity?'

She remained as she was, turned away from me, fiddling with the chrysanthemums.

'You asked me to come,' I said. 'You wanted to talk?'

As she swung slowly round I understood why she hadn't spoken before: she had been unable to, consumed by such distress that her face was swollen, her eyes all but lost in pale, puffy folds of flesh. Her voice came out thick and cracked, hollow with desolation: 'How can I bear it? Oh, Rose… He cannot be dead!'

We sat in the front pew, talking in low voices, as she confessed her love for my brother. For a long time she had adored him from a distance, never believing he might care for her.

'I had made up my mind to content myself with growing old alone, a maiden aunt to my sisters' children. And then…' Remembered joy gleamed through her tears like sunlight through showers. 'I met Victor, by chance, at the home of a mutual acquaintance. Mrs Linnet Longville, do you know her?'

I searched my memory. 'No, I don't believe so.'

'She lives in Drayton village. In a pretty little cottage with a lovely garden. She keeps bees. She gave us some honey.' Seeing that it meant nothing to me, she went on, 'Chloe and I went to call on her, with some sleeve-patterns which Mama had promised, and Victor was there, taking tea.'

Mrs Longville, wife to a sea captain who was frequently absent, was a person somewhat lacking in breeding but with a kind heart and two beautiful daughters. She had contrived to leave the pair alone for a few minutes and, 'Oh, Rose!' Fresh tears sprang from Felicity's eyes. 'Victor had planned that meeting! He felt as I did! During all my years of agony… *he had felt just as I did!*' Sobbing, she buried her face in her mittened hands.

Other meetings had followed, snatches of conversation after church, and another covert rendezvous at the home of Mrs Longville, '… who was never far away,' Felicity hastily assured me, her pale cheeks stained with magenta. 'Victor would never compromise me, you know that, Rose. He's so…' Wincing at the slip, she corrected herself with a catch in her voice, 'He was… so strong. So very strong. He fixed his mind steadfastly on his goal and he never faltered from it, however long the road ahead, however steep the climb. Stubbornness, he called it, but *I* call it strength of resolve. An innate sense of honour. Victor always did what was *right*.'

'Yes, that's so.' My brother's sense of 'what was right' had at times been uncomfortable to live with. Nevertheless, it had been part of what made him as he was, and I too had loved him.

He and Felicity had exchanged photographs as a token of their bond; she had also given him her book of poetry, with the special poem marked. She would have been happy to marry him at once, but my brother, stubborn and stiff-necked as ever, had decreed that they must wait until he had sufficient money to keep her in a manner of which her wealthy family would approve. He had calculated that, if all went well, he should accomplish that feat by the time he was thirty.

'Just a little over three years and we might have been married,' Felicity wept. 'Or even... even just a day or two more and we might at least have been betrothed. He was planning to approach my father as soon as the steam engine trial was over.' She stared at me hopelessly. 'But we were not vouchsafed that joy. I haven't even the right to mourn for him properly. Oh... I must have been a wicked sinner for God to punish me so. Now I shall be alone for ever.'

Clasping her hand, I said, 'God isn't so unkind. Don't blame yourself. Haven't you told anyone else how you feel? Your mother...'

'Yes. Mama knows, now. At first I couldn't bring myself to speak of it. But after the service, when they took him away from me for ever... then I confessed the truth to Mama.' As she looked up at me her eyes brimmed again. 'Do you know what she said? – She said that I shall forget him, that I shall find someone else. And I shall not! I have never loved any man but Victor. I never have and I never shall, though I live to be a hundred. Rose, what shall I do?'

I had no answers for her. I had only sympathy to offer, and a shoulder for her to weep on as we shared our sorrow.

–

When Father returned he continued to brood alone when in the house, and he absented himself for hours. We heard from Aunt Lettice that he was seen in Morsford churchyard, standing alone by the grave. It was as though those few feet of earth held all that had ever really mattered to him; the rest of his family – the living members of it – were of no account.

A week or so after the funeral, Father was on hand when William Turnbull arrived with some men and a sturdy wagon. Together, they supervised the loading of the pieces of the steam engine, which were going back to the works to be examined. They spent the evening closeted in the farm office, and in the morning Father announced his intention to accompany Turnbull back to Thetford. When Mama begged him not to go, he said it was time he learned more about the business in which, once Victor's estate was settled, he would be a partner.

I tried to explain this to Ned Plant when he came up to the house to see me.

'That's all very well, Miss Rose,' he replied. 'But there's work to be done and I don't know what to tell 'em to get on with. I had a man come sayin' as Mr 'amilton 'ad ordered a gang to help finish pickin' mangolds afore the frost set in. How do I know if that's so? Which field shall I set 'em to? And Benstead's goin' on about that cash prize he's been expectin' for weeks. Promised his wife a new bonnet out of it, he say. Not to mention...'

He went on 'not to mention' several other problems, until my head was buzzing. I couldn't hope to handle matters all alone. To whom could I turn?

Who else but the man who had been friend, guide and mentor ever since Father first took the lease on Orchards?

George Pooley and I walked the farm while he advised me which fields were ready for the plough, which should be planted with winter wheat, which roots to pull, which holes in the lanes should be filled with stones, which ditches needed clearing. He advised Benstead to bring the bullocks in from the marshes for the winter, while the sheep were folded on ploughed tilth, their hurdle pen moved occasionally so that the whole field would be well manured. Taggart the shepherd was preparing his hut, where he would live during lambing.

So the shortening days passed. My hands grew calloused, my nails split, my skin roughened under the assault of rain and cold winds. Often, coming in tired, cold and aching, I thought about Victor and wondered what he would think, to see me now, taking his place. Neither of us had ever dreamed of such a future.

-

In the long evenings, much to Mama's dismay, I settled myself in Father's office, acquainting myself with the account books. At first I felt like a thief, prying where I shouldn't, but as I found my way among the maze of information and began to detect a pattern, I knew that, given time, I could handle it as well as any man.

Farmer Pooley seemed to agree. 'You've got a good grasp of what's what, Miss Rose,' he told me. 'Why, I'll wager you could take over the management of the farm – if it were a womanly thing to do.'

'Why should it be unwomanly?' I demanded. 'You don't call Old Dame Rudd "unwomanly" because she runs her farm on her own.'

'Bessie Rudd.' He rubbed his cheek uncertainly. 'Aye, well, that's a different matter, Miss Rose. It's a smaller property. And she's a widow woman, and well on in years. You're a single lady – a *young* single lady. A gentlewoman.'

Though I knew that public opinion would agree with him, I argued. 'I can't see what difference it makes. I'd make as good a farmer as Victor. At least my heart would be in it. His never was, you know. He did it because it was what Father wanted.'

'Aye, gal, I know.' He perused me for a long moment, holding his ruddy nose, eyes half buried beneath bushy brows set in a weathered face. Then he laughed and slapped his thigh, 'By gar, you know who you remind me of?'

'No. Who?'

'Your father. You remind me of your father. Blast my eyes if you don't!'

He told me how Father had ridden to his door on the day my mother died – the day I was born – and declared his startling intention to be a farmer. My own ambition was just as unlikely, but, 'If anybody can do it, it's Will Hamilton's daughter.'

'If only Will Hamilton will let her,' I commented.

Pooley sobered, nodding sagely in agreement. 'Aye, gal, you'll have a hard time convincing him it's right and proper.'

'Then maybe you'll put a word in for me?'

That made him smile, his eyes twinkling. 'Mebbe I might. Meantime, I was wondering… How would it be if I asked my nephew Basil to help keep an eye on the place for a while? He'd be glad to oblige, I know.'

'Oh, please don't bother him,' I said at once. 'I can manage, with your help.'

'Trouble is, Miss Rose,' he said, pulling at his ear. 'Mrs Pooley and I hev arranged to go on a trip, to see her sister up north. I've been promising her for ages. We thought we might stay over Christmas. I'd feel easier about it if Basil was on hand, now and then. Just in case. He's no farmer, but you may find you need a man... I'll ask him to keep an eye. Just as a friend. Just to set my mind at rest.'

Though Basil was not my idea of an ideal steward, I agreed, simply to let dear Pooley go off on his jaunt with a free mind.

'But anyway,' he assured me bracingly, 'your father'll be back afore long, I don't doubt. He'll be back and take up the reins again as if nothing had happened, don't fret your pretty head about that. I've seen him like this afore. It's the way grief takes him. Hard. He takes it hard. But once he's worked through it he'll be his old self again, you'll see. Then you can forget all this nonsense about managing the place yourself.'

–

Grace's eighteenth birthday came and went in quiet fashion: her friend Maria Kinnersley stayed for a few days and there were cards and presents, but Father's absence – and the yawning gap where once Victor would have stood – were achingly apparent. Grace spent most of the day sulking. As a result, when she was invited to stay for a while with the Kinnersleys in Lynn, Mama agreed, on the understanding that she must observe her mourning obligations and not be too gay.

It became my habit to ride out every day, partly as a means of exercising Dandy, Victor's horse. At first he was uneasy with me, and with the side-saddle which had once belonged to Mama. However, after a while we reached an agreement to get along. Where the dogcart might have bogged down, the horse stepped along the verges, allowing me to oversee the farm despite the increasing muddiness of the lanes.

Yes, I knew that tongues were wagging; I was not behaving as a decent young woman should. But the farm had to be kept going until Father got over his melancholy and there was no one else to do it. Farmer Pooley had gone away and, though Basil did call about once a week, his knowledge of farming was scanty. I neither needed nor wanted his help.

But Basil did entertain poor, sad Mama. He told amusing stories and he flattered her until she turned blushing coy like a maid of sixteen.

'Really, I never before noticed what a very *pleasant* young man he is,' she remarked. 'Don't you think so, Rose? He may not, be a gentleman, but he has an engaging way with him, don't you think?'

'He can be very agreeable when he chooses,' I conceded.

'And he's very fond of *you*,' she observed.

'As an old friend of the family, he's fond of us all, I dare say.'

I took care not to give Basil any encouragement, but I confess that I was beginning to revise my opinion of him. He never became intrusive; he was polite, supportive, a welcome antidote to the gloom that often gathered over Orchards. It was a comfort to know he was there, if we needed him.

I tried to tell him as much, taking care to emphasise that it was Mama who most benefited from his company: 'She seems to blossom when you're here. You're good for her.'

'She's a lovely lady,' he said. 'The pleasure's mine.'

'Well, I'm grateful.'

He stood looking at me, hat in hand, ready to leave, his blue eyes bright as they surveyed my face. 'That's all I need to know, Miss Rose. So long as I'm being of some use to you.'

-

On 1 December, the county celebrated Princess Alexandra's twenty-first birthday, with public buildings specially illuminated in Lynn, teas and suppers held, a party for local schoolchildren at Sandringham Hall itself, and a ball at the big house in the evening. Mama and I saw some of the celebration fireworks, shooting stars sparkling across a frosty sky, rockets flaring tails of orange fire. But we didn't watch for long. Mama complained of feeling cold.

'Draw the curtain, Narnie,' she instructed, moving away to sit huddled by the fire. 'Come and sit with me, Rose. Don't you feel the cold, too? How you can be about the farm in this weather...' But the subject was distasteful, so she discarded it. 'Next year, you and Grace will be able to attend the Birthday Ball. By then, you will have put aside your mourning and be able to enjoy yourselves without feeling disloyal to Victor's memory. Oh, my dear,' she added as she saw my face, 'he would not have wanted you to be unhappy. He wanted you to have a good life, to find a husband and—'

'Perhaps I don't want a husband,' I said.

She exchanged a glance with Narnie before settling a troubled look on me. 'That's your aunt Agnes speaking, not you, Rose.'

'I'd rather stay single than have some man treat me as Father treats you.'

Behind me, Narnie muttered her agreement.

But Mama's mouth trembled and as she bit her lip a tear welled up and dripped down her cheek. She wiped it away with a handkerchief, saying hoarsely, 'Your father is out of sorts at present. That's all it is. Of course you want to be married. What else will you do – become a governess, as Agnes plans?'

'I may decide to stay and help Father run the farm.'

Her mouth formed a little 'o' of dismay and she clapped her hands to it, staring at me across them.

'Take no notice of her, Miss Flora,' Narnie said, bustling across to knead her neck. 'Mr Hamilton will never let her do that, and she knows it. She only says these things to startle you. Off with you, Miss Rose. Your mama needs to rest. Go and find something to do.'

I got to my feet, wearying of the conversation. Mama seemed to think of nothing but marrying me off as quickly as possible. She never talked about anything that really mattered. 'Someone has to help Father,' I said. 'With Victor gone, who else is there but me? And I could do it. I know I could.'

'Ruin your hands, and your complexion,' Mama fretted. 'You can't mean it, Rose.'

I hadn't fully realised it until that moment, but I did mean it. Every word.

–

The weather turned frosty, red skies at night, clear stars blazing, mornings rimed with ice as thick as snow. We kept the bullocks in deep straw in the home yard, and Benstead picked out the most promising ones, putting them in individual boxes to fatten them up. Taggart, the shepherd, wanted 'his ewes' to have some grazing on the grass of the fallow field, so I agreed that he could let them in there during the day and take them back to their fold at night.

Despite the weather, threshing was going ahead – in the old way, by flail and winnow, building heaps of golden corn in the barn – and in the lanes one passed laden carts taking roots for chopping into winter feed. I thanked providence that most of the mangolds were piled warm under straw; frost could ruin them. Some ploughing continued, and harrowing, and I kept the work-gang on to pick stones in new-ploughed fields to fill the holes in the lanes. It was a mystery where all the stones came from; some of the country folk believed they mated and bred in the night.

The shooting continued unabated. Nervous pheasant, partridge and hares, driven from their homes, haunted the orchards, and once I came across an exhausted woodcock that hardly had strength to move even when I stroked it. Occasionally a hunting horn could be heard winding, far away, the sound carrying on the still air, and once I saw the hounds streaming across a hillside like blown leaves. But, fox-hunting being incompatible with game-rearing, a finding was rare – most adult foxes were poisoned or shot by game-keepers in West Norfolk, though cubs were reared to ensure the survival of the sport.

One day I found it necessary to take the train into King's Lynn to see Uncle Jonathan at the bank and arrange for some cash to be made available. Father's continued absence was becoming an embar-rassment. My uncle provided temporary financial coverage, but he was concerned to know that Father was still away and promised to write to him at Thetford. I had luncheon at Weal House, together with Grace and her friend Maria Kinnersley. Grace was in no hurry to come home.

Once again darkness was falling as I arrived at Wolferton, but this time Benstead met me and drove me home. I was able to give him his belated cash prize from the agricultural show, for which he was pleased. He actually stopped grumbling for several minutes but soon the complaints started again – his rheumatics were playing him up; his potatoes had got the blight; there were too many hares about, they were eating all the green tops and taking food out of the mouths of his beasts… I was tired, and his litany of woe wearied me.

As we drove up the incline to the house, I saw a fine sporting gig tethered by the porch. My heart contracted painfully as I recognised the vehicle, but the door of the house opened and, against the glow of lamplight from within, a lanky figure appeared – not Geoffrey, but his father, Sir Arthur Devlin.

'What's this?' he demanded as he strode up to me with a curious hopping gait – one of his long legs didn't bend at the knee. 'What's this? Your father not here? *You* managing the farm? What next? My God, what next, I say?'

'Good evening, Sir Arthur,' I replied, climbing from the trap.

'What?' He peered at me in the twilight, head thrust out and slightly tilted, as if he were deaf. 'Ah – yes. But it's not a good evening, Miss Hamilton. Not a good evening at all. Not when your animals have broken through my hedge and got into my best turnips. It's too bad! Your father and I have had words about this before. Done it deliberately, I shouldn't wonder. Done it deliberately to aggravate me. Well, let me tell you this – I'll put my solicitor on to it if it continues. I'll take you to court and have *them* decide who's right. Good evening to you, Miss Hamilton.'

With that, he swung awkwardly up to the gig and with his stiff leg sticking out to one side was off before I could collect wits enough to reply. The thin high wheels sent a spray of mud to splatter my skirts as a parting insult.

'Oh, Lor', Miss Rose,' Benstead sighed. 'Don't say Taggart went and let them ewes get out of that field. I coulda told you that would happen, if you left 'em too long in that fallow.'

'Then why didn't you say so?' I asked in exasperation.

He looked at me in amazement. ''Tweren't my place to question orders, Miss Rose. I'm only the yardman.'

I was even more angry when I learned how Sir Arthur had harangued a bewildered Mama and left her in tears. Without pausing to change my clothes or take a cup of tea, I went down to the yards in search of Plant, in hope of explanations.

Our sheep had grown tired of eating grass and, unerringly finding their way to the place where the boundary hedge was thin, had pushed through and found a succulent supply of their favourite food – turnips. How were they to know the turnips in question belonged to Sir Arthur, and that they were a type being grown for experimental purposes with the aid of superphosphates, an artificial manure known by all shepherds to be harmful to ewes? There had been a rare to-do catching the sheep: Taggart, anxious for his stock so close to lambing, had come to blows with one of the Ambleford men; and then Sir Arthur had arrived, shouting and cursing and threatening litigation.

'Like he alluss do,' said Plant. 'No love lost between him and your father, Miss Rose, that's fer sure. If he en't over here shoutin' he's a-writin' letters, or sendin' Mr Geoffrey to lay down the law.'

As I discovered from a file in the office, a heated correspondence between Father and the baronet had ended in August with Sir Arthur saying he would see to the hedge 'as soon as my men have leisure to attend to such trifles'. In my current mood, the tone of the letters seemed typical of the Devlins – arrogant and uncaring, going their own selfish way, careless of consequences to those less able to defend themselves, I was thinking bitter thoughts of Geoffrey when I wrote to Sir Arthur, demanding that he should have the hedge mended at his earliest convenience.

–

One afternoon I rode the lanes, keeping an eye on progress. The day was cold, a brisk wind driving clouds that threatened sleet. In one field the harrows were at work, covering seed; in another a boy whirled a clapper and yelled in a hoarse voice to scare away the clouds of rooks that came hungrily reconnoitring. A mongrel dog barked noisily and went streaking after a hare and, further on, the work-gang bent along muddy furrows picking stones, tossing them into a line for others to hurl into a cart.

Most of these workers were women and children. Whatever the weather, they walked the long miles from Castle Acre six days a week; all day they pulled mangolds, or picked stones out of cold, wet, sometimes frozen, ground, until the light was failing, when they trudged the weary miles back home at night, their boots and clothes thick with mud, muscles aching, fingers and toes hot with chilblains. Rough labourers they might be, but I did not envy their lot.

Hearing a loud voice raised, I peered over the bare hedge and saw the gang-master stride along the headland to where, not far from the gate, what looked like an old, muddy sack lay crumpled. It was not a sack; as the man bent and jerked at the bundle I realised that it was a child. I heard it whimper as the man dragged it up by one arm, cursing it in language too coarse to record.

'Get up, you lazy little toad,' was his gist. 'Get up and work. What do I pay you for? No work, no snap. Hear me?!'

The child was no more than five or six, a sickly, underfed little scrap almost too weak to stand, feet encased in sodden rags buried in balls of clinging mud, coat made of sacking, belted with rope, little hands thick with the mud that clotted its clothes and hair. As the overseer cursed on, one or two of the other workers, aching backs too stiff to straighten, lifted their heads and looked on with sullen, watchful eyes. None of them made a move to intervene.

75

Thrusting the child ahead of him by jerks of a heavy hand at its shoulder, the overseer forced it back into line and stood over it, pointing at a heavy stone embedded in a clod. It was evident that the child hadn't the strength to pull the skin from a bowl of hot milk, much less a boulder from half-frozen soil, but the overseer lifted his knobby stick and the terrified child bent its small, slimy hands to grasp at the stone.

'Pull, damn you!' the man snarled. 'Pull!'

As he raised his stick again I found myself running through the gateway, crying, 'Stop, you brute! How dare you? How *dare* you?' I have seldom been so angry, or felt so impotent.

The gang-master argued and blustered but, determined to save the child, I swept all his protests aside. Seeing that the youth leading the cart was one of our own lads, I summoned him and had him lift the boy and place him on Dandy's back. I led the horse myself, all the way back to the farm.

Carrying the child in through the side door, I gave orders for hot water to be brought and then, despite Mama's cries of horror, I took him upstairs to the bathroom. The filthy rags all but fell from his thin body, exposing a mass of bruises and weals and scratches; the bindings on his feet covered boots several sizes too big, whose soles grinned away from the uppers. Beneath them his feet were encrusted with dirt, hard with callouses and red with chilblains.

The young maid Howlett appeared with two buckets of hot water which she added to the bath, fretting that I shouldn't be doing it myself, that my clothes were all muddy, that I would get wet...

I suffered her to fetch me a coarse apron, but I refused to let her take over. She could help, but it was a task I needed to do myself. I kept thinking of my own child, wondering if she too would come to degradation without my care. Perhaps I was a little mad.

As the warm water soaked away the mud, the boy whimpered, but he did not cry. I was the one who wept. His hands and feet were cracked and bleeding, his body a mass of bruises and weals where I had no doubt the gang-master's stick had landed. Even his face had not escaped; his mouth was chapped and split and under one eye the yellowing remains of a bruise showed. Seeing it, I wanted to rush out and beat the gang-master until he too was black and blue and bloody.

Later, wrapped in blankets, the boy sat in the kitchen devouring a hunk of bread and cheese, his upper lip white with cream from the fresh milk he had gulped. His clothes had been washed and now hung in front of the fire, steaming. While he ate, Mrs Benstead, the two maids and I looked on in satisfaction.

'Though I don't know whatever you'll do with him, Miss Rose,' Mrs Benstead commented, shaking her head. 'He can't stay here, he'll have to go back to his family.' Bending near the boy, she asked, 'Is your mother with the gang, my man?'

The child glanced at her with bird-bright eyes. He shook his head, then, as if he had only just understood the question, nodded vigorously and sank his teeth into the bread, tearing off a chunk that he stuffed into his mouth with his fingers.

'Poor mite don't know what we're a-sayin',' said Mrs Benstead, touching the child's hair which, now that it was clean, had a soft golden tint to it, and an appealing curl. 'Now then, my little man, what's yore name?'

The child ignored her.

One of the row of bells on the wall – the one labelled 'Front Door' – jangled tunefully. Straightening her cap and apron, Swift went to answer it, while I tried to persuade the boy to speak. He was intent on wolfing down all the food Mrs Benstead could supply.

'Begging your pardon, Miss Hamilton,' said Swift, returning in a fluster of pink cheeks. 'There's a gentleman to see you. Mr Geoffrey Devlin, if you please.'

'More trouble,' Mrs Benstead muttered.

Despite the breathless swoop of my heart, I kept my expression neutral as I turned to the maid. 'What does he want?'

'He asked to see the master. When I said Mr Hamilton weren't here, he asked to see you, miss. That's all he said.'

'Well, it's most inconvenient. Tell him I'm not at home. Tell him…' But why should I refuse to see a neighbour who had called? If I avoided him, it might cause speculation. Aware of the increased speed of my pulse, I smoothed damp palms against my skirts. 'Oh, never mind, I'll speak to him myself. Look after the boy.'

'Shall I get Miss Narborough?' Mrs Benstead asked.

'No, don't bother. She's busy with Mrs Hamilton.' Besides, the fewer witnesses to this encounter, the better. 'Where have you put him, Swift? The drawing-room?'

'The parlour, miss. There's no fire in the drawing-room. You told Howlett not to light one and be wasting coals.'

'So I did.' But I had not been expecting company.

'Your apron, Miss Rose!' the call came after me.

I had forgotten about it. As I removed it, I became aware of the state of my clothes – my oldest clothes, serviceable serge crumpled and streaked with dried mud, boots and hems crusted, sleeves and bodice damp from bathing the boy. I brushed ineffectually at the marks, and, pausing by a mirror, swept back a trailing frond of hair, then snapped my hands down. Why should I care how I looked for Geoffrey Devlin? But even in the dimness of the hall, heightened colour revealed my agitation.

He was in the homely parlour, straddled on the hearthrug with his back to the fire as he gazed round the room with its round table covered in baize, a brass lamp standing at its centre. The walls were hung with oils, engravings, and a couple of calendars from merchants, and among the fine old pieces of china on the sideboard were saucers of wheat and barley samples, and 'Prize Cattle' cards.

On that December day, with clouds low overhead, the room was dim, the fire's light gleaming on Geoffrey's polished knee-boots. Elegant in riding attire, he examined every detail of my dishevelment before his dark gaze rested on my face, questioning and anxious, seeking a response.

Despite the tension inside me which squeezed my lungs and stirred each tiny hair on my skin, I believe I managed to sound uninterested. 'Mr Devlin. Good afternoon.'

The animation in his face died as if a curtain had been drawn. He sketched me a bow, imitating my formality. 'Miss Hamilton. Forgive me, I had hoped your father would be at home by now. I find it hard to believe that he has gone away and left you with no one in charge.'

'*I'm* in charge.'

A sceptical eyebrow twitched. 'That was the impression my father received. I told him it couldn't be true, despite the rumours I've been hearing. It's hardly the proper—'

'I'm perfectly capable of running the farm,' I broke in, annoyed that he should presume to criticise. 'Was it my father you came to see?'

'Yes. But perhaps it's better if you answer for yourself, since you were the one who wrote the letter.'

'Letter? Ah.' So that was what had brought him. 'Do you intend to repair the hedge, or must I resort to a solicitor?'

He drew his brows together, mouth set and eyes sparking as he threw out an arm in a gesture of irritation. 'Must we p-prolong this ridiculous feud?'

'Feud?' I repeated.

'What else would you call it? It has been going on for too long already. Now your ill-conceived interference has made matters worse. My father was incensed – justifiably so – by the tone of your communication. I can't think what p-possessed you to write in such terms. What right had you—'

'More right than your father had in coming to this house and upsetting my stepmother!' I exclaimed. 'Especially at this time, with my father away and all of us distressed. May I remind you it's barely a month since we buried my brother?'

That reached him. He took a long breath, regarding me sombrely as he extended his hand in appeal. 'I can only apologise most sincerely, and beg your indulgence. My father doesn't always think before he acts. He's irascible, and growing worse with the years. That's why… This ludicrous b-business of the hedge…'

It had begun two years before: one of our trees, struck by lightning, had been left in a dangerous condition, so Father had ordered it felled. Unfortunately, the men had miscalculated and the tree had fallen into the boundary hedge, breaking down an entire section which had recently been plashed and layered at the cost of much time and trouble to Sir Arthur's men. He, in a temper, had blamed Father for negligence, and though our men had repaired the hedge as best they could, it had not satisfied Sir Arthur: he chopped down their repairs, and filled the gap with wicker hurdles, which were constantly being blown down, letting animals through in one direction or another, so that continuing arguments had ensued. The damaged hedge had begun to sprout again from its roots, but it was not yet strong enough to keep out greedy sheep – as we had discovered.

'It's a sorry tale, don't you agree?' Geoffrey said. 'Two stubborn men locking horns over a trifle. My father is the main culprit, that much I allow. But your father replies in kind, and your recent letter has only made my father angry, and even more determined not to repair the hedge.'

'I didn't know,' I said.

'No,' he replied with a sigh, his eyes cloudy as he gazed down at me. 'How could you?'

He was very close to me – how he had come there I do not know, for I don't recall either of us moving, but somehow he had come very close. I could almost feel the warmth of him. His nearness reached out to encompass me, calling me to touch him, lean on him, to know again the strength of his arms. I remembered too well how his lips felt, gentle on my face, how his hands would tremble, touching me, how his body blended with mine and— No!

I jerked back violently, making him blink and frown at me. He said: 'There's no need for us to quarrel over it. I hope we can be friends, you and I.'

Friends. The word was meaningless. 'Acquaintances, perhaps.'

'Oh, Rose…' he sighed, the message in his eyes, and the regret in his voice, raising shivers along my nerves. 'More than that, surely. After everything that was between us…'

'Don't speak of it!' Throwing my hands to cover my ears, I moved further away. 'Don't ever speak of it.'

'But we must, Rose,' he said quietly, stepping softly towards me. 'There are so many things I want to…'

I swung round and snatched at the door, throwing it open. 'I must ask you to leave, Mr Devlin.'

'Rose…' he pleaded, coming closer.

I stood frozen, my face averted, and when he reached past me to close the door I spun away, holding my skirts to avoid crowding tables and chairs as I made for the far side of the room. There I tugged on the silk rope that would ring the bell and summon the maid.

'You're angry with me,' Geoffrey said. 'Did you… d-did you have my letter? I wrote to you in Brighton. I wanted—'

'I had it.' My voice was flat, bitter. I couldn't look at him.

'I took the coward's way,' he confessed. 'I know I did. But if you knew what pressures…' The words trailed off and there was silence for a moment before he added with a sigh, 'I won't bore you with my troubles. But we are neighbours, Rose. We're bound to meet. If we can at least be polite with each another…'

Regarding him from my eye corner, I said stiffly, 'You will never have cause to reproach me for *my* conduct.'

He smiled a little ruefully at that. 'And are you reproaching me for mine? Do you find it strange that I am unable to forget—'

But, whatever he had in mind, its telling was curtailed by the arrival of good-natured, incurious Swift.

'Mr Devlin is leaving,' I said.

'Yes, miss.'

She bobbed a curtsey and turned to lead the way to the door. In her wake, Geoffrey exaggerated a bow that both mocked and chided me.

Then, as he started across the hall, there came a high-pitched scream, and a yelp, and a small naked body erupted from the kitchen passage, stepping on a mat that slid and spilled him, sending him tumbling headlong against Geoffrey's legs. The impact nearly unbalanced Geoffrey.

'What the—' He grabbed for the naked imp, but the boy was up and darting away, colliding with a whatnot. It toppled, shedding ornaments and a big potted aspidistra that crashed deafeningly on to polished floorboards. Shards of broken pottery appeared among a mess of spilled soil. The boy dodged away, started up the stairs – and stopped when Narnie appeared at the top, demanding to know what was going on.

'He bit me!' Mrs Benstead announced, emerging from the passageway with the assaulted finger raised. 'Bit me, the nasty little toe-rag! Do you come here, my man, and I'll learn you how to bite!'

Caught between Narnie, at the top of the stairs, and Geoffrey at the bottom, the boy looked from one to the other like a trapped animal. Quick as light, he shinned up to the banister, poised there on his bare feet like an acrobat in a sideshow, and took a flying leap. He hit the floor awkwardly, a splat of flesh against board, and sat there nursing his leg, muttering obscenities that came the more shocking from one so young.

Everyone began talking at once. Geoffrey was astonished, Narnie outraged, Mrs Benstead seething. Howlett and I looked on in mute amazement as Swift bent and wrapped the struggling boy in her apron, carrying him away to the kitchen.

'Whatever is going on?' Mama asked in bewilderment as she joined Narnie on the landing. 'Oh… Mr Devlin, good afternoon to you. Is something wrong?'

'It's that boy,' Narnie said, glowering down at me. 'I knew no good would come of it, but Miss Rose has to have her way.'

'Rose, have you offered Mr Devlin some refreshment?' As always, Mama dealt with unpleasantness by ignoring it. She came down to join us and insisted that Geoffrey must have a cup of tea before going out again in the damp chill weather.

So we sat in the parlour by the fire, like polite company, making polite conversation over tea and the first mince pies of Christmas. I found myself recounting the tale of the urchin and how I had rescued him, while Narnie tutted her scorn from a corner behind me.

'It was a kind impulse,' Geoffrey said. 'But you can't hope to improve the boy's lot by giving him a bath and one good meal.'

'I've shown him a different way of living, however briefly,' I replied. 'I've shown him that there is kindness as well as cruelty. He may remember it. It may influence him, to the good, in the future.'

His expression said he doubted this would be so, but he said, 'Perhaps.'

'What would you have had me do?' I demanded. 'Leave him to be beaten because he was too exhausted to work?'

'Was he? If so, he recovered remarkably swiftly.'

'Mr Devlin is right, dear,' Mama put in. 'Oh, I applaud your charitable instinct, but such a child…' She shuddered delicately. 'I heard the language he used. My dear, such children are beyond help.'

'Indeed,' said Geoffrey. 'You will recall, Miss Hamilton, the ingrate bit the hand that fed him.'

Glancing at him, I saw an ironical gleam in his eye and realised he was having a little fun at Mama's expense, though she remained unaware of it.

'Oh, yes!' Mama breathed. 'He bit Mrs Benstead. Such ingratitude.'

I sat staring down into my cup, tensed against a sudden desire to laugh aloud. Geoffrey had always been able to make me laugh. It was one of the things about him that I loved. *Had* loved, I reminded myself sharply. And I had been mistaken in him. I mustn't be fool enough to forget how badly he had betrayed me.

The trouble was that, every time I saw him, the present reality of him – his apparent sincerity, his undeniable charm, his disarming wish to make amends – blurred the details of memory. I even caught myself wondering if I had been wrong about him, and the next moment, angry with myself, I knew that I was falling prey to that same old spell. I wanted to cling to my dream. Deep inside, I was still a fool.

Later, Mrs Benstead reported the disappearance of the work-gang child. Waiting for his clothes to dry, he had curled by the fire, seeming to be sleeping, but in fact waiting for the moment when Mrs Benstead stepped out to the dairy. When she returned, the boy and his damp clothes were gone, and with them the blanket in which he had been wrapped, a loaf of bread, three herrings, some onions – and two silver tablespoons.

In fading daylight, I went after him, but he was not with the work-gang as they made ready for the weary trek home. 'Run off back to Castle Acre, I 'spect,' said the gang-master. 'Well, I did try to warn you, Miss Hamilton. That young Jack Huggins's a wicked sinner. But his father's dead, and his mother's sick, and three more young 'uns to raise. Will you be bringing charges?'

Though I was angry at being made to look a fool, I deemed it best to forgive. The lad was welcome to the food, and as for the spoons, well, perhaps they might procure a few comforts for his family.

Narnie told me I was a fool – a naïve fool. Charity was best kept for one's own folk, who could repay it with loyalty and hard work. It was not to be squandered on the likes of young Jack.

–

Thoughts of Geoffrey continued to haunt me. Memories, and unanswerable questions, intruded whether at work or leisure, getting into my dreams at night. He had said we must talk. Perhaps he was right. Too much had gone unspoken between us.

When he came again to Orchards, as he surely would, I resolved to listen to what he had to say. I looked forward to it.

But the days went by, and Geoffrey did not come.

–

I went down to the yards at dawn, as usual, to give the men their daily orders. To my surprise and relief, Father was there, talking with Plant and Benstead. He looked at me across his shoulder – a dour look – then went on with his discussion. I waited nearby, hearing him ascertain what work was in progress, and when I tried to intervene to correct something Plant said, Father again looked at me. 'I'll talk to you later, Rose. Go up to the house and wait for me.'

Finding myself with nothing else to do, I trailed home and waited to be called for breakfast.

'Did you know Father was home?' I asked Mama when she appeared.

'He is?' Her hand sought the comfort of her amethyst pendant as her face lit with hope. 'Oh, Rose... How is he? What did he say?'

We were at table when Father came in. Mama looked up, eyes wide and anxious over the whiteness of a napkin she crumpled at her lips.

'Will?' was all she said, and he replied, 'Good morning, my dear. Yes, Swift, I'll have coffee – and ham and eggs and kidneys.'

Nothing was ever said about his absence – not in my hearing, anyway.

My own appetite had fled, but Father seemed hungry and disposed of a hearty breakfast. Finally, draining his cup, he blotted his mouth and tossed his napkin aside before pushing back his chair. Only then did he look directly at me, saying, 'You'd better come and show me what you've been doing, Rose.'

I searched his unreadable face, wondering at the import of this. Was he angry?

'Well, girl? Are you coming? I asked them to have the horses ready for us. It seems you've been riding Dandy.'

Swallowing a lump of apprehension, I said, 'Yes. He needed exercise and—'

'I had it in mind to sell him,' Father said. 'Maybe I was wrong. You always did want a horse of your own. Well, shall we go?'

And so, in his own oblique way, he gave Dandy to me.

It was a fine clear December day, frost remaining in shaded places even though the sun was bright. As we toured the farm I remained on edge and defensive, but Father neither harangued nor criticised, only pointed out one or two errors of judgement I had made. I gained the impression that, overall, he was pleased by the way I had managed.

When I confessed about the troubles with Sir Arthur, and the letter I had written, his eyes gleamed, though the rest of his face remained stern, as if carved in weathered oak.

'He's a bad-tempered old fool,' he said. 'But I'll best him yet, see if I don't.'

Though he never openly encouraged me to help about the farm, neither did he forbid me. Whenever I chose to ride the lanes my presence was accepted and though Father resumed the management I continued to do the books, to learn and to observe, unobtrusively. I was not filling Victor's place, not completely, but I felt sure I was of use and that comforted me.

We didn't speak about my future, whether I should stay or not, nor did he mention my long exile. I was home again, and that was that: 'Least said, soonest mended,' as Narnie would have said.

As the first snows fell, confining me more to the house, Grace came home. She had learned a few new airs and graces from her stay with the Kinnersleys, and she was forever praising their taste, their house, their clothes, their friends, and quoting her friend Miss Maria Kinnersley, who had opinions on every subject from fashion to flirting. Mama found the gossip diverting.

One afternoon shortly before Christmas we were in the parlour, Grace occupied with embroidery while Mama worked on a picture she was making from scraps of coloured paper. Narnie was mending lace on a pillowslip and I had a book in my hand, a novel borrowed from the circulating library.

White light invaded through lace curtains, shining from the snow which lay inches deep on the surrounding countryside, but the sun was shining in a blue sky and I could hear a blackbird singing. I also heard a tinkling of bells, and wheels rattling up the drive. Bored with my book, I got up to look out and see who was coming.

It was a lady, all alone, driving a neat trap with a four-in-hand of miniature ponies, their harness strung with tiny bells. She came up to the porch and stopped, set her whip in its bracket and climbed down to tether her horse, glancing up at the house as she did so.

I must have made some small exclamation, for Mama said, 'What is it, Rose? A visitor?'

Surprised into immobility, I watched the lady take a laden basket from the trap, lifting her skirts clear of the wet ground as she stepped up to the door.

'It's the Princess of Wales!'

I have seldom known such fuss and bustle as they all leapt to their feet and frantically began tidying themselves and the cushions. Mama declared she was going to faint, then decided there was no time for that, while Grace went to a mirror and began to press her lips together and pinch her cheeks to bring more colour to her face.

Feeling that a personal welcome might be more pleasing on such an informal visit, rather than waiting for Swift to announce the visitor I went into the hall as the maid was opening the door. I saw her goggle and drop a wobbling curtsey before stepping back.

The princess caught sight of me and her sweet smile beamed out as she sailed across the hall with her hand extended. 'My dear Miss

Hamilton! No, no!' she chided as I automatically bent my knees in respect. 'Not here, remember. Here I am at home and we are friends. Look what I've brought – some Christmas dainties from my kitchen. I made the biscuits myself – Bertie loves them. My dear... how are you?'

That visit was the first of many. We eventually got used to welcoming Her Royal Highness into our parlour, where she made herself at home, but on that first occasion we were all over-anxious and tongue-tied until the princess's own natural sweetness put us at ease. She did not stay long, but the brief visit cheered us all.

When she had gone, we rehearsed every word and nuance over again, all of us enchanted by our visitor. Mama and Grace were thrilled to think that we were on the verge of a close relationship with the big house. We should undoubtedly receive invitations. What opportunities that would provide for Grace and me!

We fell to discussing ball-dresses. Grace, of course, knew all about current fashions and promised us that her friend Miss Kinnersley would help us to procure the very latest patterns.

'We really must take every care to be up-to-the-minute,' she said. 'All the other ladies of the district will be sure to...' She stopped as a stray thought intruded, making her face glow as she exclaimed, 'I quite forgot! One piece of gossip that Maria heard only recently... Listen to this, Rose, you may be interested. Mama, have you heard of a young lady named Lucinda de Crecy?'

The name raised unwelcome echoes for me. My heart seemed to pause, holding its breath, as memory swept me back to an autumn day three years before...

I had been on my way to meet my young lover, anxious as I took the familiar path through the woods. Geoffrey was going to Italy, where his aunt was sick. This was our last chance to meet. If he wasn't there, if he didn't come... Growing ever more desperate, I picked up my skirts and ran—

Straight into Hal Wyatt. Tall and fair, with the coldest eyes.

For a moment I struggled wildly with him, then I broke free and backed away. He was barring my path, his smile pure malice.

'You're in a hurry, Rose,' he observed. 'Where are you going in such a rush? Going to meet Dev again?'

I hung there, gaping at him stupidly, my brain paralysed with horror. 'How—'

Hal laughed at me. 'How do you think? He's a friend of mine. He told me. Men do, you know. Talk about their conquests. Their little village whores.'

Fear and anger made me lash out at him, but Hal parried the blow and swung me round against a tree. He wasn't angry, he was enjoying himself. 'Has he told you he loves you? Has he told you he'll marry you?' A rich chuckle erupted from his throat. 'You're a fool if you believe that. Marry you? He's as likely to marry a scullery-slave.'

I began to struggle, but he held me fast, his hands like bands around my arms.

'Use that educated head of yours,' he mocked me. 'Sir Arthur has financial problems. Everyone knows that. He's deep in debt and he needs his son to marry money. Didn't you know they already have a bride picked out? An heiress. A very wealthy heiress. It's been understood for years that she and Geoffrey would marry some day.'

'It's not true!'

'It *is* true!'

'Then what's her name? Tell me her name!'

'Lucinda de Crecy. The Honourable Lucinda de Crecy. Lord Elston's daughter. Why don't you ask Dev if she's real or not?'

But I hadn't had a chance to ask Geoffrey. I hadn't seen Geoffrey. The man who came eventually and found me weeping was my brother, Victor, summoned by the backus boy, who had seen me quarrelling with Hal. Victor, 'doing what was right', had taken me back to face Father.

Emerging as if from mists, I heard Mama say, 'No, I don't believe I have, my love. Who is she? Another friend of the Kinnersleys?'

'According to Maria, she's an heiress,' Grace confided, her face alight.

'And did you meet her, my love?'

'No, Mama!' Grace laughed. 'Maria *told* me about her. But I might be meeting her soon. We all might, since she's going to be living quite near. The fact is, Miss Lucinda de Crecy... is about to announce her engagement... to...'

She paused, teasing every ounce of drama from the moment, while I stared at my book, unable to move, immobilised by a hand that seemed to have fastened about my heart.

'To whom?' Mama asked a little impatiently.

'To Mr Geoffrey Devlin!'

The hand about my heart squeezed viciously. It was true then. Just as I had been allowing myself to believe again, here was proof of Geoffrey's duplicity. Hal Wyatt hadn't lied. Lucinda de Crecy did exist.

Four

'Why, that *is* news!' Mama cried. 'Mr Devlin to be married. Rose, did he mention this when he was here? Did you know about it?'

'Why should I be concerned with such inconsequential tittle-tattle?' I retorted. 'Besides, it may not be true.'

'Of course it's true.' Grace was indignant.

'Well, whether it is or whether it isn't, it's of no importance to me *who* Mr Devlin might marry.'

'But aren't you intrigued?' Grace gasped. 'I mean, everybody's been speculating about it for years. There was talk about him and Felicity Wyatt, if you remember, though Mama always said that was all nonsense – wishful thinking on Mrs Wyatt's part – didn't you, Mama? Anyway, this is the truth: Maria Kinnersley is acquainted with someone who knows the family and she's told me *all* about it. The de Crecys live a good deal in Italy, but their family home is in Kent. They're related to the Dukes of Devonshire, and they've known the Devlins for years – Lady Devlin has family in Italy, too, you know. That's where Mr Devlin met Miss de Crecy. Maria Kinnersley says the announcement has been expected for some time. Miss de Crecy is an only child, very beautiful, and very wealthy. But then that was to be expected, I suppose. Sir Arthur wouldn't allow his only son and heir to marry a nobody, would he?'

On New Year's Day, 1866, the betrothal was officially announced: The Hon. Lucinda de Crecy, only daughter of Lord Elston, to Mr Geoffrey Devlin, only son of Sir Arthur Devlin, Bt. As I was soon being informed by all the women of my acquaintance, New Year's Day was the intended bride's birthday. She was eighteen years old.

Only eighteen? – the news puzzled me. If it were true, then Lucinda had been only fourteen that summer when Geoffrey and I had been lovers. How long had the match been arranged? Just when had Geoffrey decided that he wanted to marry this wealthy child?

Not that it mattered. The announcement drained the last dregs of illusion from my heart, as surely as a pig-sticker's knife drains the blood from a sow. In Geoffrey Devlin's life I had been nothing but a diversion, a dalliance, an amusement to keep him from boredom.

Recalling our conversation in the firelit parlour, I concluded that my return to Orchards must have stirred his conscience – and his fears. What he wanted of me now was my silence.

–

Guests at Sandringham Hall that winter included members of several European royal families, together with aristocracy, artistes and any other person who happened to interest the Prince of Wales. The men went out shooting almost daily, their ladies joining them for lunch, or they would ride with the prince on inspections of his estate. Some of them joined the West Norfolk harriers for an outing after a fox. It became quite usual for us, when riding the lanes or walking the fields, to be greeted warmly by the Prince of Wales and his wife, and often introduced to their guests.

The byways were also busy with newspapermen, and spectators come for a glimpse of royalty. West Norfolk in winter had never been so frequented. However, around the end of January, when pheasant-shooting finished, our royal landlord and his wife left Sandringham to return to their court duties. The big house resumed its slumbers, life settled back to normal and winter work went on, the lambing being our main concern.

My weekly routine revolved around work on the farm and in the office. On Mondays I was usually a party to the haggling that ensued when the stock-buyers came visiting, and some weeks I went with Father to the Tuesday market in Lynn. He liked to linger, gossiping with his friends, and often dispatched me home alone on the train while he stayed behind, sometimes indulging so long at the inn that he had to stay overnight in town. I had a feeling that he saw his Tuesdays as a welcome escape from the wearying company of womenfolk.

Through a relatively mild winter the usual crop of coughs and fevers took its toll. We lost several of our own folk, among them old Beecham, the best hedger in the district; he died of influenza at the age of eighty-four, leaving his idiot son to be carted away, grinning, to the workhouse. The old man had worked all his life to prevent such an eventuality and it saddened me. But a greater sorrow was the death of children who succumbed to one disease or another.

Grace and I did what we could, visiting the sick with dainties from the killing of our pigs, or bones to make broth, or a bottle of Mrs Benstead's home-brewed elixir. We comforted the bereaved, ran errands, sent for the doctor or the rector, or sat with the ailing.

If my homecoming still caused ripples of curiosity, I discovered an equable demeanour to be my best defence – 'brazening it out', as Narnie would have said.

I did not see Geoffrey Devlin, nor did I wish to. I knew that I must forbid him even from my thoughts, but that proved impossible. When I pictured him with his beautiful heiress, pain sliced me to the heart – pain that turned into anger at myself for being such a fool.

–

In Dersingham I renewed my acquaintance with Pam Chilvers who had been in service with us. She and Ben shared a comfortable cottage with their two small daughters and the Widow Playford, relict of the old carpenter. Their parlour was clean and cheerful, cluttered with toys and photographs and cheap ornaments, with the old woman nodding in a creaking rocking chair by the fire and the children running in and out. Above the mantel an embroidered sampler read, 'Happy the Home where Love Abides'. And so it was.

The Chilvers's cottage became my oasis of peace, not least because Grace would never accompany me there: my half-sister felt it not quite proper to cultivate a friendship with such people, especially when Ben's father had been ignominiously dismissed from Orchards after protracted troubles and open insolence towards Father. The surly Amos Chilvers had never been a friend of any Hamilton. He now worked for the Devlins and had a cottage at Ambleford, so I took care only to visit his son's family when there was no risk of his being there.

That February, Pam Chilvers produced her third child – her first son, and to everyone's relief born without deformity. Only the middle child, tiny Alice, had inherited her father's club foot.

While I nursed the new baby, little Alice came hobbling to my knee and clung there, beaming up at me as I repeated nursery rhymes. Her bright button face appealed dearly to my heart, making me reach out to touch her cheek as I thought of my own lost daughter.

'You ought to get married and have one of your own, Miss Rose,' Pam Chilvers said.

Despite a knife of pain inside me, I laughed. 'Goodness, who would have me?'

'Any young man'd think himself lucky to have a wife like you. My Ben, he alluss say "Miss Rose deserve someone special", he say.'

The news made me smile. 'That's kind of him.'

'I hear as how Mr Basil Pooley is a regular caller at Orchards,' she remarked. 'And that there Mr Turnbull, too. Fine young men, both of 'em, and both doin' well for themselves, so I hear tell.'

'You hear a deal too much,' I chaffed. Concentrating on her sewing, she formed a delicate stitch and drew the thread through in a smooth, practised motion whose skill I envied. 'They say that Mr Hal Wyatt got himself wed over in America.'

'Yes, that's so,' I agreed.

Her needle bit cloth again, paused, and her hands relaxed as she looked across at me. 'That's not my place to say, and I hope you'll not take it wrong, Miss Rose. But me and my Ben, we're fond of you. You've always been a friend. So mebbe I can say... we was glad your father sent you away. Away from harm.' She glanced at old Mrs Playford, whose rocking chair had paused in its creaking rhythm. From beneath the lace of her mob cap, the old woman was watching intently. 'Pity nobody done the same for Ben's sister, Meg,' Pam added, and the silence lengthened as she smoothed out the work in her lap.

Puzzled, I tried to recall what I knew of Meg Chilvers. 'She's a housemaid at the Grange, is she not?'

'She was,' Pam amended, and as she lifted her head I saw her mouth tighten with anger. 'Truth is, Miss Rose, she was led astray. Got herself in the family way. Got herself dismissed.'

Before I could find words to reply, she went on, ''Course, he denied it all. Hopped off to America, quick as you please. Leavin' her stranded. That was terrible to see her, a-cryin' and a-mopin', wonderin' what was to become of her. Our Davy – my brother, Davy Timms... he offered to marry her and give the child a name. But she wun't have him. Well, you've seen him, Miss Rose, hen't you? You seen him at the station, the night you come home. Lost his good looks, hen't he? Meg called him a monster. She say, "I'd as soon walk the streets as wed with a man what look like somethin' out of a bad dream", she say. Then she run off. Went to London. Ben went after her, but...' Glancing at the door, she lowered her voice to add, 'They found her in the Thames, Miss Rose. Drownded. She died like a dog with no one nigh nor by to help her. All on account of that Mr Hal Wyatt.'

Hal Wyatt?! I had known he was a rake, but this... Appalled by the tragic story, I could think of nothing to say.

'She was sixteen year old,' she said bitterly. 'Sixteen, Miss Rose! How could he do that, get a young mawther in trouble and then deny it, go off and forget it? It wun't her fault, but she was the one as suffered.'

Meg's sin had been far less than mine – she hadn't had my advantages of education and birth. 'I'm so sorry. This is terrible news. But sadly it's the woman who always suffers in such cases.'

'Aye, that's so, Lord help us. But Meg wun't the only girl as had cause to regret ever meetin' Mr Hal Wyatt. I could tell you stories as would make your hair curl. And our Davy was hurt, too. He was fond of Meg. Where'll he ever find a wife, lookin' like he do? Oh, forgive me, Miss Rose, I didn't mean to sound off so. I just thought as you ought to know the truth of it. You'll be far better off with that Mr Turnbull, or even that Mr Basil Pooley.'

In some ways I was thankful for the misconceptions about my relationship with Hal Wyatt: most people seemed to believe I had been sent away to prevent any entanglement with him, and that I had been allowed to come home because he was safely married and in America. It served as a screen to cover the more shameful truth.

As I left the cottage, I ran into Ben Chilvers, covered in sawdust and chippings from the sawpit where he had been working. He greeted me with pleasure and swept off his hat, then stood brushing himself down as if embarrassed to be caught in such a state.

'Your son and heir is beautiful,' I said. 'The girls, too. Little Alice is a joy. You must be very proud.'

'Proud. And thankful,' he said with a smile. 'That's so, Miss Rose. I've been blessed, though only the Lord know why. I never did nothin' to deserve it, that I remember.'

'Didn't you? You saved my life once. I might have been trampled to death in the stable.'

'Oh...' Hot colour rushed up to stain his ears.

'And don't deny it,' I broke in. 'I shan't forget it. Ever.'

'That wasn't nuthin' I'm proud of,' he said, shuffling his feet and looking at his boots. 'I should've stopped 'im, but I was wholly scared o' the great bully. And then tryin' to cover up for 'im...' He let his eyes meet mine again. 'Truth is, Miss Rose, Amos witched them hosses.'

'Witched them?'

'That's what he call it – witchin', puttin' a spell on 'em. He knows all the owd magic. Got a book full of receipts that he never lets nobody see. Healin', drawin', jadin'... He wanted to mek mischief and get back at Mr 'amilton. So he took a dead mole and he rubbed it on the stable doors, all up and down the jambs, and on the lintel. Hosses won't go nowhere near the scent of a dead mole. It frights 'em. So when he let 'em loose in the stable, they got scareder and scareder, frit to escape through the doors, frit to stay with that scent in their nostrils.' He paused and shook his head at me. 'You don't look as if yer believe me, Miss Rose, but that's the truth. That's why I had to wash that scent off, afore anybody found out. I was scared what 'ud happen. And I was shamed – shamed of my own father. You could have been killed, but he wun't have cared.'

Shaken by the fierceness in him, I said, 'Nevertheless, Ben, you saved me, and I shall never forget it. I'm only sorry someone wasn't there to help your sister Meg. Your wife just told me.'

His brown eyes clouded with sadness. 'She was a foolish girl, but she didn't deserve that fate.'

'*No one* deserves such a fate!' I replied. 'Oh, Ben, I had no idea. What can I say?'

He shrugged his broad shoulders and looked down at the hat he held in his hands. 'Nothin' anybody can say, Miss Rose. Just that Mr Hal Wyatt better stay in America, that's all, for if he show his face in Dersen'am agen...'

For a moment the breeze blew extra cold. Was he threatening violence – he, the gentlest of men?

He must have read my thoughts, as he so often did. He said in an undertone, 'Davy Timms have a long memory, Miss Rose. A long memory and a bitter grievance against the world.'

–

As most of the district had observed, William Turnbull had become a regular visitor at Orchards on Sundays, arriving in time to join us at church, have lunch and spend the afternoon before catching the train back to Thetford. We often walked the fields with Father, or if the weather was bad we strolled, accompanied by Grace, in the roofed arcade between the bullock pens, where it was warmer, or took tea with Mama and played cards. The engineer sometimes called during the week, too, when he was about the district negotiating sales of his engines. In his own quiet, self-effacing way, he was paying me court. I did nothing to dissuade him. Nor, I think, did I actively encourage him.

Basil Pooley also took to calling on Sundays, a fact which irritated me and amused Grace; she loved to watch the two men covertly squaring up like stags at the rutting season.

'You should be flattered,' she told me. '*I* certainly should be, if two men came dangling after me, all but coming to blows over my favours. I just wish you would make up your mind which one you'll have. Mama won't let me have followers until you're settled.'

'Then you may have to wait a very long while,' I said.

–

During haying, I tethered Dandy to a post and climbed a field gate to sit and watch the scythes sweep and the tossers lift the grass to air and dry it. It was a bright day of chasing cloud and blue skies, birds calling, hares bobbing, the air full of the sweet scent of cut hay. As I breathed in the day, rejoicing in its splendours, the sound of horses and wheels drew my attention along the lane. A carriage was coming from Ambleford village. I recognised the uniform of the coachman and the footman on the box: Devlin retainers.

The carriage was open to the sun, gay parasols lifted to shade the faces of two ladies who sat together. One of them was Lady Ophelia Devlin, erect and haughty; she had been a great beauty in her youth and even now, turned sixty, remained a handsome woman. Her aristocratic nose lifted as she met my gaze and looked through me with no sign of recognition beyond a flicker of disdain.

The young woman beside her had her head turned to look at something beyond the far hedge, her arm extended as she pointed to draw the attention of her companions. All I glimpsed was a slender figure clad in brown silk, the turn of a youthful cheek behind a veil, and hair swept into a netted chignon beneath the straw and feathers of a fashionable pork-pie hat.

The carriage wheels tossed up stones and a whirl of dust, making Dandy shake his head and stamp, so that I reached to soothe him. And then, as the vehicle swept by, I saw the man who accompanied the ladies – it was Geoffrey. He was smiling at whatever the young woman in the feathered bonnet was saying. I froze with my hand on Dandy's coarse mane, seeing Geoffrey glance towards me, his smile dying as his eyes met mine and held across widening distance.

Even after the turn of the lane took them out of sight I sat there, my stomach churning, my heart beating so fast I thought I must faint. I knew who that young woman must be. All at once I was conscious of my crumpled, serviceable clothing, my straw hat tied on by a length of old muslin, and of my inelegant perch on the gate. No wonder Lady Ophelia had looked through me as if I were a peasant. I must have been mad ever to believe that her son cared for me.

Untying Dandy, I threw myself into the saddle and urged him into a trot and then a gallop, riding wildly down the lane, into the woods, with sunlight glimmering through trees. I drove the horse across the heath where rabbits darted back into their burrows in alarm and pheasants rose in a whirr of wings. Down the long incline among young pine trees we raced, and out to the watery wastes of the marshes, where bullocks grazed on lush grass threaded with dykes and bounded by banks. There, with the wide blue skies above me, with gulls flashing white wings, I half fell from the saddle and threw myself down among tall grasses to weep out the desolation that had been building in me for months.

How long I lay there in the tall marsh grasses I do not know, only that it was long enough for the racking sobs to give way to deep, shuddering breaths, and for misery to ease to numb despair.

Half dozing, I heard the grasses brush. 'Miss Rose?' the voice came from regions over my head. Then a hand fell on my shoulder and, as I jerked round, away from him, I blinked up into a face made indistinct by the brightness of the sky behind him.

'You all right, Miss Rose?' I knew the voice, and as he moved his head so that he shaded me from the sun I saw him gazing down at me in concern – Basil Pooley, roughly dressed in corduroys with a linen shirt and jerkin, a yellow kerchief tied at his neck.

I sat up, wiping with my hands at my futile tears until he reached into a pocket and presented me with a large handkerchief that smelled faintly of fish. I used it to dry my face, while he crouched beside me.

'You're a long way from home,' he said. 'Come out to see after the bullocks, have you?'

Since I could not be truthful, I grasped at the explanation he offered. 'That was my intention. And then I fell to thinking… about Victor, and…' It wasn't entirely a lie: Victor had been in my thoughts, his loss one of my greatest sorrows.

'I know,' he said. 'I do know how it is, Miss Rose.'

Angrily, I blew my nose, dried my eyes and stroked the dishevelled hair from my face. 'I didn't expect anybody to come by. Not here.'

'I've been fishing.' He lifted a pole that lay close by, showing me the five or six dabs that hung there. 'I was on my way back to share them with Old Fenny when I saw Dandy standing here.' In answer to the question on my face, he added, 'Old Fenny Jakes, the cockler. You must've heard of him. He lives in a cottage in the wood there.' He gestured at the trees clustered by the horizon, where the land began to lift towards the ridge, perhaps half a mile away across the flatness of the marshes. 'Why don't you walk with me? The old man doesn't get much company. We could beg a cup of tea. You look as if you need it. And Dandy here'll be glad of the rest.'

I let him help me up and then, like one in a dream, I walked beside him, lifting my skirts clear of the long damp grasses. Basil held his fishing pole jauntily over one shoulder, his free hand leading Dandy by the rein. I forget what we talked about. I only remember feeling empty, incapable of making any decision for myself.

We climbed up to the lane that wound around the edge of the marsh. It followed the contours of the wood, flanked by broad, deep ditches full of water after a rainy spring. Where the lane took a sharp turn, the pungent scent of wild garlic assailed us. Onion Corner: now I remembered hearing of an old cockler who lived in the wood here – in a cottage owned by Basil Pooley.

A pheasant called harshly from the thickets as we made our way down a rutted track where trees met overhead. Beneath them, ferns and blackberries tangled, half choking the course of a narrow ditch that drained on to the marshes.

The cottage lay deep in the woods, behind a broken fence and over-grown garden. A dog came barking out, its noise sending pigeons clattering among the trees until Basil spoke to it sharply and it subsided, sidling round us as we trod the uneven path. Honeysuckle clustered over the door, trailing fronds around the window on whose sill stood jars half full of water and dead wasps, and either side of the path a litter of old traps and creels lay discarded among trails of tattered fishing net and rusting buckets. Two cats lay sunning themselves against a wall where straggling foxgloves bloomed.

However, despite the surface air of neglect, a ladder was propped against the wall, and up on the roof a man was laying fresh thatch of Norfolk reed. Basil was evidently a thoughtful landlord.

'Can't leave the old man with rain dripping in, can I?' he said, and greeted the thatcher, 'Going well, Tam?'

'Goin' bootiful, Mr Pooley, sir,' the man replied. 'I'll have it done afore you know it.'

The cottage door stood ajar. Basil pushed it further open and stepped back to let me go first. 'After you, Miss Rose.'

Inside the cottage, as my eyes adjusted to the gloom, I saw an old man seated in an armchair by the hearth. Despite the warmth of the day he was well wrapped, red flannel pinned around his chest, his hands encased in ancient fingerless mittens, a blanket of knitted squares about his knees and on his head a shapeless cap from whose edges protruded wisps of thin white hair. A fire burned low, barely a red glow through a mound of ashes, with a kettle on a hook above it; objects lay about haphazardly, and several more cats slunk soundlessly, twining round chair legs and under the hang of oilcloth on the table. The place smelled of cats, and of unwashed human being, but on a wooden drainer by the stone sink a pile of cups and plates stood drying, so someone had made a small effort at housekeeping.

'Well now, Fenny,' Basil said loudly, tapping the old man on the shoulder. 'I've brought a young lady to see you.'

'Oh, aye?' the old man's voice was high and cracked. 'Who might that be, then?'

'It's Miss Rose Hamilton. I've told you about her. Miss Hamilton from Orchards Farm.'

'Oh, aye?' Old Fenny cocked his head, as if listening, and only then, as faded eyes stared into the distance, did I realise that he was blind. 'Your lady-love, is she, bor?'

Basil glanced at me sidelong, embarrassed. 'Take no notice of him, Miss Rose, he talk like a fool at times.' At this, the old man threw back his head, opening toothless gums to let out a cackle of laughter.

'You sit and talk to him while I make some tea,' Basil suggested.

And so I sat on the edge of a sagging horsehair couch, the cats prowling round me, and attempted to make conversation with the gnarled, wizened old man who had spent his life hunting for cockles on the shores of the Wash – and smuggling when the opportunity arose, so gossip had it. He refused to talk seriously, but kept making obscure, teasing remarks and then laughing loudly at his own nonsense. Behind my back, Basil made a sign that said the old man's mind was wandering.

Covertly, I watched as he made himself at home, raking over the fire until it glowed hotly, then lowering the kettle to heat. The cupboard on the wall, with its ill-fitting door, was well-stocked with dry goods, as I saw when Basil opened it to get out a tea caddy. From remarks passed between them I gathered that he had been at the cottage earlier, and that it was he who had washed the dishes and made some effort to tidy the place. He evidently came there frequently, presumably to check on the old man's welfare; I had a feeling that he was responsible for the good supply of food and fuel.

'You need some new cups, Fenny,' he told the old man as he poured the tea. 'These are all cracked or chipped. Here you are, Miss Rose. This one's the best – if you drink out of that side you'll be all right. I'm sorry that's not best china, but the tea's a good blend.'

'So long as it's wet and warm,' I said, taking the cup.

I was touched by his solicitude, both for me and the old man. I had never thought of Basil as the caring sort.

After a while, the tea drunk and the afternoon waning, I took my leave of Old Fenny.

'I'll see you to the gate,' Basil offered, adding to the old man, 'I'll be a couple of shakes and then I'll fry those dabs for our tea.'

Outside the June afternoon was golden, the scent of garlic heavy on the warm air. The thatcher had moved his ladder and could be heard hammering pegs in on the far side of the roof while, by the gate, Dandy pricked his ears, seeming rested and eager to go.

'D'you feel better now, Miss Rose?' Basil asked.

'Yes. Thank you.' Grateful to him, I looked into vivid blue eyes that searched my face with concern. 'I'm only sorry I've inconvenienced you.'

'Oh, you've not,' he said at once. 'You could never be an inconvenience to me. Miss Rose…' He hesitated, his expression unhappy in the moment before he blurted out, 'Miss Rose, it's probably not the right time to ask, but you may as well know… Old Fenny wasn't so far wrong. What he said about you bein'… I mean, you must know how I feel about you, and I just wondered if you could ever…' The sentence trailed off as he read my face and looked away, unlooping Dandy's reins from the fence, his mouth compressing in self-disgust. 'No. I see you couldn't. Didn't think as how you would, not really. Well, so long as I know. It's to be the engineer, is it?'

'No!' I spoke by instinct, too flustered to think straight. 'No, it's… it's not to be anybody, not yet. Maybe not for a long time. Mr Pooley, I… I'm flattered by your declaration, but… Too many other things weigh on me. Victor's death, Mama's illness, the farm… I can't possibly think about marriage. Not yet.'

Blue eyes narrowed incredulously, a light blazing behind them. 'But you're not turning me down? You're not leaving me without hope?'

'I…' What could I say? At that moment the thought of marriage with anyone made me want to run away, but in the end, inevitably, I must make a choice. Since love was not to be a factor, did it matter which man I chose? 'I'm not sure. I don't know. Please don't force me to make promises that I may not be able to keep.'

'Oh, I won't. I won't!' But even as he spoke he grabbed my hand and brought it to his lips, kissing my knuckles before folding my hand in both of his own, saying fervently, 'It's enough that you'll think on it. It doesn't matter for how long. I'm a patient man. You'll see that. I'll prove that I'm worthy of you. I'll wait. Until you're ready. However long it is. I'll wait.'

Disturbed by such intensity, I said, 'And if the answer's no, after all? If the waiting is for nothing?'

'Then I'll be content that you thought about it. I'll know I had a fair chance. Oh, Miss Rose…'

What he might have said, or done, I do not know; but at that moment I glimpsed the thatcher watching us, his head just visible beyond the ridge of the roof. I pulled my hand from Basil's grasp.

'Blast!' he muttered, his eyes flashing. 'Forgive me, Miss Rose. I'd not have folk talking. There's been enough of that.'

'Yes, indeed there has.'

'Groundless talk. I know that. I never believed—'

I felt chilled suddenly, and angry with him for no good reason. 'I'd better go. Help me, please.'

He laced his hands for my foot and I leapt up to the saddle, settling my skirts about me.

'I'll see you soon,' he said.

Unable to reply, I lashed the rein against Dandy's flank and he set off back down the track, where hares ran for cover among undergrowth scented with garlic.

My thoughts ran for cover, too, darting here and there seeking escape from the corner into which Basil Pooley had backed me. I didn't want him waiting and hoping; I couldn't bear the thought of having him come calling with that bright, eager look in his eyes. Why hadn't I had the courage to turn him down?

—

After much discussion, Grace was allowed to accept an invitation from the Kinnersleys to travel with them through France that summer. They departed in June, with the result that Mama fretted and grew ever more querulous.

The doctor could diagnose no specific illness, but despite all his efforts Mama had lost weight until she was almost skeletal, her face all eyes and cheekbones, her neck like a chicken's, her hands mere skin-covered claws. I remained convinced that the laudanum with which she dosed herself was partly to blame, but she and Narnie were adamant that she needed the drug if she was to sleep at all.

Soon after Grace went away, Narnie had a letter saying that her niece in Northumberland was desperately ill and her presence was required to comfort the girl's mother, her only sister. Since Johnny planned to spend most of the summer with friends, and Grace was in France with the Kinnersleys, the prospect of losing Narnie, too, sent Mama into transports of distress.

'Now, now, my lamb,' Narnie soothed her. 'It won't be for long. You'll have Miss Rose.'

'But Rose is no company. She won't sit still and talk to me like Grace does. Like you do, Narnie. She's always wanting to be out in the fields, or off to the village.'

Narnie shot me a look that said, There, now see what you've done. 'Never you fret, Miss Flora. Why don't you go and visit Mrs Jonathan in Lynn? The change would do you good. You could have some new gowns made while you're there. You always say Mrs Jonathan's dressmaker is as good as any seamstress in London.'

This prospect interested Mama so that she put aside her tears. 'Why, yes. Yes, you're right, Narnie. I must have some new gowns ready for the Birthday Balls at Sandringham. Rose and Grace must have some, too. Oh, but – we mustn't have them too early, in case the fashions change. Perhaps we should wait until Grace comes home, and see what she and Maria know of the latest styles.'

'We can still go to Lynn,' I said.

'We?' Mama looked at me blankly. 'You mean, you'll come with me?'

'But of course. I'd enjoy a stay at Weal House. There's so much to do in Lynn. The library, the shops, magic lantern shows, concerts in the park, walks by the river… We'll have a wonderful time.'

My offer was not entirely unselfish. Staying at Weal House would give me an excuse to avoid Basil, and stop me thinking about Geoffrey. Every horseman riding by along the lane, every gig or carriage to and from Ambleford had me gazing from windows, pausing in my work, watching, hoping… I despised myself for it, but my heart wasn't listening.

I wrote a letter to Basil, informing him with maidenly modesty that he had taken me by surprise, that I needed time to think about his declaration of affection. Besides, I would not be at Orchards for the next few weeks; I was to accompany Mama on a visit to my uncle and aunt in Lynn and we expected to be away probably until Grace came home from her extended trip to France.

However, in the way things have of turning back on one, Mama changed her mind about staying with Aunt Beatrice. On the evening before our planned departure I discovered her feverishly unpacking the clothes which the maids had prepared for her sojourn at Weal House.

'I cannot go!' she wept, throwing herself into my arms. 'Oh, Rose, I cannot go away. I dare not!'

'Dare not? Mama, what do you mean? What are you afraid of?'

But she wouldn't tell me. I helped her into bed, pitying her. Poor sick, helpless Mama.

'My medicine,' she cried. 'I must have my medicine!'

For the sake of peace, I dosed her with laudanum and sat with her until she sank into a snoring stupor. And in the morning I had the servants complete the unpacking.

Naturally Basil got to hear that I was still at Orchards, and naturally he took it ill; he did not come near the farm again for months. His uncle, Farmer Pooley, said that important business had taken Basil to London and in order to deal properly with it he had taken a house and planned to stay in town for a while. I felt guilty for my part in chasing him away, but at least his absence saved me from any further unwanted attentions. Sincere as he might be, I could not take him seriously as a suitor.

—

With Narnie away, I was surprised to find how much there was to do – seeing to the ordering, keeping a check on the kitchen, the dairying and the brewing, generally overseeing both domestic servants and yard-workers. Mrs Benstead ruled the kitchen, of course, with Swift and Howlett in the house; an old laundry-woman came in to do the washing; two other women saw to the dairying and brewing, besides a gardener and a man-of-all-work, with various lads and girls to assist them. And there was that mine of miscreance, the backus boy, who received the sharp edge of everyone else's temper.

I also played companion to Mama, listening to her inconsequential chatter, plans for wonderful marriages for Grace and me, visions of social triumphs at Sandringham Hall. When letters came from Grace, telling of adventures in France, Mama read them aloud, building fantasies from a turn of phrase: Grace had met a rich Frenchman; Grace was invited to stay at a chateau; Grace was obviously in love and would probably be married before the year was out. More and more Mama lived in a world of imaginings; the real world seemed to hold too many terrors for her.

During that summer, men appeared in our fields without so much as a 'by your leave', and began planting shrubs and young trees across both crop and fallow. The trees were designed to provide shelter for the prince's game birds and we had no right to interfere. We were not even permitted to clear the weeds around the saplings, for fear of disturbing nesting birds, though seeds spread among our crops and the resulting wild growth threatened to choke both root and wheat. Our hoers were kept busy dawn to dusk.

Hares were another increasing annoyance. 'Kangaroos' the village folk called them or, more often, 'blasted kangaroos'. They chewed on the choicest swedes, bit tops off mangolds, feasted on corn and battered down leaves. They nibbled the bark of our apple trees, and in our garden they picnicked on freshly-planted rose bushes and finished off with a dainty dessert of flowers.

But protests to the land agent brought the same reply – the game belonged to the prince, who was only exercising his rights, as landowner, to use his acres for the rearing of birds and animals that would provide him and his friends with good sport. The law that allowed him this privilege had obtained for centuries.

–

The time of the Royal Norfolk Agricultural Show approached. It always caused a buzz of excitement in the farming community and that year it was of especial interest to me because William Turnbull was to exhibit some of his firm's latest engines. He had presented me with a printed invitation to visit the Turnbull stand at the show ground.

Father planned to spend a day or two at the show, but he decreed that Mama, even had she been interested in things agricultural, was not well enough to go with him. With both Narnie and Grace away, that meant that I must stay behind too. Much to my irritation, I had to be content with William Turnbull's recollections, recounted to me when he called the following Sunday.

'A great success!' he beamed as we strolled in the dappled shade of the orchards, ducking under branches where young fruit swelled. 'We have several orders already – firm orders for some of our most expensive engines. And, beyond all my hopes, an invitation to hold a demonstration when we shall be able to show what our engines can really do, on the ground, in a real farming situation.'

'I'm so glad,' I said. 'I've been afraid that, after what happened to Victor...'

'I, too.' Stroking his luxuriant beard, he regarded me gravely. 'But I believe we have proved that that was just a freak accident – a most terrible, unfortunate accident, but an accident just the same. Now we must put that behind us. Victor would have wanted us to go on. To look to the future.'

'Yes. Yes, he would.'

There was a pause. During it, I heard him draw a long deep breath. 'Speaking of the future...'

'Where is the demonstration to be held?' said I.

He hesitated, but I feigned not to realise that I had interrupted a portentous speech. His innate good manners came to my aid, obliging him to answer my question and set aside his own intent.

'Quite near here. On the neighbouring estate. Ambleford.'

'Ambleford?' My dismay must have shown itself.

'Have I done wrong?' Turnbull asked anxiously. 'Sir Arthur Devlin was most accommodating. I could hardly refuse his offer to allow us the use of his estate. He visited our stand at the show more than once. His son was agreeably interested, too. They stayed for hours.'

'Indeed?' Troubled by thoughts of Geoffrey, I moved away to lean on the fence that separated orchard from meadow.

Benstead and his boy, both dressed in Sunday best, were driving heavy-uddered cows across long grass merry with buttercups. I hardly noticed the familiar sight. My thoughts elsewhere, I nudged the toe of my boot against the sacking barrier nailed taut along the bottom of the fence in an effort to keep the nibbling hares out of the garden.

'I'm conscious that your father has certain problems with Sir Arthur,' Turnbull said, following me. 'Will he raise objections to my accepting the invitation? A good many West Norfolk landowners are eager to watch our engines in action, but… I thought it hardly tactful to suggest trying again at Orchards.'

'And you were right! Father wouldn't want that. Nor would I.'

'Then… is Ambleford too close? Will it raise too many painful memories for you? Sir Arthur plans to make it a gala day. I had hoped that you and your father would do me the honour of attending the event, as my personal guests.'

His anxiety not to cause offence, to Father or to me, revealed a sensitive nature, but it also irritated me beyond reason. He was pompous, a man of little humour or imagination. But he was also considerate, steady and reliable, and he had excellent prospects. One day he would be a wealthy man. And he cared for me – he kept coming all the way from Thetford just to spend a few hours in my company. I ought to be flattered to be courted by such a man. He would make a fine husband.

A visit to Ambleford in his company might not be a bad thing; it would show Geoffrey Devlin that I was not still yearning after him. Turning with a smile, I said, 'You're right. Victor believed in your engines. He'll be there in spirit, cheering you on. I can't speak for my father, but… I shall be honoured to be your guest, William.'

His eyes lit up and his beard parted as he smiled with genuine delight. 'It will be a special day, Miss Hamilton – Rose. A most special day, if you are there beside me.'

Flattered by his evident devotion, I promised myself that, before the day came, I would make up my mind about William Turnbull.

–

Since Narnie had departed for Northumberland, I had been trying a remedy for Mama's indisposition: I watered down her phial of laudanum, just a little, hoping in time to wean her off the drug. One of her doctors had recommended this course to Narnie, but she, swayed by Mama's frantic pleading, had ignored his advice; she thought she was helping Mama, believing that her 'lamb' really needed the medicine.

Aware of the responsibility I had assumed, I remained alert for every change in Mama's emotional stability. I propped my door ajar and, most nights, lay awake until after I had heard Father go in to her. In the morning I was ready to tend her as soon as Father left at dawn. Often she would still be sleeping, under the influence of her medicine, and when she woke her mind remained fogged by the drug.

'I do wish you would try not to take the medicine every night,' I frequently told her. 'I'm sure it's not good for you to take so much.'

'I try,' she would say in her helpless little-girl way, with a shrug and a quick touch to my hand. 'I do try. But then I lie awake and my heart pounds so and I get palpitations and I think I'm dying and… I can't do without it, Rose. I can't!' Her voice would rise, her thin hands clutching at me.

Surreptitiously, I added a little more water to the phial, though I had begun to think that curing her of her unhealthy addiction was beyond my powers. Yet if she didn't stop she would surely die of it.

'I'm afraid she's really sick,' I told my father, who was poring over the books in the office. 'Perhaps we should send for the doctor.'

Drawing deeply on the glowing nub of his cigarette, he pressed it out in an ash-tray full of stubs and let the smoke trickle from his nostrils as he watched me over the half-moon spectacles he had lately affected. 'She's seen more than one doctor, Rose. You know that. They find nothing wrong. This sickness… it's in her mind, not her body. My wife, your stepmother, is a hypochondriac, and since the state is of her own choosing she must live with it, as must we all.'

'There must be some cause,' I said.

'There is: her overworked imagination.' He sounded ineffably weary as he removed his glasses and pinched the bridge of his nose. 'She's always been afraid of illness. You know that as well as I. Rose, don't bother me with this now. I've tried. There's nothing I can do.'

'But surely—'

His hands came down flat on the desk and he rose to his feet, glowering at me. 'I said don't bother me with it! Why will you never learn when to leave well alone? I have work to do. Don't burden me with women's problems. You see to it. What else are you here for? I allowed you to stay – much against my better judgement, when many another man would have sent you from his door. I allowed you to stay because my son begged me to forgive you and for the sake of his memory—' His voice grew rusty and his mouth snapped shut as he fought to hide his emotion. 'The least you can do is shield me from these petty household concerns,' he finished, and sat down, beginning to sort irritably through his papers.

I felt as though he had slapped me. So this was why he had let me stay – because Victor had pleaded for me. Unable to find words to express my feelings, I spun on my heel and snatched the door open, slamming it behind me.

'Rose!' he shouted after me. 'Damn you, Rose...!' The words caught in his throat, and as I climbed the stairs I heard him coughing.

—

In the darkest hours before dawn, something woke me. Still half asleep, I listened to the wind in the woods tossing summer leaves, whispering like the sea; then as I came further awake, I heard the sound that had really disturbed me – Mama was weeping.

Barefoot, I crossed the hall, dragging a wrap about me as I hastened to her door and knocked there, calling softly, 'Mama? Mama?'

The sobs lessened, as if she were trying to hide them from me, but her distress was too deep to be silenced. As I opened the door I saw the bedroom dimly lit by a low-burning lamp at her bedside. The bed was empty, the covers thrown back. Small snufflings, interspersed with wrenching shudders of breath, came from beyond the darkened doorway of the dressing-room.

In the edge of light from the bedroom, I saw her kneeling by the couch, lying half across it, her arms outstretched to embrace its leathered seat. Her night bonnet drooped askew over trailing, tumbled hair, and her thin body looked pitiful in its voluminous, lace-trimmed cotton nightdress.

'Mama!' I hurried to her, laying a hand on her bird-thin shoulder. 'Mama, what is it? Are you ill? Where's Father?'

She raised a wan face that, even in the almost-darkness, looked haggard with tragedy, and her hand fastened about my arm like the teeth of a man-trap. 'He has not come home!' she cried, her voice so wild with despair that I scarcely recognised it. 'He has gone to her!'

Resorting to practicalities, I lifted her to her feet – not a difficult task when she was so frail – and half carried her back to bed, where I tucked her in much as Narnie would have done. All the time she wept inconsolably, throwing her head from side to side, mopping at her face with a sodden handkerchief which I wrested from her and replaced with a fresh one from her drawer.

I pleaded with her to try to rest, but still she thrashed from side to side on her pillows, wailing and exclaiming incoherently.

Concerned as I was, yet a part of me seemed to stand back and watch, mind wrestling at the inconsistencies of what I had found. Where was Father? Why had Mama been embracing the couch in the dressing-room? As for the reference to some unknown 'her', I refused even to believe that I had heard it. Mama was evidently more sick than I had realised if she had begun to imagine such things.

I found the smelling salts and held them under her nose, making her wince and push the bottle away. But at least it broke through the hysterical tossing and wailing into which she had worked herself. She lay still, her head turned away from me, sobs dredging up from deep inside her, as I wet a cloth in the ewer and wrung it out, to cool her brow. The room seemed stiflingly warm and I went to open the window, seeing the muslin curtains billow gently in a breeze. I also saw, with relief, that the eastern sky was lightening.

'It's almost dawn,' I remarked, leaning over the bed to turn the cloth so that a cooler portion lay on her brow.

She seemed calmer, staring up at me with eyes buried deep in bruised sockets – eyes from which tears still seeped to trickle down her temple and into her hair. 'I don't think I can bear it, Rose. If he doesn't come home—'

'Of course he'll come home,' I consoled. 'He always does.'

Her face contorted as her agony returned and fresh fits of sobbing shook her. A bony hand came out and fastened painfully in the flesh of my upper arm. 'I must have my medicine! I must, Rose! I need my rest!'

I tried to loosen her grasp. 'Please let go. You're hurting me.'

At that she released me and threw her hand over her eyes to hide the flow of more tears. As I rubbed my sore arm, she muttered, 'I'm hurting, too. I hurt all the time, knowing he doesn't want me. He never wanted me, Rose. He married me because he pitied me. And even then I failed him.'

'Mama—'

'I did. I did! You mustn't blame him, Rose. It was *my* fault! Oh, dear God, how can I go on bearing it, year after year? Rose. Rose! Help me! I must have some sleep or I shall go mad.'

Because I feared that I was partly to blame for this, because of diluting her opiate, I mixed another thin draught of it and helped her take it. She drank it down as greedily as if it were the first liquid she had tasted in days. The mere taste of it seemed to calm her.

The breeze through the window caught the small flame in the lamp and, the oil being low, snuffed it out, leaving only the faint dawn light creeping grey into the room. I sat with Mama, holding her hand, hearing her breathing grow more even as her distress faded and she lay watching me with agony in her eyes.

'I tried so hard,' she croaked. 'I tried to be a good wife, even though...' Her fingers tightened on mine as she added in a voice choked with distaste, 'Marriage has its dark side, Rose. Men... men have needs and desires. Animal desires. Do you know what that means?'

'Yes, I believe so.'

Her nails bit urgently into my flesh. 'I thought so, too. But nothing had prepared me for the reality. I could not believe that such... Oh, I cannot describe it to you, I haven't the words. You cannot possibly know what a wife must endure.'

Dear innocent Mama. If ever she had suspected the reasons for my disgrace, she had long ago sealed them off from her conscious mind.

More tears welled in her eyes and dripped over to run in rivulets down her face. In a small, breathy voice cracked with despair, she said, 'I wanted so much to give your father another son. But after Grace came, every time I conceived, after a few months the pains would start. So much pain, Rose. So much blood. Every time, I thought I must surely die! And then, when again it happened, when I started with Johnny... I lived nine months of fear. Terrified of losing the baby. Terrified of dying – as your mother did. And then the birth...' Remembering, she writhed and laid a hand on her stomach. 'I gave your father his son. But I couldn't have gone through that agony again. I couldn't, Rose! I had to deny him my bed, didn't I?'

Horrified as I was to be offered such intimate secrets, yet pity surged through me – pity for them both. I glanced at the yawning darkness that was the open doorway to the dressing-room on whose couch, I guessed, my father usually slept.

'You mean you haven't...' I could hardly frame the shocking words, 'you haven't lived as man and wife since...'

'Since before Johnny was born.'

How had I gone through life without realising that so much was wrong between my parents?

'Only Narnie knew,' Mama said, and her lips formed a strange little twisted smile. 'I tell Narnie everything. I always have. I need someone to talk to. Someone who will listen to me. *He* won't. He never would.' As she stared at me, fresh tears formed in her eyes and she thrust the back of her hand against her mouth, saying unclearly, 'Oh, Rose! Does he talk to *her*? Does he? This woman... this *whore*—'

A tiny sound made me turn and straighten, seeing Father standing in the doorway, one arm braced against the jamb. I had the impression he had been there for some time. He looked tired, his body drooping, his clothes creased, his hair dishevelled. In his still face his eyes glinted as they rested on me without expression.

I heard Mama catch her breath. 'Dear God!' she whispered. 'Will! I didn't mean... Oh, dear God. Oh, dear sweet God!'

Five

His voice low and even, Father said, 'Leave us, Rose.'

'No!' With a high yelp of panic, Mama caught my hand and held on, digging her nails into my flesh, crushing the bones of my fingers together. She pulled herself over in the bed, so that she was behind me, out of Father's sight.

I stood between them, facing my father, feeling that I must defend Mama. 'She's sick. She's delirious. I tried to tell you—'

'That's right!' Mama breathed. 'That's right, I don't mean it. I don't know what I'm saying. It's just… I'm frightened, when I'm alone. I shouldn't have listened to wicked gossip. I'm sorry, Will. I'm sorry. It was Narnie. Narnie told me.' She sounded like a child, terrified of a beating, telling tales to deflect a parent's anger.

Father's thin brown face hardly changed, but all at once disgust was written clear amid his weariness. 'Dear Narnie,' he said softly. 'Dear, good old Narnie. The serpent in my Eden. Working against me, poisoning my wife's mind.'

My hand was going numb from the grip Mama had on it. She huddled on the bed behind me, sobbing and muttering to herself. Afraid for her, I said, 'Father, please… Not now.'

'Then what is it she wants of me? A divorce? Is that it?'

'No!' Mama whispered, clinging even more tightly, her legs drawn up as if she were in agony. She rubbed her face hard against my hand and I felt the warm flow of her tears on my skin. 'Don't let him leave me, Rose. I can't bear that. Anything! I'll do anything.'

Two strides brought Father within inches of me, glaring into my face. 'Get out of my way, Rose.'

I held my ground, though I was shaking. 'You're not to hurt her.'

'What do you take me for?' He thrust me aside. The force of it pulled Mama, still holding tightly to my hand, half out of the bed. I sprawled to the floor, jarring my hip and the wrist I landed on.

As I righted myself, rubbing my strained wrist with a hand that tingled as blood flowed back to it, Father helped a weeping Mama back into bed. His solicitude was strangely at odds with his recent temper. He drew the covers around her and sat beside her, stroking the damp hair from her face, saying in concern, 'Flora…'

'Only don't leave me!' she wept. 'Only don't leave me, Will. I can't lose you. I need you. I need you!' Taking his hand, she drew it to her lips and kissed it fervently, in an agony of love and despair that was painful to watch.

Father turned his head, looking over his shoulder at me. 'You can go back to your room now, Rose. I'll look after your mama.'

In the morning, Father gave me a letter to take to the post office in Dersingham. 'See that it's posted,' he said. 'See to it yourself, don't trust it to one of the servants.'

The letter was addressed, in Mama's hand, to Narnie at her sister's home in Northumberland. Judging by the ill-formed, spidery writing, it had been written in distress.

I hurried upstairs and found Mama at her dressing-table, listlessly brushing her hair. She gave me a tired smile.

'Rose… My dear, I was having such bad dreams in the night. I don't know what I said. You must discount it, whatever it was. I was not myself. All is well now. Your father and I… we have come to an understanding. I feel so much happier. Yes, much happier.'

'Then I'm glad.'

Through the mirror, she managed another tremulous smile, though panic peered from behind her eyes. 'I do wish dear Grace were here. I miss her. I don't know how I'm going to tell her… You see, Rose, your father… your father *and I* have decided that that it's time for Narnie to retire.'

I caught my breath. Narnie was to leave us? Was that the price my father had exacted?

'We're going to find her a cottage,' Mama added, 'though she may prefer to stay with her sister, in the north. What do you think?'

'Oh, Mama…' Awkwardly, I rubbed her shoulder, feeling the bones beneath thin flesh. 'Narnie won't desert you. I'm sure she won't.' I was sure of nothing. Being summarily dismissed after forty-odd years of dedication, Narnie might easily decide to take umbrage and stay away. 'Oh... how can Father do this to you? I don't understand him!'

She laid her hand over mine, watching me through the mirror. 'It's all right, Rose. I don't mind, really I don't. If it means he will be happy... He's right, anyway – Narnie is growing old. She deserves a rest. Besides, with the farm doing well, we can afford a proper lady's maid. Your father has promised to advertise at once for a suitable person. Won't Grace be pleased! But for now... would you mind?'

Knowing the futility of trying to talk to her, I took the hairbrush and began to stroke it through soft dark hair in which thick threads of grey were showing.

–

Only two days later, I came in from exercising Dandy to be informed by Howlett that the carrier's cart had arrived, and with it Narnie, returning from her stay in Northumberland. She had started on her journey before the letter could have reached her.

'She's in the parlour with the missus,' Howlett said.

Mama was on the sofa, her hands clasped at her lips, staring over them with tear-bright eyes at the rigid figure standing framed by the lace curtains at the window. Evidently the awkward news had been told.

Narnie looked grim. She was still dressed in her travelling outfit of black and grey, her figure made broader by a cape that trailed down to meet crinolined skirts, her grey kid gloves – a present from Mama – in her hand. She drew them slowly through her fingers as she glanced at me, her mouth set in angry lines that I knew well.

'So this is my thanks for all the years of faithful service,' she said. 'Soon's my back's turned, you set my Miss Flora against me.'

'Narnie...' Mama croaked. 'Don't blame Rose.'

'Why not? Did she speak up for me? Well, did she?' Regarding me balefully, she took a step towards me. 'After all I've done—'

'Please,' I broke in, afraid that some indiscreet word might betray things I had hoped forgotten. 'I know you're upset, Narnie, but it will be for the best. We'll look after you, I promise. There'll be a cottage, and an allowance. I'll bring Mama to visit you, frequently, and you can come here to see us.'

'I wouldn't set foot in this house again if the devil were after me with a red-hot poker,' she said, and stumped towards the door.

'You're not leaving?' Mama cried.

Narnie looked round. 'No, my lamb, not yet. Never you fear, Narnie'll be here for a while. I've my things to pack, and there's a cottage to be found. Or will he throw me out on the street?'

'Of course he won't!' But, fearing that he might, she added defiantly, 'I shan't let him!'

'Calm yourself, my lamb,' the old woman soothed. 'Narnie won't be deserting you yet awhile.' With a look at me that bade me follow her, she made for the door.

In the hallway, with the parlour door closed so that Mama couldn't hear, she turned on me. 'What've you been doing to her? She's sick. Anybody can see that.'

After her long journey she smelled unclean, of sweat and elderly flesh, and for the first time I noticed the liver spots that were beginning to show on her brow and on the hands that still toyed with her gloves. Her deep-set eyes fixed on my face in a stare as hard as stone.

Narnie's stare had often unsettled me, turning me to jelly inside despite my outer defiance. Now, for the first time, I saw her as a helpless old woman, a servant, reliant on my father for her existence. Beneath her bluster, she was afraid of being cast out to loneliness.

'Mama's distressed because she's losing you, that's all,' I said. 'Don't make it worse, Narnie. If you care for her—'

'Care!' she spat. 'I've cared for her all her life, since she was a tiny scrap of a thing, all great brown eyes and baby softness. I've cared for her more than you can ever understand.'

'I know that,' I said.

'You know nothing! Miss Flora looks worn out. If Miss Grace had been here, it would have been different, but you... All you ever think about is yourself. Have you been taking proper care of her? Seeing she takes her medicine? Or has she been lying awake, exhausting herself?'

My temper snapped. 'That "medicine" was destroying her. Don't you realise that? She hasn't been sick, she's been unhappy. You were helping her to kill herself.'

Narnie paled, her mouth working in a fury of real distress. 'That's a wicked thing to say. I'd never hurt my Miss Flora. Never in this world. She's all I've ever cared about. How dare you say—'

'I don't doubt you were doing it for the best. But you were acting in ignorance, Narnie. Laudanum, and all drugs of that kind—'

'Ignorance!' she spluttered. 'Well, that's a fine word to throw at an old woman that hasn't had the education you've been allowed, young lady. I'll have you remember it was this ignorant old woman who taught you how to dress yourself. Who stood for hours doing your hair? Who fretted over you, trying to make you into a young lady when all you wanted was to be a hobbledehoy? And when you finally went and disgraced yourself, who was it held her tongue and kept her counsel?'

Casting a glance at the door to the rear passageway, I grasped her arm and drew her further away, for fear the servants might hear. 'We were talking about Mama. Narnie… she's unhappy because things are not as they should be between her and Father. He seems to blame you for it. So you must help her by leaving without fuss.'

'And what's your precious father going to do to make her happy?' she raged. 'Force himself upon her again? She always hated that side of it. But he never cared what she was feeling. He never cared for anybody. Except your mother, God rest her. No mortal woman could hope to take Hester Colworth's place. How d'you think it's been for my Miss Flora all these years, having to live with another woman's portrait in pride of place over her mantel? It's broken her heart, but does he care? Not he! Oh, yes, he'll get rid of me, and gladly. He's been looking for an excuse for long enough. And if it kills Miss Flora, well, that's probably just what he's hoping for. If she were dead he could marry his fancy woman!'

I was so angry I wanted to hit her. 'Don't try your lies on me! I know my father. He would never—'

'Wouldn't he?' Her face pinched into ugliness. 'Little you know! He was never good enough for my Miss Flora. But she was in despair after the squire died and left her penniless, and she had the misfortune to be in love with the only man who offered for her. Oh yes, she loved him, if ever woman loved man. Loved him so much that she gave up the life she was born to and agreed to be the wife of a common farmer. She should have wed a gentleman of means, that she should. But she loved your father. She couldn't see that he never felt anything for her beyond pity – and fleshly, filthy pleasuring.'

'That's not so!' I denied.

'Of course it's so!' She shook her gloves at me in a bunched fist. 'She was young and alone and he needed a mother for his children, and a woman for his bed. He used her until she was worn out, and when she was too frightened to let him use her any more, when she asked him to be patient, what did he do? He went and got himself a more willing vessel to be used at his pleasure and convenience. That's the way men are. Haven't you learned that?'

I found myself shaking, my hands clenched in my skirts, my heart so unsteady that its loud thudding in my ears made me feel ill. No wonder Mama had been terrified of the marriage bed, with this twisted old woman as her only guide. Father had been right. 'You hate him. You really hate him.'

'He earned my hatred for the way he treated Miss Flora. She was brought up sheltered, nurtured like a tender flower by her dear father, and by me. Why, we'd both have died sooner than see her hurt. And then along comes Will Hamilton, when she was most helpless...'

'He gave her a home. He gave her his protection. Without it, she'd have had nothing – and neither would you, Narnie. Don't you owe him some small loyalty?'

'I owe him nothing but contempt!' she spat. 'That's what he's earned, for turning my sweet young lady into a sick and sad woman.'

'And haven't you played your own part in that? Haven't you worked on her, trying to turn her against him? It was you who told her there was another woman, putting fears into her head so that—'

A bitter laugh cut me off. 'You think I made it up?'

As I glanced again at the baize door to the rear passage, Narnie grasped my arm and swung me round, saying maliciously, 'Don't fret who may be listening, Miss Rose. This isn't news to the servants. Everyone knows about Will Hamilton and the widow Stead. Everyone!'

Disquiet pricked my skin and brought sweat out on my palms. If this 'other woman' had a name...

Her nostrils flared as she glared at me from under drawn brows, saying in a low, steady voice, 'She lives in King's Lynn, on St James Street, not far from the Walks. Stead is her name – Jane Stead. She was widowed by the war in the Crimea. She takes in sewing for a living. And every Tuesday market day she takes in your father for—'

'No!' The low gasp made us both look round. Mama was leaning weakly in the parlour doorway, her face ashen as she clung to the jamb. 'How *could* you, Narnie! I didn't want the children to know. You *knew* I didn't want them to know!' A trembling hand stretched out as she came unsteadily towards me. 'You mustn't blame him, Rose. It was my fault. I drove him to find consolation elsewhere. But he won't see her any more. He has promised me. It was a part of our bargain. Oh, Rose, don't think badly of him. Don't...'

Before I could reach her, she crumpled to the floor.

—

Narnie had made a bad mistake. Her hatred of my father, spilling over as it had, caused a rift between her and Mama; filled with remorse, she made no more complaints about her enforced retirement. A cottage was swiftly found for her, a pretty little place beside the church in Feltham village; she left Orchards House within two weeks, a sad and subdued woman desperate to win back her place in Mama's affections.

Without any real discussion of the matter, I stepped into Narnie's shoes, and there was no more even the hint of my leaving to take a teaching post. Orchards House needed a housekeeper and Mama needed a companion; I was elected to the post.

Small signs in the main bedroom told me that Father no longer slept in the dressing-room. Nor did he overstay at the Tuesday market, but spent noticeably more time in or near the house, and he was kinder to Mama. He even, much to the delight of the rector, started to attend church with us on occasion: he was trying.

And I... I hated him. Loathed him. For when I, in innocence and ignorance, had loved unwisely...

The scene came back sharp in every detail: Father's study in the old house, with the pigsty outside. Grey snakes of tobacco twining in the air. The pigs' odour, strong but familiar, and a fading glow of reddish light from the western sky. Gloom gathered in corners, thickening into dusk. Father had not lit the lamp.

When I thought the beat of my heart might suffocate me, he leaned to stub out his cigarette. Only when it was ground to powder in the ash-tray did he turn to look at me through the shadows, his face unreadable in that light. 'I've only two questions to ask of you, miss,' he said. 'Just answer Yes or No. First: is it true what Victor tells me – have you been meeting young Wyatt in the woods?'

I moistened my lips, feeling that my whole body was one vast pulse. 'No, Father.'

'No?' His voice was low, like a rumble of thunder along the horizon. 'I warn you, miss, if you don't tell me the truth—'

'Not Hal Wyatt,' I said.

That gave him pause. 'The boy Finch saw you.'

'The boy Finch saw me arguing with Hal, that's all. When Victor found me, I was alone.'

'But you were expecting someone.'

'Not expecting, exactly.'

His frown carved deep furrows in his brow. 'Don't trade words with me, miss. This is your father you're speaking to, not one of your fancy Academy friends. You've been meeting with a man. Is that so?'

'Yes, Father.'

'What man?'

I thought on that, considering all the possibilities. What good would it do me to confess the truth? It would make no difference. It might make things worse.

'*What man?!*' Father repeated, his voice louder now.

'His name isn't important. It's all over. It's finished.'

'You'll tell me, miss, or by God—'

'Or by God you'll do what, Father? Beat me? Do, if it will please you. It won't make me change my mind. And don't swear by God when you don't believe in him. That's profanity.'

Father went rigid. I heard him draw a rasping breath, his hand a tight fist at his side. He let the breath out slowly, said, 'I knew it was a mistake to have you educated, girl. Is that what they taught you – defiance and insolence, to your own father? Very well.' Without haste he reached to unfasten his belt, while I watched, mesmerised.

The belt slid from its loops. 'Will you tell me his name?'

I shook my head, scraped a cobweb of fear from my throat. 'No. Never.'

He took the belt buckle in his palm, wrapping the leather once about his hand and flexing it as if testing its strength. 'One last chance, Rose. The name.'

'His name doesn't matter! I shall never see him again.'

'You've been seeing him until now! Good God! That a daughter of mine should—'

He stepped forward, lifting the belt. I turned away, my arms over my face. A cry escaped me as the belt bit across my shoulders. I leaned on the door and sank my teeth into my sleeve, feeling a stripe of pain start to burn.

'The name!'

Tears hot behind my eyelids, I shook my head.

Again the belt spat, writing another line of fire on my back. 'Tell me his name!'

Even if I had wanted to, I couldn't have spoken. It had become a battle of wills. If he beat me unconscious I wouldn't tell him what he wanted to know.

A third time the belt lashed, dragging a low moan out of me.

I waited, tightened into a knot of anguish as I tensed myself for another blow. In the silence I heard Father breathing harshly.

'Now go to bed,' he rasped. 'Go to bed and be thankful I was able to control myself. I'd like to beat you until you bleed. It's what you deserve. You'll never see him again. Do you understand me? If he sends word—'

'He won't,' I wept, swinging round to face him. 'I told you, it's over. It's over and done with!'

A breath of satisfaction escaped him. 'Good. And you'd better pray it stays done with. If you're with child, Rose, I swear I'll disown you.'

My hands clenched into fists as I stared at him through my tears, hating him. 'You're so certain I've done wrong, aren't you? You've always expected the worst of me, Father. Always.'

'You mean… you didn't give in to him?'

The hope in his voice made me hate him the more. I wanted to hurt him as much as I could, so I said, 'Of course I did. I was in need of love. I never had any from you!'

His face contorted and he lashed out again. This time I saw the blow coming and dodged to avoid it. The folded belt sliced at my cheek and my ear, sending me sidelong across a chair, and while I lay there half dazed my father stood over me, saying, 'You wanton bitch! You call it love? Filthy, disgusting, wicked… God, that your mother should have died giving birth to such as you! I warn you, I'm raising nobody's bastard in my house. If you're with child it'll be the streets for you. The streets! Do you understand that, miss?'

Oh, I hated him – hated him for the burning, raging pain that invaded my back from shoulder to waist, for the crimson fire in my ear and the side of my head; I hated him for his coldness, for the love he had denied me all my life.

Father stared at me in the twilight. What he read in my face I don't know, but whatever it was it made him step back. 'Go to bed,' he said. 'Go to bed. We shall not mention this again.'

No, we didn't mention it, not out loud, but neither of us forgot. And now I knew what a hypocrite he was. When I had most needed his understanding he had taken his belt to me, cast me out into exile and disowned me for three long years. Yet he himself – my perfect father – had a mistress. He had committed adultery. How could he? How *could* he?!

–

In the way she had of ignoring the unpleasant, Mama rarely mentioned Narnie. She made valiant efforts to be less weepy, more positive, but she developed a horror of being left alone even for a few minutes; I had to be with her most of her waking hours.

Mealtimes, when the three of us were obliged to be together, became models of good manners, stilted conversation and acute awareness. We stepped carefully around one another, as if we walked barefoot in a field of fresh cow dung. Father and I were polite to each other, but our glances seldom met, and when they did they slid away again without real contact. Often he snapped at me for no reason, as if he blamed me for his pain.

My feelings for him were in turmoil. He was no longer the man I had believed him to be.

–

In answer to an advertisement which Father had printed in various magazines, replies from prospective lady's maids began to arrive. Father suggested that Mama and I might spend a few days in Lynn and interview the applicants there. The change would do Mama good; she might take the opportunity to look at patterns and material for evening gowns, with the Sandringham winter balls in mind. Father was all largesse. Guilt made him generous.

If Mama had doubts about his motives for sending us off, she hid them well, but then she was always good at playing ostrich. I had the impression that Father was tired, that during the rigours of harvest, when days could last from dawn to starshine, he would be pleased to come and go as work demanded, not bothering with formal meals and other politenesses necessary when his womenfolk were at home. Little I cared. So long as he didn't go running to his doxy.

I no longer doubted that the woman existed. Her name had leapt out at me from the columns of the *Lynn Advertiser*: 'Seamstress requires work. Anything undertaken. Dress-making, make-overs, repairs. Latest patterns. Unexceptionable references. Mrs Stead, St James Street, Lynn Regis.' I pictured her as loud, coarse, painted, the archetypal 'loose woman' of novel and melodrama. The thought of Father's turning to such a woman, however great his need, disgusted me.

–

King's Lynn, and the company of Aunt Beatrice, Uncle Jonathan and other friends, made Mama bloom. She began to eat well. She was even putting on weight. She ventured out in the carriage to take the air by the river or in the park; she enjoyed shopping with the generous allowance Father had given her. She and Aunt Beatrice spent hours gossiping, discussing the merits of various candidates for the post of lady's maid at Orchards, or speculating about the plans of Geoffrey Devlin and his Lucinda – a subject which kept many ladies enthralled.

William Turnbull called one Saturday morning and was invited to lunch. He had been to Ambleford to make final arrangements for his Great Steam Engine Demonstration: he talked of little else. For hours.

Desperate for a change of subject, Aunt Beatrice said, 'And is there to be a wedding?'

Turnbull blinked, giving me a startled glance. 'Wedding, ma'am?'

'Why, yes! Or is it to be a long engagement?'

Again Turnbull looked at me, wondering if some decision had been made without reference to him.

I said, 'I believe my aunt is referring to Mr Geoffrey Devlin and Miss de Crecy.'

'Ah.' With a long forefinger, Turnbull stroked the hairs of his beard away from his full lips. 'Ah, yes. No, I've heard no mention of a date having been set.'

'Is there any hint of Miss de Crecy's visiting Ambleford again?' Beatrice asked.

Turnbull blinked. 'Why, ma'am… she's been at Ambleford all summer.'

Mama gasped. '*Has* she? Then why is she never seen?'

'I understand she goes out only on rare occasions.' His glance flicked uncomfortably from one to the other. 'She's a shy young lady.'

Timid. I've only briefly glimpsed her once, from a distance, when I was up at the house discussing the transport of our engines for—'

'Well, that *is* intriguing!' said Beatrice and, turning to Mama, drew her into further speculation about Miss de Crecy.

After a while, not being much entertained by the mystery of Geoffrey Devlin's fiancée, Turnbull asked me if I would like to take a stroll to the Walks with him. I was glad to escape.

It was a cool September Saturday, a day of chasing cloud and sunlight, cobbles wet, gutters full of puddles, streets noisy with people, carts and carriages. The wind toyed with my bonnet and fluttered my cape as I walked beside the burly figure of my admirer, my hand lightly tucked under his arm. Striding out in unison, we rounded the corner past the chequered façade of the ancient Guildhall, coming out in the Saturday marketplace. In the shelter of dark yews edging a churchyard, with the church tower rising in a grey wall of knapped flint, the stalls of the small market were thronged with eager shoppers, women with laden baskets, boys bowling hoops.

All at once I realised we were in St James Street, where Father's paramour had her lodging. Turnbull was talking again about the coming demonstration, but I stopped listening. I was glancing in shop windows, noting numbers on doors of terraced houses.

Just ahead of us, a neatly-dressed woman emerged from a house, a big wicker basket over her arm. The pavement was so narrow that we had either to pause or step into a puddle of water, the drain being blocked and the gutter flooded after overnight rain. Even as Turnbull and I came to a halt, a carriage came by, its wheels sending up a spray of filthy water. My escort shouted angrily at the coachman as I flinched my spattered skirts aside. The woman swung her heavy basket out of danger, but lost her balance. She would have fallen had not Turnbull lunged to save her. The cover slid off her basket, revealing its contents to be bedlinen, trimmed with fine lace and embroidery. I found myself rescuing the linen from slipping into the dirt, helping the woman settle her wares again while she thanked us breathlessly.

She appeared to be in her early thirties. Shorter than I, with a slender figure and a ready smile, she was plainly dressed, but neat and clean. There was nothing gaudy or tasteless about her. Though not beautiful, not even pretty, she had a sweet face and kind eyes.

'Some coachmen have no care for pedestrians, I fear,' my escort said, raising his hat in salute. 'Are you hurt, ma'am?'

'I've grazed my elbow a little,' she admitted with a rueful smile, rubbing the soreness. 'What Mrs Heron would have said if her linen had gone in the dirt, I do not know. Thank you again, sir.'

'The pleasure was mine.'

Smiling, inclining her head, she moved on. And then I saw it – the printed sign in the window of the house she had left: 'J. Stead, Seamstress.' So this was the 'scarlet woman' of my imagination. The warmth of her smile stayed in my memory long after she had gone.

—

The new lady's maid chosen by Mama was named Ellen Earley, which gave rise to many a joke among the men, whose country wit delighted in puns and word play. The backus boy was frequently heard singing a song whose refrain included the line, 'Oh, Lord, but she was early,' and after Mrs Benstead clipped his ear for him he took to whistling the tune instead. Earley herself remained stoically indifferent to the clowning and merely said, 'Yes, madam,' when Mama suggested we should call her 'Ellen'.

She was a taciturn person, rather plain in looks but with a taste for fancy dressing, and she was skilled at making and trimming bonnets, as we discovered. At the importuning of Swift and Howlett, Ellen was inveigled to create fashionable bonnets for them; they were beside themselves with joy, until their appearance in church caused a scandal among some who thought such headwear unfitting for housemaids.

The lady's maid did her work efficiently, without fuss, but she kept herself to herself; she never became part of the family as Narnie had been.

Ellen had been with us only a few days when Grace's return set the household alight. Three months on the continent had burnished my sister into a fashionable young lady and she was so delighted with the change in Mama, and with Ellen's skills, that she barely reacted to the news that Narnie had left.

'I shall go and visit her tomorrow,' she declared. 'I can't wait to tell her all the news of my travels. Oh, Rose, dear, your nails! And your hair! I must take you in hand. If we're to attend the Birthday Balls at the big house this year…'

The Birthday Balls were all she thought about. We must have gowns in the latest fashion. Our crinolines were so *passé*, the latest *cages americains* were capable of being drawn up, in the manner of a window blind, to prevent one's skirts from trailing in the street, and they were straight in front, with more fullness at the back supporting a sort of train. Orders went out to London outfitters and dressmakers – Father was in a mood to be indulgent, probably thinking that a little expense on fripperies would win him a quiet life.

Grace chattered endlessly about the things she had seen and done in France, the parties she had attended, the important people she had met, and the hearts she had broken. Listening to her enthuse, I felt more than a pang of envy. While she had been off enjoying herself, I had been witness to painful dramas whose shadows remained.

'If I had the chance to travel,' I said sourly, 'I'd study the landscape, and the architecture, and the history. I wouldn't fritter away the time preening myself, and flirting!'

'But, my dear,' said Grace with a laugh, 'if it had been *you*, there wouldn't have been anything else to do but study the landscape, the art, the history… Would there?'

I deserved the jibe. My envy of Grace was something I despised myself for. Nevertheless, I was as thrilled as she when the material samples and the patterns arrived, and then the dresses themselves. Final adjustments of fit were made by our local dressmaker, Mrs Todd, with the aid of Ellen Earley.

–

After the merriment of harvest home, we found ourselves with surplus provisions – pies and preserves and lardy cakes – that we planned to distribute in the village.

'Shall we take some to Narnie?' I suggested as Swift and Howlett stowed the victuals in the dogcart. The old woman had been on my conscience ever since she left.

'Why, yes!' Grace agreed. 'I want to tell her about my adventures in France. Perhaps Mama would like to come.'

Mama was reluctant, probably fearing Narnie's reproach, but we overcame her objections.

Willow Cottage was tucked away behind Feltham church, half hidden from the lane by trailing willows that flanked its gate. Holly-hocks grew in a garden thick with scented roses, forget-me-nots, and lavender. An old broken wall, a mixture of flint and chalk and brick, overgrown with ivy, separated the cottage from the churchyard, where dark yews grew tall.

As I helped Mama down from the dogcart, I saw the lace curtains at the cottage window twitch, but Narnie didn't come to the door: she made us knock and wait, so long that I began to think she would refuse to see us. Then a small tabby cat emerged from the undergrowth to leap lightly up the steps and miaow expectantly at the door.

'What a dear little creature!' Grace exclaimed, scooping it up into her arms just as the door opened to reveal a sour-faced Narnie. 'Narnie, is she yours? Isn't she – Ow!' With a little scream, Grace dropped the cat, which hung by its claws in her skirts until she shook it off, saying, 'Beastly creature, it scratched me. I'm bleeding!'

Narnie tried to maintain her cold dignity, but old habits of affection proved stronger and after a moment's hesitation she said, 'Come in and let Narnie tend it. Come in, all of you.'

'Oh, Narnie…' On the threshold, Mama paused as emotion caught at her and she held out her arms. 'Oh, Narnie…'

A tearful reunion ended with us all seated by the fire drinking tea and eating Mrs Benstead's lardy cake while Mama and Grace recounted all the gossip.

It seemed to me that, while Mama looked younger, Narnie had visibly aged. Her face was more lined than I remembered, her hair greyer. She didn't pretend to be happy: she said that her neighbours were unfriendly, her rheumatics were bad, she wasn't sleeping well.

'And that graveyard out there is no easy neighbour. You should hear the trees moaning at night. Like lost souls. Makes me shudder to hear them. Still, it won't be long before I'm under one of those old stones myself.'

'Oh, don't say that!' Mama begged. 'We shall come to see you often. Shan't we, girls?'

'If you're allowed,' said Narnie dubiously. 'If that husband of yours doesn't put a stop to that, too.' Seeing that the reminder had hurt Mama, she added grudgingly, 'Still… I'm glad to see you looking more your old self, Miss Flora.'

'Yes,' Mama said, her mouth trembling in a half smile. 'I'm much better. Very much better.'

The day of the Great Steam Engine Demonstration loomed imminent. This time, to show his faith in his product, William Turnbull himself was at the footplate of one of his self-moving machines as it drove through the West Norfolk lanes, though tactfully he did not bring it close by Orchards. Even so, I hardly slept that night because of irrational fears of another explosion. In the early hours of an October morning I heard the alien noise in the distance, chugging and rattling on its way to Ambleford. I lay listening, hardly breathing, until long after the sound had faded.

For a day or so before the show, Turnbull was a guest at Ambleford Hall; Sir Arthur was being most accommodating, probably in the hope of acquiring an engine at cut price. He held a dinner party on the eve of the big day; Turnbull wondered if he should ask for an invitation for me, but, things between Orchards and Ambleford being what they were, my father thought it inappropriate. I didn't argue. The last thing I wanted was to be forced into polite proximity with Geoffrey Devlin and his fiancée. Besides, to accept such an invitation would have been tantamount to announcing my own engagement to Turnbull.

'I only wish he'd asked *me*,' Grace said. 'Imagine turning down an invitation to dine at Ambleford Hall! Aren't you just *dying* to meet the mysterious Miss de Crecy? Everyone's talking about her. They say she's horribly deformed. Maria Kinnersley heard that she had huge warts all over her face.'

'Oh, really, Grace,' I sighed. 'Not long ago you were telling us how beautiful she is. It's all silly gossip, just because she doesn't go out much in public. Use your intelligence, do. Would Geoffrey Devlin marry a girl who wasn't at least pretty?'

'"Sightings of her are as rare as the bittern",' Grace quoted. 'That's what they say. Do go to this dinner party, Rose. You can find out the truth, and I'll be able to tell Maria—'

'With Sir Arthur constantly threatening Father with litigation over some silly disagreement or other, I wouldn't go even if they *did* invite me. It's not as if I were engaged to Mr Turnbull.'

'Not officially, perhaps. But as good as. If he weren't such a boring *bourgeois* he'd have asked you before. Everybody knows one only needs six months' mourning for a brother.' Seeing my incomprehension, she threw out her hands, exclaiming, 'He's waiting for the full year to pass. Good gracious, Rose, didn't you realise that?'

I hadn't realised it, but she was probably right. Being the man he was, William Turnbull would walk the finest edge of convention and respect my mourning for a full year. After that, I had better be ready with my answer.

-

On the day of the demonstration, Father was in a bleak mood because of a letter he had received from the Prince of Wales's agent. He didn't say what it was about; he tried to make light of it, but as he hurried us into the carriage he had hired I sensed his irritation.

A thick wet mist blanketed the landscape, making the autumn trees drip, churning the ground to mud under wheels and hooves and boots. Mama, Grace and I were all garbed in waterproofs and galoshes, with umbrellas at the ready. The Ambleford park was crowded, half the landowners and farmers of the county turning out. Some brought their wives, though most of the ladies elected to remain in the marquee, out of the inclement weather. The Prince of Wales's duties obliged him to be elsewhere; however, he sent his land agent Edmund Beck to take notes. Father kept watching the agent, seeking a chance to speak to him, but among the crowds Mr Beck proved elusive.

To my delight, Farmer Pooley joined us, and we met other friends. There were a few labourers present, too, come to watch and assess how much of a threat to their jobs the new machines might be.

Sir Arthur Devlin played host in his eccentric way, making an enthusiastic if incoherent speech to welcome his guests and raise hopes of a bright future with machinery to aid the farmer; then William Turnbull had his turn on the dais, telling us what we might expect to see. I must confess that I felt immensely proud of him that day, though some of my attention was elsewhere, watching the crowd, wondering if Geoffrey might appear.

Perhaps he was away. I hoped he was, for I certainly didn't wish to encounter him. Or so I told myself.

But I did glimpse another familiar face, this one totally unwelcome. I had forgotten that Father's old adversary Amos Chilvers now worked for Sir Arthur. I hid myself among the crowd before he could see me.

Mama and Grace decided to stay in the shelter of the marquee, where the chance to gossip and criticise other women's clothes was more to their taste. It suited me to be out in the mist and the mud, watching the fun. Some of the Ambleford men acted as marshals: Amos Chilvers seemed to be in charge of them. As we moved about, he often came quite close and once I heard him say loudly to his companion, 'Blood will out. Like father, like child.'

From the corner of his eye, he surveyed me insolently. What was he doing – spreading rumour about Father and me? Or was it my own guilt that read too much into a comment overheard out of context?

Demonstrations began in the barns, with smaller engines that could chop roots and hay, implements for digging drains and laying pipes, for reaping and mowing, and a noisy threshing machine that separated the grain, lifting the straw on an elevated conveyor belt that rattled and pulsated. The damp conditions were unfortunate – threshing is best done on a dry, breezy day – but as Turnbull pointed out to his audience, the machine took only hours where men with flails took weeks to accomplish the same result.

'And where'll that leave us, then?' a man behind me muttered.

'Out o' work, bor,' came the laconic reply. 'That's where.'

The labourers misliked this whole show, foreseeing the workhouse for themselves and their families if these machines took over. But then, as Farmer Pooley often said, men always grumbled, if not about wages then about their cottages, and failing anything else they'd grumble about the weather. It was their way of making conversation.

The misty air was thick with the smell of smoke and hot coals, the hiss of steam and the tooting of whistles. It was exciting, but I half feared the engines, their noise and their heat, their contained power. Every time one expelled steam with a whoosh and a hiss I jumped and backed off, my heart thudding. One of these monsters had killed my brother. I should never entirely trust them.

At lunch in the crowded marquee, smelling of crushed grass and clammy with the steam from wet clothes and umbrellas, William Turnbull was surrounded by would-be buyers all wanting to ask questions. Mama looked a little tired, but a bright-eyed Grace watched everything with the condescension of one who had seen wider horizons.

'The English are so terribly provincial,' she remarked, and, 'Dear me, isn't Mr Turnbull the thing today? Quite "*je ne sais quoi*".' Despite her facetious tone, she was eyeing William with interest. 'Victor always did say he was a coming man.'

'And *you* always said he was a pompous bore,' I reminded her.

Grace merely pulled a face at me.

Summoned back to the business of the day, those of us who were following the demonstrations made for the fog-shrouded field where a double-engine plough was getting up steam, ready to show how it could haul a coulter back and forth without need for horses. The far side of the field was lost in grey mist, so that the cables, strung between the engines to pull the ploughshare, appeared to vanish into nothingness. Several blue and red wagons had been ranged along the headland for spectators to have a grandstand view, and kind hands helped me up to stand with Pooley beside me and others crowding round us. I had lost sight of Father.

'Tha's a expensive old do,' someone remarked. 'Spend a fortune to plough a few field? Why, here in Norfolk all you need's a brace o' rabbit an' a clasp knife.'

A ripple of amusement passed through the listeners, all of whom knew the notorious lightness of Norfolk soils. Most of us had seen a March gale send top soil, seeds, and guano dressing drifting like snow against hedges and along lanes. However, the power of the engines, slicing the blade through the wet ground, and the way the ploughshare and its rider kept appearing and disappearing in the fog, was better than a magic lantern show, the spectacle appreciated even if the machinery was beyond the pockets of most.

As the crowd began to disperse back through the gateway and down the lane, I waited on the wagon as George Pooley climbed down, going slowly and awkwardly, stiff from standing still. Puffing with pain, he gained the ground and paused there, groaning, forcing his bent back to straighten while I watched in concern.

'May I...?' Offering a hand to help me, someone else stepped in – someone whose grave slate-blue gaze made me stop, as if all the breath had been driven from my body. So he was here, after all. He had grown a moustache. It suited him. All at once I was conscious of the inelegance of clambering about in my crinoline, my skirts all muddied. I wished I had never got up there.

Convention stepped into the void, causing me to say, 'Thank you.' Reaching a foot to the wheel-rim, I used Geoffrey Devlin's hand to steady myself as I climbed out, searching with my other foot for the hub and cursing my hampering skirts, which had caught up on the wheel and hidden everything below me.

'Allow me.' Geoffrey's hands came at my waist and with easy strength he conveyed me to the ground. Discomposed, I made a show of straightening my cape and skirts, unable to look at him.

'Blasted arthritis!' Pooley cursed. 'How I hate getting old!'

'You'll never be old, Mr Pooley,' Geoffrey said, a smile in his voice.

'Don't you believe it, bor!'

'Well…' Doffing his hat, he made us a bow. 'If you'll excuse me… A pleasure to see you again, Miss Hamilton.'

He walked away, leaving me with the burning imprint of his hands at my waist, and in my heart a fresh memory of the way he looked, with a smile on his lips and sorrow in his eyes. The neat dark moustache gave his face a new maturity. How I wished my heart would stop its silly galumping.

'Fine young gentleman, that,' said Pooley. 'No side to him at all.' Then he laughed aloud, teasing me, 'By gar, gal, you're blushin' like sunset. Don't let Turnbull see.'

William Turnbull, however, was occupied with several of the more prosperous landowners who had gathered to question him about the plough. Suddenly aware of the thick mud weighing down my hems and clodding my boots, of the damp state of my hat and hair, and my general lack of grooming, I started for the gate. I felt bitter and angry, irrationally furious with my beau for being so preoccupied.

'Made up your mind to have him, have you?' Pooley said.

Well aware that my answer would go back to Basil, I glanced back at the bulky, bearded figure of the engineer, seeing him in command, impressive, at ease with the gentlemen around him. One of those gentlemen was Geoffrey Devlin, making some point that made Turnbull and the others roar with laughter.

'Yes, I think I have,' I replied, and moved on.

In the gateway, my father was arguing with Mr Beck, the agent for the Sandringham estate. Father barred his path, gesticulating angrily with a letter he held in his hand.

'…too much! Those damn coverts… weeds all among the crops… hares destroying everything… I wrote and asked for compensation before next year's rent was settled, but you didn't deign to reply. And now you're asking me to pay for…'

'You sound surprised,' Beck replied. 'Yet you agreed that—'

'When? I don't recall signing any paper.'

'It was a gentleman's agreement. A handshake with the prince. I'm amazed that you can have forgotten.'

'There was no mention of five per cent—'

'You expect His Royal Highness to quote figures?' the agent exclaimed with a lift of eyebrows. 'My dear sir, he employs others to deal with such details. Five per cent on the cost of the house and buildings. Another three hundred pounds for carting.'

My father's eyes blazed. 'Damnation, man! The work isn't even properly finished.'

'Indeed. His Royal Highness has mentioned the unkempt look that disfigures your property. Your pond needs digging out. There's that unfinished wall… And all the sacking draped about your fields.'

'To keep the blasted hares out!'

'It was His Royal Highness's opinion that it looks like a laundry. Get it tidied up. The prince likes to find his estate presentable when he shows his guests around. Good afternoon.'

With a nifty side-step, he got past Father and hurried on down the lane. Father made to go after him, but stopped and slammed the side of his fist against the gate. Shoulders sagging, he leaned on the gate as if all his strength had drained away, defeat written in every line. My heart contracted with anxiety as I read his weariness, his despair. He no longer had the reserves he had once been able to draw on. He looked old, and he looked ill.

'Tek no notice, Mr Will,' Pooley advised. 'It's the organ grinder you want to deal with, not his monkey. Talk to the prince when next he come.'

The chill, clinging dampness of that day at Ambleford gave me a fever that confined me to bed. I did not feel well enough to entertain Turnbull when he called the following Sunday to see me. Grace told me later that, it being a beautiful day, she and the engineer had taken a stroll through Poacher's Wood. They had found an injured hare, an escapee from the shooting, and at Grace's pleading Turnbull had bound its injury with his handkerchief. However, as they carried it home the 'poor creature' expired. One less pest to decimate our crops, thought I. But the incident of the dying hare proved to be more significant than I thought: it formed a first bond between my sister and my gentleman friend.

Unsettled by three months of high adventure in France, Grace found the farm dull; she needed novelty. The Birthday Balls might have provided the necessary excitement, but there were to be no Birthday Balls at Sandringham that year: the Waleses didn't come to Norfolk. The prince was in Russia, being fêted, going hunting, generally enjoying himself, and also attending the wedding of his sister-in-law, Princess Dagmar of Denmark, to the Archduke Alexander of Russia. The Princess of Wales did not accompany him; being pregnant again, and unwell, she remained in London with the Queen. The news of their enforced absence came as a disappointment to many of us, but poor Grace, who had set her heart on social triumphs, was desolated. She raged and wept every time she thought of her beautiful new dresses going to waste. How could she ever face Maria Kinnersley again?

Needing some other diversion, she started to flirt with the susceptible William Turnbull. She always swore she didn't deliberately set out to steal him away from me. Perhaps that was true. But whether she did it consciously or not, the result was the same.

–

Around the turn of the year, we were all stunned to learn that our dear Princess Alix was seriously ill. She had contracted rheumatic fever. Her symptoms were exacerbated by the difficult birth that February of her third child, the little Princess Louise. And then she developed 'white leg', one of the many dangers attendant on women after childbirth. As she told me in later years, she had several times been sure she would never see her beloved Sandringham again.

Bland bulletins assured the nation that she was 'improving', but in fact she was bedridden for months; it was well into the summer before she regained anything like her usual strength.

That winter my relationship with my father was fraught. He suffered feverish colds, but he kept working. When a bout of influenza forced him into confinement, he left his bed much sooner than he should have, which sapped his strength and left him with a dreadful hacking cough. He relied on me to act as his assistant, but he resented me for it.

At times I pitied him; at times I loathed and despised him. My father, the man who, throughout my life, I had both feared and loved, but always respected… I could not decide what I thought of him now.

Though I could not forgive him for betraying his marriage vows, I could see that Mama was no sturdy helpmeet for a man to lean on:

she was a weak vine, needing constant support. Was it so strange that Father had turned to Jane Stead? Even in that one brief meeting, I had sensed her warmth, her gentleness, the quiet strength that was part of her nature. I believe Father sorely missed the comforts, both physical and emotional, that she had given him.

Being in no position to cast stones, I came to understand and even sympathise with his dilemma. It's painful to realise that one's father is not a superior being, all-knowing, all-powerful, all-prescient, but a mere mortal man, weak and vulnerable like the rest.

–

Aunt Agnes had a new passion – women's right to a vote – and in Cassie she had a bright and willing student. I, too, enjoyed political discussion. It was stimulating to envisage a future when a woman might emerge from her bondage and have a voice in her own destiny. When such talk flowed, my aunt and I found much to agree upon.

'You two are so alike!' Cassie said one day, smiling from her pillows. 'I'm so glad we're all still friends.'

By saying it, I suppose, she hoped to make it true.

Felicity found our discussions a waste of time and breath; the lovely Chloe, who had fallen in love, was happily content to submerge her own life in that of her future husband, and the three youngest of the Wyatt sisters refused to enter the argument.

'Papa says we shouldn't talk unless we know something about the subject,' Kitty informed us loftily.

Poor Mr Wyatt, deserted by his sons and left with only womenfolk, couldn't abide idle chatter. Perhaps that was one reason why he had taken up politics, to the extent of going canvassing for our local Member of Parliament, who was often a guest at his home. Mr Wyatt had staunchly supported the changes in the Poor Law but he was sympathetic to the farmers' cause, too, and would always listen when I complained about the hares and the trouble the shooting gave us. I did not, however, foresee that his kindly, well-intentioned interest would one day rebound on me.

Niggling quarrels with Sir Arthur Devlin continued, most of them too petty to recall; I only remember that they kept Father in a state of constant tension and irritability, so that the men and I came to detest the very sound of the names 'Devlin' and 'Ambleford'.

In the early spring of 1867, however, the problem escalated, with an incident that I do remember.

Sir Arthur, for all he constantly pleaded poverty, had bought two Turnbull steam-engines and various implements to go with them. He spent the winter playing with these new toys, so we heard. To fuel the engines he needed coal, which was carted from the railway in heavy wagons that chewed the lanes to ruts during the autumn, before the ground froze and snows came. When, at the thaw, one of his laden coal wagons splintered a wheel and spilled its load almost at our gate, Sir Arthur blamed Father for the bad condition of the lanes. Solicitors' letters flew back and forth.

In the end, Geoffrey Devlin came over to Orchards. I happened to be at an upstairs window, watching men erect the new wrought-iron gate at our entry, when I saw Geoffrey arrive astride a fine hunter. I drew back behind the curtain, covertly watching as he walked his mount up the slope.

By the time Swift answered the door I was near the head of the stairs, keeping out of sight. I heard Geoffrey ask if Father was at home. Swift asked him to come in, and showed him into the front drawing-room.

Father, who was in the office, evidently refused to see Geoffrey. His voice got louder, until I distinguished words: '...got anything to say to me he can do it through my solicitor! I'll not have him coming here and accusing me of...'

The better to hear what was happening, I was leaning over the banister rail when Geoffrey strode from the drawing-room. Startled, I must have made some small sound, or perhaps the rustle of my petticoats reached him. He looked up. He stopped. In the act of backing away, I stopped too, frozen as a mouse under a cat's bright glare, a pulse throbbing heavily in my throat.

His mouth tightened with anger under his dark moustache, and then he was gone, striding for the office where I heard him say, 'Mr Hamilton, I beg you to spare me a few minutes of your time. I've discovered what happened and I've come to offer you an apology.'

The office door closed. I heard no more. I leaned on the wall feeling weak and ill, my heart beating so hard and fast it near suffocated me – all because Geoffrey Devlin was nearby. Though I took care not to be seen again, I was watching from an upper window when he rode away.

At dinner that evening Father told us that Geoffrey had asked Ben Chilvers to take a look at the broken wagon wheel; in the carpenter's opinion, the stopper in the wheel's hub had been loosened, so that the wheel wobbled slightly, throwing great stress on the spokes. When he examined further, he found that, before they were splintered in the accident, the spokes had been partially sawn through.

'You mean...' Mama had paled, a hand going to her breast, 'someone did it deliberately?'

We were in our familiar dining-room, the four of us, lamps glowing, the fire bright, the table full of good things to eat. We were safe in our house, in our dear West Norfolk. It seemed incredible that such unpleasantness could come so close to our haven.

'What nonsense!' Grace scoffed. 'Why on earth would anyone go to such trouble to spill a load of coal? I can't imagine why Mr Devlin took the least notice of anything Chippy Chilvers had to say. What does he know?'

'He's an expert with wood,' Father said, and took breath to explain further but, glancing from Grace to Mama, decided against it. 'Well, never mind. It's nothing for you to worry your heads about.'

Later, however, he called me in to the office, asked me to sit down and, when he had got his pipe going, advised me to keep my eyes and ears open for signs of unrest and dissatisfaction.

'Sir Arthur may still hold me to blame,' he said, 'but then he blames me for every ill that befalls him. His son has more sense. It appears that some trouble-monger is about, Rose. Someone whose purpose it suits to stir the feud between us and Ambleford. I don't like to think one of our own men is behind it, but I couldn't swear to the loyalty of them all, and there are enough malcontents around who might find amusement in this sort of mischief. Be on the alert, will you?'

It flattered and cheered me to be taken into his confidence – to be told, implicitly, that he needed me as his lieutenant. He had no one else. He couldn't talk to Mama, or to Grace, not about this; he would have shared his worries with Victor, but Victor was no longer with us, and Johnny was too young. So he had turned to me. At last he had turned to me. How proud I was to be honoured with his trust.

But my joy was short-lived.

One April afternoon we were in a field of young beet, examining its recovery after rolling to consolidate the roots, when Father bent to pluck a tiny dandelion shoot that the hoers had missed. Holding it on his palm, he said abruptly, 'By the way, I've engaged a new farm steward. He'll be moving into Wood Lodge next week.' With that he moved away, leaving me feeling as if I had been slapped.

I ought to have expected such an eventuality. As Farmer Pooley had said, young, single, marriageable ladies did not manage farms; unless forced by poverty, ladies were not supposed to work at all, except at accomplishments designed to pass time or to please a future husband. I saw the looks I got when I drove out alone, or rode Dandy about the lanes, or asked questions of the men, or the stock-buyers, or the solicitor. But still Father's abrupt announcement hurt me.

I watched him pause and speak to the workers. He was limping slightly, easing his back as if it ached, his shoulders slumped where once he had stood proud with his head up and his eyes full of fire. I knew why he hadn't told me about the new farm steward before – he had lost the energy for arguments. Yet he was only fifty-one. That wasn't old, surely?

Six

The new steward, Ian McDowall, was a wiry Scotsman, affable enough at first meeting, with a ready laugh, crafty eyes and a pale freckled skin to go with his sandy hair. It seemed strange to me that he should have been available for work at the busiest time of year, and that his previous employer could have borne to lose such a treasure – his references were impressive. But Father said I was prejudiced against the man and it was not my place to question.

With his wife and two children, McDowall moved into Wood Lodge, which lay at the corner of the lane on the edge of Poacher's Wood. The house had been empty for years until it was renovated as part of the prince's improvements. After the agent's remarks about untidiness, Father had set some men to trim its trees, plash its hedges and paint its woodwork dark green. I had naïvely thought he was going to offer the house to Ned Plant.

Soon fresh washing could be seen drying in the garden and the McDowall children walked to and from the new school built by His Royal Highness in West Newton. The lodge's steps were scrubbed daily, its windows gleamed, with clean lace curtains backed by potted plants, and as spring advanced the flower garden bloomed in kaleidoscopic colours. Mary McDowall was evidently a worker, but when I called on her she did not invite me in; she was polite enough, but anxious to be getting on with her cleaning and polishing, her baking and making. Caring for her house and family appeared to be her sole interest.

In the village, Mary McDowall became known as 'a quiet sort o' mawther', living her life almost as a recluse. The children, too, were subdued and nervy; they did not play out with the others. Neither they nor their parents seemed to encourage friendship.

I did not take to McDowall. He was almost too willing; he had a habit of appearing suddenly, as if he had crept up silently, waiting behind corners, and though he was nothing but respectful in front of Father I often detected hostility in his eyes when he glanced at me. Probably he resented my interference – as I resented his. I felt that he had usurped Victor's place, and mine.

That year the hares were more numerous than ever, in the woods, on the fields, even in the garden. Every time I went out of doors, one or more of the little beasts would scamper for cover, leaving some plant half chewed. In common with our men, I began to sympathise with poachers, and to dislike the arrogant 'velveteens' – Sandringham's army of green-coated gamekeepers.

I made some remark about the hares to McDowall one day, and he looked at me in amazement. 'You didna' imagine they all bred in Norfolk, surely? Lands, lassie, the prince buys live hares by the score, and has them brought here. Everyone knows that.'

As ever, he managed to make me feel like an ignorant female: I hated being addressed as 'lassie' in that patronising way. However, as I discovered, 'everyone' did not include my father. When I told him about the importation of hares he sighed, 'I thought it was strange that they were breeding so prolifically.'

'But isn't it a shameless breach of the game agreement?'

'Yes. But I'm tired of trying to fight the big house. I feel like Canute, ordering the tide to stay back. The prince refuses to hear what he doesn't want to hear. And his minions – when they deign to listen – only fob us off with words and half promises.'

'But if we don't do something our profits will be way down! We have a right to compensation.'

'I know that!' he snapped. 'Don't try to teach me my business, girl. You know nothing about it.'

'I know more than you'll admit!' I returned. 'I know as much as McDowall. Oh, why did you have to employ him? I was doing the job, wasn't I?'

My answering back always made him angry. 'Farming's no job for a—!' the roar choked off as breath caught in his throat and set him coughing – the loud, hacking, wrenching cough that made me wince for him as he held his chest, pain tearing at his lungs. He sank into his chair, gasping for breath, swallowing thickly, pallor spreading under weathered skin that suddenly seemed stretched across his bones.

'You're ill,' I said worriedly, laying a hand to his clammy brow. 'Shall I send for the doctor?'

'No.' Roughly he brushed my hand away and leaned his head in his hands. 'No, it's just my cough. It catches me wrong at times, that's all. Don't fuss me, Rose.'

'But—'

He lifted his head to glare at me. 'I said don't fuss me! Go and... go and do some sewing. Or practise at the piano – heaven knows you need it.'

To relieve my sore feelings, I went for a long, hard ride, along the lanes and through woods still fresh with early summer. Waves of the ubiquitous hares fled from me at every turn, their bobbing tails mocking me.

Somewhere ahead, distantly at first, and at irregular intervals, a gun cracked – someone shooting rabbits, I guessed. After a while I came out of the trees on to the edge of Sandringham Warren. The landscape of gorse scrub, sandy banks, bracken, bramble and blueberry was pockmarked with rabbit holes and bounded by plantations of pine. Fifty yards from me, the Prince of Wales stood by a cluster of hazel bushes, accompanied by one of his keepers carrying a game bag and spare guns, and one of his aides holding two horses. His Royal Highness was taking aim, but my arrival startled his quarry and several white tails bobbed frantically. The gun spoke, but the rabbits all safely vanished underground.

'Damn it all!' the prince complained loudly, turning to shout at me, 'What d'you mean by charging around like that? Completely ruined my shot. Well, don't just sit there. Come over here. Can't talk to you from a mile away, girl.'

I slid down from the saddle and, leading Dandy by the rein and wishing I had been more cautious, picked my way across the heather scrub. Perhaps this meeting was fortuitous. I had been thinking for some time that if only the prince knew what a bother his hares were becoming he might do something about it. His land agent was evidently unable or unwilling to do so.

His Royal Highness had put on weight. At twenty-six he was portly in tweed knickerbockers and sack coat, his deerstalker cap pulled low over his eyes so that he peered out at me from under its peak, eyes narrowed in his bearded face, the broken gun over his arm. The equerry beside him moved closer, murmuring something which made the prince shrug irritably and say, 'I know. I know. I recognised her at once.' Then his face changed, his smile beamed out like sun after rain. 'My dear Miss Hamilton! What an unexpected pleasure to find you here!'

'I fear it was more a case of my stumbling across you, sir,' I said with chagrin. 'Please forgive me for—'

'Oh, nonsense, nonsense. What's a rabbit or two between friends?' He turned to the man beside him for agreement. 'Eh, Hamilton?'

'Indeed, sir.'

To my astonishment, the equerry was my youngest uncle, Captain Henry Hamilton. It was some time since I had seen him and in the interim he had grown luxuriant Dundreary whiskers that puffed out either side of his jaw, though the rest of his face remained clean-shaven. He bore a fraternal resemblance to my father in colouring and feature, but he was eighteen years younger, and decidedly more handsome.

This was the first inkling I had had that Uncle Henry had been transferred to the prince's household.

Seeing my expression, His Royal Highness burst into laughter. 'She didn't know you, Hamilton! Damn me, don't you keep your family informed of your whereabouts?' His amusement increasing, he slapped my uncle's shoulder, adding slyly, 'Getting as bad as me, what?'

His look invited me and the keeper to share the joke, which of course we did – one did not offend the heir to the throne by openly finding his humour in poor taste, though I couldn't help but remember stories about his unsuitable friendships and the way he neglected the sick princess. One had only to glance through the pages of *Punch* to know all the gossip.

'Well, Miss Hamilton,' the prince said, pleased with himself. 'And what are you doing out here without a chaperon? Pretty young woman like you shouldn't be out on her own. What do you say, Hamilton?'

'I'm sure any young lady is quite safe on your estates, sir,' my uncle murmured.

'Even so. Even so...' He gazed at me speculatively, gleaming eyes narrowed. 'I'm surprised your father lets you out, Miss Hamilton.'

'I think he's given up trying to train me to convention,' I said ruefully, which made him laugh again.

'Like to kick over the traces, do you? I like that in a woman. Like a girl with a bit of rebellion in her.' That was probably why he had fallen in love with Alexandra of Denmark, I thought. 'Sir, may I ask... Is Her Royal Highness's health improved? We've all been so concerned for her.'

He drew gravity round him like a veil. 'Ah, yes. My dear wife and I have been touched by the messages of goodwill that have come from all over the kingdom, many of them from our beloved Norfolk. Be assured that the princess is recovering, Miss Hamilton. It goes slowly, I fear. She was *very ill*, you know.'

'Yes, sir, I know. And I'm very glad to hear that the news is good. I hope to see her at Sandringham again before long. Sir, since happy chance has brought me into your company, would it be in order for me to speak to you about—'

'Rose,' Uncle Henry intervened sharply, his expression warning me not to stretch the prince's patience too far. 'His Royal Highness is here for a private day or two, alone, to recoup his strength before returning to his duties. I trust you're not going to be so thoughtless as to bother him with matters of business.'

I recognised the rebuke, and felt ashamed of myself. 'Forgive me. I didn't mean...'

'That's what Mr Beck is there for,' Henry said. 'Yes, I know. But Mr Beck—'

'Rose!'

I subsided, shrugging uncomfortably. 'I... I'm sorry.'

'So I should hope. You forget yourself.'

The prince was trying to look stern, though the twinkle in his eyes betrayed him. 'I think we should see that she makes proper amends in order to earn forgiveness. What do you say, Hamilton? Shall we insist that she joins us at dinner on Saturday?'

I gaped at him, aghast. 'Oh, but—'

'You can't refuse,' he told me blithely. 'It's a royal command. Your uncle here will come and fetch you, and be your partner. No harm in that, surely? It's only to be a small party. Very informal. Just a few close friends. As it happens, we need one more lady to make up the numbers. Don't we, Hamilton?'

My uncle agreed that that was true, and so it was arranged. How could a mere farmer's daughter refuse an invitation from her future king? I rode away in a daze, hardly believing what had happened. Grace would be livid with jealousy. And what would Father say?

—

Father had doubts about the propriety of the invitation; the prince's reputation with ladies was already the subject of disquiet, though most people, including Mama, thought it was malicious gossip about a lively young man who couldn't answer back. If Uncle Henry was to be my escort, I should come to no harm.

Grace was certainly envious but, as she said with a sigh, 'William wouldn't be pleased if I attended such a party without him. Anyway,' she assured herself, 'we shall no doubt be invited to one of the Birthday Balls this year. They won't miss them two years running.' Cheered by the thought, she agreed to advise me on my toilette on the under-standing that I should tell all to her on my return.

In the event, few details of the house, the women's gowns, the food or the conversation remained to me. I was too mesmerised by nerves to be observant. That, at least, is what I told Grace.

Mrs Todd, the dressmaker, made over an old lilac silk gown of Mama's for me. She made the fullness all in the back, lengthened the skirt with flounces and lace trimmings, kept the bodice low-cut and off the shoulder. It probably made me look like the gauche country girl I was, but at the time I thought it wonderful. Ellen did my hair, sweeping it up and back, using curling tongs to tame its wiry exuberance. She fixed white roses among a cascade of ringlets caught up at my crown, matching the flowers at the décolletage, and Mama lent me her diamond necklet. Seeing the elegant creature who stared back at me from the mirror, all creamy shoulders and floating silk, I felt like Cinderella on her way to the ball. A pity my Prince Charming had to be my uncle.

The whole family gathered on the doorstep to see us off, Father issuing instructions to his younger brother to take good care of me.

'I don't wonder you run wild,' Henry said with sympathy as we settled together into the carriage and the coachman cracked his whip. 'So should I, hemmed in so tightly by anxious parents.'

'They mean well,' I said.

'Quite so. But tonight, little niece, forget them. You're about to have an experience for which many women would do murder. So enjoy it.'

I was amazed to find him so understanding. But of course he was more of my generation than Father's – he was only a little older than Basil Pooley – and he moved in wider, more sophisticated circles.

Excitement rode with me, making my pulse beat faster as we drove through the darkening lanes and came at last to the wrought-iron gates which had been presented to the prince and princess as a wedding gift from loyal residents of Norfolk. Beyond the gates and the police guard, the drive swept round under trees, dark giants humped against a pale sky where the evening star hung bright, and in the distance I saw the oblong shape that was the house. Tall Tudor chimneys lifted over stuccoed walls, with light gleaming a welcome from many windows.

Liveried footmen waited by the ornate red and white porch that looked so odd against the severe white ugliness of the rest of the house, and inside was a confusion of light and colour, polished wood and silk brocade, oil paintings with gilt frames, Chinese porcelain... I was overwhelmed with nervous awe.

My memory of the early part of that evening is a jumble of impressions – a maze of rooms, a maelstrom of strangers. I recall a drawing-room full of laughing, chattering people in evening dress, where the prince kissed my hand, told me I looked charming, and left my uncle to introduce me to other guests. The 'small' party consisted of about forty people. Among them were persons whom later I came to know as identifiable names and faces, some destined to hold high office. There were actors, a poet, a Bavarian baron, and one Colonel Valentine Baker, later cashiered for indecent assault on a governess in a railway carriage. With them were as many ladies, some married and some single, though whether the married ones all belonged with the gentlemen present I wasn't sure. Half a dozen of the young women were actresses of one kind or another, and I was astonished to recognise one girl as Kitty Hambledown, younger daughter of the local miller. She winked at me across the room, as if we shared a merry secret.

Among the company I felt swamped, tongue-tied and self-conscious.

When dinner was announced, Uncle Henry had the job of dividing the party into pairs. The prince took in Lady Filmer, I remember. Other gentlemen claimed their smiling partners.

'Rose, you're with...' Henry consulted his list. 'Ah, yes. You do know Mr Devlin, don't you? Devlin, you take my niece in. Now, Betsy dear, I've put you with...'

I could feel shock trickling from my scalp, cold rivulets down my neck, across my face, like ants rushing to cover every inch of my skin. Geoffrey looked equally startled. Turning from conversation with a dark-haired girl with pearls in her hair, he stopped dead, the smile freezing on his face as his glance swept me, as if he could scarcely believe his eyes. The sight of him, tall and lithely elegant in evening dress, made me feel as if I were choking.

After one frozen instant he regained his composure and strolled forward, offering me his arm.

'Miss Hamilton. Good evening. I hadn't realised you were here.'

'Nor I you,' I managed.

'I've only just arrived.' Then, under his breath, he muttered, 'Well, do we go in, or do we set the entire company wondering?'

Because there simply was nothing else to do, I laid my hand in the curve of his arm and we turned to follow the procession.

Under cover of the noise of voices and shouted laughter, Geoffrey muttered, 'What the d–devil are you doing here?'

'His Royal Highness invited me. Personally.' I didn't dare look at him. 'And my uncle Henry brought me. It's all quite proper.'

'Proper? You think so?'

'And what about you?' I countered. 'Where's Miss de Crecy?'

'She had to go up to town,' he said stiffly. 'With my mother.'

'How very convenient!' I shot him a look that told my contempt of a man who could attend a party of this nature without his fiancée, and Geoffrey returned with a sparking glare. We walked on, not speaking, not looking at each other.

The evening progressed in a haze of unreality. My consciousness seemed to be splintered. My outer self was a mannerly party guest, replying when spoken to, laughing when jokes were made, eating and drinking in moderation… My inner self was self-conscious and ill at ease, cruelly aware of Geoffrey Devlin beside me, and of the chasms between us.

Around us voices grew louder as courses progressed and wine flowed. Geoffrey spoke to me only in monosyllables when politeness obliged him to it. It was like sitting too near a fire, being scorched but unable to move. I could hardly eat; my stomach was too taut to welcome food. But a growing thirst made me glad of the wines that kept being poured into the array of glasses before me. The wine made me aware of how unhappy I was; it also made me wonder if it mattered what people thought.

About me, people kept up a flow of talk to which I had no need to add much, except, 'Really?' and, 'How strange!' or, 'Good gracious!' The man on my left, called 'Dickie', was heir to a dukedom. At the end of the table, the prince laughed uproariously, flanked by Lady Filmer and one of the actresses, and elsewhere Uncle Henry was giving most of his attention to Kitty Hambledown.

The prince was on his feet, moving down the table to exchange a few words with each guest. He bent over me, his gaze on my shoulders and bosom as he made some joking remark and moved on. As he spoke to Geoffrey and those beyond him, I fingered Mama's necklet, trying to conceal the fact that the prince's straying glance had made me feel naked. Most of the other women didn't appear to mind being leered at, or even fondled – down the table, across from us, one of the gentlemen had his hand on a lady's bare shoulder.

'You should never have come here!' Geoffrey said.

Momentarily, I met glimmering dark eyes that sparked anger at me. 'Why not?' I demanded. '*You're* here!'

'That's different.'

'Why is it?'

As he sought for a reply, I thought how fine he looked in formal evening dress, his dark hair falling softly either side of his brow, his face enhanced by the growth of hair on his upper lip, and by the tiny mole on his chin. I had never forgotten that mole, or the slight crookedness of one front tooth. Chills of awareness ran through me as I remembered our intimacy and caught myself imagining how it would feel to kiss him now that he had grown a moustache.

'Enough of that, Freddie!' The prince's amused roar was aimed at the gentleman with straying hands, over whose head he tipped a glass of wine. The red liquid ran down the man's face, on to his white shirt and tie. Shouts of approving laughter encouraged the prince to enlarge the jest and, enjoying himself, he reached for a dish of ice-cream. 'Maybe this'll cool your ardour.'

'Damn it!' the butt of the joke cried. 'You drunken buffoon, Bertie!' and he charged out of his chair with such force that he sent the prince lurching backwards. The dish of ice upended itself in a lady's lap. As she screamed in dismay the gathering's hilarity crescendoed: the heir to the throne had tripped, landing flat on his well-cushioned backside.

Servants rushed to help him up, and as he got to his feet the noise subsided; the prince was furious. Hilarity choked into spreading silence, leaving the atmosphere tense, watchful. I saw people glance apprehensively at one another as every sound ceased. We held our breath, waiting for the storm.

Glowering blackly, the prince jerked at his jacket to straighten it, then shot out his arm to point at the offender. 'I said you need cooling off, sir.' A jerk of his head summoned all the men present. 'Toss him in the lake!'

A whoop of glee greeted this order, followed by a rush to leave the table and swoop on the wine-stained victim. He protested and struggled, but was lifted head high. French windows opened before him.

I found myself on my feet, not knowing what to do. No use relying on Uncle Henry to help – he had been one of the first to grab the unfortunate Freddie. Maybe Geoffrey…

'Lend a hand, Devlin!' the prince cried.

Beside me, Geoffrey hesitated, then strode to join the rowdy rabble crowding to get out of the French doors and on to the terrace.

I followed, finding myself in the middle of an excited group of stragglers. They pushed and jostled, eager not to miss the fun, then the crush eased as the main party got through the doors. Beyond them I glimpsed the darkness outside, the lake in its hollow cloaked by trees, with moonlight shimmering on its dark surface.

Among the last to leave the dining-room, I felt the night air cool on my shoulders. My head swam a little from the wine.

'Miss Hamilton?' One of the footmen stopped me. 'His Royal Highness would like a word with you, miss. If you'll come with me…'

I don't believe I even thought about it. I simply went with him.

Beyond a maze of passages lay a cosy sitting-room. A single lamp burned there, shedding its soft glow on armchairs and low tables, on exotic wood carvings grotesque in the shadows, and on Prince Albert Edward, standing with his back to an embroidered firescreen. The footman closed the door behind me, leaving me alone with the prince. I stood there, feeling a little unsteady on my feet.

'I hope the behaviour of one ill-mannered gentleman has not spoiled your first evening among us, Miss Hamilton,' he said with an apologetic smile. 'It will do them good to get some air, anyway. They were all getting over-heated. Meanwhile, I thought you and I should have a talk. Get to know each other better, what?'

Grace, I thought blearily, would not believe this. 'Yes, sir.'

'Excellent!' He beamed at me. 'Then come and sit down.'

Since his gesture indicated a velvet-covered *chaise-longue* to one side of the hearth, I moved across to it, walking carefully erect so as not to set off the whirling in my head. Wide skirts whispering about me, I sat down demurely, saying, 'I've been wanting an opportunity to speak with you, sir.'

'Have you indeed?' he murmured with a smile.

'About the hares.'

The smile faltered. 'Oh, come now, Miss Hamilton,' he chided, and before I knew what he intended he had seated himself close beside me. 'Not boring business talk. Not now.' He leaned his arm on the back of the *chaise*, his gaze on the swell of my breasts. His face was flushed, his breathing quickened. I saw him moisten his lips. 'You interested me very much the other day. When you spoke of kicking over the traces. Being a bit of a rebel. I like that in a woman. I've always been a bit of a rebel myself.'

I wished I could think straight. My head seemed to be cloudy. It didn't seem right that I should be here alone with the prince – a married man – and yet it all seemed to be quite routine to him, and to the servant who had brought me.

Without warning, he lunged for me. His hand plunged down my dress and his mouth fastened on my neck. A cry escaped me as I was pressed backward and a hot, wet mouth came searching for mine. 'Sir!'

'Damn it, hold still!'

Panicking, I wriggled, turned over, slid to the floor on my knees, squirmed out from under him and scrambled free, adjusting my gown as I backed away. 'Sir, please!'

'Blast you!' he raged, and would have flown at me, but some thought stopped him. He turned abruptly away, his hands on the back of the *chaise*, his face hidden. In the dim light I saw a fist clench, and feared his anger. Then, as I glanced at the door, wondering if I could escape, he made a sound. His shoulders were shaking. After a moment I realised he was laughing. Or pretending to.

'Ah… ha, ha, ha, ha, hah! Ah… ha, ha, hah!' Turning to look at me, he crowed, 'You thought I was serious! Hee, hee, Miss Hamilton! Did you really think I was about to seduce you? What a silly goose you are.' He eased himself to his feet and, smiling, advanced on me. 'It was my little joke. I only wanted to see your face. I'm a naughty boy, aren't I?' Head on one side cajolingly, he reached for my chin and tutted when I flinched away. 'Oh, come. Don't look like that. Don't be angry with me. It was my joke. I didn't mean to upset you.'

'I'm sorry, sir,' I muttered. 'I'm just not used to—'

'Not used to horseplay, I suppose. Not used to enjoying yourself.' Playfully stern, he wagged a finger at me. 'It's time you were married, Miss Hamilton. Yes, that's the answer. We shall have to find you a husband.' His gleaming glance was roaming again as he murmured, 'Married ladies have more freedom to enjoy themselves, you know.'

An involuntary shiver ran through me and, seeing it, he stepped away, his eyes narrowed. His expression said he was tired of the game, and of me. 'You may as well go home. Good night, Miss Hamilton.'

The door slammed behind him. I was alone in the private sitting-room at Sandringham Hall.

Thinking that I could easily walk – run! – home, if I could find my way out of the house, I went out into the dim–lit passageway and turned towards what I believed to be the rear of the house. Nowhere could I find, as I had hoped, an outer door that would lead to cool night air and safety. Nor did I meet any servant who might have helped. That part of the house seemed deserted. Perhaps the prince had arranged it so.

Then I heard a squeal. At the far side of a hallway one of the ladies who had been at the party appeared – the girl in blue, with pearls in her dark hair. She was laughingly evading the clutches of the gentleman who pursued her. With her skirts lifted to reveal a flutter of many-coloured petticoats and a pair of red–stockinged ankles, she dodged away, starting up a flight of stairs, while he, growling like a bear, went after her. Neither of them noticed me.

I blundered back the way I had come and found myself back at the door of the small sitting-room. It was set in an angle of the passageway and, from around the corner, in some distant area of the house, I could hear laughter and music. There was nothing for it but to venture in that direction and hope I might find a way out.

But as I stepped around the corner I collided with a man in evening dress. I cried out in alarm. The man took hold of me and pressed me back behind the wall, saying anxiously, 'Rose! Where have you been? My dear... what's wrong?'

It was Geoffrey. Relief surged through me, then as I realised what it all meant I was consumed by rage.

'"What's wrong?"' I repeated. 'Don't you know what's wrong? Oh...' I shuddered away from him, 'Don't touch me! Don't ever touch me again. I hate you. I hate you all!'

'Who was with you?' Geoffrey said sharply. 'Who brought you here? Tell me and I'll—'

'You know who it was,' I cried. 'You know! Didn't you tell him all about me? You're such good friends. Didn't you tell him how easily you had seduced me? Isn't that why he invited me here – and got my own uncle to… Oh, God! Oh, God! Uncle Henry was in it, too.' Tears burst from my eyes and I flung my hands to contain them, my face turned to the wall.

'I think,' Geoffrey said, 'that I had better take you home.'

With his arm about me he led me through passageways and darkened rooms to a side entrance where he said, 'I shan't be long. Wait here,' and vanished.

In the shadows of that little porch I leaned on the wall and wept, certain that I was ruined for ever. I knew now what sort of party it was, why I had been invited, and why Uncle Henry had told me to enjoy myself. No wonder Lucinda de Crecy wasn't there; a lady such as she would hardly be included in a night of debauchery. But Geoffrey was here. Geoffrey, who was obviously on familiar terms with both the prince and this house. How often did these orgies take place?

Picking up my skirts, I started to run along the gravelled path but had not gone far when wheels crunched and a light, one-horse vehicle bowled up behind me, its lamps agleam.

'Rose!' Geoffrey's voice shouted. 'Rose, don't be foolish.'

I veered away on to a lawn, heading for the shadow of trees not far away, aware that he was coming after me on foot. As I reached the trees, he caught me, spinning me round. For a moment we struggled together, I trying to fight him off and he trying to gain a hold; then all at once I found myself in his arms.

Emotion exploded inside me as our mouths met and commingled. I clung to him, my fingers driving into his hair, holding him down to me, feeling my body press itself against him, hampered by the crinoline. I wanted him so badly. Needed him. And I knew he shared my need. Yet somewhere in the still-sane part of me I knew also that to give in to it would only bring more shame.

Weeping with despair, I pushed at his shoulders. 'No. No!'

He released me at once and as I turned away, my hands to my face, his arm came about my waist. 'Let me take you home. Come.'

Despairing of myself, I let him lead me back to his gig.

The vehicle was narrow, cramming us together so that my crinoline billowed out like a mettlesome horse until I got it under control. Geoffrey had brought my cloak and I huddled it round me, wishing the vehicle had more room; his proximity in the darkness beneath the hood of his vehicle was unbearable, though he sat forward and I sat back, behind his shoulder as he held the reins. What must he think of me? If only my head would clear!

He didn't speak until we were past the guard at the Norwich gates and clopping slowly down the lane; then he said, 'Did he... D–did he actually—'

'No, he didn't. When I fought him off he seemed suddenly to remember that I was unmarried. And then he pretended it was all a joke. He said I should find a husband. Presumably married women make less fuss about being debauched.'

'I'm sorry.'

'I feel sick just thinking of it. I feel unclean. Poor Princess Alix...' The words choked off as I swallowed a sob.

'She's been ill a long time.'

'Does that excuse him?' I cried.

After a moment, he said quietly, 'No. No, it doesn't.'

Tears slid from my eyes, wetting my face. Making no attempt to stop them I huddled behind him in the darkness, aware only of my intense misery. What would become of me now?

'I have not discussed you with the prince,' he said eventually. 'Not at all. I have never told anyone about—'

'Not even Hal Wyatt?' I cried.

He twisted to look at me over his shoulder, saying fiercely, 'Especially not Hal Wyatt!'

'Then how did he know about us? Oh, you must have said something, Geoffrey, even if you didn't mean to, you must have given him some hint – enough for him to guess. Oh...' Impatient with my tears, I wiped at them with my hands, but more came behind them, flowing warm and free. I couldn't seem to stop crying.

Bringing the horse to a halt, Geoffrey secured the reins and turned to me, saying, 'Don't, love. Please don't.' And, as if it were the most natural thing in the world, he gathered me into his arms. I didn't resist; I wept helplessly against him. I needed comfort and he gave it to me, holding me warm and safe with his cheek on my hair.

It was so good to be with him again, there where no one else could see, where only he and I existed. Clinging to him, I nestled closer, breathing in the familiar scent of him, feeling his guardian arm tighten as he stroked my hair and my cheek. He bent his head closer, rubbing his face against mine, his breath warm on my neck.

'I never told anyone about us,' he said. 'I swear I did not. I would not. It was our secret, Rose. Too precious to be shared.'

'I know. I know.'

He was silent for a long while, holding me close while the mood between us softened to a familiar intimacy. 'I didn't tell you how beautiful you looked tonight,' he murmured. 'I was so glad your uncle partnered you with me. I couldn't have borne to watch another man have the pleasure of your company.' His lips brushed the lobe of my ear. His moustache felt soft, adding to the sensual pleasure of touch.

In some detached part of my brain I was aware that wine was making me behave as I would never have behaved had I been sober, but at that moment I knew only that I ached for him, that I had missed him, that I needed the comfort of his nearness. I burrowed my face into the curve of his throat, kissing the pulse that throbbed there. My lips tasted the angle of his jaw and his cheek, until I found his waiting mouth and gave myself up to the soaring joy that filled me.

He loves me, I thought. He has loved me all this time. I was wrong to doubt him. I should have told him about the child. The child. Our daughter. He doesn't even know that she exists. If I tell him—

Then a pheasant cried alarm, its croak harsh in the night. Undergrowth rustled loudly. Geoffrey lifted his head. For long moments we were both still, listening.

'Poacher?' I breathed.

'No, I don't think so. A fox, maybe. Or a weasel.'

I shifted myself upright and sat back, shivering, drawing the cloak about my shoulders. Reality was seeping back through the haze of alcohol. 'It might be one of the keepers. Perhaps we should go.'

'Perhaps we should.'

Turning away, he took up the reins and slapped the horse into motion, faster than before. I had the impression that he was as anxious as I to end this impossible evening.

Wood Lodge, where the McDowalls now lived, was all in darkness. As we turned the corner to go under the tunnel of trees, I said, 'Set me down at the gate. My father will be waiting for me.'

Geoffrey made no reply, but I knew he understood. He stopped the vehicle just beyond the gates, so that the new wall hid us from the house, and then he leapt down and came to help me alight. Neither of us knew a graceful way to accomplish our parting.

If I were to tell him the truth, perhaps even now there was hope for us. He might go and find our child, bring her back, acknowledge her – and me. 'Geoffrey...'

He said, 'Lucy and I are to be m–married in August.'

I stopped as if he had driven a dagger into me. I wanted to scream, or fly at him like a Fury. I did nothing. I only stood there, staring at him, dying a little.

'Rose...' He took me by the shoulders, peering down into my face in the darkness. 'Please understand. Whatever I may have done as a single man, I intend to be a faithful husband. I can't let Lucy down. I've made promises to her. Whatever I feel for you—'

'I know what you feel for me,' I broke in, my voice thick with self-loathing. 'And you're right. I'm a fool.'

'You're warm and sweet and true,' he said in a low voice, his fingers gripping, almost shaking me. 'I know that. I envy the man who wins your heart. I pray you will be happy, Rose Hamilton.'

Hot tears splintered my sight as agony pierced me. How could he keep up the pretence? I broke free and backed away, saying hoarsely, 'You don't care whether I'm happy or not. You never did. Don't lie to me, Geoffrey. I know it's all lies!'

With tears running down my face, I fled.

In the house, a few lights were burning. If Father saw me, he would probably kill me. Little I cared. I sat down on the step, careless of my lilac silk, and waited until the night air had cooled my swollen face. How was I to explain my dishevelled appearance?

But for once in my life fortune was with me. I saw no one as I went up to my room – Father had fallen asleep at his vigil in the parlour; even Grace had grown tired of waiting and given herself to dreams. The only person I saw was Ellen Earley, who was dozing in a chair in my room. She jumped awake and came yawning to help me undress, but she didn't seem to notice anything amiss; she was just eager to get the job done and find her own bed. I let her go as soon as she had loosened my stays.

Left alone, I stood before the mirror staring at my reflection. My hair was like a bird's nest, my face blotched, my eyes so bleak with hopelessness that I couldn't face them. Then as I began to turn away I stopped and looked closer, seeing a long red scratch mark that stood out against the whiteness of my breast. My fingers discovered its raised shape, and its slight soreness. The Prince of Wales's fingernail had caused it when he had lunged so clumsily at me.

Sickened by the memory, I blew out the lamp, climbed into bed, and cried myself to sleep.

Seven

On the day following his 'quiet' dinner party, the Prince of Wales returned to his official duties. Presumably my uncle Henry accompanied him. Later, newspapers reported that the Prince and Princess of Wales were to spend a few weeks in Wiesbaden, the German spa where, it was hoped, the princess would recover her health.

Life went on, as though that shattering evening at Sandringham Hall had never happened. I told no one about it. In time, I half convinced myself it had been a bad dream.

One consolation was the fact that Mama seemed better. Her marriage was more secure, her relationship with Narnie mended, and Grace was being earnestly courted by Turnbull; Mama was, if not exactly happy, at least more settled.

On occasion I took her and Grace to visit Narnie, leaving them at Willow Cottage while I went on to the Grange to see the Wyatt girls. My life seemed meaningless. I was haunted by thoughts of my child, my little lost daughter, imagining how she must be growing, wondering if she was happy, if she was healthy. Thoroughly unsettled, ill-tempered with little provocation, I quarrelled with Grace, was impatient with Mama, and even had words with inoffensive Felicity when she chided me for wishing aloud that I had been born male.

'You can't mean it, Rose,' she said. 'That's your aunt Agnes speaking, not you. God made you as you are, for his own reasons.'

'What reasons?' I demanded. 'Why is his purpose always so obscure? While he was creating me female, why didn't he also create me compliant like you and your sisters? *You* may be content to moulder away without purpose to your life, but I hate it.'

Felicity looked as if I had slapped her. 'I don't choose to moulder as an old maid. If Victor hadn't been taken…'

I was sorry to have hurt her. To Felicity faith was an anchor, to cling to without question. To me it was a string of mysteries whose enigmatic nature was an irritant to my restless, questing soul. That summer, everything irritated me. When Johnny came home, he too tried my limited patience. At fifteen, already as tall as I and still growing, he had reached a difficult time between boyhood and manhood. And he was bored. Most days he simply went off somewhere, and all too frequently the backus boy went with him. We heard about their escapades later, from villagers whose children had been frightened, or whose windows had been broken, or from farmers whose hens had been scattered. It all made an extra annoyance.

Father's health continued to concern me. He had started to add, 'God willing', to every sentence concerning the future, and he came more often to church, as if seeking answers that had so far eluded him. In that, he and I had much in common.

Between haying and harvest, Father went to Norwich on business for a few days, leaving McDowall in charge. In his absence, I decided to take a good look over the farm while exercising Dandy. August had begun, bringing the date of Geoffrey's wedding ever closer.

The day was hot, the flies swarming and biting, and the crops were in a sad state, wheat and barley broken down, green tops chewed, legumes drooping and dying – all because of the hares. What they didn't nibble they battered down. We had tried everything: tarring the runs, stuffing gorse into holes in hedges, erecting more sacking barriers... Nothing stopped the furry predators.

Arriving home in a fret of concern for the farm, I discovered that Johnny had been up to yet more mischief. He had come in filthy, refused to say where he had been, then sworn at Mama, leaving her in tears and Grace outraged. I didn't wait to hear the details; I hurried upstairs and burst into his room.

Angry remonstrances died in my throat as I saw my young brother standing stripped to the waist, twisting towards the mirror in an effort to see his back – which was covered in livid blue and red weals. Someone had beaten him.

'Johnny!'

Startled, he whirled to face me, clasping his shirt to cover his chest. His face was streaked with dirt and tears. 'Don't tell Father! Don't tell Father!'

'Who did it?' I strode across to him and grasped his shoulder, making him wince with pain as I turned him so that I could see the marks more clearly.

'It was Sir Arthur.'

'Sir Arthur Devlin?!'

'He took his riding crop to me.'

For a moment I couldn't think coherently through my anger, then: 'For what?' Again I took hold of him, making him look at me. 'What did you do to annoy him, Johnny?'

'I was only walking on his land. Only walking. Truly, Rose! You won't tell Father, will you? You won't tell—'

I heard no more; just as I was, in my working clothes, darned and dusty, with my hair caught in a snood beneath a broad-brimmed straw hat, I swirled out and ran down the stairs.

—

Ambleford Hall was a gracious old house of mellow red brick, its earliest parts dating from Elizabethan times. It was approached by a long drive flanked by towering oaks that met overhead, hiding the view until one came round a bend and out of the trees, into open parkland where sheep grazed. The park spread right up to rose-red walls with pointed archways, buttresses and leaded windows, the whole topped by tall twisting chimneys reminiscent of our old farmhouse.

I galloped Dandy up the drive and threw myself to the ground, tossing the reins around a hook by a mounting block hollowed by the feet of centuries. Tugging on the brightly-polished brass bell-pull, I waited, tapping my foot, bitter thoughts fuelling my temper. A part of me hoped that Geoffrey would be there, so that he could witness the confrontation. How dared his fine family treat Hamiltons like serfs to be whipped and scourged!

A butler appeared. I demanded to see Sir Arthur. Inviting me to wait in the small entry hall, where a dark Jacobean cupboard had pride of place, the man disappeared along a gloomy hallway, reappearing after only a few minutes to inform me that his master was 'not at home'.

'Then I want to see Lady Devlin,' I said. 'And don't tell me she's not at home either, for I'm not leaving until I've seen one or the other of them.'

'Very well, miss. If you'll be so kind as to wait here...'

But this time I went after him, covertly, planning to disconcert the Devlins if, as I fully expected, they should refuse to see me.

The dark-panelled hall, narrow and full of shadows, led past a stairwell and a gun-room whose open door allowed me to see the weapons ranged in their cases. There was a tang of expensive tobacco in the air: Sir Arthur might not be 'at home' – not to me – but he wasn't far away. Ahead of me, the butler opened a door which let more light into the dark hall. I heard him speaking with someone, heard a woman's voice answer, and with that I was pushing past him, saying, 'Lady Devlin, I must insist that—'

Lady Devlin wasn't there. The only person in the room was a girl who jumped up in alarm, oversetting her tapestry frame. It clattered to the floor with a thud that made her wince visibly, a hand flying to her mouth.

'Miss Hamilton!' the butler exclaimed in outrage.

'I'm sorry.' The apology was for the startled girl, who looked as if she might faint. I hurried to pick up the frame for her and set it back on its stand. 'Forgive me.'

'I shall summon Her Ladyship at once,' the butler warned, and went away.

The room was long and narrow, bright with sunlight pouring through tall windows. Two marble pillars helped to support an ornate plaster ceiling. There was no fashionable clutter here; no ornaments and photographs, no antimacassars, bobbled velvet, or draperies to hide the 'limbs' of chairs, tables or piano. To my eyes the room with its exquisite Georgian furnishings looked half empty, but in that first moment I hardly saw it: all I saw was the frightened girl.

I took her for a companion, maybe an impoverished relative being cared for by the Devlins. She looked to be about sixteen, a small, slender person with grey eyes set wide apart in a pallid face. She wore her mouse-brown hair drawn back into a netted chignon spangled with jet, matching the necklace that hung down the front of an afternoon gown in grey trimmed with black. The tapestry sampler she had been working on was equally colourless, worked in shades of brown, grey and black, with a few stitches of dark blue.

'I didn't mean to startle you,' I said. 'But it's important that I see Lady Devlin.'

She stared at me with worried eyes, her hand still cupped as if to protect her mouth. 'Do I know you?'

'My name is Rose Hamilton. I'm a neighbour, from Orchards Farm.'

'Oh. Yes.' She glanced down at my clothes, reminding me that I was still dressed as I had been when I came in from the fields.

'I came out in rather a hurry,' I said with chagrin. 'You're right, it's hardly the proper way to come calling, but I was so angry that—'

'Miss Hamilton!' The imperious voice made me stop and take a deep breath as I turned to face Lady Ophelia. She stood erect and severe, her face, though thin, still striking, set off by greying fair hair, with a frothy jabot at the throat of a black gown. 'How dare you burst into my home in this way! Leave at once. You're unwelcome here.'

'Lady Devlin…'

'I told you to leave.'

My courage faltered. She was a formidable woman, with a way of looking down her thin nose that made me feel like a beetle she was about to squash. But I remembered Johnny's back, marred by blue and red weals. 'I shan't leave until I've said what I came to say. This feud between Sir Arthur and my father has gone far enough. Today your husband beat my younger brother – viciously used his riding crop on the boy – merely for walking on Ambleford property.'

The girl behind me made a small sound like a choked-off moan. She looked sick, her hand still hiding her mouth.

'Crimmond!' Lady Devlin snapped.

The butler, who had been waiting behind her, advanced on me.

'If he lays hands on me,' I said, 'I shall take pleasure in charging him with assault.'

The butler stopped, looking uncertainly at his mistress.

Breathing angrily through her nose, she looked me up and down with disdain. 'I've heard about you, Rose Hamilton. You're a disgrace to your sex. How dare you come to my house looking like a field-worker, forcing your way into my drawing-room, upsetting Miss de Crecy? If you don't leave of your own free will I shall have you ejected from this property. And if you dare to lay a complaint then I shall be glad to see you in court and have you explain this to a jury. I know with whom they will sympathise.'

What had she said – 'upsetting Miss de Crecy'? Stunned, I looked at the pale girl beside me. Was this frightened creature the 'beautiful heiress', Geoffrey's intended bride?

'Leave us, Lucy,' Lady Devlin said.

The girl looked relieved. 'Yes, Aunt. Thank you.' But before she left she gave me a troubled glance. The hand that had been guarding her mouth dropped away, and I saw the scar that cut across her upper lip, puckering and disfiguring it.

'*They say she's horribly deformed,*' Grace's voice echoed in my head. The story had been exaggerated in the telling, but it was evidently based on truth. Wealthy as Miss Lucinda de Crecy might be, some accident had destroyed her chances of beauty. Now she was afraid to be seen in public. Poor girl. My heart contracted with pity as she hurried away, her slippers pattering on the polished floorboards that edged the room.

And then with a chill I thought of Geoffrey – my Geoffrey – planning to marry that sad, timid creature. '*I shall be a faithful husband,*' he had vowed. Did he love the girl? Perhaps he pitied her. Or perhaps the truth was that she was heiress to great wealth, while Sir Arthur's experiments in farming had drained his own resources and put him in debt. Was Geoffrey marrying her merely to restore his family fortune?

'Well, Miss Hamilton?' Lady Devlin reminded me of her presence.

'I'm leaving,' I said, starting for the door. But as I passed her I paused and looked her in the eye, saying, 'I apologise for the way I burst in, and for my appearance. I was angry. I didn't think.'

'That would appear to be an unfortunate trait in your character,' she replied loftily.

'I didn't mean to cause offence. I came to try and settle this stupid feud. We're tired of it. My father's unwell and... Lady Devlin, you must know as well as I do that if your husband doesn't curb his temper he may do something that—'

Her eyes sparked at me. They were slate-blue, like Geoffrey's. Though she was turned sixty, grey-haired and female, I saw clearly where her son had acquired his good looks. 'My husband,' she said coldly, 'is perfectly in control of his temper. Unlike yourself, by your own admission, Miss Hamilton. As for your brother, I suggest that next time you listen to him whine you might stay to enquire a little more deeply into the truth. Yes, he was found on Ambleford land. He had a shot-gun with him. He was shooting pheasant. Which would you prefer for him, Miss Hamilton – a beating, to teach him a lesson, or a jail sentence for poaching?'

'I would have preferred it if Sir Arthur had had the courtesy to explain it to me himself,' I said. 'Good day, Lady Devlin.'

When I tackled Johnny about it, he confessed. Yes, he had taken a shot-gun with him, but he had been after rabbit, not pheasant. He wouldn't be such a fool as to go after pheasant. I believed him. I was furious with him for lying to me over the gun, but for the rest I believed him. I still do.

And – no, we didn't tell Father. Not about any of it.

-

Geoffrey married his heiress later that month. At the bride's request, the wedding took place at Ambleford church, followed by a vast reception to which most of county society – including the Wyatt family – was invited. The only notable absentee was, apparently, Lucinda's father, struck down by illness at the last moment.

I spent the day at home, in a daze, hardly knowing what I was doing, all my aching thoughts concentrated on what was happening a few miles away, my imagination conjuring the scene in painful detail. I kept dreaming that news would come of some last-minute change of heart by one of the parties. Only will-power prevented me from making a spectacle of myself by riding over to Ambleford to witness the event.

Felicity Wyatt later told me how wonderful the bride's gown had been, all lace and pearls; how handsome the groom had looked, and how exciting their honeymoon was going to be – six whole months in Europe.

'Lucinda looked quite beautiful,' she kept saying. Felicity seldom spoke an unkind word about anyone.

But others had been at the wedding, and had got their first good view of Lucinda de Crecy. Gossip spread, like a flood-tide across the marshes, as people speculated about the truth of the affair. General feeling was summed up by one matron who was heard to remark, 'Well, she's rich, and in the dark I dare say her equipment's the same as every other woman's. Geoffrey Devlin's no fool. Once he's got her in the family way he'll be free to carry on with his philandering. She's not the sort to ask too many questions. Only too pleased to have got herself a husband of any kind, I should think.'

-

After harvest, when the cost of damage to our crops became calculable, the angry farmers called a meeting. Father attended it and, seeming disturbed by what had happened, recounted the story to me as we walked in the orchard, checking the fruit, with the sun low and clouds of screaming swifts darting over the meadow after midges.

The annual audit of farm rents was due at Michaelmas; as a matter of custom, it was preceded by a tenants' dinner held in one of the large hotels in King's Lynn and attended by the Sandringham agent and the prince's London lawyer. At this year's dinner, the farmers intended to rise as one man and demand proper compensation for damage by game. The longest-standing tenant had sworn that, if he didn't get fair treatment, he would resign his lease.

'A sight of good it will do him,' Father said in weary disgust. 'He'll lose his home, that's all, when he's spent years of toil and a fortune in good money consolidating and improving the land. Beck won't be blackmailed by threats of that kind. There are farmers lining up to get a place on the royal estate.'

'Is that what you think, or what McDowall says?' I asked – our farm steward was known for his pessimism.

He shot me a dark look. 'It's a fact. I don't need McDowall to point out what's plain as a pikestaff.'

'Then you won't join the protest?'

'Oh, I'll join it – God willing. I'll complain as loudly as the next man, never you fear. And then I'll listen to Beck explain why there won't be compensation, and why the rent's going up again.'

'But it's not right!' I exclaimed. 'Our profits are being eaten up by those rotten "kangaroos". If it goes on—'

'So what do you want me to do about it, Rose? Maybe you'd like to go to the audit and have it out with Beck yourself.'

'I only wish I could!' I said fiercely.

'Oh, don't be such a fool,' he sighed, and turned away, coughing, hawking up mucus that he spat over the fence. 'It's coming up damp. Best come in and have your dinner.'

–

The following Sunday, when William Turnbull arrived, he asked to speak to me alone. In his solemn, pedantic fashion, he was seeking my permission to approach Father to ask for Grace's hand in marriage.

'I thought it only right to speak with you first,' he said. 'You have known for some time that my affections were turning towards your sister. Even so, I should be in your debt if you could find it in your heart freely to give us your blessing. I was always most fond of you, Miss Hamilton. And while fondness may have been enough, had you returned it, my feelings for your sister are such that—'

When he was embarrassed, it made him more pompous than ever.

'Mr Turnbull… William, dear,' I sighed. 'If you're in love with my sister, shouldn't you be telling her, not me?'

He looked down at the hat he was turning in his hands. 'I have done so.'

'And will she have you?'

'Her only fear is that, by marrying one who was formerly so bold as to call frequently on her older sister, she may offend you. And, you being the older, you might expect her to wait until such time as you yourself are in the happy position of—'

'She might die of old age, waiting for that,' I said. 'Oh…' Reaching on tiptoe, I brushed a kiss against an unbearded area of his face. 'Go and put her out of her misery. I'll dance at your wedding and be glad for you both.'

As he hurried away to give the news to Grace, I was prey to a momentary pang of regret. But if I had married William Turnbull his stiff formality would have irritated me to fury. He deserved better.

Father gave his consent, and so a delirious Grace became engaged and began to make plans for a spring wedding. Not only was she stealing a march on me, she was going to the altar ahead of her dear friend Maria Kinnersley, who was beside herself with envy. Grace's cup was full.

-

On the day of the tenants' dinner, tense and unable to settle, I took Dandy for a gallop through the autumn woods. A big shoot was being held in the Dersingham area, so I went the other way, towards Ambleford, and found myself following familiar pathways. Hares ran ahead of me, and birds flew complaining as I raced along, my mind on the rent audit and what might come of the farmers' protest at their dinner. Without consciously intending it, I came to the refuge.

I sat on Dandy's back staring at the mean, tumble-down hut that had witnessed so much youthful passion, so many hopes and heartaches. It was a desolate place now. Weeds grew waist-high, inside and out, and a sapling had somehow grown, poking its way through the thatch. Hurdle walls were broken, sagging askew. And on one of the nearby trees was nailed a gamekeeper's gibbet – a long pole on which, impaled on metal hooks, the dead bodies of stoats, rats, squirrels, jays and magpies hung rotting. It seemed a comment on the nature of my relationship with Geoffrey Devlin.

I had avoided the place before, because of an illogical fear of facing my memories. But my memories were with me all the time. And now I had to face the present: Geoffrey was far away, in Europe with his new wife; my sister was to marry the man whom once I might have had for my own husband; and I…

A rustling of leaves jerked me out of my reverie. I started, making Dandy dance uneasily beneath me, as one of the Sandringham game-keepers ducked out of a thicket and stood glowering at me.

I knew the man by sight. His name was Pyke, and he was reputed to be ferocious with anything, on two legs or four, that threatened his precious pheasants. A shifty-eyed, unshaven man, he wore a jaunty hat with a feather in it, crammed down near to bushy eyebrows, and on his scrawny frame the uniform of cord breeches and green velveteen jacket hung lank and oversized. Over his arm he carried a broken shot-gun, while his other hand restrained a shaggy wolfhound by a short leash.

'What the 'ell d'you think you're doin' 'ere?!' Astounded to be addressed in such a coarse, hostile manner, I said, 'I beg your pardon? How dare you speak to me in—'

He gestured with the gun. 'Go on! Get away from 'ere. You're disturbing the game.'

'My good man,' said I, 'I happen to know that the shoot is over at Dersingham.'

'So it is. Today. They're shooting these woods tomorrow, as you know very well.'

'Indeed? And how should I know that?'

''Course you know! Why else are you 'ere? Thought you'd come over and stir up the birds, did you? Scare a few of 'em away? I know what you'd like to do, if you had your way. Blasted farmers! At 'em, Tyke! At 'em!' With that, he loosed his dog.

The wolfhound came leaping, barking and snapping round my stirrup. Dandy reared in fright. I clung on, trying to keep my seat, trying to control him. Then he thudded to earth and shot off, almost unseating me. Above the snarling of the dog, I heard the keeper call out in derision as low branches slapped at my face. I bent close to Dandy's neck. I shouted at him, hauling at the reins, but he was out of control. He would have to run it out.

He stepped into a hole. I heard the bone snap, and then I was flying headlong into a thicket of bramble and bracken. Tossed head over heels, I lay winded for a moment, then scrambled up in a fury. Dandy was whinnying piteously, threshing in pain. The dog stood over him, still giving tongue.

Hampered by thorns and briers, wrenching my skirts free from their clutches, I went to throw myself down near the horse, speaking to soothe him, seeing his eyes roll wildly.

Pyke had come up. He said, 'Only one thing for it. Move aside, miss,' and I heard him prepare his shot-gun.

'Don't you—' Leaping up, I wrested the gun from him. He was so surprised he didn't even try to stop me. I stood over Dandy, sighting down the long double barrel, waiting for a moment when he was still enough for me to be sure of a clean shot. The gun boomed. The kick hurt my shoulder, drove me staggering back a few steps. As Dandy died, such pain twisted inside me that I swung round, levelling the gun at the man who had caused Dandy's death. I had one barrel left.

The dog went wild. The keeper went pale. He held out his hands. 'Wait, miss. Don't!'

I swung the gun, pointing it straight up in the air, and discharged the shot. Ears ringing from the noise, I threw the gun at the keeper and whirled to kneel beside Dandy. Around us the shot pattered like hail on leaves and branches.

Blinded by tears, I stroked Dandy's neck, hating the keeper, hating the prince. 'Damn them! Damn them all!!' I raged, having no better vocabulary to express my feelings.

They had robbed me of my last living link with Victor.

When eventually I looked up, the under-gamekeeper and his dog had gone. Good! I didn't need his help. If he had offered it I would have refused. In anger and distress, I ran to summon other hands to help bring Dandy home.

My way led me along a sorry field of mangolds whose hare-bitten tops were as sparse of leaf as the roots were thin beneath them. The sight only added to my bitter sense of injustice. It wasn't right! It wasn't fair! Father had worked hard to build up the farm; just when he was prospering, along came the Prince of Wales and, all for his own private sport and amusement, allowed our livelihood to be jeopardised. There had to be some way of bringing the truth home to him.

We buried Dandy in a corner of the meadow, within sight of the orchards where the ladders were out, the fruit being cropped. Johnny and Grace were there, and the men who had dug the grave, with McDowall observing in his non-committal way. Mama didn't come out; she said it was all too sad to bear and she would watch from a window. She had one of her weepy moods on, perhaps because Father had gone to Lynn. He was attending the tenants' dinner, and would be staying overnight at Weal House before meeting with the agent and lawyer next day to agree the rent figure for the coming year. I guessed that Mama wondered who else he might be seeing in Lynn; she was still haunted by the existence of her rival, Jane Stead.

'We'll have a headstone made,' Grace promised through her tears, holding my arm to comfort me as the men shovelled soft dark earth on to the old blanket which covered Dandy's body. 'Don't weep, Rose.'

I wasn't weeping, not then. My eyes were dry, my tears done. I felt hard and angry, bitter with the whole world, and determined to do something about it. If Father didn't have the energy to fight for our rights, then I would. *I* would!

–

Unable to sleep for thinking of Dandy, and the coming audit, I got up at first light. I was stiff from my fall the previous day, my right knee sore and bruises showing on several parts of my body; it all helped to fuel my determination. Going out to the decimated field of mangolds, I pulled several of the sorry roots and put them in a willow basket. Then, dressed in my best coat of pine-green cloth with Russian frogging, I took the dogcart and drove to Lynn.

Early as it was, the town was busy. Horses and vehicles jostled for space, carriers' carts and farmers' buggies, village women carrying laden baskets, all on their way to the Tuesday market. I negotiated the dogcart through the throng, down King Street and under the carriage arch to the yard behind Weal House.

As I entered the house, Aunt Beatrice was hurrying down the stairs with her skirts billowing and an anxious look on her face. She paused in surprise on seeing me.

'Why… Rose, were you expected? Oh, no matter, I'm glad you're here. Your father's been taken ill. He went to the dinner last night and came in quite late. Then this morning the maid found him collapsed in his room. No…' As I made for the stairs, she drew me instead towards the morning-room, 'don't go up. He's sleeping now.'

'But what's wrong with him?' I asked anxiously.

'The doctor says it's a stomach disorder. It may take a few days to clear up. But he's welcome to stay here. You know that. I'll look after him.'

In the sunny morning-room, Uncle Jonathan was at breakfast in company with Uncle Seward, who had come over from Morsford to offer his support at the audit. Being directors of Hamilton's Bank, both of them could claim to be Father's financial advisers.

'Stomach disorder!' scoffed the portly Seward, tucking into a plateful of devilled kidneys and fat bacon. 'Why not call a spade a spade, Bea? Truth is, Rose, your father had too much to drink.'

'Seward!' Aunt Beatrice reproved. 'Have some charity.'

He made a face at her. 'Can't stand mealy-mouthed humbug. You know that, Bea. Besides, Will was bound to get falling-down drunk. He never did take disappointment well.'

'Disappointment?' I queried.

Uncle Jonathan, thin and lugubrious as a stork, explained: 'Mr Beck and the solicitor both found themselves unable to attend the tenants' dinner last evening owing to other engagements.'

'You mean they heard there was going to be trouble and they both turned coward,' said Uncle Seward. 'So the farmers' guns were spiked, Rose. No point in taking aim when the targets weren't in sight.'

'And now your father has made sure of losing today's fight, too,' Uncle Jonathan added. 'There's not a great deal of purpose in our attending the audit without him.'

'Why not?' Seward demanded. 'I'm game to beard the lions in their den. And won't that fellow Pooley be there, if we need agricultural argument? We all agreed to add our voices to Will's cause. We can't let him down.'

'We shall simply look foolish without the presence of the chief complainant.'

I couldn't bear the thought of letting this opportunity go by without a fight. 'Then if Father's not well enough to go, *I'll* represent Orchards.'

'You?' Jonathan uttered in shock.

My boldness amused Seward. 'And why not? Our Rose is no soft milk-and-water maiden to quail before a couple of pen-pushers, however illustrious their master may be. Made of stouter stuff than that, eh, girl? Like your mother before you.'

He could not possibly know how that final comment gave me heart. I would show Father that I really was Hester's daughter. 'Only give me a chance to speak face to face with that land agent. Not even he can talk his way out of it with *these* as my witness.'

They both stared as I produced the nibbled, wilting leaves, still attached to wizened knobs of mangolds. Jonathan looked aghast, but Seward was so entertained that he laughed aloud and slapped his thigh. 'By heaven, Rose, that'll show 'em.'

'You can't possibly go in there waving those things!' Jonathan objected. 'They'll think you're threatening violence.'

The argument was continuing when Farmer Pooley arrived. In his opinion, the evidence of the mangold tops 'couldn't do no harm'.

I was still carrying my basket as the four of us set out down King Street.

The audit was being held at the Duke's Head Hotel, an imposing building which overlooked the expanse of the Tuesday marketplace. On the cobbles, under the shade of a few scattered trees, gay stalls had been erected and vendors cried their wares to dealers and housewives and maidservants: fresh eggs, live eels, bread borne in trays on men's heads, milk straight from the cow, oranges and lemons brought from the docks, and vegetables dug at dawn from cottage gardens. The further part of the square was taken up by cattle pens, where bullocks, sheep and a few horses were being bartered over. Chickens squawked from cages and a duck had got loose. It took wing, chased by a barking dog, scattering feathers. I hardly noticed the hubbub; my thoughts were on the meeting ahead, on crops ruined by furry kangaroos, and on Dandy screaming in pain because of a few disturbed pheasants.

I felt like an avenging angel, determined to speak up for my family's rights. With three staunch men to support me, how could I fail?

Staunch? Well, maybe they were, by their own lights, but in their own way each of them was cowed by the eminence of our opponent. Though Prince Albert Edward wasn't there in person, his puissant presence pervaded the interview.

As an office for the audit, the hotel had provided a room on the first floor. The noise of the market was a murmurous hum, caught and held beyond lace curtains and thick velvet drapes.

On greeting us, the London solicitor, a Mr Partiger, newly come to the prince's service, was all charm and politeness. Land agent Beck seemed nervous, but relaxed when he realised Father wasn't there. His patronising smile grated on me as he brought a chair for me and saw Uncle Seward and Mr Pooley settled either side. Uncle Jonathan, ill at ease, remained standing, while the agent resumed his seat behind the desk.

'Well, gentlemen…' he began, addressing the three men around me as if I were not there. 'In respect of the rent for Orchards Farm…'

'Whatever rent is due, Mr Beck,' I put in, disconcerting him, 'it may prove to be beyond my father's means. How shall we pay rent without income? Our wheat is all chopped down, and this…' with a satisfying thump, I slapped the pitiful mangolds and their chewed tops on the desk under his startled nose, 'this is a specimen taken from our best mangold field. All of our crops are in a like condition – because of His Royal Highness's hares.'

Mr Partiger's brow furrowed and he eyed my exhibits with distaste. 'I know very little about root crops, and even less about the habits of hares. What we are here to consider—'

'What we're here for at this time o' day,' Pooley said, 'is a man's right to compensation for damage done by game raised on account of the landlord's shooting rights. Plain simple justice – that's what we're here for today, sirs.'

'Well, yes indeed, that is one of the matters which must be settled, but…'

The argument proved convoluted and tedious, but with the mangold tops lying between us, silently accusing, and with my three stalwart heroes to aid my cause, eventually our opponents agreed, reluctantly, to pay for damage to Orchards' crops that summer. A thrill of triumph made me want to cheer. I could hardly wait to tell Father.

'That's good of you,' Uncle Jonathan murmured, glancing at the door as if anxious to be gone. 'Yes, that's very fair.'

'But we haven't settled a figure,' I objected.

Mr Beck, on the point of rising, looked at me over his spectacles, his nostrils flaring as if he scented bad drains. 'Naturally we shall need to verify the extent of the damage before we calculate a figure.'

'Howsomever,' said Pooley, stroking his nose, 'that ought to be agreed that no rent shall be paid until you settle on a fair sum for damages, agreed by both parties.'

'Oh, come...' the lawyer sighed.

'Mr Pooley's right,' I said, in a mood to be stubborn. 'If we pay our rent now, how can we be sure we shall ever get our damages? And what of extra compensation for the importation of live hares? They're not all being bred on the estate, they're being brought in directly – in breach of the game agreement.'

I heard Jonathan draw a disapproving breath, and Seward gave me a sidelong, raised-eyebrow look, both amused and amazed by my rashness.

The agent got slowly to his feet, drawing himself up, eyes glinting behind his spectacles. The silence thrummed with threat. It reminded me of the party at Sandringham, when the prince's temper had been aroused and everyone had stopped breathing.

Into that silence, Edmund Beck enquired in a tone edged with ice, 'Do my ears deceive me, or is Miss Hamilton questioning the integrity of the Prince of Wales?'

'No, indeed not,' Uncle Jonathan said at once, and bent to take my arm. 'My niece is overwrought because of her father's illness. She was always a headstrong child. Come, Rose, we've attained our objective. Let us not be foolish and say things we shall regret.'

'We ought to have it in writing!' I protested.

But Uncle Seward took my other arm, smiling at me pacifically. 'It will be all right, Rose. Don't worry. It will be all right.'

I glanced at Pooley, who winked and nodded, seeming to say that enough had been said for one day, and with that we were being bowed out by the obsequious land agent. As the door closed on his palpable relief, I shook free of my uncles' restraining hands, wishing the meeting had left me with some more tangible result. The Prince of Wales's integrity was known to be as reliable as a wax bridge in a heatwave.

–

Father's illness confined him to bed at Weal House for several days, after which he was brought home and put into his own bed. Grace and I nursed him for another week before he was able to be up and then slowly resume his work. Whatever was wrong, it was caused by more than a bout of drinking, but when I tried to find out the truth Father grew annoyed with my questions. He said only that he had seen a doctor while at Weal House and that a few days' rest, with proper sustenance, would find him well again.

As to the outcome of the rent audit, he anticipated no real victory. 'I'll believe it when I have the money in my account.'

Because of his illness, I found myself fighting shadow battles with an elusive Edmund Beck, writing letter after letter, making appointments to see him only to find him out when I called. The land agent tried every trick to squirm out of paying fair damages.

Naturally I spoke of this perfidy to my friends at Feltham Grange. Mr Wyatt was particularly supportive and concerned. I recall strolling in the yew walk with him and Felicity one late October day of gusting winds and scattering leaves, recounting the story and thinking how good it was to tell someone who understood.

'It's an outrage!' Mr Wyatt agreed. 'For the prince to quibble over a few hundred pounds, when your father's so ill and you bravely trying to cope alone, why it's... it's insupportable. Don't worry, my dear. I shall take up the cudgels on your behalf.'

He was a small, lightly-built man, looking ill-suited to putting up a fight, or indeed to having sired eight children, but he possessed a determined chin and a way of slapping a clenched fist into his open palm to emphasise points. I was grateful for his concern.

He wrote to his friend the MP, but because of a misunderstanding the letter was read out, verbatim, in the Houses of Parliament. It caused a storm of abuse to be aimed at the prince, at a time when he was already unpopular because of rumours about his womanising and his gambling. Several journalists called at the farm to obtain more detail – one even accosted me in the lane. Contributors to *Punch* magazine, in particular, had a merry time composing articles and sketching cartoons lampooning the prince.

Already offended with me for what had occurred at his party the previous spring, he now had good excuse to scowl ferociously when he encountered me about the lanes. His friends also cut me dead, making me burn with humiliation. But the worst blow of all was when the princess drove by, in her charming little trap, and behaved as though she hadn't even seen me – she who had been so friendly and sweet.

Norfolk society divided itself around me. Only a minority of the 'quality' dared to take my side openly; the rest were too afraid of being outcast from the charmed circle that might hope for invitations to Sandringham Hall. Even in church people ignored me, except to talk loudly about me, saying how wicked was 'she' who caused trouble for the prince, so ungrateful for favours shown, and so hurtful to the poor princess, barely recovered from her illness and worried over her babies.

I coped with my new disgrace as I had done before, by brazening it out, holding up my head and defying the gossips, however much it hurt in private. My true friends stood by me – the Pooleys, the Wyatts, Ben Chilvers and his wife, and most of the villagers. It was only the social climbers who were too afraid of upsetting the prince, but unfortunately it was the social climbers whom Mama and Grace counted as friends.

Father took it all stoically, seeming detached from the traumas. More and more he existed inside himself, concentrating on his work to the exclusion of all else, and when he wasn't working he was reading, hour after hour by winter lamplight, devouring books with a steady determination designed to shut out the world and, I afterwards guessed, his own fearful thoughts.

One day, when she and Grace returned from a fundraising at the rectory, Mama exclaimed, 'I can't bear it! They look at us as if we were unclean. I spoke to Mrs Harper and she turned her back on me – the *verger's wife* turned her back on me!'

'It's Rose's fault!' Grace tore off her hat, leaving her hair in disarray. 'Oh, now we shall never be invited to the Birthday Balls! This was my last chance. I shall be married and living in Thetford next year.'

'But you can come home for the balls,' Mama cried.

'It won't be the same!' In a passion of disappointment, Grace threw herself down on a settee and beat her fists on red velvet. 'I shall never forgive you for this, Rose. Never!'

'All I did was stand up for our rights,' I said stiffly. 'Perhaps you'd prefer it if Father was bankrupted? Or doesn't it matter to you, now that you've found yourself a rich husband?'

Grace jumped up, her pretty face contorted. 'That still infuriates you, doesn't it? That I stole him away from you? You couldn't have kept him anyway. He says you're headstrong. And foolish. He's ashamed of having to associate with you.'

'Girls!' Mama pleaded. 'Oh, girls, don't! Rose… Rose, surely this trouble can't last? We shan't be outcast for ever, shall we?'

When I hesitated, Grace stepped in, saying, 'No, of course we shan't, Mama. *We* shan't.' She glanced over her shoulder at me, her look saying clearly, But you will.

'See if I care!' I responded as she led Mama away to lie down and rest. 'I can do without Birthday Balls, and I can certainly do without William Turnbull.'

Mother's portrait, gazing serenely from over the mantel, seemed to smile agreement.

Eight

It was a Sunday in December, a clear frosty day, the earth streaked with ice under a crystal blue sky. Turnbull was not with us; he had taken to arriving too late to go to church, in order to avoid the atmosphere. By the lych-gate of Sandringham church we encountered the princess with her companions. I saw sympathy in her eyes, but she turned her face away and swept by. Her companions ignored us, too. I watched her go, seeing the dipping limp that her illness had left and wondering how much of the truth she knew. She had said we would be friends, but between a royal princess and a farmer's daughter simple friendship is difficult.

We followed them down the path and took our usual pew, amid stirrings and whispers. Everyone whose glance I encountered looked away at once, and all through the service my neck prickled with awareness of hostility. The prince himself appeared late, as was his wont. On his orders, the sermon was never very long.

The service ended, the royal party left first. Reluctant to face the wall of silence which would greet us, Father, Mama, Grace and I lingered, finding gloves, settling capes, using every tactic to delay until the crowd had dispersed. But on that day, while half the congregation still waited to leave the building, a man came striding down the aisle to greet Father. 'Mr Hamilton, sir, good morning to you. I hope I see you well?' The cheerful sound of his voice in the hushed church made many heads turn.

I had never thought I would be so pleased to see Basil Pooley again, though it wasn't so much the man himself that pleased me as the way he boldly declared himself an ally, at a time and place designed to cock a snook at the gossips.

He was smartly dressed in dark suit and coat, well-groomed and muscular, tow-coloured hair curling long in his neck with bushy, scimitar-shaped side-whiskers of a gingerish hue. He couldn't alter the skewed angle of his nose, or whiten his ruddy skin, but I thought again that he was an attractive man, growing more attractive as the years rubbed off rough edges.

'Mrs Hamilton!' he cried, taking Mama's hand. 'A sight for sore eyes, as ever, ma'am. And Miss Grace – a joy to behold, a breath of spring on a winter's day.' Twinkling at my sister, he added, 'I gather you're to wed Mr Turnbull. Ah, but what a lucky man he is. He'd best be good to you – tell him so from me. Won't that make him mad!'

Blooming rosily under his gaze, Grace laughed and told him to stop his nonsense, though I could see she was flattered by his compliments. Even Mama had a touch of pink in her cheeks and a smile on her lips.

'Miss Hamilton.' As I stepped from the row of pews he sketched me a bow and I gave him my hand. We hadn't met since that encounter at Fenny Jakes's cottage eighteen months before. He had at first avoided me and then, according to his uncle, gone to London on business and found reason to remain there.

'I'm glad to see you,' I said. It was the simple truth.

His expression, as his eyes met mine, was wary, questioning, his glance searching my face for a brief moment before his smile beamed out. He said, 'The pleasure's mine, Miss Rose. If you'll allow me...' and he tucked my hand into the curve of his arm, leading me out from the church.

The royal party was making away across the park, the path lined by the usual crowd of onlookers who came to stare. Most of the congregation still lingered, exchanging gossip and saying farewells against a background of departing carriages. Chatting happily, Basil led me among the crowd, greeting this one and that with an air of unconcern. A fierce surge of elation made me laugh with him, defying the surprised looks and whispers that followed us.

'Brazen hussy!' a female voice hissed.

The epithet stung me, but I went on smiling at Basil, clinging closely to his arm. Yes, I was glad to see him again. In the depths of my despair, he had dared to stand by me.

Basil continued to champion us, joining us in church, sometimes meeting Father at the market and occasionally accepting an invitation to Sunday lunch, usually when he knew William Turnbull would not be there. He and Turnbull could not seem to like each other; to have them both at the same table caused friction.

The planning of the wedding fully occupied both Grace and Mama that winter. Their main concern was how many of the guests would stay away because of my 'difficulty' with the prince.

The ceremony was to take place at Eastertide, at the church of St Margaret's in Lynn, in order to allow distant guests to put up easily in the town and not have the trouble of travelling out to Sandringham. It also meant that more people would see Grace in her finery, that she would ride through a busy town instead of quiet country lanes, that she could leave from the grandeur of Weal House, and that Maria Kinnersley, living next door, would witness all the preparations.

By the time the day arrived, most of the guests had accepted the invitation. They evidently pitied my family for the recalcitrant changeling nurtured in its midst. Showing off new dresses and hats, exchanging pleasantries with all about them, they filled the church, smiling and nodding to greet Mama as she took her place. Few of them looked at me, fewer still acknowledged me. Smiles died when they lighted on me. If a glance inadvertently met mine it would pause, glaze, and slide beyond me, becoming a greeting for another acquaintance. I even sensed it in my own family, particularly the Morsford cousins, and some of the Turnbull relatives looked askance – heaven knew what tales they had heard. But Felicity stayed close, and Basil Pooley, with his aunt and uncle, forming a kind of loyal guard to shield me from hostility. With their help I managed to smile through most of the day, even if my heart felt dead inside me.

'In sickness and in health, to love, cherish, and to obey, 'til death us do part...' They were solemn words. In order to say them aloud, one would have to be sincere. All I could think of was Geoffrey, saying those words to Lucinda. Making promises before God. Had he meant them? 'I intend to be a faithful husband,' he had said. 'I can't let Lucy down.' What did that mean?

They were back at Ambleford now. They had arrived back a week ago, so village gossip said. After seven months touring Europe. Seven months of days spent together. Seven months of nights...

Father gave a rasping cough, his thin shoulders heaving as he stuffed a handkerchief to his mouth. I felt the pain that racked him. Grey hairs grew thick now in the curls about his ears, and his cheek looked sunken in coloured light from a stained-glass window.

A party of us saw the bridal-pair off at the station, bound for London and then for Brighton town. Grace stood on the steps of the carriage, laughing, lifting her bridal bouquet to throw it. Her eyes met mine as she tossed the flowers. She meant them for me. But one of the ribbons caught on her finger and as I lifted my hands to receive it the bouquet veered away. Squeals of delight erupted as Chloe Wyatt caught it, her eyes bright as she laughed over the flowers at her sisters. 'I'm next! I shall be next!'

I saw the little moue of regret that Grace made at me, then she blew me a kiss as recompense and was off on her adventure into married life. Smoke from the funnel made my eyes water as the train edged away with couplings clanking and steam sighing, the whistle giving a final salute.

A handkerchief appeared before me, proffered by Basil Pooley. 'Here you are, Miss Rose. It's clean.'

I used the handkerchief to dab my eyes and blot my nose. 'It's the smoke.'

'Yes, I know.' He crooked his arm for my hand. 'Well, they're away. Let's go back to the party, shall we?'

–

Rebuilding work began that spring on Sandringham Hall. The Prince of Wales had finally decided that the old house was too full of draughts, too cold and damp, to be habitable. He blamed it in part for the terrible illness which had left his wife lame and slightly deaf; so he gave orders that the house was to be modernised, given all comforts and conveniences. Architects set to work to draw up their plans and submit them for royal approval, and meanwhile the old hall was shut up and left to dream alone.

To Mama's distress, Grace's marriage and the hospitality enjoyed at the wedding did little to soften our neighbours' attitude towards us. People continued to cut me, glare unspeaking, or draw aside as if I had leprosy. Because of this, because she missed Grace's company, and probably for other reasons too, Mama grew querulous again. She was always complaining of something or other, wanting me to spend more time with her, wanting me to take her to see Narnie, or wishing she could see her dear, dear Grace. She started taking her medicine frequently, on the grounds that she couldn't sleep without it. Because of her restlessness, Father moved out of their room.

This time neither of them tried to hide their physical separation; Father transferred his things into the room which had belonged to Victor. Not a trace of my brother remained there, which was as Father had wished, but I wondered if the room held memories. However, the only time he alluded to it was to remark that, 'The shades are friendly here.'

–

Grace had hardly returned from her honeymoon when Mama decided that she must go and visit the newlyweds and see how they were settling down. She wrote at once to suggest it, and back came a letter saying that the Turnbulls would be delighted to have her stay. Whether their delight was shared in equal measure I don't venture to guess, but no doubt Grace was eager to show off her new home and Turnbull was new enough at husbanding to indulge her.

The invitation included me, but I declined on the grounds of spring-cleaning duties, and haying in prospect. It was true, but it was only one of my reasons: with Father's health deteriorating I didn't want to leave him alone, and besides I was in no mood to have my younger sister flaunt her status as a married lady in my face. I already knew from her letters that Mrs William Turnbull rejoiced in her affluent new life.

In the end, much to their mutual satisfaction, Mama took Narnie with her to Thetford, with Ellen Earley in attendance.

–

That same month, May 1868, Hal Wyatt's wife gave birth to a son in California, making Mr and Mrs Wyatt grandparents for the first time. They planned a ball to celebrate, a Midsummer Ball with all their friends and neighbours to share their joy. And, since they had so many marriageable daughters, they planned to invite an ample supply of eligible young men.

'You'll be able to take your pick,' Felicity laughed as we sat one day in the rose garden, under parasols, with a jug of lemonade on a table nearby and the fountain playing its cool undersong. 'I shall make sure your card is filled for the entire evening. You're twenty-four years old, Rose. You can't let these chances slip by.'

I almost pointed out that she was four years older than I, but we had been over that same conversation many times. She always averred that, with Victor gone, she would never love again. For me it was different. She wanted to see me married and happy – in her mind, the two were synonymous.

'I haven't danced for years,' I said.

'You danced at Grace's wedding – with young Mr Pooley. I saw you.'

'Once. I danced once.'

'At least it shows you haven't forgotten how. But you can't come alone. It looks so bad. You must have a proper escort.'

'Some brave bold knight susceptible to bribery, perhaps?'

My voice and my expression made Felicity tut. 'Now, Rose! You know very well that any number of young men would be only too happy to… There's James Freshing, for a start. He was most complimentary after you met last year. And there's Gordon… what's his name? – the tall thin one with the spectacles, who likes to talk politics with you.'

'Making conversation over tea in your drawing-room is one thing,' I said, 'escorting me to a ball is another – the not-quite-respectable Miss Hamilton, pariah of this parish.'

'Don't speak of yourself in that way! It's not true, Rose. They're all wrong about you. It's so unchristian of them. That's why we want to show them that you're still a good friend to us. We don't care who we offend by it. We intend to stand by you.'

Dear Felicity. Dear Wyatts all. How I loved them.

'Papa has especially invited the Devlins,' she told me.

She might as well have tossed her lemonade at me, complete with ice; I felt suddenly cold, my ears singing, my head buzzing. I watched a ladybird alight on the edge of my glass and crawl there, each wing showing five red spots, while in some other part of my mind I heard Felicity saying something about mending the feud between my father and Sir Arthur before it got out of hand, and that a social encounter might help to heal the breach.

'Are they coming?' I asked. 'All four of them?'

'Well, of course. It's a pity your father won't be there.'

'No,' I said, my thoughts fragmented. 'I mean – yes. But Father's not one for parties.'

She sighed. 'I know. Oh, this isn't helping to find you an escort, Rose! It looks as if it will have to be Mr Pooley. I know he's not exactly a gentleman, but he has made real efforts to improve himself. As Papa always says, you have to respect a man with character enough to pull himself up by his own boot-straps. Yes, I'll make sure Mr Pooley has an invitation. After all, you don't have to be with him all evening.'

Basil Pooley called at Orchards House a few days later, on a pretext which I forget; his real reason was to tell me that he had had an invitation to the Wyatts' Midsummer Ball, and to ask me if I were going with anyone, or if he might be allowed the honour...

'I should be delighted,' I replied, and he bent to kiss my hand and smile at me, blue eyes gleaming, pleasure shining out of him.

'It'll be the proudest day of my life,' he said.

-

On Midsummer's Day I was out with our workers as soon as the dew had cleared, tossing hay all morning as the sun rose clear and hot. When the horn blew to announce a pause for elevenses, I walked back to the farm and ate a bite of dinner with Father. I intended to rest a while during the afternoon before getting ready for the party, but Mrs Benstead was so busy picking and preserving the glut of strawberries we had that year that I found myself helping her, and so the afternoon fled. It was always so in spring and summer, so much work that one hardly had time to draw breath.

However, that evening I indulged myself in a long cooling bath and sat by an open window to brush out my hair and let it dry in the lilac-scented breeze. Hoping to lace my waist down to twenty-one inches, I took only a cup of tea while Swift dressed my hair and helped me put on my party self. I was thinking of Geoffrey, dressing for him, grooming myself for him – and despising myself for it.

Though I was never a beauty, being too tall and angular, and freckled from the sun, I could look striking when I made the effort. That night I felt at my best as I went lightly down the stairs to where Basil and my father waited in the hallway. My dress floated about me, a dress that Mama had ordered when she ordered Grace's trousseau, pale green tarlatan, the skirt boasting thirty-two flounces, the ribbon edging embroidered with leaves and violets – why do we women remember such silly things? – all under a long cloak of pine-green velvet. Gloves of fine green net hid most of the scratches and fruit-stains on my hands.

I saw, with satisfaction, the admiration that widened Basil's eyes, though Father remained inscrutable, gaze narrowed in his thin, weathered face. I can see them now, the contrast between the two of them: one wearing immaculate evening dress, full of youth and life and hope; the other in linen shirt and old trousers, looking thin and drawn, a poor sketch of himself.

Basil looked as if he might burst with delight as he surveyed me. 'Why, Miss Rose, you're… you look…'

'He means you'll do,' Father said huskily, breath catching in his throat. He turned away, coughing into a handkerchief.

Worried, I laid a hand on his shoulder. 'Perhaps I shouldn't go. If you're not well…'

'I'm perfectly well!' he rasped. 'It's just my cough. It catches me now and then, that's all. Take her away, Basil.'

'I'll take good care of her, sir,' Basil said.

'Yes.' Father had himself under control as he looked at us with hooded eyes. 'Yes, boy, I know you will. Well, go. Go!'

Basil had hired a victoria, and a coachman to drive it. Such thoughtfulness impressed me as, with princely courtesy, he handed me into the open carriage and settled himself beside me.

Though it was past nine o'clock the evening remained light, and with the hood of the carriage thrown back we could see the sky shading from gold to red, promising another fine day tomorrow. The warm air smelled of hay. Swifts zoomed after flies above the meadow where the milk cows grazed, and the hayers were still at work, loading up the carts, tossing the cut hay, scything yet more for tomorrow.

We found the Grange alive with bustle, carriages arriving, people being greeted. Interconnecting rooms rang with laughter as skirts swayed, whiskers bristled, graceful shoulders slanted and fans fluttered their message of coy flirtation. All the windows were thrown open so that warm air billowed through the house and music flowed across the lawns and gardens. As the dusk grew, lanterns twinkled from all the trees.

Mr Wyatt met us and drew us into the throng, introducing us to his guests with a flourish – almost daring them to be impolite. Most of them managed at least a semblance of courtesy, especially the gentlemen; it was the older matrons who remained disapproving.

Among them, the most formidable was Lady Devlin. She stood with her husband and a small group of others in a corner of the drawing-room where a chandelier sent glittering light across rose brocade walls and gilded furnishings. My champion led me straight across to them with an air of cheery unconcern. To my relief, neither Geoffrey nor his wife was with them.

'Ladies and gentlemen,' Mr Wyatt began, 'you do know Miss Hamilton, I believe? And Mr Basil Pooley?'

Sir Arthur harrumphed and muttered something to the effect that he was, yes, ah, acquainted with… and the other guests nodded, murmuring appropriately. One of the women, I noticed, slanted a sidelong look at Basil, assessing him from head to toe with evident appreciation before holding out her hand, 'I don't believe we've met,' at which Mr Wyatt introduced them formally and they fell into conversation. Only Lady Ophelia remained silent, regarding me with flared nostrils and eyes like frosted slate.

'Lady Devlin,' I greeted, sketching the briefest of curtseys.

She drew an audible breath and turned her shoulder to me, continuing a conversation which our arrival had interrupted.

'We shall move on.' Mr Wyatt drew my hand through his arm, patting it comfortingly. 'Don't mind Lady Ophelia. She's out of sorts. Her son and daughter-in-law don't seem to have turned up. Young Mrs Devlin is prone to headaches.'

'Is she?' Did he mean she was pregnant?

He pulled a wry face. 'That's the excuse she uses. She's not much of a social animal, is she?'

How could I have forgotten Lucinda Devlin's disfigurement? 'No, of course… Poor girl.' But mingled with my sympathy was disappointment. Deep in some secret part of me, hardly admitted even to myself, I longed to see Geoffrey again.

My dance card, though not filled, held a respectable number of names, and when sitting out there was Felicity to talk to, and Basil ever nearby.

I escaped for a while and went to see Cassie, who lay in her room with Aunt Agnes for companion. She wanted to know about the party, but where once her questions had been eager, probing for a full picture, now she asked them in order to please me, not because she wanted to share the experience. She had ceased trying to be part of the world outside her room.

'Don't let me keep you,' she said after only a few minutes. 'You go and enjoy yourself.'

'Did you say you had come with Basil Pooley?' my aunt enquired. 'Is that wise? What do we know about him?'

'He's the nephew of a dear friend; he was my brother's best friend; Father and Mama both like him.'

'Yes, but what do you *know* of him? What *is* he?'

'Kind, honest, generous, thoughtful, amusing… He's a businessman, if that's what you mean, with various properties bringing in rents. And doing very well from it. What else do I need to know?'

'Do you intend to marry him?'

'I could do worse. In fact, my reputation being what it is, I couldn't really hope to do much better, could I?'

Agnes settled back in her chair, smoothing the open pages of her book. 'In your present mood, you deserve no better. Go back to your estimable Mr Pooley, then. Good night, Rose.'

There was no more to say.

Intending to refresh my toilette, I made for the dressing-room which had been set aside for that use with a maid in attendance to supply whatever might be needed – a pin, a stitch, a glass of water. The maid was busy folding towels, and by a cheval glass a young woman in a frothy gown of lemon lace nervously stroked the flounces that disguised the flatness of her bosom. She caught sight of me through the mirror, and instantly her hand darted up to conceal her mouth. My stomach twisted on itself and my heart leapt as I recognised the pale, fearful face. Lucinda de Crecy, now Mrs Devlin.

Geoffrey must have arrived, too.

The room felt hot: the window had been closed, presumably to exclude the moths that danced beyond the glass, though one or two darted about the lamps on suicide forays. Sweat damped my palms and beaded my forehead as I said, 'Good evening. It's… it's Mrs Devlin, is it not? I'm Rose Hamilton. You may remember—'

'Yes. Yes, I do. Thank you.' Even through the mirror I glimpsed her distress, her fear – and the fact that after ten months of marriage there was no sign of any thickening at her waistline. She was as thin as a boy. She cast a final glance to check her appearance, and, without looking at me, swept past me, nervously stroking her nose – the need to conceal that scar on her lip was habitual.

I took my time, washing my face and hands, damping down shiny patches with powder, aware of my heart pulsating audibly. Why was Lucinda Devlin so unhappy? Was something wrong between her and Geoffrey?

As I went down the stairs, back to the gleam of candles and lamps, to the music and night air dancing with moths, every dark-haired man I glimpsed made my heart lurch. Geoffrey was here somewhere. I saw him everywhere, in a turn of head, a breadth of shoulder, an elegant curve of calf…

'So there you are!' The voice made me whirl, dizzy for a moment, staring into a face that didn't fit, until my senses cleared and I saw that it was Basil, his smile fading. 'Is something wrong?'

'I was thinking of something else,' I said.

'Obviously.' But he didn't pursue it. 'I was looking for you. This is our dance – the supper dance.'

'Oh – yes, of course.' I found a smile for him as I allowed him to lead me into the dining-room, which had been cleared for dancing, chairs pushed to the walls, the carpet lifted and the floor polished. The small orchestra, arranged in one corner, bowed busily at a polka while energetic couples whirled about the room.

It was then I saw Geoffrey, standing in the far doorway, engaged in conversation. There was no time to think. Basil twirled me into the dance. The room revolved behind his fair head, portraits, windows and doors on a whirligig of splintered light. I had to think about the steps, trying to keep my footing on the slippery floor, trying to keep up with Basil. Geoffrey was watching but I didn't dare look at him. I kept on dancing, jigging round and round.

When the music stopped I swayed, feeling sick and giddy as I clutched at Basil for support. Working since dawn, no food since noon, stays laced too tight out of sheer vanity…

'I must get some air,' I gasped as the dizziness increased and my ears roared. 'Please…'

His arm about me, he led me through crowded rooms to where doors stood open and the night air caressed my heated face. Under trees hung with lanterns, couples strolled taking the air. A distant gong sounded and voices called, 'Supper! Come along, it's suppertime!'

I shook free of Basil and hurried on, making for the cool shade of the yew walk, where there was just enough light for me to see my way. Gulping in fresh air, a wispy handkerchief blotting my brow, I felt the faintness recede. Forcing my lungs to expand on a deep breath that strained against my stays, I laid a hand to my throat, feeling an artery throb.

'Are you all right, Miss Rose?'

I had forgotten Basil was there. 'Yes, thank you. The dancing made me... It seemed airless in the house.'

'We should have sat out. I'm sorry.'

'Oh, no – no, don't apologise.' My voice sounded breathless, the wisp of lace in my hand fluttering as I gestured nervously. 'You go inside. They're serving supper.'

'I'm in no hurry.'

We were alone in the yew walk, the house a distant gleam of lights through a growth of trees, lanterns flickering here and there. Above us in a column of sky between the yews hot stars shimmered, and a hidden moon added pale light to the scene. The air around us seemed alive.

Then a movement to one side startled me. A harsh scream made me throw my hands to my ears and step back, colliding with Basil's sturdy body. As his hands came at my waist to support me, I saw that the screech had been uttered by a large bird, which came picking a delicate way between the yews. With a soft rustle it spread a great fanning tail, painted eyes shining ghostlike in the darkness.

'It's only the peacock,' Basil's murmur came in my ear, vibrant with laughter as he leaned closer. 'You're not scared of a peacock, are you, Miss Rose? Why, look at him. He's a beauty. Showing off.'

The peacock turned in a slow circle, shaking his magnificent tail in arrogant display. I watched him, but my other senses were concentrated on Basil, aware that he was holding me as close as he dared, breathing in my scent, letting his cheek touch my hair. His hands felt hot at my waist, his chest solid behind my shoulder. Warm breath fanned my cheek and throat.

'We ought to go in,' I said.

'If you're feeling better.' Slowly, he removed his hands from me and stepped away.

'Perhaps we could walk around the house. There's a way across the front. We can get that way to the supper room.'

'Whatever you say, Miss Rose.'

He offered me his arm, and laid a hand over mine as it lay in the crook of his elbow. Our path lay down a flight of steps and across a moonlit lawn where light streamed from the house and figures could be seen moving beyond the open windows; then through a gateway in the wall and across the gravelled front courtyard to a similar gateway on the other side of the house, where lay the rose garden and the terraces. Here lanterns lit the scene of tables set under the stars, with guests enjoying their supper. Laughter and light spilled from a French window which led into the morning-room, where the food had been laid out.

'Shall I fill a plate for you?' Basil asked. 'You find a quiet place somewhere. There's space by that pool, look.'

And so we ate supper, sitting on the low stone surround of a pool where golden carp slid through weedy shadows. Other people came to sit around us on steps and terrace edges, enjoying the warm evening and the chance to relax over food and drinks and light conversation.

Basil and I said hardly a word to each other.

As we finished supper, a breeze sprang up, cooling the air and sending goose-pimples along my bare arms and shoulders. Other ladies shivered and exclaimed, beginning a general drift towards the warmth of the house, and as I stepped into the brightness of the morning-room I heard thunder roll distantly. A dark band of cloud was advancing to shut out the stars.

'It'll probably pass over,' Basil said.

'I hope so.' My thoughts were on the hay, fearing another disaster if storms set in.

And then, without warning, I found Geoffrey standing in front of me, smiling with social grace, saying, 'Ah, Miss Hamilton. May I claim a dance? I hope your card isn't full?'

After a moment of total incomprehension, I recovered my wits and fumbled for the card looped on its ribbon round my wrist. 'No, not quite.'

'Excellent.' He perused the card, scribbling his initials in one of the spaces. 'That one, I think, if I may. Our host seems anxious that we should bury hatchets, and since my father doesn't dance...' he laughed at the thought. 'That is, he does, but he'd probably t-tread on your toes. I shall try to be more circumspect. Well, Pooley? How are you? Was that thunder I heard? Is it going to rain? Just when the hay's coming in nicely, too. Oh – but you're n-not a farmer, are you?'

He was all charm, all gracious politeness. I hated him for the ease with which he conducted himself when I was all worms and wires, though his stammer told me he was not as relaxed as he appeared. He chatted for a few minutes with Basil, neither of them saying anything of consequence, then he turned his smile on me.

'Well, if you'll excuse me…' and he spun lightly on his heel to go back to where his mother was standing, with Lucinda behind her trying to make herself invisible. Lady Ophelia was engaged in conversation with Mrs Wyatt; nevertheless, her gimlet gaze flicked to Geoffrey, and beyond him to me, and I knew she had witnessed our encounter.

'Mr Wyatt's a regular Cupid,' Basil said.

My head snapped round. 'What?'

'Trying to make peace between Orchards and Ambleford by getting Devlin to ask you to dance.'

'Oh. Yes.'

Lucinda's colourless countenance had lit up, her eyes fixed on Geoffrey's face as he spoke to her. He seemed to be asking her to dance, a hand held out in appeal. She shook her head, drawing back further into her corner, one finger stroking her nose so that her hand veiled her scarred mouth. He pleaded with her, every line of his body cajoling and tender as he caught the hand that she hid behind. Her other hand came up as if to replace it, but stopped, and she allowed him to ease her out from behind his mother and lead her towards the distant dining-room, where music played again.

'Handsome couple they make,' Basil said. 'From a distance, at any rate.'

'Don't be unkind.' Whatever I might feel for Geoffrey, I was achingly sorry for his young wife. 'Can't you see she hates all this? It's torture for her being in company. Poor girl…'

'Well, what's a man supposed to do? Let his wife hide herself away? If he was seen out without her there'd soon be talk. Not that there isn't talk enough. He could have had his pick. Why did he choose a bruised blossom when he could have had a perfect rose?'

Basil had a knack of making remarks that set my nerves strumming like telegraph wires in a gale. But it was chance, that was all, an ill-considered choice of phrase. He couldn't possibly know the truth.

As a chill of doubt wafted over me, Basil said, 'If you're not engaged for this dance, may I…?'

While I waltzed with him, over his shoulder I watched for glimpses of Geoffrey and his wife among the swirl of dancers. She was petite in his arms, not reaching his shoulder, hanging her head and hiding her face. Geoffrey watched her, talking softly to her, and once I saw her look up and smile at him in a tremulous way before her head dipped again. As they turned I saw his face, his mouth tight under the moustache, his eyes dark, turned inward on himself. Another turn and, between the heads of other dancers, his eyes met mine. It lasted no more than a second and then the gap closed, the dance swirled us on, but I knew as surely as if he had spoken that Geoffrey was as unhappy as Lucinda was.

His initials on my dance card burned themselves into my consciousness as the orchestra played on.

A rising wind sent cold draughts eddying, making curtains billow and ladies shiver. Servants came hurrying to close the windows, and within minutes the house felt airless; gentlemen eased their collars, ladies' fans flickered madly. I felt sweat soak my undergarments and my stays dug into me.

Two dances ended, then three. I was with Felicity when, in the lull between music, I saw Geoffrey approaching.

He stopped beside me, smiling at Felicity. 'Miss Wyatt. You look splendid this evening.'

'And you're as gallant as ever,' Felicity returned, tapping his arm with her fan. 'You're too much a stranger, Mr Devlin. You must bring your wife to visit us. We should make her very welcome in our female circle, shouldn't we, Rose?'

'Indeed we should.' His presence robbed me of all wit.

'You're most kind,' Geoffrey said on a deep note of gratitude and I saw him exchange a look of private understanding with Felicity before he smiled at me and held out his hand as the orchestra struck up another waltz. 'Our dance, I believe.'

He held me lightly, almost at arms' length as we swept about the floor, and I stared over his shoulder, avoiding his eyes. We probably appeared to be nothing more than two acquaintances engaged in social niceties; if we seemed stiff with each other that would accord with the known feud between our families. Only we knew of the currents that flowed hotly between us, unspoken but inexorable as the storm that gathered outside.

Basil didn't appear to be in the dancing room, nor Lucinda, but I had glimpses of Mr Wyatt, nodding his head in time to the music, his plump wife smiling beside him; Lady Devlin, stiff with disapproval behind her busy fan, and others, amused or curious over the spectacle of Mr Geoffrey Devlin dancing with the notorious Miss Hamilton. The thought brought a wry curve to my lips.

'Something amusing?' Geoffrey asked.

'It occurs to me that I've taken over my aunt's mantle. They used to refer to her as "that Miss Hamilton". Now they use the same tone for me. More so, indeed. Agnes may have offended a convention or two. *I* offended the Prince of Wales.'

'I had heard. It was brave of you.'

The music swept us on, *step*, two, three; *step*, two, three…

How could he be so calm? I felt vicious, wanting to hurt as I was hurting. 'I offended your mother, too. I'm sure she told you how I burst in upon her in such ill-bred haste. Though I fancy she detested me long before that. My mere existence offends her. You should never have danced with me. You'll be in for a scolding when you go home.'

'If I were afraid of my mother,' he said tightly, 'I wouldn't b-be here at all.'

Beyond the west lawn, a flare of blue-white lightning crooked from sky to earth and stood there, connecting the two. People exclaimed in alarm and wonder. Geoffrey and I paused in our step as the music faltered and the musicians stopped playing. All eyes turned to the window. The jagged light remained, imprinted on my retina as darkness returned. Thunder cracked, making curtains shudder and candle flames twist, and a torrent of rain threw itself against glass panes.

The hay! I thought despairingly.

'Why do you hate me?' Geoffrey said.

For the first time since we had stepped on to the floor, I looked fully at him, and as I did so his face dissolved behind tears I couldn't control. I didn't want to quarrel with him. I loved him. My heart was breaking for him. And yet I distrusted and despised him…

'Rose…' His voice thrummed hoarsely in my ears as his hand tightened about mine and the arm at my waist drew me in closer. 'This c-can't go on. We have to talk it out. My dear—'

'Don't!' Panic tugged at me. Everyone would see. Everyone would know…

But the storm had caused everyone to forget about Geoffrey and me. In the brief confusion I pulled away from him and fled to find Basil and ask to be taken home.

Nine

Rain beat down on the hood and apron of the victoria as our coachman picked his way along dark lanes. The storm centre had moved on, leaving in its wake a steady, soaking downpour.

I could smell brandy on Basil's breath. Locked beside him in the confines of the vehicle, I wiped spatters of rain from my face and thought of the evening with all its events and undercurrents. We had left quietly, stealing away without spoiling the Wyatts' celebration – that, at least, had been my excuse. Now we were silent, both keeping our own thoughts.

Reaching Orchards, we ran through the rain to the door, which was always kept unlocked, and into the hall where a single lamp burned. The house was silent, sleeping.

As I fumbled with the cord that fastened my damp cloak, Basil lifted the heavy velvet from my shoulders and placed it across the banister, saying softly, 'Thank you for your company tonight, Miss Rose. It's been a good evening. I enjoyed it.'

'Yes, so did I.' I moved a little away on pretext of shaking out my skirts, starting to peel off my gloves. 'But I'm tired, as you must be. Don't let me delay you.'

He watched me for a moment. 'Is that all?'

'What else do you want me to say?'

Moving softly closer, he said, 'I'm a patient man, Miss Rose. I promised I'd wait until you were ready, and – don't mistake me – I'm still prepared to do that. But it seems to me a man ought to expect a bit of encouragement now and then. You're glad enough to cling to my arm when we're in company. You'll allow me to dance with you. But when we're alone it's "keep your distance, Basil Pooley". A man might be forgiven for wondering if he's being used.'

'I don't recall ever asking you to wait,' I said in a low voice. 'I am grateful for your support these last months, but... I don't know what it is you want. Would you have me pretend to feelings that—'

'No,' he said at once, shaking his head. 'No, I'd not have you pretend anything that's not real. Only...' he reached for my hand, holding it gently between his own, 'these things have to be nurtured. Like plants. Fed and watered. Given the right ground. There's got to be a bud before there's a flower. If you never let me close, how will we ever know what might be waiting to grow between us?'

He could be right, I thought. I had made use of his affection; I owed him something in return. I owed it to myself too, to try to break free of the spell that Geoffrey Devlin had cast on me. Whatever had happened in the past, he was married to Lucy now. Was I to go through life longing for a man I could never have when another man might ease my pain, perhaps even make me forget?

Slowly, as if afraid to startle me, he lifted my hand to his lips, watching me over it. Then he turned it over and, bending his fair head, pressed his lips to my palm.

'Basil...' I began.

'Sssh,' came the whisper as he laid a hand along my face, brushing my cheek with his thumb, his glance studying my every feature. He looked at me as if I were beautiful. He looked at me with awe and wonder, making me wish that I could feel the same for him. He was a good man; he deserved better than I had so far given.

'I want to kiss you, Miss Rose,' he muttered. 'I want it so much I can hardly bear it. Will you allow me the liberty?'

I suppose I made some sign of assent. Watching my mouth, he bent closer, until I was obliged to close my eyes and I felt his warm, brandy-scented breath on me. His lips touched mine with a soft, chaste pressure that withdrew almost at once. To my surprise, that was as much as he dared. I found him watching me as he gently withdrew his hand from my face.

'That's all right, Miss Rose,' he assured me, gathering my hand and holding it to his breast. 'Like I said, I can wait. You've things to do, things to think about. I'll be near, though. I'll never be far away. You can count on me.'

–

Luckily the storm did no lasting damage. It was followed by a brisk wind that helped to dry the hay, so that haysel was accomplished with only a minor delay.

Mama returned from Thetford full of news about Grace; for a while she was almost happy again. I kept myself busy managing the household; there was soft fruit to be preserved, village visiting to attend to, watching the corn ripen, watching the weather, cursing the hares, arguing with McDowall and, that year, worrying about my father.

When Ned Plant let slip the fact that Father no longer tended his own horse, I knew my fears were justified. He had always taken pride in rubbing Harry down with his own hands, feeding and watering him at the end of a busy day. Now he no longer had the energy. In fact, it soon became evident that even riding was too much of a chore. If he had to go out, he would take the dogcart, but more and more he stayed in the house, or within sight of it, going only as far as he could walk. He even suggested that *I* should take Harry for exercise: 'I don't feel up to it today', or, 'He'll enjoy a good gallop and I've got these books to tally.' While such chances delighted me, for I loved to ride, they troubled me too. Father left most of the overseeing to McDowall and he seldom chided me for interfering or being less than conventional. He hadn't the energy. But he would never admit when he was in pain; he always had some explanation or excuse. I watched him, I worried and I waited. Sad to say, we couldn't talk about the things that mattered most.

The summer proved warm and dry. As ever the furry 'kangaroos' did their share of despoiling despite our efforts in blocking the runs, smearing tar or stuffing them with briers. A considerable amount of poaching went on, winked at by farmers, and many a village family dined illicitly on jugged hare.

During the school holidays, Johnny had new friends to occupy him. A boy he knew at school came to spend the summer with cousins whose father had leased East Esham Hall; Johnny spent most of his time there. East Esham being Mama's old home, she sighed many a sigh over the 'old days'. Her reminiscences were encouraged by visits from General Hall, a contemporary of Squire Ferrers who continued to keep an avuncular eye on Mama from time to time. Dwelling on the past with this old friend saved her from facing the present: she knew Father was ill but she refused to think about it, let alone discuss it.

Johnny must have told his new friends about the beating he had taken from Sir Arthur. Making mischief at Ambleford became the boys' delight. Not that they had to do much in order to set Sir Arthur on the rampage. If they so much as walked along one of his headlands he sent men to chase them off. So, naturally, they took to walking along his headlands at regular intervals.

Eventually, the furious Sir Arthur sent his son to make complaint. Trying to shield Father, this time I invited myself to witness the interview. 'My father isn't strong. If you upset him...'

'I have no intention of upsetting him unless I'm driven to it,' Geoffrey answered. 'By all means join us. Perhaps you can help control that young brother of yours.'

He had come seeking a truce. He too suffered from his father's irrational temper, so he sympathised with Johnny, but he was afraid of what might come of the mischief-making. The latest development was the chalking of insults on barn walls – the boys had been interrupted while scrawling 'Mad Devlin lives here'. If it went on, either Sir Arthur would drop dead of apoplexy or the boys would commit some real felony. None of us wanted that.

'I'll do what I can,' Father said. 'Yes, I'll talk to him.'

'I should be grateful,' Geoffrey replied, gathering up his hat and riding crop.

I saw him to the door, where we said only polite, formal words such as any two neighbours might exchange. But beneath the conventions our eyes held more intimate conversations. The forces that bound us were as strong as ever.

Father had a long talk with Johnny, and later I too had words to say to my brother, begging him to avoid Ambleford if only for Father's sake. Father was ill, I told him; he mustn't be given extra worries. Johnny promised that he and his friends would find other amusement and leave Sir Arthur alone.

'But there were words on the barn before we wrote any,' he said. 'And they weren't chalked, they were painted.'

'What words?'

'Things like "tyrant" and "machine lover". And in another place it said "remember Captain Swing". Who was Captain Swing, Rose?'

I didn't know, but George Pooley told me that 'Captain Swing' was the name coined by activists in the farming troubles in the thirties. That had all died down, but now a farm labourers' union was being formed, with strikes and lock-outs occurring in the south, where conditions were particularly hard. Was the unrest beginning to stir in Norfolk, too?

One thing was sure – it wasn't Johnny and his friends who had written that particular threat.

–

One August afternoon, returning home from a visit to Narnie, Mama and I were horrified to see a column of white smoke rising over the woods and fields, lifting straight into a depthless blue sky. At first we feared a conflagration at Orchards. I whipped up the pony, but as the dogcart moved along the lanes it became apparent that the blaze was further away. On Ambleford land.

Our gates were open, another dogcart waiting by the house with beside it two figures – Father, and a gesticulating Sir Arthur Devlin, strutting, shouting, waving a stick. Father had his arms up to protect his head. As I stopped the cart, he collapsed and fell.

'Oh, no! Oh, Will!' Mama gasped.

I leapt down and ran to where Father lay with Sir Arthur hopping near him, saying in angry bafflement, 'I never touched him. Never touched him! Damme, I'd have been justified...'

He ranted on but his voice was just a noise in the background. Father lay on his side, one arm flung over his face, his whole body contorted as if in agony. I gently moved his arm, and saw how ghastly pale he was under the weathering of his skin. He looked at me with eyes full of pain, saying almost inaudibly, 'Don't move me. Not yet. Let me lie here a minute.'

From Sir Arthur's ravings I gathered that he blamed Johnny for the fire that was even now raging through a field of wheat. He shouted incoherently, wagging his stick, raining curses down on us all. Mama stood by the dogcart, hands to her face, fright in her eyes.

Then a horseman came galloping, a whirl of dust and motion as he threw himself from the saddle. He came running towards me, all concern. Geoffrey.

'I came as soon as I could. What happened?'

His father ranted: 'Happened? Happened, you say? Dammit, sir, the Hamilton boy fired my wheat, that's what happened! Blasted limb of Satan! Ought to be horse-whipped within an inch of his life. If he was a son of mine...'

He went on, but we ignored him. We were both too concerned for Father.

'He's in terrible pain,' I said. 'Can you help me get him into the house?'

Geoffrey knelt and gathered my father bodily into his arms. Father moaned a little, then clamped his lips against the pain as Geoffrey stood up with his burden, nodding at me to lead the way. 'Oh, be quiet!' he snapped at his own father, who was astounded into silence, and then we were in the house, making for the stairs.

Thin as Father had grown, the effort of carrying him made Geoffrey breathe hard. Even so, he spoke kindly, reassuring Father, and when we reached his room – Victor's room – he laid him down with infinite care and stepped back, wiping his brow.

'Thank you,' I whispered.

Geoffrey shot me a lightning look. 'Good God, don't thank me! I wish I'd got here sooner. Did my father attack him? Is there a wound?'

'I don't think so. I don't believe your father actually hit him. He just collapsed. You... you'd better go back. I can manage now.'

'Yes.' He glanced down at Father, back at me, caught my hand and pressed it hard, then without further words he left.

When Father recovered enough to speak, he insisted that he would be all right after a rest. No, he wouldn't let me undress him, or help him in any way. He would manage.

'You stay with your Mama, she'll need you,' he said, his voice threaded with pain. 'And when Johnny comes in I want to see him straight away. Straight away, Rose. Now leave me. I'll try to get some sleep. I'll be all right.'

But this time I knew he would not be 'all right'. I sent for the doctor, and I sent for Aunt Agnes – the backus boy went running over to the Grange to fetch her and she was with us inside an hour. One look at Father and she became brisk, ignoring his protests. We stripped him of his clothes, sponged him down and put him into a fresh nightshirt. He hated it, but bore it in silence, needing all his strength to fight off the pain that racked him with every movement.

'You're so stubborn, Will!' Agnes chafed. 'You always were too stubborn.' But while she scolded there were tears in her eyes.

Basil Pooley arrived, summoned by the drifting smoke in the sky. I told the maid to ask him to sit with Mama; Agnes and I remained with Father until, in the early evening, he seemed to be sleeping; then Agnes told me to go and see to Mama.

'Is Johnny home?' Father wheezed as I was leaving. 'Rose, find out if Johnny's home.'

Johnny was not home. He had not been seen since early morning.

–

In the drawing-room silence lay like creeping mist. Mama stared at her embroidery, her needle scarcely moving. Basil sat on the edge of a chair, elbows on spread knees, his head hanging as he counted the threads in the carpet, while I stood by the window staring on to bleak vistas in my own mind. The window was open, lace curtains stirring. The smoke from the wheat-fire had dissipated, only a few wisps still curling up, forming small cloudlets that drifted away to eastward. Somewhere over the meadow a lark flew in the evening sky and sang for joy of living. The high, twittering song jarred in my ears.

Into the silence, Basil said, 'Shall I go and look for Johnny?'

'Johnny will be home soon,' Mama said, not looking up. 'He'll want his supper.'

Basil's glance sought another reply from me. I shrugged: 'Where would you start looking? He could be anywhere.'

'He's never late for supper,' Mama said. While she ignored it, it couldn't happen. Father would be well, Johnny would come home, nothing would change. But Johnny was already late. The hours were ticking by, the sun had gone and dusk was gathering.

Leaving his seat, Basil came to stand by me and indulge in low-voiced speculation about what had happened at Ambleford. He had been over to see the fire before he came to us; he had heard what they were saying – that Johnny and his friends had been caught smoking along that hedgerow before, that today spent matches and a tobacco pipe had been found right by the spot where the fire had started, before the wind took it and whipped it across the field of ripe, dry wheat that stood ready for harvest. Another few days and it would have been gathered. Now it was lost, and with it a sturdy length of hedge and a cart that had been left on the headland. The boys were held to blame, by accident or intent. Sir Arthur was determined to have them charged with wilful fire-raising.

'If it's true, and he's run off,' Basil said, 'he'll be in trouble. Shall I go over to East Esham Hall?'

'No. Not yet. Wait a while.'

'But they might know...' He stopped, squinting out of the window as something by the gate caught his eye. When I looked, I too saw the riders coming – Geoffrey Devlin on his hunter, Johnny astride his pony. The sight made me spin round and rush for the door, out into gathering twilight.

'It's all right,' Geoffrey greeted me, reining in as I ran out to meet them, with Basil a pace behind me. 'He's safe and all's well.'

'I was nowhere near Ambleford today,' Johnny added. Judging by his clothes, he had been somewhere muddy. With an arrogant swagger he swung his leg over the pony's head and leapt down, tossing the rein to the boy who had appeared. 'And I can prove it.'

From the doorway behind me, Mama said, 'There! What did I tell you? I knew he'd be home for supper. Come, Johnny, my love. Come and wash your hands. Are you hungry?'

As they went inside, Basil wrinkled his nose expressively, rubbing his ear much in the manner of his uncle George. Geoffrey's eyes, too, said that he understood the difficulties I had with Mama. He sat gazing down at me, framed by a bright evening sky streaked with primrose and pink, where the invisible lark still trilled.

'I went over to East Esham,' he said. 'The boys had said something about going fishing. They spent all morning around the pond at Rising Mill – John Hambledown had them under his eye all the time. They had a picnic, and then they made off downstream. I found them with one of the fishermen, where they'd been all afternoon. The man – Davies – vouched for that.'

'That'd be Clam Davies,' Basil said. 'After dabs, I expect. That's a fine way to while away a few hours. Often done it myself.'

'Yes, so have I,' Geoffrey agreed.

Stroking the hunter's soft nose, I said, 'It was kind of you to take the trouble. I'm grateful.'

He pulled a face. 'I was sixteen once, not so long ago that I've forgotten. And I felt responsible. How is your father?'

'We're waiting for the doctor now.'

'What about the fire?' Basil wanted to know. 'They were saying they'd found a pipe, and matches.'

'Yes, they did,' Geoffrey said grimly. 'It looks very much as though someone wanted to throw suspicion on the boys, not knowing they'd have a solid alibi for today.'

It took me a moment to understand what he was saying. 'You mean… it was arson?'

'It begins to look that way.'

'But who…?'

He gave me a humourless smile. 'My father has a knack of making enemies, Miss Hamilton. Don't let it worry you. At least we can be sure it had nothing to do with your brother. Good evening.'

As we watched him ride away, Basil said, 'I knew I should have gone over to Esham. There was no need for him to bother himself.'

'He meant it kindly.'

'He meant it to butter you up! Don't forget who it was caused your father's collapse. You could have that old fool for assault. Or slander. He can't go around accusing people of fire-raising without proof. It's time he was locked up. That's why his son's being so considerate. Blood's thicker than water. Don't let him fool you.'

Wafting at a cloud of midges dancing by the honeysuckle on the porch, I returned to the house, where Agnes and the doctor were coming down the stairs. Their grave expressions told me all I needed to know. I stood quite still, chilled by dread.

'How long?'

'Three months. No more.'

Three months? I must have swayed; Basil's arm came about my waist to support me and I let myself lean on him, glad he was there.

'I shall stay, of course,' Agnes said. 'We'll nurse him together.'

–

Father didn't have three months, or even three weeks. He had fought valiantly for a long time, keeping his pain to himself, but in the end he gave up. The cancer that was eating at every part of his innards conquered even his stubborn spirit. He hated being so weak, hated his body for letting him down, for forcing him to need services that robbed him of all dignity. The illness stripped him of everything, even his pride.

Mama stayed away from the room where he lay dying. She went about like a wraith, silent and wan, dark eyes like bruises in her pale face. Johnny, too, though he did come to see Father now and then, seemed afraid of what was happening.

It was a relief to us all when Grace arrived. Her presence allowed Mama to weep and they wept together. Agnes and I contained our grief behind walls of practicalities.

After only three days he slipped into delirium, hardly knowing us, and we summoned the rest of the family. I consoled myself that at least Father was unaware of what we had to do for him, though he often cried out in unbearable pain. He clutched at my hand, near breaking my bones in his agony, while I moistened his mouth and cooled his head, murmuring through my tears, 'I love you, Father. I love you.'

'I love you, too, Hes,' he muttered.

He took me for Mother. Perhaps he sensed her near.

One evening I went in and found him lucid. The skin stretched tight on his face, but his sunken eyes were focused and aware. I took his hand and smiled at him, smoothing his hair. 'Father?'

His fingers dug into me, dragging me closer. For long moments he searched my face, trying to find words to convey some important message. The struggle filled his eyes with tears.

'It's all right, Father,' I breathed, my voice cracking on the words. 'It's all right.'

He lifted his free hand to rub the moisture away, his mouth twisting in a wry, trembling smile. 'You should have been a boy,' he croaked. 'Yes, you should.'

Would he have loved me better if I had been a boy? My throat closed up and I could find no reply.

He said, 'I've not been a good father to you, girl.'

'Oh, but—'

'Listen!' His hand tightened, conveying his urgency. 'Let me speak. For once in your life, listen! You're my only hope now. If you let me down, it will all have been in vain. That's what I fear most – that it was all for nothing. Maybe that's why you were born. For this. Hester's girl.' Tears gathered again, making his voice a whisper. 'You're so like her. Did you know that?'

Biting my lip, feeling my own eyes grow hot and wet, I watched as his face contorted with anguish and sobs shook through him. But even in that extremity his will won through; he steeled himself against his distress, breathing deeply until he regained control. He lay for a while as if seeking sleep, still holding tightly to my hand.

Beyond the window, daylight waned. I could hear sounds of laden wagons creaking home, stacked with sheaves, of men and horses heading for food and rest. Sounds of voices, and a woman's laughter, floated from that other world where life went on.

When his eyes opened again they were calm and clear. 'Fight for me, Rose. Don't let it all go for nothing. Fight to keep the farm. It's all I've got to show for my life. Johnny's too young yet. If only I'd been given a few more years… There's only you now. Promise me. Promise me you'll keep the farm until Johnny's old enough to…'

'I promise,' I vowed, holding his hand. 'I promise!'

The effort of talking seemed to drain him. He sank back on his pillows, closing his eyes, but his hand clung to mine and after a while he looked up at me again, muttering something that sounded like, 'Hester… wait.'

He sank into a coma. For twenty-four hours we sat with him, Mama and Grace weeping, Johnny silent, Agnes and I outwardly calm. My uncles too kept watch, even Seward sombred by what was happening; their wives flitted in and out supervising necessities.

The end came so peacefully that we were hardly aware of it.

'He's gone,' Agnes confirmed.

As Mama gathered her children into her arms, wailing out her grief, I left the room. Without conscious intent I went down to the shadowed dining-room, to stand before the portrait of my mother, seeking answers but receiving only her steady, enigmatic smile. Were they together at last? She, and Father, and Victor.

'Miss Rose?' Basil had been a regular visitor during the past days; it didn't seem strange that he should be there now.

'He's gone.'

He made no reply. He simply came to stand near me, a hand at my waist, and I, needing solace, leaned on his shoulder and let the tears come.

—

During the lying-in, Geoffrey Devlin came to pay his respects. It was no more than any neighbour would have done, but though we spoke no private word I knew he came for my sake, and that if circumstances had been different he would have held me and comforted me. The bonds between us were almost unbearable that day.

At the funeral he didn't try to speak to me, though I saw him exchange a few words with Grace and Turnbull. Later he wrote to say that he would be available if we needed help from him, but he wouldn't call at the farm to 'trouble' me in my grief. He was right. If he had come and found me alone, I might not have been able to be strong.

We buried Father at Morsford, with Mother and Victor, as he had requested. The gravestone, removed and leaning against the church wall, was already carved with his details – he had had it done after Victor died, adding his own name and date of birth along with his son's; all it wanted was the final date: 28 August 1868.

You never forgave me for being born, I thought, but in the end I was your only hope. You needed me, Father. At the last, you had to admit that you needed me.

It was enough. Despite hail and storm, wind and fire; despite hares and princes, I would keep Orchards Farm for Johnny. That was the legacy my father left to me.

–

That winter was one of the blackest periods of my life. Some things stand out stark, others are obscured by the shock and grief which, at the time, I did not recognise for what they were. I thought I was being strong and resolute. In retrospect, some of my actions seem wilfully perverse.

Father's death seemed to stun Mama. She couldn't accept it; she spoke about him as if he were expected hourly. Soon after the funeral, Grace took her back to Thetford, where she and Narnie planned to nurse her through her grief. They left Ellen Earley behind, ostensibly to be my chaperon and companion, but also because Narnie resented the woman and considered that she herself could care for Mama much better.

Ellen was better than no company at all. She was a good worker, always sewing, looking after my clothes and my personal accoutrements, but she had no conversation; she knew nothing about farming.

–

My father's will included a small legacy for me, but he left most of his estate in trust for Johnny to inherit when he came of age. My uncles, and the bank, were the trustees. The estate included the remainder of the lease on the farm, which, having been renewed only three years before, had another eighteen years to run.

Mr Beck, however, evidently considered this his chance to ease the troublesome Hamiltons out of Orchards Farm. To my fury, he wrote to my uncles and offered to buy the lease.

Jonathan was for considering it, but Seward sympathised with me: Father had put years of effort, and incalculable capital, into improving the land, the buildings, the drains... And Victor had died there because of his dream of introducing modern methods. The farm was ours by moral right, to hold and keep, so long as we paid our rent in due time. No one was going to throw us out.

The matter was still unsettled when, at the rent audit, my uncles and I once again demanded fair compensation for game damage.

'I'm sure we could come to some amicable agreement on the sum due,' Beck said. 'Now, as to this business of the lease...'

'It's not for sale,' I said before either of my uncles could speak.

Beck appealed to Jonathan, aware that he was the weakest link. 'Then who do you intend shall take charge of the farm in the interim?'

'My niece will,' Seward answered. 'Well, don't look like that, man, she's perfectly capable of it. She has a good manager in McDowall, as you very well know, and we shall be here to advise.'

'But a single woman...' Beck demurred. 'It's most irregular. His Royal Highness really cannot be seen to be condoning... I must look into it. I must take advice.'

I doubt that he bothered his royal master with such a minor matter. Since their Royal Highnesses were about to embark on an extended tour of Egypt and Greece, Beck probably hoped to greet their return with the news that the 'little difficulty' at Sandringham had been given her marching orders.

In November he wrote again to my uncles, two pages of hyperbole embossed with the royal crest: the request had been considered with sympathy, but consensus came down to the view that to allow a lady to undertake such an onerous task without the day-to-day support of a husband, or at least a male relative of an age to take responsibility, would so contravene the spirit of the agreement that His Royal Highness, on whose behalf the writer penned this letter, must deny my right to hold the lease, even nominally. Mr Beck was sure we would understand that he had to consider the whole picture, and for His

Royal Highness to be seen encouraging such unconventional practices, when he was already a target for vicious rumour and innuendo...

What he meant was that I was not wanted at Sandringham and if I persisted he would make things awkward for me. Mr Beck had never forgiven me for making a stand over our game rights.

I didn't doubt that he could do what he threatened. With my reputation already besmirched, the gossips would welcome any chance to throw yet more mud.

Now that I was alone at the farm, those same gossips could not have failed to note Basil Pooley's frequent visits. He had become my sturdy champion, spending long evenings with me playing cards and helping me outface the gossips, at church or walking out.

There was, then, an obvious answer to my problem.

One evening McDowall and I were in the parlour, poring over samples of our wheat and barley to assess the yield and choose seed for next year. When Basil arrived, I dismissed the steward, asked Basil to sit down, poured him a glass of brandy and showed him Mr Beck's letter.

He sat in a corner armchair, a page of the letter in each hand as he studied it in the light from a lamp on the bookcase, squinting at it, his lips forming some of the words syllable by syllable – his schooling had been rudimentary, the rest he had taught himself. Another lamp with a pink glass shade shed its soft glow across the plush cloth and the assortment of saucers where lay the corn samples. Rubbing the grains absently through my fingers, I waited. It was quiet in the room, but for the crackle of the fire.

'I suppose this means you've got to get out,' Basil said at last.

'In effect, yes. My uncles have to find a tenant who'll hold the place until Johnny's of age. Naturally, if a stranger came to live here Mama and I would have to leave. We couldn't possibly stay like lodgers in our own house.'

'Would this hold up in court?'

'My uncles think it probably would, given the skill of the prince's lawyers. Either way, it would make an ugly scandal. I'm already out of favour. If the prince's minions decide to start another campaign of whispers... As your uncle once said, single ladies do not run farms.' The idiocy of it made me angry. 'Presumably my lack of a husband would be too much of a temptation to all the men about me.'

'So what do you mean to do? Will you go to Weal House?'

'That's one possibility.' Aunt Beatrice had already told me that, if ever I needed a home, I should find one with her. But that would mean my leaving Orchards. That was unthinkable. To keep the farm for Johnny was all Father had ever asked of me; I had to do it, whatever the cost.

I sifted the grain, watching it shower through my fingers into the saucer in order to avoid looking at Basil. 'You said once that you were only waiting for me to say the word...'

He stared at me blankly, as if working through all the alternative meanings to what I had said. In the silence, the clock tocked to itself, the fire spat. Then: 'You'll marry me?' he asked in a voice fraught with incredulous hope. 'D'you mean it? You'll marry me?'

'If you're willing.'

'Willing?! Blast, Miss Rose, don't you know...' Eyes blazing, he came out of his chair and started towards me.

'Wait!' I threw up my hands, stopping him a few feet away. 'Before you say any more, you should know... you should know...' I had sworn that I would let no man marry me without telling him the full truth. I didn't want to deceive Basil. He deserved better than that. 'Mr Pooley, I have to tell you...'

'Why, bless you, Miss Rose,' he put in with an unsteady laugh, 'you don't have to say it. I know. I know it's for the farm. But there's worse reasons for getting wed. You won't regret it. I'll be good to you. Blast, but my uncle George will be pleased.'

If I told him the truth about myself, he might despise me for it – he might not marry me, and then I would lose the farm. Did it matter if I left him in ignorance? I would be a good wife, a faithful wife. I would put Geoffrey Devlin from my mind. If Basil was willing to marry me, knowing that my only reason was to keep Orchards, then surely that was all that mattered? Had I the right to hurt him for the sake of my own conscience? The sin was mine; let the hurt be mine too.

I told him nothing.

Part Three

Mrs Pooley

One

We planned to marry early in the New Year, when the first three months of my mourning had passed. At first we planned to do it openly, in defiance of the gossips. But when I thought of the uproar that would follow a formal announcement, or a public reading of banns, my courage failed me. There would be gossip enough once folk knew I had married Basil Pooley. And so we decided to do it as discreetly as possible.

I spent Christmas in Thetford with my family, in the gracious Georgian mansion which William Turnbull had bought when he was courting me. It stood amid wooded suburbs, sash windows symmetrically set either side of a colonnaded entry, fronted by chestnut trees and a lawn dotted with flowerbeds.

The Turnbulls kept a carriage with a coachman; they employed a butler and a basement full of servants. Grace was happy. She was also pregnant. But, for almost the first time in my life, I didn't envy her. I should never have been content in Thetford with Turnbull.

Mama worried us all. She behaved as though she wasn't quite sure what was happening, or who we all were. I suspected her regular doses of laudanum were back to full strength. Perhaps I should have protested more strongly, but I hadn't the energy. If she and Narnie chose to go down that road, then how could I stop them? I was only human. Keeping the farm was going to take all my resources.

Johnny too was with us, so quiet and unobtrusive he often went unnoticed among the company. At sixteen he was already taller than I, with Father's lean frame and soft brown hair tending to curl, but where Father's eyes had been ice-blue Johnny's were hazel, flecked with gold and fringed by long lashes. Those eyes had a steady, enigmatic regard that made him difficult to read.

'I hate it here,' he confided to me one day when the house was loud with Turnbull's family and friends, most of them *nouveau riche* bores. 'Mama's not going to stay, is she?'

'Only until she's well enough to come home.'

'That's good. I want to spend my summer holidays at Orchards.'

'At Orchards? Or with your friends at East Esham?'

Johnny looked at me, hazel eyes meeting mine unblinkingly. 'I belong at Orchards. You have told that man Beck that we're not selling the lease, haven't you?'

'Yes, I have. I'll be holding the farm for you, Johnny. But first you must complete your education. There's more to farming than knowing the old ways. Our advancement in the future depends on you.'

'Father wanted me to go to university,' he recalled. 'He said it would make me a better farmer. But he thought he was going to be there to work with me. Still, there'll be McDowall, and Ned Plant – and George Pooley…'

'And me,' I reminded him.

Johnny slanted a look through his lashes, doubting my efficacy as a source of wisdom. 'But in the meantime, when I'm not studying… I'll be there to help and to learn. I'm the man of the family now.'

Touched by his earnestness, I almost told him that that burden was soon to fall on Basil's shoulders, at least until he, Johnny, was older. But again I said nothing. Which was another mistake.

–

At ten o'clock on a bitterly cold January morning, shortly before my twenty-fifth birthday, Basil and I were married by special licence in the Pooleys' home parish of East Esham. I had played coward, unable to face our own rector, Mr Lancaster. Our only witnesses were George and Eliza Pooley, to whom we had told the news the previous evening. It was a strange wedding, the church cold and echoing, the bride in mourning, no flowers, no music, no guests…

I felt perfectly calm and clear-headed, knowing exactly what I was doing. Putting the past behind me, giving my future into the hands of a good man who cared for me.

As he made his vows, in a firm, assured voice which rang around the empty church, Basil watched me with bright eyes, as if he still couldn't believe his luck. I replied, quietly but steadily: 'I, Rose Mary Hester, take thee, Basil Joseph, to be my lawful wedded husband. For better, for worse; for richer, for poorer; in sickness or in health; forsaking all other… 'til death us do part…'

We did have a wedding breakfast of sorts: Eliza Pooley insisted that we go back with them to their farm to have a bite to eat and to drink a toast in home-brewed ale.

Afterwards we returned briefly to Orchards, where I wrote a letter informing my uncles of my marriage and asking them to confirm to Mr Beck that, with their agreement as trustees of my father's estate, my new husband would lend his name to the tenancy. Legally, Beck had no good reason to refuse the request. And if he tried – if he forced me to it – I was prepared to start another scandal and accuse the prince of persecution. My reputation was about to decline again because of my hasty marriage to Basil. Further fury from Sandringham could hardly hurt me. Legally and morally the farm was mine.

I had already let it be known that I intended going away for a few weeks. Now I called the house servants into the hall – Mrs Benstead came wiping flour from her hands – and, with Basil beside me, I showed them my wedding band and told them that when we returned from our trip to London my husband would be living at the farm with me.

They greeted the news in silence, staring at me in disbelief. Only Ellen showed no sign of surprise, but then she rarely showed sign of any emotion. I could see Mrs Benstead frantically thinking it through, posing questions and reaching conclusions, but all she said was, 'Good luck, Miss Rose. And you, sir.'

Within a day or two, the whole of West Norfolk would know that I had become Mrs Basil Pooley.

—

London was in the grip of a fog that clung to the windows of the crawling cab and gave no hint of the city outside, except for the strangely muffled sounds of hooves and wheels and the occasional distant shout. Once the cab rocked wildly and three small, grinning faces appeared as three boys leapt to the side of the vehicle and clung there, pressing their noses against the glass so that they resembled gargoyles. Basil's shout of anger mingled with a roar from the cabby as he cracked his whip. The urchins vanished, their raucous laughter following us.

'Blasted beggars!' Basil said. 'The city's full of 'em. They didn't frighten you, did they?'

'Startled me a little,' I admitted. In truth, I was beginning to wish we had stayed at home instead of venturing to the city. I was cold to the bone after the train journey, heading to a place I couldn't visualise, with a man who was now my husband.

My husband. So far he had been considerate, diffident and almost shy. Would he know that I was no longer a virgin?

The house where we were to stay lay in Camden Town. It belonged, Basil told me, to an acquaintance of his who no longer came up to town very often but who liked to have his house occupied and kept aired. A carriage would be at our disposal, too, and servants to ensure a comfortable and pleasant stay. My husband, I was discovering, had connections in many unexpected areas.

It was almost dark when we arrived. Gas lamps glowed through the swirling mist, making the street even more murky. When Basil helped me down from the cab I incautiously breathed too deeply. Lungsful of dank, smoky fog made me choke, and I was still coughing, tears in my eyes, when a butler opened the door.

A huge aspidistra stood under an ornate gilt mirror, but that was all I noted as a solicitous Basil led me upstairs, into a bedroom with a four-poster bed, silken tassels adorning rich blue hangings. Blues repeated everywhere, on the sprigged wallpaper and the patterned carpet, contrasting with the deep red of mahogany furniture. A fire blazed bright in the grate, and with lamps gleaming, curtains drawn against the foggy dusk, it was a cosy, welcoming place, far more splendid than I had expected.

'Oh, my... my goodness!' I croaked. 'How lovely!'

As I made for the hearth, wiping streaming eyes and taking off my gloves to warm my hands at the blaze, Basil stood regarding me with a slight smile, enjoying my surprise. 'I told you you'd like it.'

One of the servants, a tall, lanky man in a black jean jacket, came in with some of our luggage, and behind him a maid appeared with a tray of tea.

'I'll go and have a word with cook,' Basil said. 'You drink your tea and settle in. Marcie will unpack for you. Won't you, Marcie?'

The maid bobbed a curtsey, aimed somewhere between us. 'Yes, sir.'

Left alone, I divested myself of coat and hat and sat by the fire, feeling cold to the soul. Not only because of the season. I seemed to have become trapped in a strange dream, going through the necessary actions like a puppet, with no will of my own, nor real feeling.

I would have liked to question the maid about the house and its owner, but one did not cross-question servants unless one wished to raise untoward speculation below stairs. So I sipped my tea in silence while Marcie unpacked.

'Will that be all, madam?' she asked at last.

'Yes. Thank you, Marcie.'

She bobbed another curtsey and went away. She hadn't looked directly at me once.

Now I finally sat down and wrote one of the most difficult letters of my life, to Mama, telling her of my marriage and the reasons for it. Putting it into words, seeing it written in black ink on white paper, made me realise at last what I had done. I had rushed into this marriage while still in a state of shock. What had seemed like rational thinking now appeared to be madness. But it was too late now to go back. It was done. I was Mrs Basil Pooley.

Adjoining the bedroom was a dressing-room, which Basil used to wash and change for dinner, allowing me the privacy of the main room. I donned my best black silk with its big, pointed white collar.

Over an excellent dinner in a panelled dining-room made intimate by candle-light, Basil asked me what I would care to do while we were in the city. He proved to be full of suggestions, mentioning the great houses, the palaces and churches, the museums, the parks...

'You know the city well,' I observed.

'Oh, yes. I'm here a lot, for reasons of business.'

'And this is where you stay, in this house?'

'Generally. The servants are used to me by now. I lived here nigh on eighteen months after... well, after I made a proper fool of myself that day at Old Fenny's.'

He had never mentioned that day before. 'You didn't make a fool of yourself. It was I who...'

'Yes, well, that's done with now. We're wed, and that's more than I dared hope for. If...' His gaze faltered and dropped to the glass he twisted by its stem, watching candle-light dance in the pale wine. 'If you want me to wait a while before... I mean, I'll sleep in the dressing-room if you want. For a night or two.'

I shook my head, pressing a linen napkin to my lips. 'No, there's no need for that.'

'You're sure?'

'Yes, I'm sure.' I had married him in full knowledge of what it meant, pledged heart and soul and body in return for his name and his guarantee of my tenure of the farm. I would not deny him his rights.

With a hand that was not quite steady, he lifted the wine glass and drained it. 'Why don't you go up? I'll be there directly.'

The maid had left my nightgown laid out. Trimmed with lace, its voluminous folds covered me from throat to wrists to ankles as I removed two hot stone bottles from my side of the bed and climbed between stiff starched sheets. I don't remember feeling anything beyond a numb passivity.

Eventually I heard the door of the dressing-room open and Basil came in wearing a nightrobe of flamboyant red velvet. He moved about the room pinching out candles, until only a small lamp by the bed remained alight. Leaning over it, he blew it out, leaving the room so dark that phantom images moved across my eyes.

I heard movement and imagined him disrobing, then his weight came on the bed. Discovering the two bottles which still warmed his side he gave a little grunt and tumbled them out to thud upon the floor. Cool air flooded in as he lifted the sheets and lay down, settling the covers over him.

'Are you asleep?' he asked.

'No.'

Moving closer, he lifted himself on one elbow, touching my face, bending over me to kiss me. I could feel that he was naked, already roused to erection. Alcohol fumes assailed me on breath that came swift and excited. 'It'll be all right,' he said as he reached beneath the sheets, his fingers catching in the fabric of my nightdress, drawing it up. 'It'll be all right, Miss Rose. Oh, Miss Rose...'

Despite my mind's resistance, my flesh began to respond. I was no untried virgin, nor he an inexperienced boy. He was skilled in the calculated art of rousing a woman and I could feel the excitement building in him as he discovered my readiness. All at once with a great gasp he rose up in the bed like some leviathan from the deeps, throwing back the covers. 'I can't wait,' he groaned. 'I can't wait!' His knee forced my thighs apart as he threw himself on me, all consideration forgotten, muttering, 'Blast it! Blast it! Aagh!' With a violence that slammed at me like a fist, he thrust deep inside me.

Afterwards, he lay exhausted, his head heavy on my breast. Sweat curdled between us where our bodies met, and I felt a sticky warmth trickling out of me. Would there be a child from this night? Dear God, did I want Basil Pooley's child?

Letting out a long sigh, he moved away, composing himself for sleep. I pulled my nightdress down to my feet, as if by covering myself I could shut out the memories. My body throbbed, aching for a release that never came. Yes, he was skilled, but for his own gratification rather than mine. He had long desired to possess me. Now he had his wish. But it wasn't love. Not for either of us.

He said, 'Are you in pain? Did I hurt you?'

'No.'

'No. Not with all the riding you've done. It stretches a woman, so they say. But it was good. And it'll get better. I'll show you. Good night. Good night, my dear.'

–

In the days that followed, I often wondered if I had ever really known Basil. He was far more at ease in the city than I was, known in all the best establishments, greeted by name in many places.

'I've got a finger in many pies,' was his explanation. 'Property, merchandise… My interests change, depending what pays best. Don't worry your head about it. Didn't know you'd wed a wealthy man, did you?'

He enjoyed my astonishment at his revelations, as he enjoyed spending his money on me. He took me about the city, showing me the sights despite the fogs and sleet of the chill January days. He sat patiently while dressmakers pinned and tucked, their assistants bringing pattern after pattern, bolt after bolt of cloth for our approval. There were hats, and shoes, wraps and shawls and gloves such as I had never hoped to possess. And there were jewels – every day he found excuse to buy me some new gewgaw, as if I were a concubine to be rewarded for her favours.

By day he seldom touched me except to offer his arm or extend a helping hand. By day he played the old-fashioned gallant, even when we were alone. And at night, in darkness, he made love to me with a sensuous, half-violent enjoyment.

My physical self responded to the assault he made on my senses, though most nights when he fell into exhausted snoring I was left wide awake, my body on fire with frustrated need. On other nights I felt nothing at all, except a faint disgust. And every morning I took a bath or a strip wash and scrubbed myself clean. More and more my mind revolted.

London was exhilarating with its noise and bustle, its streets full of costermongers and traders in all kinds of goods, from old clothes to cat-meat to muffins and live eels. And the traffic – cabs and coaches, omnibuses and wagons, crammed wheel to wheel in a dense stream along all the main streets. People of all classes rubbed elbows with each other, young and old, rich and poor. Urchins swept the street crossings, held horses, ran errands for pennies – and picked pockets, so Basil warned me.

We saw a hue and cry one day, a well-dressed gentleman gasping after a skinny, sickly-looking lad who skipped away into an alley and was lost, along with the gentleman's purse. The lad looked familiar to me, but rack my brains as I might I could not decide whom he reminded me of – one of our old backus boys, probably.

Apart from wishing to acquaint me with the city's sights, Basil had business to conduct; some mornings he went out early, leaving me to myself until lunchtime, but for the rest of the time he was attentive, always ready with some idea for my amusement and delight. We spent hours poring over exhibits in museums; we visited the waxworks and the menagerie; we saw extracts from Shakespeare and attended the music hall; and one evening we dined in a private room at an exclusive eating house patronised by the Prince of Wales. 'Good job he's abroad,' Basil said with a grin. 'Wouldn't want to run into him with one of his doxies, would we?'

The days were interesting and varied. It was the nights that troubled me.

I began to wish we could go home, face the gossip, put it behind us and make a start on the rest of our lives. I half-believed that our relationship would revert to the old comfortable ways once we were at home, when Basil had to put his mind, and his physical energies, into helping me run the farm.

On a particularly raw morning when the fog hung thick and sour, causing people to hold their scarves across their noses, Basil and I crossed Piccadilly, our way through the horse muck cleared by a small child of indeterminate sex, dressed in clothes three sizes too large, with a cap tilted to one side of its greasy locks. Hooves clopped in the mist, hansom cabs looming up like black ghosts; even the bawl of the street traders was muffled. Outside one of the shops, a lad was holding the reins of a fine Arab horse whose master was evidently inside the emporium. The lad looked to be about ten, though thin and half-starved, shivering in inadequate clothing. He looked ill, dark shadows under sunken eyes, his lips near blue with cold. I recognised him as the boy who had fled with the gentleman's purse. More than that, I recognised him as—

'Basil...' I caught his arm to draw his attention to the lad, but as I did so a well-dressed man came striding out of the store in a fine temper, shouting at the boy to bring his horse. He leapt up to the saddle, and would have ridden away at once had not the lad hung on to the bridle, saying weakly, 'Sixpence, mister! You said sixpence!'

'Six penn'orth of good leather!' the man snarled, and lashed his riding crop across the boy's head, his boot kicking out to land in the lad's ribs and brutally shove him away.

'Don't interfere!' Basil grasped my arm as I started forward, and in the same moment the horseman was away, hooves striking sharp on cobbles. The boy fell into the streaming gutter, thick with dung and some indescribable liquid ooze whose origins I didn't care to guess.

The little street-sweeper looked on dispassionately. 'He shoulda stayed wiv Gypsy Jim. Won't last long wivout a guv'nor.'

I had no idea what the child meant, except that the sick boy had no one to turn to. None of the passers-by even bothered to break step to help him.

'Leave him!' Basil ordered.

'How can I leave him? He's ill. Can't you see?' And I bent beside the boy, who was all but unconscious. 'Jack. Jack Huggins! Can you hear me?'

'You know him?' Basil asked in astonishment.

'He used to come with a work-gang from Castle Acre. We must help him. Basil, please let us help him!'

-

We took the boy Jack back to the house in Camden Town and put him to bed. I tended him myself, with the aid of Marcie, and it soon became apparent that rest, warmth and good food would work the miracle of restoring him.

'And he'll repay you the way he did before,' Basil snorted.

'No, not this time.' I was confident.

'Well, at least keep his door locked. I'm not having him wandering about the house. He'd be away with all the valuables. He's not Oliver Twist, you know.'

I wished I had never told him how much I had enjoyed Mr Dickens's story of the poor lost boy.

Jack's story was similar in many ways. When his mother came to London she had hoped to keep her family together, but poverty had forced her to send the oldest boy away. She had descended to prostitution, dragging her two daughters down that same road. The girls vanished – Jack didn't know where. Then his mother had taken sick and he had been forced to beg and steal, which had brought him into the orbit of 'Gypsy Jim', a villain who kept a band of youngsters doing petty crimes to keep him in gin. When Jack's mother died, the boy had moved into the rookeries – the crowded stews of the city's backstreets where families lived ten to a room – and there he had continued to thieve and lie for his meagre bread until Gypsy Jim caught him trying to conceal a golden guinea with other coins he had secretly been collecting. Jim stole his treasure, beat him soundly and threw him out to fend for himself. He had been living on scraps and sleeping rough for two months when I found him.

All of this emerged slowly as he learned to trust me. At first he was too sick to care, then as he began to recover he was like a wild animal, fearful and distrustful. When he discovered himself to be locked in he accused me of keeping him for the police. He didn't remember coming to Orchards, not at first, but as I sat with him and talked with him about Norfolk his memories of his childhood expanded. Yes, he recalled the lady who had taken him and bathed him; he remembered running naked, jumping off the stairs – he had hurt his ankle; it had been swollen for days. And, yes – with a furtive, sidelong look – he remembered stealing the food and the spoons. But he had needed them, for his mother!

'Why didn't you tell on me?' he wanted to know.

'Because I understood why you'd done it – you didn't know any better. You still don't. But there's a better way, a better life, Jack. If you'll let me, I'd like to help you.'

'Why?'

'Because I believe it was intended. Have you heard of fate? Do you know what it is?'

He didn't, but he was eager to learn. He was an intelligent boy, if only someone would give him the chance.

One thing intrigued me – when he had been living in such poverty, half-starved and poorly clad in the tender care of Gypsy Jim, why had he been trying to save money? Why hadn't he spent it on extra food and warm clothes?

'It was my escape money,' he said. 'I was going to get away. I was going back home. To the country. To look after horses.'

Such a simple wish to have. 'We have horses at Orchards. Would you like to come and work for me? But if you do I must have your word – no more stealing. No more lies. First time I catch you taking something that doesn't belong to you...'

'Oh, I won't, Miss Rose!' he promised. 'I swear I won't!'

-

We had been in the city about three weeks when a letter came from Basil's uncle, George Pooley. Among ill-spelled and hardly legible comments on the weather and happenings in Norfolk, he included the news that Cassie Wyatt was 'ailing bad'.

'I must go back,' I said at once.

'What?' Basil looked up from his breakfast. 'Why must you? Cassie Wyatt's been ailing for as long as I can remember. He doesn't say she's dying, does he?'

'I must go, Basil. I have a feeling I'm needed.'

He muttered something, but when I asked him to repeat it he said only, 'I can't go yet, I haven't finished my business.'

'You don't need to come with me.'

He stopped and frowned at me. 'That would look fine – coming home alone from your honeymoon. What do you take me for? I'm not just a name on a marriage certificate.'

'I know that.'

'And don't you forget it. You're a married woman now, with a married woman's responsibilities. Your husband comes first – ahead of your fancy friends.'

'I don't know what you mean. Of course you come first. But if Cassie's ill, then—'

'That's just an excuse to get away. You've been fretting for one – no, don't deny it. I've known it ever since we got here. You're sorry you married me, aren't you?'

'No!' How had the conversation become so hostile?

'Well, that's good, because it's too late for regrets. Married we are and married we'll stay. I'm the best husband you've got and you might as well make up your mind to it, for you'll not get another.'

He was adamant. So it was another week before we started home.

The boy Jack Huggins travelled back with us, warmly wrapped in decent clothes. It was a long, slow, bitter journey. A great tree had fallen across the railway line outside Ely and in other places there were floods, though by the time we arrived in Lynn it was freezing. Basil hired a carriage to take us home through lanes whose ruts were thick with ice.

At Orchards, Mrs Benstead greeted us with a sad face.

'You've heard, then, Miss Rose?'

'Heard?'

'About Miss Wyatt. Miss Cassie Wyatt. God rest her sweet soul… She passed away, day before last.'

Hardly able to look at Basil, hating him for keeping me away too long, I went alone to Feltham.

–

In the morning-room at the Grange, heavy drapes were drawn against the daylight. Candles lit the scene, and Cassie lay peaceful, free of pain at last, doll-like in a box lined with blue satin. Mrs Wyatt and her five remaining daughters sat keeping watch over the coffin, but my aunt remained apart, moving restlessly about the room amid shadows, occasionally stroking back her curtain of grey hair to send a bright darting glance at me.

With tears glinting under her eyes, Mrs Wyatt removed the square of white linen, allowing me to see Cassie's face, pale as marble but wonderfully serene. 'We don't like to leave her alone,' Mrs Wyatt said. 'While she's still with us, we'll stay with her.'

I stood beside my oldest friend, unable to believe she wouldn't move, breathe, open her eyes. But what lay there was not Cassie, only the empty shell she had used. Cassie herself – the essence of Cassie – was free at last from pain and earthly shackles.

'She's gone to a better life than this,' Felicity murmured as we embraced in our mutual sorrow.

'Had she been very ill?' I asked, head and heart heavy with the pain of losing yet another dear friend.

Mrs Wyatt wiped a tear from her eye with a man's linen kerchief. 'Not especially. But she was tired. She simply slipped away from us. In her sleep. We should be glad it was so easy, for her sake. Oh, my child. My poor child!'

As tears overcame her, Felicity gestured to a brocade settee. 'Sit down, Rose. It was kind of you to come.'

'Kind?' I managed. 'No, not kind. I only wish I had come sooner.'

We sat like figures in a play, some of the girls employed in sewing mourning bands as we talked of Cassie, of the details of her passing. But eventually an awkward, expectant silence spread. None of them liked to voice the questions that were in their minds.

I found myself toying with my wedding band, twisting it round on my finger. 'You will have heard that Mr Pooley and I are married,' I said, looking from one to another of the waiting faces. 'I know it may appear that it was done in unseemly haste, but… The fact is, we should have been obliged to leave the farm if Mr Pooley hadn't offered to take on the tenancy. Poor Mama was already so distressed, I couldn't add that burden to her woes.'

That was enough for Felicity, who smiled a tearful but sympathetic smile. 'So that's the answer. My dear, we did wonder. But… you would have married him in time, anyway, would you not?'

'Oh – yes. Yes, I probably would,' I agreed.

'And would you, indeed?' The hiss came from Agnes, who strode suddenly to the centre of the room. In her unrelieved black with her grey hair flowing wildly, she reminded me of one of Macbeth's witches – Basil and I had seen the play in London. '*Would you?!* I must speak with you, Rose. I must speak with you alone. Come…'

She stumped to the door, went out.

'Yes, go with her,' Mrs Wyatt said. 'Maybe you can ease her mind. She's taking it hard.'

Agnes had gone ahead. I followed her receding figure up the main stairs, around the gallery, along the bedroom corridor and up the bare back stairs. Seeming anxious to put as much space as possible between us and the family, she led me all the way up to the old schoolroom in the attic.

Two small windows looked out under eaves, across a parapet roofed with lead, to distant woods veiled behind a flurry of falling snow. It was cold there, echoing and dusty, filled with memories, the desks still set in two rows, the board still bearing scrawls of chalk; even the pointer that Fraulein Griebel had used to emphasise her lessons lay as she might have left it minutes before. 'Now come, my young ladies, you will pay attention to me please!' Her voice came clear in my head and I saw dusty sunlight stream, and the three of us – Felicity, Cassie and myself – sitting at the desks. Those days of a merry long ago were almost tangible.

'And where were you?' Aunt Agnes's cry seemed to come from far distances, as if she were the ghost in this scene. 'Where *were* you when she was asking for you so pitifully? Off in London, with that… that creature you call a husband. It's unforgivable. Unforgivable!' The bare floor echoed to the thud of her heels as she strode, her arms wrapped about herself as if she were in pain. 'You helped to kill her. Do you know that?'

The charge brought me back to the present. 'What?'

'When she knew what you'd done – when she heard that you'd married in secret and run off – she wept bitterly for you. She blamed herself for it.'

'Why should she blame herself for what happened to me?'

'She felt she should have been able to save you from yourself. She wouldn't accept that you have always gone your own wilful way, that no one on this earth could ever divert you once your mind was made up. God knows I've tried often enough. And your father. You were his despair.'

'No!' Lifting my head I faced her squarely in the dim weird snow-light. 'No, don't make me feel guilty about that too. I won't accept it. I know you're grieving. But you're not alone in that. If I had known Cassie was so ill…'

'You never cared how ill she was!'

Watching her eyes glimmer in her pale, lined face with its frame of lank grey hair, I felt only a numb bewilderment. 'Why do you hate me so, Aunt Agnes? I know I disappointed you, but—'

'Disappointed! That tells only half of it. I believed you were truly sorry. I believed you had learned your lesson. Once I could forgive. But twice is too much. Twice is wilful stupidity.'

Knowing well what she meant, I straightened my back, feeling calm and clear-headed. 'I'm sure I don't know what you mean.'

'Are you going to make me say it – what the entire county is saying – that, with her father scarcely cold in his grave, Rose Hamilton went and got herself in the family way and had to get married, in secret and in shame?'

I was trembling, but my voice sounded level enough. 'Is that what Cassie believed?'

'Yes!' As the cry hung between us she seemed to feel it turn on her. She sank down on one of the small chairs, leaning her elbows on a desk, head in hands, saying in a muffled voice, 'No... No, Cassie never believed ill of you. She always made excuses for you. Cassie was an angel. Too good for this earth.'

Drawing a long, deep breath, I let it sigh out of me. 'Thank you. I needed to know that.'

She flung me a scornful glance as she stood up again and paced away. 'I had to tell the truth for her sake. Not for yours. She was a saint. So sweet and good herself she could never think ill of anyone – even if it was so blatantly obvious that—'

'I married Basil because of the farm, because my father asked me to keep Orchards. No other reason.'

Agnes stared at me, reading my thoughts, believing me and yet still finding reason to hate me.

Fierce emotion welled up in me, a mixture of grief and anger and deep hurt. 'I never did understand what you expected of me, Aunt. Something I couldn't give, evidently. Did you expect me to be a replica of you? To live the life you planned for me? But I'm not you. I never could be.'

'God forbid!' she got out, choking on the words. She stood erect, a statue with grief hammered into every line, and then her whole body shook, shuddered. Sobs dredged up from deep within her and she fell to her knees, her mouth an ugly shape letting forth ugly sounds.

I stood beside her, awkwardly stroking her shoulder, not knowing how to cope with my aunt in this strange state. 'Agnes... Yes, weep for her. Weep for us all. We shall miss her. You're right, she was a good sweet soul. And now she's at rest. Gone to a better place, where she'll be whole again, able to run and ride and laugh...'

A cry jerked out of her and she threw back her head, laughing bitterly. 'You don't believe that. You don't believe it any more than

I do. There's no heaven. There's a hell, but that's here on earth and we create it for ourselves. Beyond the grave there's nothing. Only darkness, and silence – and peace. That's so, isn't it?' She clutched at my hand, holding it in fingers like clawing talons, her eyes full of fear. 'Tell me that's so. It can't go on, surely. Oh, it can't!' The last words came on a deep, shuddering cry of despair as she sank back on her heels, hiding her face in her hands.

Fearing that grief had made her mad, I bent over her, trying to persuade her to her feet. 'Come, Aunt. It's cold in here. Get up and come back where it's warm. Cassie wouldn't have wanted you to distress yourself. For her sake...'

She allowed me to help her up. She seemed feeble, like an old, old woman, weeping softly and quietly now as if all her defences were gone. Leaning on me, she let me guide her down the narrow back stairs to her room, where a fire burned and her familiar books crowded every space.

I rang for the maid and ordered hot chocolate to be brought. While we waited I brushed Agnes's coarse hair, braiding it so that she looked tidier, less like a witch.

'Cassie used to brush my hair,' she said as if to herself, then reached up and caught my hand, lifting her face to look at me. 'Tragedies come in threes, Rose. Your father, now Cassie... Who will be next, I wonder? Who will be next?'

Could this be my aunt – my practical, logical aunt? 'You're upset. In a few days you'll see it differently.'

She gazed at me with anxious, brimming eyes. 'Is there a heaven, Rose? Is there? Tell me it's not so! Because if there is... if there is, then there must also be hellfire and damnation waiting for wicked sinners like me.'

By the time I left she seemed calmer, but even so the memory of the encounter troubled me deeply.

–

A letter from Mama awaited me at the farm. Sentences wandering off in strange directions, she wrote that she understood about our being married, that she was happy to welcome Basil as her son-in-law.

> *I was always exceedingly fond of him, as you know, Rose, and his dear uncle George who has always been so kind and brought*

those tasty pheasants that first Christmas. Grace sends her love and good wishes. She is becoming a little heavy round the waist but that's only to be expected. I only pray she will not have the troubles I had. I shall be staying with her, of course, until the baby is born. Some time in May, the doctor tells us...

In her usual vague way, Mama glossed over difficulties, like a skater scribbling over the surface of ice until the depths are hidden beneath a white frosting.

Meanwhile the boy Jack settled in. He ate in the farm kitchen and slept in a corner of a store-room over the stables, from where he acted as a general yard-hand for both Benstead and Ned Plant. They complained of his cheekiness, but they both agreed he was a good worker. Mrs Benstead reported approvingly that the boy had a good appetite; she had seldom seen a child eat so heartily. It made her feel proud to see the way he tucked in, and to hear the way he praised her cooking.

Jack Huggins flourished. He had an easy charm, a silver tongue. I doubted he would ever contend for sainthood, but he worked hard and, as far as I knew, he never stole again. Not from me, anyway.

–

They buried Cassie in Feltham churchyard, with full pomp. Young girls dressed in white accompanied the coffin. It pleased Mrs Wyatt to dress all her daughters in white, too, as a tribute to Cassie's purity of mind and body. My aunt wore deepest black, and behind her heavy veil her eyes were dead. She remained aloof, distanced by some extremity of emotion that was more than grief. I could not reach her.

During the ceremony I thought about Cassie and our long friendship: the accident, the years of girlhood when she and I had been so close, and the events that had separated us. I had not been a constant friend, that I knew. My own selfish needs had come first. Now, too late, I wished I had taken more time to talk with Cassie and benefit from her gentle wisdom. And I wished I had come home in time to say goodbye to her.

All the time, in the back of my mind, I wondered if Geoffrey was there. I tried not to look for him, but as we moved from church to graveside, umbrellas raised against a cold, persistent February drizzle,

I caught a glimpse of his profile among the crowd and pain skewered through me. Pain, and shame, and the damning knowledge that I would go through life in this same way, catching glimpses of him and hurting for what might have been. Fate drove us ever further apart, but nothing changed my feelings for him.

Later, at the Grange, I happened to be crossing the hall with Felicity as Geoffrey was taking his leave of Mr Wyatt. Felicity paused to speak to him while I stood apart watching them, wondering why Geoffrey looked so drawn and tired.

'Everyone who knew Miss Cassie will sorely miss her,' he said.

We all murmured our assent to that.

A footman approached, bearing Geoffrey's hat and coat which he took, saying, 'Well, if you'll excuse me. My wife...'

'Of course, dear boy, of course,' Mr Wyatt murmured. 'Give her our best wishes. I trust she'll be fit again very soon.'

'Thank you. Goodbye, Mr Wyatt. Miss Wyatt. Mis... Mrs Pooley.'

Once we had read each other's thoughts with uncanny ease, empathy flowing between us. Now the slate-blue eyes were shuttered against me, like opening a familiar door and finding a blank wall.

When he had gone, I said, 'Is young Mrs Devlin unwell?'

'Just a slight indisposition,' Felicity replied. 'Poor Lucy is not the strongest of women, I fear.'

Her father blew down his nose, shaking his head. 'Geoffrey's too protective, that's the trouble. She should be drawn out of that shyness of hers, not allowed to indulge it.'

Returning to Orchards, I remained enwrapped in a cocoon of hurt and grief, having no appetite and no wish for conversation. I went early to bed, but such were my thoughts that I was still wakeful when Basil came up. We exchanged a few desultory words as he undressed, but when he put out the candles and climbed in beside me, reaching for me, I moved away.

'Not tonight.'

'That's what you've been saying since we got back! Wait until after the funeral, you said.'

'But not *immediately* after! Can't you understand how I feel? Cassie was my best friend.'

Making his reluctance clear, he drew away and turned over, thumping the pillow angrily before settling down.

How strange the mind is. On that night of all nights, I dreamed vividly of Geoffrey, of running through sunlit woods with him, laughing with him, embracing him. In my dream I knew we were about to make love. I ran to meet him through a house with long, echoing corridors, where I burst into the attic schoolroom knowing my young lover was waiting for me – and found there a coffin set on bare trestles. Pierced by the unbearable thought of Geoffrey lying dead, I approached with fearful step. But the man in the coffin was my father, and as I saw him he opened his eyes and sat up—

I woke with a gasp, relieved to find it just a dream, breathing hard to calm my pulse and drive away the lingering shreds of fear. It was dawn. Grey light filtered between the curtains, turning the furniture in the room to murky shapes.

It was then I heard a sound, faint and far away. I identified it as a shot – a single distant blast. It made me sit half up, listening.

'Whassup?' Basil muttered.

'There was a shot. I heard a shot.'

'In the middle of the night? Don't be stupid, Rose. Go to sleep.'

'It's not the middle of the night. It's time we were up.' I threw the covers back, reaching for my wrap.

'What?' He groped for the pocket-watch he had left on the bedside table, peering at it in the dim light. 'It's not yet five-thirty!'

'We ought to go down to the yards and see the men. We can't leave it to McDowall much longer. He needs guidance.'

Basil lay down, wrapping the sheets close about his neck and over his face. 'Then you go.' After a moment, goaded by my silence, he threw himself round to look at me. 'I'm no farmer. You knew that when you married me. You've got a steward to manage the place. If you can't trust him to do the job properly, then you'll just have to see to it yourself. I've got other fish to fry.'

'But I thought…'

'What did you think?'

'Nothing,' I sighed. In truth, I hadn't really thought about it at all. I had just assumed that he would at least take an interest. On reflection, it suited me not to have him interfering. With McDowall's help, I was perfectly capable of running the farm.

Before eight o'clock, a messenger came from the Grange to enquire if my aunt was with me. A maid had found her room empty, her rumpled bed cold. A search of the house had discovered no trace of her. Yet her belongings remained – including all her clothes. It appeared that she must have gone out in her nightdress and blue velvet wrap.

All that might offer a clue was a sealed envelope, addressed to me. But the note inside it read only, '*Forgive me, Rose. Please forgive me.*'

The search ranged across fields and through woods, which was where she was eventually found. Lying cold and dead. Shot through the head.

Afterwards, my own imagination supplied the details of Agnes's last walk through wet winter woods, as the sky lightened with dawn. Her bare feet muddied and scratched, her nightgown wet and torn, her hair wild and her eyes empty, she had wandered from the Grange and sought the shelter of the woods that lay between Orchards and Ambleford. In her hand she had carried one of Mr Wyatt's shot-guns.

It could not have been an accident. She placed the muzzle of the shot-gun in her mouth. She used a cord to pull both triggers. A gamekeeper found her – not far from the place where an old hut stood rotting.

Two

Battered by all the blows of recent months, I sat with Basil in the parlour at Orchards as shadows gathered and the fire blazed brighter through the gloom. Because I needed to talk of it, I told him about my last conversation with Agnes. 'She talked about hell. As if she was afraid of it. Do you think she meant to kill herself, even then?'

'Who knows?' he replied. 'She was always half mad.'

'Don't say that!'

'Well, she wasn't normal. I remember tales being told about her from the time I was knee-high to a grasshopper.'

'She was unconventional. People didn't understand her, any more than they understand me. People are so narrow-minded. Break one or two of their petty rules and you're outcast for ever.'

He looked at me sidelong, under his lashes. 'It was more than a petty rule or two she broke, if what they say is true.'

'Oh?' I felt myself bristle, ready to defend my aunt. 'And what do "they" say, pray?'

'Never mind.' He looked uncomfortable, as if he wished he had never said anything about it.

'But I do mind. I want to know.'

'You won't like it.'

'I'll decide that for myself. Tell me. What are they saying about Agnes?'

Before replying, he took a cigar from a leather case and lit it with a spill from the hearth, drawing in a good lungful of smoke. I watched him with distaste. My father had always kept his smoking to the office and until now Basil had respected that tradition. Just as I was about to object, he said, 'Never had any men-friends, did she? Always preferred women.'

'And so?'

'There's a word for immoral practices like that.'

Rumours of such things had been whispered at school. Now the implications so frightened and incensed me that I threw myself at him, raining blows on the arms he threw up to defend himself. 'How dare you! How *dare* you!'

He leapt up, easily fending off my attack. He drew back his arm and hit me. My head seemed to explode as his open palm spat against my cheek.

I staggered back and hung there, staring at him in disbelief, a hand cooling my aching flesh.

'You forced me to do that,' he said levelly. 'Some things I'll take. Some things I'll not. Being slapped by my own wife's one of them. You asked me to tell you.'

'It's not true! It's not!'

He looked about to argue, but his expression changed and with one step he was beside me, his hands grasping my arms. 'It's not true about you, anyway, and that's all I care.'

'Me?' I managed. 'Did they say that I...?' My grief and despair rose up and I turned away from him, a hand to my stinging eyes. 'I'm going to rest for a while.' Basil didn't attempt to delay me.

In the room we now shared, I removed my outer clothes, loosened my stays and lay down under the coverlet. Agnes... Memory produced a hundred tiny glimpses – things my aunt had said, looks and caresses she had exchanged with female friends; her antipathy towards men, her delight when I seemed to be like her; her cold fury when I allowed myself to be seduced by a man. And... and, yes, dear heaven, her intimate closeness with Cassie which had made me feel so uncomfortable.

Through half-closed eyes I saw Basil come in. I didn't want to talk to him, not then. Feigning sleep, I heard the lock click as he turned the key, then the floor creaked. The bed gave under his weight. He leaned over me, stroking my hair, touching the cheek he had lately abused.

'That didn't please me to have to hit you,' he said. 'But don't you ever go for me again. I won't stand for it, Rose. And don't ever talk to me in that hoity-toity manner, either. Those days are gone. If it weren't for me, where would you be, eh?'

'I'm grateful,' I murmured.

'Are you? Show me.' Without haste, he pulled the coverlet away from me and, as I opened my eyes, he slid a hand inside my camisole.

'Please!' Hot with unease, I grabbed that errant hand and tried to push it away. 'Please, not now!'

'How long do you expect me to wait? I've waited, out of respect for Miss Cassie. I won't wait any longer.'

'Do you expect me to make love to you with my aunt unburied? It's not twenty-four hours since she died. I can't—'

'You can and you will! You're my wife. Or are you trying to drive me away? Do you want me to leave, and have your uncles take someone else on for the tenancy?'

'You wouldn't!'

'Blast, and I would!'

He fell upon me, forcing me to suffer the grindings of his body. But I felt dead inside. For the first time there was not the least flicker of response in me.

At last, when he lay replete and exhausted from his exertions, I rolled away and began to dress myself, my back turned to him.

'I'm a man,' he muttered. 'A man has his needs. You're my wife!'

'Indeed, I am. You used me as is your right. I'll not complain.'

He was silent for a while, then, 'I didn't expect it to be like this.'

'Nor I.'

'Then what did you expect?'

'I don't know. Tenderness, perhaps. Kindness.'

'Kindness? Aren't I kind to you? Haven't I bought you clothes and fancy doings?'

Sighing, I laid a hand to my aching head. 'Yes, you have.'

'Isn't that enough? What else do you want?' He scrambled from the bed and stuffed his shirt tail back into his drawers, doing up the buttons – such had been his haste that that was as far as he had gone in undressing.

I watched the performance, despising him, tired of humouring him. 'I wanted your name, Basil Pooley, that's all. You knew that. You agreed to it. It was more than you ever dared to hope, remember?'

He stared at me, bristling. 'My God...'

'I'll keep to my vows, never fear, so long as you keep to your part of the bargain. I'll warm your bed and keep your house, so long as you let me keep this farm. That's the pact we made. And one thing more – I'll thank you not to smoke in the parlour in future. My father never did. If you want to smoke, you can use the office, or go outside. I'll not have my house tainted with that smell.'

'*Your* house…' His mouth closed like a trap, lipless and grim as he glowered at me. 'Right, then, if that's how it's to be…' He sat down on the bed, pulled on his boots, and stamped for the door. 'I'll be at The Feathers. I may be late. Wait for me. Don't go to sleep. And don't wear your nightgown!'

Having vowed to obey, I obeyed. To the letter. Long after the servants went to bed and the house was silent, I waited, in a chair by the dying fire in our room. I did not sleep, nor did I put on my nightgown – I did not undress at all but sat with a shawl about my shoulders as the room grew colder. A single lamp burned beside me. By its light I read Wordsworth, finding peace and comfort in his images of nature.

It was after one when Basil finally came home. I heard his step in the hallway and then he was standing in the open doorway, regarding me with a tilt of brow, a slight curve to his lips. I felt a pulse jerking in my throat, evidence of my nervousness, though outwardly I remained cool and resolved.

Slowly he closed the door and leaned on it, taking wry note of the way I had concurred with his orders. He had been drinking, but the drink had mellowed him. 'You always were a stubborn woman, Rose Hamilton Pooley. But, blast my eyes, that was one of the things that drew me.' He walked wearily to the bed and sat down, taking off one boot and then the other, letting them thud to the floor. He threw off his coat and waistcoat, undid his tie and his collar, loosened his shirt, and as he fumbled with his cufflinks he looked again to where I was sitting.

'We're wed, you and me. For better or worse. Neither of us knew what we were getting, that's plain. But it's done. It's a fact. No going back. What d'you say we make the best of it, hey, Mrs Pooley?'

'We don't seem to have any other choice,' I replied.

'Then come to bed, before you catch your death. I'll not bother you tonight. I'm too tired for it. Come on, girl. Let's make peace.'

Our marriage had found its level. From then on we enjoyed – if that is the word – an uneasy truce. We lived our different lives. He had his work and I had mine. What went on between us when we were alone in our bed was, for me, a necessary evil.

Agnes's death brought the family to conclave at Weal House. Only Uncle Henry was absent, off in warmer climes with the Prince of Wales.

My hasty marriage, and Basil's presence as my husband, caused only minor disturbance among that gathering. Of far greater import was the inquest, and the storm of publicity that accompanied it. To complete our humiliation, when the coroner returned a verdict of suicide, the Morsford vicar refused to bury Agnes in the family plot. She had not been a regular churchgoer, he pointed out. Indeed she had openly declared agnosticism, if not atheism. However, a kindly veil might have been drawn over that had she not also committed the unpardonable sin of taking her own life.

My uncles argued fiercely that Agnes had not been in her right mind, but the vicar and his bishop remained obdurate. My aunt was granted the briefest of services, followed by interment on the dark north side of the churchyard, the place marked only by a stone embedded in the ground, just large enough to bear her initials. Even the church turned its back on Agnes at the last.

In the upstairs drawing-room at Weal House, I sat reading black-bordered letters of condolence, while Grace stood by the window, holding the lace curtain aside as she peered down King Street. Her tea-cosy silhouette, lacy shawl meeting wide skirts, disguised her advancing pregnancy. She was restless, working herself up to say something.

'Rose…' she began at last. 'Rose, dear, William and I have been talking and… and we really do think that Mama ought to go home with you. I mean, William and I have had hardly any time to ourselves since we were married, what with his relatives and mine always visiting. His mother appears nearly every day. Narnie doesn't like her, and makes it obvious. And Mama frets over me…'

Understanding all too well, I said with sympathy, 'I'd be happy to have her come home. I've mentioned it several times, but she doesn't respond. You know how she is when she doesn't want to face reality.'

'But I wish you would try harder to persuade her. She… she might be more willing to go if you let Narnie—'

'No!' I looked up sharply. 'No. I'm sorry, Narnie must go back to Willow Cottage.'

Her underlip thrust out, trembling. 'Why?'

'Because Father would have wanted it.'

'But Father's not here now!'

'Quite so. And I won't betray his memory by having her back.'

A baffled silence followed. Then: 'He hated Narnie – just because Mama loved her. He was always unkind to her.'

'That's not true, Grace. Whatever story she may have told you… well, it doesn't matter. I can't have her back. I won't have her back. That's an end to it.'

Stamping her foot, she swung away and jerked the curtain aside, peering at the street for a moment before she tossed the lace back into place, saying fretfully, 'This is too bad of William! He promised he would take the early train. Why doesn't he come?' Moving heavily, flat-footed with a hand to her aching back, she came to sit in an armchair near the fire, sighing in relief as firm cushions supported her. 'Some *business* kept him, no doubt.'

'Yes, probably.' I was only half listening.

'With men, it's always business.'

'That's how they support their wives and families.'

'Oh, you! You don't care whether your husband's away or not.'

As I looked up again she began to fuss with her skirts, brushing at imaginary crumbs, her mouth sulky in a face puffed with pregnancy. 'Well, it's true. I haven't heard you complain about him going off to London again. Not that he seemed sorry to leave.' Her brow furrowed as she watched me. 'Why *did* you marry him? He's so uncouth. He doesn't even know how to hold a knife and fork properly.'

'Don't be so sniffy, Grace.'

'But it's true! All the family are saying it. How can you bear to…' Her mouth twisted and she gave a little shudder. 'I mean, I know how it is. Now that you're married you're obliged to share his room, and his bed, and…' Her face contorted with distress as she whispered, 'It's horrible, isn't it?'

The sudden change in her caught me unawares. 'What is?'

'You know – *that*. What Mama calls the dark side of marriage. I do love William, but even so, sometimes… Sometimes I dread the nights when he wants to…' Tears started from her eyes as she cried, 'Oh, Rose, I'm so afraid! When the baby comes… I might *die*!'

'Nonsense!' Putting the letters aside, I went to crouch beside her and comfort her. 'Grace, what has Mama been telling you? You mustn't listen to her. It's not so bad, I promise you.'

'Oh, what do *you* know of it?' she cried.

Fortunately, she was too distressed to notice the pain her careless scorn brought me, I too had feared the birth of my child. But I had not had a loving husband and family around me.

Through bouts of tears she repeated all the dreads that Mama and Narnie had managed to plant in her mind. In return, I reminded her of women who had borne children successfully – from the Queen herself to Pam Chilvers; and what of Mrs Wyatt, who had given birth to eleven?

'She only raised eight of them though,' Grace fretted. 'Three of them died. Even the Princess of Wales nearly died with her little Louise, and Mama... Mama miscarried four times after she had me. Did you know that? And then she nearly died when she had Johnny.'

'But you're not Mama. You're much stronger than she is.'

What became clear as we talked was that during the last weeks of her pregnancy Grace needed a respite from well-intentioned 'advice' that was frightening her half to death.

Unfortunately neither Mama nor Narnie wished to leave Grace's side until after the child was born. Narnie, of course, much preferred being with her 'lambs' to being alone in her cottage, and Mama, I knew, was afraid of going back to a place that echoed with Father's absence.

When Turnbull arrived he added his voice to mine. 'I'm sorry, Mother Hamilton, but you heard the doctor say that Grace must take care of herself. She has to rest, and she can't do that when she's concerning herself with looking after you.'

'But *I* shall look after *her*,' Mama protested. 'I – and Narnie. Grace needs us with her.'

His eyes glinted and behind his beard the full red lips tightened. 'Grace needs peace and quiet. My mother will take good care of her. You'll go home. You have another daughter who will take care of you. I'll brook no more argument where my wife's health is concerned.'

I don't suppose he had ever used that stern tone with her before. Mama blinked at him, her mouth trembling, but she said, 'Why... yes, William, of course. If you say so. But—'

'No "buts",' he broke in. 'Orchards is where you belong. Orchards is your home. And I dare say Rose will be happy to have Narnie stay for a while until you get settled. Won't you, Rose?'

Wondering if I were being manipulated, I surveyed them all – Turnbull expectant, his arm protectively about his pale, tearful wife, Mama bewildered and Narnie with a little smile of triumph playing about her lips. She thought she had won her way back.

'Narnie will be welcome,' I said levelly. 'For a day or two. Just until we can make sure that Willow Cottage is properly aired for her.'

Her face twitched, the smile blinking out as her eyes narrowed to slits.

Mama's breathy voice put in, 'Yes, a day or two. Just a day or two. That's all I ask.' She laid a hand on my arm, her face lifted anxiously. 'Your father won't object to that, will he?'

–

Mama's return to Orchards was accomplished amid tears and petty panics, but within hours of arrival she had performed her usual trick of closing her mind to unpalatable facts. She appeared to believe that Father had gone away for an unspecified time, as he had done after Victor died. 'When your father comes…' became her watchword.

Narnie's 'day or two' at the farm stretched nearer to a week. Though I sent our two housemaids to clean and air the cottage, she grumbled that she didn't trust them to do it properly. However, she would not go to check for herself – she seemed to feel that if she clung on at Orchards House for long enough I would give in and let her stay. It was a battle of wills I determined to win.

On a day of blustering wind, with rain showering from leaden skies, I drove over to the cottage myself and found it neat and sparkling. Even the feather bed smelled sweet, with not a trace of damp. Swift and Howlett had worked hard. The living-room hearth was still warm, with glowing embers from which I built another blaze to lighten the gloom.

As I riddled out the ashes, Narnie's little cat appeared and came rubbing round me, purring.

'Hello, where did you come from?' I stroked her head, enjoying her warm softness before I removed the pan from the grate and carefully stood up, trying not to spill the ashes.

But as I turned I heard a step in the kitchen. A tall caped figure loomed in the doorway. A cry escaped me. The pan slipped in my hand, sending a shower of ashes to the rug. The intruder's cape was dark with rain and beneath the dripping brim of a leather hat his eyes glimmered at me from a pale face adorned by a dark moustache.

'I apologise,' Geoffrey Devlin said. 'I didn't mean to startle you.'

My heart hammered with alarm. My mouth was dry, my throat tight. 'What are you doing here?'

'I wanted to see you.'

'Are you mad?'

He didn't reply at once. I saw his lips tighten beneath the dark curve of his moustache as he swept off the hat and ran a hand through his flattened hair. 'Perhaps so. Yes, perhaps I am. That would appear to be the only p-possible explanation.'

The bitterness in him made me uncertain. 'You shouldn't be here. If someone saw you…'

'No one saw me. I came by the hedge-sides, and then through the churchyard.'

'How did you know I was here?'

'I've been watching for you. As I did the day you came home. Like a lovesick schoolboy. Watching, waiting… I wanted to tell you how sorry I am about your aunt. I wanted to write to you, but…' He threw out his arm, scattering water from his hat. 'Damnation, Rose! Why did you marry Pooley? Why?'

Still helplessly balancing the pan of ashes, I said, 'You must know why. Surely you've heard?'

'Are you having his child?'

'How *dare* you ask me that?'

'I want to know.'

Suddenly my face was burning. 'I am not with child, and time will witness to the truth of that, whatever my enemies may be saying. I married Basil Pooley because it was the only way Mama and I could remain at Orchards.'

That gave him pause. His eyes narrowed as he considered, then emotion built in him again and, 'Do you care for him?' he demanded.

Wounded, I hit back. 'Do you care for Lucinda?'

With an impatient gesture he took a step towards me but stopped when I drew back. 'We're not d-discussing Lucinda. When it came to marriage I had no choice. I told you that. Good God, don't you

235

know that if I'd been free to follow my own inclinations…' He stopped himself, took a deep breath and added bitterly, 'But no, evidently you don't know how it is with me. You accused me of lying to you. Did you ever truly believe in me, Rose?'

'Geoffrey…' What did he mean?

'Answer me! D–did you ever believe that I cared for you?'

'I…' How could I tell what I had believed so long ago? It was part of some other life. 'I don't know. Perhaps I did. I wanted to. I was lonely. I needed to believe that someone loved me. But I was never foolish enough to think it might be forever.'

'No. *I* was the fool. I see that now.'

Why was he so angry, so upset? 'I don't understand.'

'You say you needed to be loved. But did you love in return, Rose?'

'Of course I did. How can you think—'

'Did you believe in me? Did you trust me? Why did you say it was all lies?'

It seemed important that I should be completely honest with him, and with myself. I tried to think back, past years of pain and separation, but the memories wouldn't hold still. 'Geoffrey…'

'Thank you!' His voice shook, deep with disgust. 'I believe I have my answer.'

My hands were trembling, tiny showers of ash falling from the corners of the pan. 'Please…'

'I never lied to you, Rose,' he said. 'Between us, only truth would ever do. So I thought. You and I… it was s–something… something apart. S–something unique. I thought you felt the same.'

'I did!'

His look was like a knife-thrust. 'Goodbye, Rose.'

The doorway yawned empty. I heard the back door open and close, and in the tingling silence the fire cracked, the cat yowled softly.

Trembling all over, I sank to my knees and set the still-warm pan down on the hearth. My hands smelled of stale ashes as I flung them to my face and swayed back and forth like a child needing comfort. I didn't understand what I had done wrong. I only knew that I hurt – and that I wished he would come back and hold me – and that if he did I would be forced to send him away.

It was never going to be possible for us. Never.

'The cottage is in apple-pie order,' I told Narnie flatly. 'You may pack your things and be ready to go home tomorrow. I'll have Benstead drive you.' I could not go back to the cottage myself. Not yet.

Mama made no open protest, but she shed tears and hugged Narnie closely, while over her shoulder the old woman glowered at me.

As I saw her out to the cart where Benstead was waiting, she said sourly, 'You've more of your father in you than I ever dreamed. You've grown hard, Miss Rose. Very hard.'

'I do what I have to do.'

'Tell that to Master Johnny,' she said, grunting with effort as she climbed up to the cart, aided by Benstead.

'Johnny?' I asked. 'Why, what—'

'You'll see. Hurry up, man, don't stand about gawping, I want to be going home. I've a lot to do. Those maids can't be trusted to do anything right. If my bed's not aired through, I'll die of pneumonia. Not that anyone'll care.'

'What did you mean about Johnny?' I persisted, remembering my young brother at Weal House at the time of Agnes's funeral, silent and withdrawn, suffering from yet another tragedy – so I had thought. Having concerns of my own, I hadn't interfered in what had seemed to be his grieving.

'Don't you know? You've upset him good and proper. Still, it's none of my concern. You've made that clear. I'm out to grass and there I'll stay, and mind my own business. Least said, soonest mended. Come on, Benstead, let's be off before it rains.'

He cast her a look that tilted up to the windy sky. 'That don't fare to rain just now, Miss Narborough, ma'am. That's wholly too wild for rain.' Then something caught his attention and he pointed. 'Why – look! Look there, in the meadow. See 'im?'

An old dog fox came loping slantwise across the meadow, half hidden in long grass. Behind him, beyond a copse that topped the rise, the brassy bray of the hunting horn called the hounds to pursue. The fox ran for the wooden fence, found himself baulked by the anti-hare sacking and scrabbled there for a moment. He found a hole. He wrenched at it with frantic teeth and claws and pushed through. Wriggling free, he darted down the driveway, through the open gates and across the lane, heading for the trees around the pond.

As I picked up my skirts and hurried after him, consternation cried havoc among the fowl by the pond. Ducks and geese went complaining in all directions. Chickens scattered squawking. But the fox was not after them. While they flew yelling their silly heads off, the sleek red body with its grey muzzle and rippling, white-tipped tail slipped across the farmyard. The bullocks in their pen looked askance and moved aside as he sped through their pungent straw and made off between the barns.

'Blast that varmint!' Benstead clambered down from the cart and came loping on rheumaticky legs to join me, anxious for his beasts. Both of us knew that nothing could stop the hounds in full cry. I could hear their music now.

Along the lane, climbing trees and perched on gates, men and boys appeared, leaving their work to watch the hunt. The hounds came into sight, streaming over the hill in a long fluid column. Behind them rode the huntsman, blowing liquid notes of pursuit, and in his wake came the first of the riders, two men with a woman close behind, then another man, and another, two more…

'He's gone away!' Benstead yelled, waving his arms. 'Away!'

The hounds milled, yelping, behind the meadow fence, seeking a way through the sack barrier. One found the hole the fox had made. It tore more as he pushed through. Others followed, leaving the sacking shredded. Meanwhile the huntsman opened the meadow gate. The pack divided, some coming through the fence, others pouring for the easier exit of the gate. All of them made for the pond. More terrified birds rose with a great carfuffle of squawking, quacking, beating wings, flying feathers… and then the dogs were at the bullock pen, confused by the strong scent of dung and urine, making the bullocks bawl and back away, rolling their eyes.

The first two riders elected to use the meadow gate. The woman behind them drove her horse at the fence. A cry escaped her as she took the jump and landed with a jolt that all but shook her from the saddle. She recovered, whipped up and came galloping on, intent on being first into the farmyard behind the pack. Her face was contorted with effort, her eyes glittering. She didn't see me. She had no thought in her head except to follow the pack and be in at the kill.

If I had not seen it, I would not have believed it. The woman was Lucinda Devlin – sad, timorous Lucy, riding headlong after a fox with the light of blood in her eyes.

One or two of the other leading riders followed her example and leapt the fence, though most took the less showy route through the gate. The dogs were still sniffing about the yard, the bullocks stamping and snorting, backed into a corner. Horses danced, voices shouted…

The horn called a triumphant note – one of the hounds had refound the scent, on a path through Poacher's Wood. Baying in answer, the pack made off through a narrow gap between the barns, leaving the riders to find a way round, back to the lane and off into the wood. As they departed, Benstead made for the yard to check on his bullocks.

Another party of riders came galloping across the meadow, with a few last stragglers behind them. The gate had swung partly closed, creating a bottleneck that delayed them. Among them, I saw, was Geoffrey Devlin, caked with mud down one side of his coat – he must have taken a fall to put him so far behind the leaders. He looked impatient as he wheeled his horse, waiting for the others to clear the gate; then, as if he couldn't wait any longer, he set his mount to jump the fence. The hunter took the leap effortlessly, hooves striking sharply on gravel as it was driven on towards me. Nearing the gate, Geoffrey drew rein with such force that the horse was startled into rearing. I flinched away from the flailing hooves, seeing how unsettled the animal was, sweating heavily, with rolling eyes. Its rider was no less disturbed – his face dark with angry blood under smears of mud, his eyes sparking fury. I had a feeling he had deliberately made the horse rear to frighten me.

'Did you see my wife?' he demanded.

'She was up with the huntsman. They're in Poacher's Wood.'

Gritting his teeth on a silent curse, he spurred away with the others, down the lane and away.

Having ascertained that his beasts were unharmed, Benstead came stumping back across the lane. 'That old fox have larned a few smart tricks,' he said. 'He've led them hounds a dance this past three year and more. Gamekeepers, too. He know all their ruses.'

'Yes, well, I hope he doesn't come back in this direction.'

'Benstead!' Narnie called impatiently. 'I'm waiting.'

'I'm now comin',' said he.

In the kitchen, I found the servants chattering excitedly about the hunt, recalling small incidents witnessed when they left their work and went out to watch.

'Pull you the other one!' said Swift in scorn.

'That was!' Howlett insisted.

Swift turned to me for confirmation. 'Is that right, Miss Rose? That lady in the plum-coloured riding habit... Was that Mrs Devlin?'

'Yes, it was.'

She shook her head in amazement. 'Well, I never.'

'Told you, see,' Howlett said, and exchanged a knowing look with Mrs Benstead, who nodded sagely.

'Why, what's this?' I enquired. 'What about Mrs Devlin?'

'Oh, that's nothin', Miss Rose,' Mrs Benstead replied. 'Prob'ly just a load of old squit. Howsomever... since you ask, that young lady have been causin' some specalation roundabout, on account of her havin' taken to ridin' so wild. Takin' leaps over fences and ditches that most of 'em think twice about – even Mr Geoffrey, and that's sayin' something. They've had words about it. Mrs Cary heard 'em as they rode by her cottage. He say to her, "You'll kill yourself," he say, and she say, "So what if I do?" There. What do you make o' that, Miss Rose?'

Swift had been taking all of this in with wide eyes. 'Maybe it's not herself she's tryin' to do away with. Maybe it's the bairn she's carryin'. Maybe that's why Mr Devlin gets so angry at her – 'cos she's tryin' to kill his child. I heard about a lady what done that. In the end, her husband strangled her!'

This melodramatic pronouncement was greeted with a shocked silence into which I said firmly, 'I think you're right, Mrs Benstead – it's a load of old squit. And I'll thank all of you not to repeat such gossip about our neighbours. Now, isn't there any work to be done?'

I heard later that the hunt had no luck that day. The fox led them all the way to the marshes, and there he vanished amid the flooded ditches. I felt a certain sneaking respect for him. But what remained with me, bothering me for months, was the kitchen gossip, and the memory of the expression on Lucinda Devlin's face, and on Geoffrey's. Something was badly awry between those two.

But one thing became clear with time. Lucy Devlin was *not* expecting a child.

–

Business continued to take my husband away, to Lynn or to Hunstanton for a day, or overnight, and occasionally he would be gone

240

for longer periods, off to London or somewhere. He owned properties here and there, such as a tenement in Norwich, Fenny Jakes's place at Onion Corner, and the boarding house in Hunstanton which he and Victor had built as an investment. As landlord, Basil had to pay regular visits to all his properties to collect the rents and see what repairs were needed. He acted as agent for other landlords, too, and 'did a bit of buying and selling, as and when', as he put it.

With the holiday trade booming, thanks to the coming of the railways, Hunstanton had grown from a hamlet to a thriving town, and in summer the beach was crowded with bathing huts and children with spades. Once or twice Basil took me for a day out to Hunstanton when business called him there, or we might travel together if his business coincided with market day, or one of the cattle fairs in Lynn.

When he was at home he helped to amuse Mama. And he indulged her, to the extent of hiring, for the summer months, a carriage and an extra man to act as coachman and general hand. The luxury delighted Mama and she often went visiting, accompanied by Ellen Earley.

For me, Basil bought a spanking new trap to replace the ancient, heavy dogcart. He still thought that he could make me happy by spending money on me, but I suppose he meant well. I did appreciate the trap. I had it painted red, with lines and curlicues in black and white, and when I drove out behind a smart black pony I felt as grand as the Princess of Wales.

Though I did visit the Grange now and then, more often it was Felicity who came to me, alone or accompanied by one of her sisters. Their visits helped to divert Mama and, to give Basil his due, if he was there he played host with diffident charm.

'I must admit I did have my doubts about your marriage,' Felicity confided. 'But Mr Pooley can be quite… quite disarming, in his way.'

She might not have been so generous if she had known how bored Basil was by her visits. 'That frumpish old maid,' he called her. 'What Victor ever saw in her I shall never know.'

–

My first nephew, Grace's son, Thomas William Turnbull, was born on 19 May that year of 1869. His mother had, so she assured me, scarcely had time to lie down before tiny Tommy was born. 'Like shelling peas!' So relieved was she that she invited Mama and Narnie to stay for a while and share the joys of the new baby.

Basil and I went over for the christening, a joyous occasion that helped to lighten some of our gloom, though we were all sad that Father couldn't be there to see his first grandson.

'The first of many!' Grace predicted as she and I bent over the crib one evening to admire the sleeping heir. Her glance slid sidelong at me, surveying the state of my waist. 'Your turn soon.'

'Not yet a while. In spite of rumours.'

She cast me an uncomfortable look. '*I* never believed that was why you got married. I didn't, Rose.'

That was probably true. My sister never did understand how any decent woman could do what she called, with delicate distaste, '*that*' without being obliged to it by vows of marriage.

In Dersingham, Pam Chilvers was awaiting her fourth confinement, afflicted with fainting spells, backache and an ulcerated leg. Her younger sister was staying at the carpenter's cottage to help, but her task was difficult, with old Mrs Playford ailing and lively children about the house. Annie, who was now six, attended school, but little lame Alice, and her brother Benjamin, aged respectively four and three, remained at home, constantly being chided to be good and to be quiet. One day I took it upon myself to rescue them and take them back with me to Orchards, where they played happily under the apple trees until their father came by in his wagon to fetch them.

After that their visits became a regular occurrence, for my husband too adored them. Benjamin with his gap-tooth grin was Basil's darling, but it was Alice whose small, bright face caused my own heart to melt. Watching her, I wondered about my own daughter. What had they called her? What did she look like? Knowing that I would never know the answers was a continuing sadness deep inside me.

My concern for the Chilvers family came to the notice of the Sandringham rector, who told me I was 'most kind' to take an interest. Mr Lancaster was a gentle, kindly soul not much older than myself, who lived at the rectory with his aged mother. Quiet as he was, I found him disconcertingly perceptive and I had always tried to avoid him. He was concerned that I no longer attended church.

'I haven't been made to feel very welcome at Sandringham church lately,' I said.

'I'm aware of that. Things have been difficult for you.'

To my own surprise, I found him easy to talk to. Perhaps I needed such a friend at that time. We had long discussions – that is to say, I talked and he mostly listened – about my father and my aunt and Cassie, about my faltering faith, about my quarrel with the prince and the gossip that hounded me.

Being domestic chaplain to Their Royal Highnesses at Sandringham, Mr Lancaster promised to try again to improve my relationship with the big house, though I privately doubted his ability to do so. However, it was good to know I had found another friend and ally.

I started going to church again, and on the second Sunday of my return to the fold the gentle rector preached a sermon about the evils of gossip, so pointed that half his congregation shifted uncomfortably in their seats and cast covert looks to where I sat with my husband beside me.

–

Another hint of lightening skies came when the gamekeeper, Pyke, arrived at the back door of the farm bringing a box in which lay curled four small fox-cubs.

'They say you raised some cubs once,' Pyke said. 'Mr Beck wondered if you might agree to do it again.'

'Mr Beck did?' What was this – another clumsy attempt to put me out of favour? Foxes were not welcome at Sandringham; the prince's keepers waged constant war against anything that threatened their rearing of game birds. 'Why?'

Pyke said that the previous year, while out with the West Norfolk, His Royal Highness had directed the master to the Sandringham woods, where good sport was sure to be found. Since his zealous keepers had made sure that no foxes remained at Sandringham, His Royal Highness was proved wrong, which annoyed him. He ordered Mr Beck to see to it that another time when he offered a neighbour sport there was sport to be had. Poor Mr Beck. The prince never appreciated the work and worry his contradictory orders caused for his servants. The desired cubs had been found but, when Beck looked round for someone to raise them, no volunteer was forthcoming. And so he had thought of me.

It was an imposition and I almost refused. However, the cubs regarded me with huge fearful eyes, beautiful creatures, slender and agile. Too young yet to have acquired the familiar red coat, their fur was brindled, sand and black, their chests and throats downy white, their shoulders a darker, ragged brown, their huge ears cocked alertly... Their raising might help to dispel the shadow of royal disfavour.

I housed them in an old shed, and hand-fed them with the help of Jack Huggins until they were old enough to start taking mice and pieces of meat. They caused me a deal of extra work and a deal of annoyance, constantly trying to dig out of the shed and escape my loving care. But Alice and Benjie Chilvers adored them.

–

Sadly for the carpenter and his wife, their fourth child was stillborn. Pam Chilvers herself lay dangerously ill for days during which Basil and I kept the children with us. We might have kept them longer had not their grandfather, Amos, come blustering to fetch them away, accompanied by Pam's brother, Davy Timms, who stayed in the cart with a slouch hat pulled low over his ruined face.

'Bloody Hamiltons!' Chilvers muttered. 'Our little 'uns want no part o' you. They've family of their own that'll do better by 'em.'

'Watch your tongue, Chilvers!' Basil returned.

'And you're no better, Pooley! Right nest of scorpions here.'

Amos Chilvers's charm was undiminished by the years.

Later, Ben Chilvers came to our door. Hat in hand, head festooned in trailing fronds of honeysuckle that overhung the back porch, he apologised for any offence his father had caused. 'Don't think it was the missus and me that sent 'em, Miss Rose. Him and Davy did it off their own bat. Whatever they said, I'm sorry for it.'

'It's already forgotten,' I replied. 'How's your wife?'

He stared at me for a long moment, his face clenched against some fierce emotion. 'Better,' he managed at last. 'Praise the Lord, she's turned the corner and come back...' The words trailed into husky silence as tears welled in his brown eyes and he turned away, muttering, 'Good night, Miss Rose.'

My own eyes were misty as through evening light I watched him go, watched the familiar lop-sided gait that looked so awkward and yet swung him along at speed. He was a fine man, tall and strong, honest, true and faithful. I hoped his wife knew how lucky she was.

–

Whilst my own marriage was not ideally happy, most of the time we managed to rub along contentedly enough. I was fond of Basil; certainly I was grateful to him. But I obviously wasn't the wife he had expected, nor was he the companionable kind of husband I had hoped for. He was often away, and when he was at home he never sat close beside me, took my hand, put his arm about me, or kissed my cheek – except when we were in bed, and then his attentions were designed not to comfort but to rouse me. Still, I tried to appreciate the good things we shared.

Though Basil had enjoyed the visits of the Chilvers children, he could not be persuaded to show a similar interest in the fox-cubs, whose care devolved mainly on me, though Jack Huggins did his share too. As the cubs grew they became ever more troublesome and, having too much work already, I hoped that Johnny might take over the chore during the summer.

My brother, however, elected to spend most of his holiday at Weal House, though I discovered he often took the train out along the coast. 'To visit his friends at Esham,' Aunt Beatrice said. 'He likes to sketch the countryside, and the birds. You should see his notebooks – crammed with lovely little drawings, and notes about nature and farming. The Lord gave him a lot of talents. I hope he'll use them for good.'

However, when I saw my brother and expressed a desire to see his sketches, he said, 'They're not for public viewing.'

'I'm not the public – I'm your sister.'

'Half-sister,' Johnny said with a look that raked me, and went away, closing the door in my face.

He wouldn't let me get close to him.

But I didn't begin to suspect just how secretive he had become until one day in July.

Basil and I drove over to Ingoldisthorpe in the trap to visit his aunt, Eliza Pooley, who was unwell. On our way, we encountered a hay wagon. It pulled aside and stopped to let us pass, the youthful driver jumping down as if to adjust the load, putting himself out of our sight.

Basil called a greeting and a mumbled reply came from behind the load of hay. Then as we drove on I looked back, puzzled, and saw the youth emerge from hiding and climb back to his perch, keeping his hat well down.

'It's Johnny!' I exclaimed. 'Driving that wagon... It's Johnny.'

'Can't be,' Basil argued, turning to squint over his shoulder. 'Same build, maybe.'

'I think I know my own brother! He was hiding from us.'

Basil's uncle, with a deal of head-scratching and earpulling, admitted that, 'The boy do come some days. Well, he's welcome. Good hand he make.' I didn't mind that. George Pooley had helped both my father and me learn about farming, so why shouldn't he also teach Johnny? It was the secrecy that hurt me – the fact that Johnny was happy to spend his time with Pooley, but he wouldn't come home to help at Orchards. At Christmas he had seemed eager to do just that.

I couldn't ask Johnny straight out about it, however, for fear of having him rebuff me again, and so, when next I saw him at Weal House, I remarked that I missed him, and that Mama, returned from Thetford, would enjoy his company.

'You don't want *me* there,' he retorted.

'Of course we do.'

'You don't need me to help when you've got Basil Pooley.'

'Basil doesn't help on the farm.'

'But he's the tenant!'

So that was it – in his eyes, Basil had usurped his place. 'Only nominally. *I* run the farm. We keep it separate from Basil's concerns.'

'Then why is he buying a steam engine for Orchards? You never told *me* about that.'

'I was going to tell you. That's one of the reasons I came into town today. Oh, how does tittle-tattle fly so fast? I suppose you heard it from Uncle Jonathan?'

'Uncle Jonathan never tells me a thing. Time enough for that when I'm of age – so he always says, the pompous ass.'

'Johnny!'

'Well, it's a fact. It's true about the engine, then?'

'It's true that Orchards is to have an engine, but not that Basil's buying it. He's extended a loan at minimum interest. We shall pay him back over two years. Oh, why won't you try to understand? I married Basil in order to keep Orchards in the family. I did it for you, Johnny.'

'No, not for me. You did it for yourself. You always wanted to run the farm, Rose. Well, you've got it. For now. But I warn you, when I've finished my education, then I shall come home and I shall take over. That's what Father planned. You're only acting "in locum ego".'

The ferocity in his voice made me blink. 'In what?'

'It's Latin,' he said, flushing. 'It means "in place of me". So don't get too settled, Rose. Your place at Orchards is temporary.'

He didn't mean it, I told myself. He was hurt and angry. When he was older, he would come home and we would run the farm together. He would need me there to advise him. He didn't mean he was going to put me out, did he? Oh, of course he didn't. He was only seventeen. He didn't know what he wanted.

–

As the summer drew on, I became aware of strain between McDowall and Ned Plant. It had started over the haying, when Plant had agreed with me that we ought to delay but McDowall had said we should make a start: 'Who's the manager here – me or yon Norfolk dumplin'? Ye're undermining my authority if you side wi' him.' So I had given in and the hay had been cut, still green in places. (One of the stacks went sour and rotted, I recall.) Now my manager complained of Plant's insubordination; he threatened to dismiss the man if his attitude didn't improve. But when I tackled Plant about it all he would say was, 'If you tell me to leave, I'll go, Miss Rose.'

'I don't want you to leave,' I told him. 'You're the best man we've ever had. Why don't you get on with Mr McDowall?'

He wouldn't tell me. When I asked Benstead, he said he'd not noticed anything amiss, except, maybe, that Mr McDowall was a bit picky with Plant and criticised everything he did. I told McDowall that Ned Plant would be staying, and they had better find a way of settling whatever differences they had.

The problem didn't go away completely but I heard less about it as we all concentrated on the summer's work. August and September proved wet; harvest lasted into October. Weeds grew riot and soft fruit went bad before it could be picked. Every day brought more headaches, and our battles with the hares continued – crow-scaring in spring was a regular chore; at Orchards we now had hare-scaring all through the summer.

Afflicted by a hundred different worries, I was relieved when Mr Beck called to inspect the young foxes and directed that they be turned out to a brick earth on the edge of Poacher's Wood, in a covert thick with gorse and swarming with young rabbits. There the cubs could learn to hunt and fend for themselves. I was to keep an eye on them, but they were no longer such a daily responsibility.

—

Sandringham Hall being uninhabited due to prolonged rebuilding and renovation work, that autumn the Prince of Wales rented distant Gunton Hall and moved in with his family. From there he held his regular shoots, using Gunton's preserves, sometimes bringing parties by train to his own estates, or visiting neighbouring squires to sample their sport. When the prince was expected locally I took care to keep my head down lest sight of me remind him of past differences. I was beginning to hope he had forgotten that I existed.

Perhaps he had, but he was about to be reminded.

The first I heard of it was farm gossip. In the yard, with the thresher going full throttle, the belt rattling and clanking with its burden of sheaves, the air full of dust and flying bits of straw, the men were saying something about a big fuss among the Sandringham gamekeepers over some trouble with the pheasants. I didn't pay much heed. I was still too nervous of engines to want to stay around the yard while ours was working.

That evening, when McDowall came up to the farm office for his orders, he told me of the consternation over what appeared to be a major calamity. 'Hundreds of birds gone, so they say.'

'Poachers?' I asked.

He shrugged. 'Who knows? Mebbe so. Mebbe we have a gang moved into the area. We'll all be murdered in our beds next.' He was implying that I was a foolish, frightened woman, jumping at shadows. 'So… I'll send Plant off tomorrow with that load of barley and get Ward to make a start on drilling the Upper Half 'un. It's gae wet down at Batty's Bottom.'

'Yes, I noticed.'

'Aye, I was sure ye would have.' It was spoken with just enough sarcasm to grate on my nerves.

We talked of the weather, the sale of our last lambs to the butcher, the pig-sticker's imminent arrival, the digging and carting of beet and carrots... but all the time I was aware of his subtle insolence: he didn't ask me, he told me; he failed to say please or thank you; and, if he no longer patronised me as 'lassie', neither did he afford me the courtesy of 'Miss Rose' or 'Mrs Pooley' – he didn't address me by any name or title. Trivial things. Petty things. Basil told me I was looking for insult when none was intended, but McDowall's discourtesy remained an irritant.

When he was gone, I rubbed my aching eyes and stretched my shoulders, wondering whether to strain the first with household accounts or the second with checking on the summer curtains that had been washed and now hung in the drying-room awaiting inspection. The curtains had been waiting for two days, but the accounts were urgent if bills were to be paid. Perhaps they took priority. I could do the curtains later, having no other call on my attention. Mama had gone early to bed and Basil was away again.

The accounts took me some hours and I had no idea what time it was, except that it was late, when I heaved myself away from the desk. Then as I left the office I heard a disturbance in the front hall, where a visitor was trying to force his way past a protesting Swift.

'Really, sir, I can't let you in without announcing you.'

'Oh, of course you can, woman!' came the impatient reply. 'You know me. What do you suppose I'm g-going to... Ah, there you are, Mrs Pooley.'

The visitor was Geoffrey Devlin, top hat in hand, wearing evening dress beneath a long cloak.

'Oh, Miss Rose!' Swift turned to me in distress. 'I'm sorry, I did ask the gentleman to wait, but he said—'

'That's all right, Swift,' I soothed her. 'It's not your fault. After all, Mr Devlin is his father's son.' The flash of Geoffrey's eyes said the barb had gone home, but I kept my chin up, assuming a poise I did not feel. 'What may I do for you at this late hour?'

'I need to t-talk to you.' His face betrayed his frustration at not being able to control that stammer, though to me the stammer itself was revealing – it always got worse when he was agitated. 'I know it's late, but I thought you should know... Seventy-one pheasants were killed in the Sandringham plantations last night.'

'Only seventy-one? I'd heard it was hundreds. If that's what you came to tell me—'

'It's not!' He stared at me, torn between temper and concern. 'What I rode thirty miles to t-tell you – t-to warn you, is… The head keeper claims you're responsible for the deaths.'

Shock doused me like icy water, driving away my weariness of mind. Aware of Swift hovering, I bade her, 'Bring some apple wine, Swift. Mr Devlin, there's a fire in the parlour, if you'd care to…'

I led the way into my familiar, homely parlour, where I began to turn up the lamps with a hand that shook. Too upset to think straight, I resorted to chatter. 'It's not the best place to entertain visitors, but the drawing-room's cold at this time of year and—'

'To Hades with that!' Geoffrey caught my wrist, forcing me to look at him. 'Did you hear what I said? Do you know what it means? The prince is spitting fire. He believes you deliberately slaughtered those birds.'

Three

I hardly knew whether to lose my temper, laugh hysterically, or weep with frustration. Just when I had thought I might win my way back into favour, malign fate had turned the prince against me yet again.

'He can't believe it!' I exclaimed. 'Seventy-one pheasants? How am I supposed to have killed them – with a shot-gun? Or was it poison? Maybe I tore their heads off with my teeth. Or does he think I cast a spell and bewitched them all to death?'

'The keeper said you let your foxes loose.'

I stared at him, feeling stricken, my stomach churning with acid. 'He said what? Dear heaven...'

'It's not true, then?'

'What?' I became aware that he was still holding my wrist, standing so close to me that his nearness threatened to swamp my sanity. 'Of course it's not true! You surely don't think I'm petty enough to...' I wrenched away, putting space between us, my reason returning as I faced him from behind the defence of the velvet-draped table. 'It can't have been my foxes. My cubs wouldn't stray that far away from home. They're amply supplied with rabbits right on their doorstep. Oh, this must be Beck's doing – another lie to discredit me! But nobody in his right mind would believe it.'

'The prince believes it.'

'Then the prince is a fool!'

Swift, arriving with the apple wine and glasses on a tray, gave me a pop-eyed look at this piece of treason, but said only, 'Will that be all, miss?' and took herself away, no doubt to recount the tale to Howlett.

Into the silence, Geoffrey observed, 'They still call you "miss".'

'It's habit.'

'She said Pooley's away.'

'Yes, that's so.'

'And your stepmother?'

251

'In bed. Fast asleep by now, I trust.'

'Good.' He put down his hat, threw off his silk-lined cloak and swirled it across a chair. 'Then we can talk in private. We can work out a strategy.'

'We?'

'You're going to need allies. There's to be an enquiry into this b-business of the pheasants.'

Closing my eyes tightly, I faced the prospect of more notoriety. It frightened me, it made me feel helpless – and that angered me into wanting to fight. 'Will you sit down? Will you have some apple wine?'

'Thank you.' He chose an armchair by the fire and, when I had poured us each a glass of the amber liquid which Mrs Benstead and I had fermented the previous year, I placed myself opposite him, perched uncomfortably on the edge of the chair, while he told me what had happened at Gunton Hall.

The Prince of Wales had been entertaining his guests after a day's shooting when his head keeper had arrived and, in front of the entire company, made his allegations. Prince Albert Edward, who always believed the first story he heard and seldom fell prey to second thoughts, had leapt up, ranting and raving, shouting curses on my head. But thankfully some of those present were friends of mine – the Reverend Mr Lancaster, for one, and dear old General Hall, who had known Mama's father and who often came by Orchards for a chat. They had both spoken up for me, as had my uncle Henry. But the prince wouldn't listen until others of his guests, disinterested parties, had argued that in the cause of fairness I ought at least to be given a chance to defend myself.

'The prince was wavering,' Geoffrey told me. 'Then the Duke of Cambridge settled the matter by suggesting a formal enquiry. They've selected Mr Lancaster to question you and write a detailed report to General Hall.'

'What – so that Beck and the gamekeepers can brand me a liar as I'm carted to the Tower? I'm already an outcast. Who's going to listen to me? I've made too many enemies.'

'You also have friends. Good friends. But for them, you wouldn't have been given even this small chance of defending yourself.'

When I thought about it, I realised how much courage it must have taken for any of them to speak out for me against the prince's rage. The good old soldier, the gentle rector, my uncle Henry, and…

From the corner of my eye I surveyed Geoffrey's evening attire. 'How did you get away? He doesn't like his guests to leave early.'

'I said I was unwell.'

'Ah.' So he had lied for me. 'And then you rode thirty miles from Gunton.'

'I had to come and warn you.'

'You were taking a risk.'

'The game seemed worth the candle.'

All at once the air felt alive between us. The room sang with unspoken nuances that made my chest tight and my heart unsteady.

'I think you ought to go.' I got to my feet in such haste that I slopped my wine and jumped back, away from the drips that plopped to the carpet.

Placing his own glass in the hearth, Geoffrey too rose, his eyes on me saying he understood my unease. He draped his cloak over his arm, picked up his hat. 'When Mr Lancaster comes... you won't...'

'I won't mention that you were here.'

'No. Thank you.' He turned to the door, stopped, looked back at me with dark, unhappy eyes. 'I owe you an apology. Several apologies. That day at Willow Cottage... I had no right...'

'It's not important. Don't speak of it.' I didn't want to remember that day. I was already remembering far too much. '*I never lied to you, Rose. Between us, only truth... something apart...*' I wanted him to go before one of us said or did something that would threaten the balance of all our lives.

'I must speak of it! I can't bear to have you think... I expected too much from you. It was puerile. C–crassly romantic... I blamed you, when the fault was mine. I was angry with you, when someone else had caused my pain. Forgive me, please.'

The hurt in him reached out to me, penetrating all my defences. I heard myself say, 'Are you really so unhappy?'

He shook his head, not so much in negation as to say that he wouldn't talk about it. 'You're not to blame for that. Don't think of it. It was my choice, my cross to bear. If only...' He stopped himself, but the tension was strong between us, a force trying to draw us together, and when he spoke again his voice was low and passionate: 'I never knowingly lied to you. I just wasn't free to...'

'It doesn't matter.' I shook my head, holding up a hand to fend off his confessions. 'Go now. It was good of you to come.'

'It wasn't good of me! Rose, I know I hurt you. I know I did wrong by you. But I meant every word of that letter. It's still true. You have only to call and I'll be here, whenever you need me, for whatever reason.' What was he talking about? 'Letter?'

'The one I wrote to you in Brighton. You said you had it.'

'I did, but… I didn't read it all. I was upset. I… I threw it in the fire without finishing it.'

'I see.' Dark blue eyes held steady on mine. 'Then you didn't read the ending.'

I shook my head. 'What did it say?'

'Something like… I'd always be there if you needed a friend. You had only to send word and I'd come. I asked you to reply – to let me know if you were well – and to tell me what really happened.' His mouth twisted. 'I heard the rumours, of course, though I knew it had nothing to do with Hal Wyatt. I—'

'Oh, but it did,' I said, my voice thick with distress. My mouth trembled as tears came hot behind my eyes. 'My father… my father found out I'd been meeting someone. I let him think it was Hal – even when he tried to beat the truth out of me. It seemed easier. I didn't want to make trouble for you. You always made it plain that you weren't making promises. I knew the risks I was running. So how could I ask you for anything? Even when…'

…*even when I found I was going to have your child*… But I couldn't say it. My tears spilled. Through them I saw him put down his cloak and hat and start towards me.

'Don't!' As I flung out my hands to stop him, apple wine described an arc between us, painting a wet stain down his starched white shirt-front, his waistcoat, his evening trousers… He stopped, glancing down at his clothes, while I hung there in sick dismay. 'Oh… Geoffrey, I'm sorry. I'm sorry!'

Without a word, he came closer, eased the wine glass from my nerveless hand and placed it on the mantel. Then he took my face between his hands, making me look at him.

'I'm sorry for all the distress I caused you,' he said. 'If I had known then what I know now… Let me tell you once and then I'll go away and never mention it again. I just want you to know – I love you, Rose. I love you.'

I couldn't move. I felt mesmerised as glowing eyes studied my face for long, agonised moments. 'Please don't!' But it was only the breath of a whisper as he bent his head. His lips met mine softly, shockingly, sending jolts of awful lightning through me. My mind seemed to swoop, common sense retreating in face of my irresistible need. No one else had ever made me feel that way. No one else ever could. Only Geoffrey...

When he felt my response his mouth hardened, claiming mine as of right. We clung together as if we would become part of one another, our mouths hungry, our bodies striving...

Air gasped into my lungs when at last he lifted his head to look at me.

'That's all I need to know,' he muttered hoarsely. 'I'll ask no more, love. The knowing must be enough. But remember, I'm there. I shall always be there.'

He released me so abruptly that I was left swaying, as if the apple wine had gone to my head. I stood there, dazed, long after he had gone, and then I took a lamp into the laundry room and began to examine every inch of the summer curtains, looking for any small holes or imperfections that needed attention before the white linen was stored away ready for next year. That is what I did with my hands and eyes, but my mind was with Geoffrey, and my heart was breaking.

–

Reverend Lancaster came the next day to tell me of what had happened at Gunton and to assure me of his faith in me. He wanted his report to be correct in every detail. He even employed a man to watch by the brick earth in the covert until it could be proved beyond doubt that the little foxes were still there. They were not old enough, or hungry enough, to have wandered the three miles or so necessary for them to have killed those particular pheasants.

Since the cubs were demonstrably not guilty, we concluded that the villain in the case must be the wily old dog fox from Ambleford.

Basil, arriving home from a business foray in the north, also took up my cause. Through his efforts, and through Jack's lurking behind corners and listening to village gossip, we discovered what was probably the truth of the affair.

The under-keeper Pyke had failed in his duties, by falling asleep or perhaps by deserting his post for some warmer pursuit. Later, upon discovering the dead pheasants, and knowing that the estate held no foxes but mine, he had covered his own culpability by accusing me of avian murder.

It took Mr Lancaster some weeks to write his full report, and in the meantime word reached us that the prince was treating his friends and acquaintances to a version of the story in which I figured as something between a traitor and a witch. In Norfolk I was once again chief pariah, variously whispered about, pointed at, or ignored… This distressed Mr Lancaster. Wishing to clear my name as soon as possible, he volunteered to convey his report to the prince in person.

I waited, hardly able to concentrate on anything for thinking of the gentle young rector walking, like Daniel, into the lion's den. If he failed in his mission, he too would earn the prince's displeasure and might even lose his living.

After a few anxious days, I saw his little pony trap come up the drive through December rain. I hurried to open the door and found him smiling at me under a large black umbrella.

'Good news?' I cried.

'Let us rather say – not bad news,' he demurred. 'The prince is more tempered now. More inclined to listen. I believe we shall have a fair hearing at the enquiry. It's to be held at Sandringham early in the New Year. His Royal Highness promises to attend. He'll be staying at Holkham with the Earl of Leicester, who has agreed to act as umpire.'

'I see.' Crestfallen, I grasped at his cricketing analogy in an attempt at humour. 'And who's bowling for my team?'

'Why, I am! Now don't you worry, my dear Mrs Pooley. I shall muster the best field I can find. We shall have your Mr Beck caught in the slips before you can say Jack Robinson. Mark my words.'

Which was all very well, but we were not embarking on a friendly game of cricket. My future rested on the outcome of this enquiry.

–

On a clear cold January day, when the wind blew across the Wash direct from the North Pole, Basil and I rode together in our carriage to our appointment with the prince at Sandringham. The big house was still undergoing renovations, with scaffolding obscuring its outlines, half the roof missing, and piles of bricks and rubble lying about. A footman met us and conducted us through the chaos to an ante-room bare of all furniture save for a row of chairs and what looked to be an old pew from a church. Here we were joined by Mr Lancaster.

We waited a good half-hour before being called into a larger room whose walls were draped in sheeting to contain the dust of work going on above. Since the hearth was full of rubble, four braziers warmed the room. A long table had been placed at one end, with behind it the Earl of Leicester, while to one side, in tall-backed armchairs, sat the Duke of Cambridge – the Queen's cousin, commander-in-chief of the army – and beside him the scowling figure of the Prince of Wales.

His Royal Highness slouched in his chair, bearded chin in hand, eyes narrowed, lips pushed out. Like the spoiled brat he still was, I thought. But that spoiled brat was heir to the throne, and as such he could make or mar my life for ever.

What sort of mood was he in? Not good, I imagined. Lately scandal had surrounded his name – he had been cited as co-respondent in a divorce case; the proceedings promised to be vastly embarrassing for the royal family. I pitied the poor princess.

Throughout the hearing I kept half an eye on the prince, watching his reactions as witnesses came and went. Then Pyke came on.

He could not resist embellishing his tale to make himself the hero – how he caught the three culprits red-handed, or rather, red-mouthed, and recognised them at once; how he set his dog Tyke to chase the foxes off, and how he followed them all the way to the earth in Poacher's Wood – all this in the dead of a moonless night. Cross-questioned by the Earl of Leicester, Pyke talked himself into a pit, for he was making the whole thing up. As this became apparent, the prince's scowl darkened, but now it was directed at the under-keeper. When Pyke left the room, the prince was heard to mutter, 'The fellow's a damned liar.'

After that, my own witnesses were almost an anticlimax – Benstead and the boy Jack stepped in to tell how carefully we had kept the foxes, and there were others who had had some knowledge of the cubs and my handling of them. As a finale, to my astonishment Reverend Lancaster summoned Geoffrey Devlin, who strode into the room and took his place in a determined manner.

'What's it got to do with him?' Basil muttered, but subsided when the prince glared at him and the earl said, 'Quiet, please.'

We exchanged no more than a swift glance of acknowledgement, but my cheeks grew hot and something inside me quirked with insatiable longing. Geoffrey, tall and lithe, elegant in country tweeds, light slanting on his dark hair...

Invited to give his account of my character, he did so in firm tones with no hint of hesitation: 'Mrs Pooley is among His Royal Highness's most loyal servants. She would never wish him harm in any way, and certainly not in the petty, underhand manner of which she is accused. I can assure this court that if Mrs Pooley has a point to make she will make it openly, not sneak about causing malicious damage. It's not her way. Her straightness, her courage, her honesty and her steadfastness are beyond question. Anyone who knows her will most vehemently defend her against these ridiculous charges.'

Hearing him speak out so publicly on my behalf was disconcerting, not to say embarrassing, and I wondered what harm he might be doing his own reputation. However, it seemed that his evidence reminded the prince of other encounters with my 'straightness' and by the time Geoffrey finished I fancied that His Royal Highness was regarding me in a not disapproving manner.

The evidence for the defence was irrefutable. Indeed, before the earl had properly concluded the business, the Prince of Wales was on his feet, coming to shake my hand.

'Mrs Pooley, I can't tell you how delighted I am by this verdict. The whole thing was due to a misconception. Of course I suspected it all along, but justice has to be seen to be done, as I'm sure you will agree. At times one is morally obliged to stand up and defend oneself, if only to clear the air.'

Perhaps he had the coming divorce case in mind.

Geoffrey did not wait to be thanked. He let his eyes meet mine across the room in an intimate, speaking glance, and then he was gone, which may have been as well since Basil seemed put out by what he called 'Devlin interference'.

'He was trying to help,' I said. 'It was kind of him to support us.'

'Seems to me he's always interfering in your affairs,' my husband objected. 'Time he looked to his own wife and left mine to me. *I'd* have defended you – if I'd been asked.'

Overhearing this, Mr Lancaster put in, 'Oh, but as a good husband you're expected to defend your wife, Mr Pooley. Since everyone knows that there has always been a slight... shall we say "rivalry"?... between Ambleford and Orchards, it was far more meaningful for Mr Devlin to speak up.'

Basil scratched his chin, grudging, 'P'raps so, Rector. I hadn't looked at it like that.'

The under-keeper Pyke was dismissed. He didn't leave the area at once but stayed around spreading spite and rumour. He said that I had once threatened to shoot him when he caught me in the pheasant preserves, which was near enough true, but he also claimed, among other calumnies, that I was leader of a gang of poachers. It got so bad that, one night at the local inn, the gentle Ben Chilvers lost his temper in my defence. Pyke ended up with a bloody nose, but when he made complaint all the witnesses swore he had been so drunk he had walked into a door. After that, Pyke vanished from my ken.

Word of my vindication spread. The cloud of suspicion lifted. People couldn't wait to smile on me again and Mama blossomed in the light of social approval: she and Ellen seemed to be out in the carriage half the time, paying and returning calls.

I received many letters – from friends delighting in my return to grace, from acquaintances trying to flatter, and from enemies seeking to cultivate me now that I was in favour again. After the first few, Basil lost interest in them.

Which was fortuitous since one of those messages was definitely not for his eyes. Recognising the handwriting, I hid the envelope under the pile of others on the breakfast table.

'More of the same?' Basil enquired. 'I'll look at them later. I'm off to Lynn. Anything I can bring you?'

'No, nothing, thank you.'

'What about you, Mother H?'

Mama looked up, smiling vaguely, saying, 'Yes, very well, dear, thank you,' which caused us to exchange a covert glance of mingled amusement and dismay.

When he had gone, I looked again at the envelope I had hidden. It was addressed in Geoffrey's hand. Unable to wait, I slit it open with fumbling fingers, making sure Mama remained unaware.

The letter itself was innocuous, a formal message such as any neighbour might have penned. Not even Basil could have objected to a word of it. But Basil might have wondered why there was a small photograph enclosed. My face felt hot as I secreted that photograph in a pocket, while Mama chattered on unheard.

From then on I frequently wore Geoffrey's likeness near my heart in a gold locket brooch. Only I knew it was there, but its nearness comforted me. It was little enough to ask, surely? It wasn't hurting anyone.

However, my conscience troubled me when I heard that Lucy Devlin had taken a bad fall while out hunting. She broke her collar bone – 'Lucky it wasn't her neck,' said the villagers. She was known to be unhappy. Everyone speculated as to why that should be. But, whatever it was, it had nothing to do with me. That marriage had been doomed from the start.

So I argued with myself, but in my heart I did feel responsible, in part. Lucy might not know there was another woman in her husband's life, but she must certainly be aware that Geoffrey didn't love her as he should.

I could only renew my vows never to do anything to hurt her – never again to be guilty of encouraging Geoffrey in any way.

He appeared to have reached a similar decision. That spring, he took his wife off to Italy to convalesce after her accident. They stayed away for most of the year.

–

During the early part of 1870, the involvement of the Prince of Wales as a co-respondent in the Mordaunt divorce case exercised the vitriolic pens of Fleet Street. Although the petition was dismissed, for months afterwards the prince was subject to abuse and jeers whenever he went out in public. Magazines lampooned him in vicious caricatures; scurrilous pamphlets circulated; he was called a 'louse' and it was hoped that he would 'never dishonour his country by becoming king'.

In Norfolk these stories were received with concern, largely on account of the princess, but elsewhere a general ill-feeling against royalty was abroad. The Queen herself caused mutterings – she cost the country a fortune, she and her brood of German brats, and what did the people get in return? Not even a glimpse of her. She remained incarcerated at Windsor, her excuse being continuing grief for her Albert, but there were shocking rumours about her relationship with her Scottish manservant John Brown.

Events in Europe added to the disquiet. The French monarchy fell and a new *République* was declared. Its spirit crossed the Channel. One read of Republican Clubs being formed all across the country – there was one in Norwich – and at a crowded meeting in Trafalgar Square,

French-style caps of liberty were raised and 'The Republic of England' announced. Even in Lynn you could hear anti-royalist remarks, and anti-royalist leaflets blew on the wind down King Street.

Perhaps it was his anxiety over these threats that made the prince so irascible when he visited Sandringham at harvest-time. Despite the inscription which declared that the new house was 'built by Albert Edward and his wife Alexandra in the Year of our Lord 1870', heaps of rubble remained and ceilings were unplastered. The prince was furious and let it be known that he would cancel the Birthday Dinner which he gave to his labourers every 9 November, unless the house was finished by then.

His annoyance galvanised the workers. The remodelled mansion, now called Sandringham House to distinguish it from the old building, was ready for occupation by the time the prince's birthday arrived.

To celebrate the rebirth of his country home, the prince planned a whole series of house-warming celebrations. For Basil and me, and for Mama, came gilt-edged invitations to attend a ball on 2 December.

When Basil came in that evening, Mama and I were in the parlour, she excitedly talking of what we must wear. 'Grace says that crinolines are most definitely out. Oh, we must go up to London, Rose, we really must, to be sure of having the latest pattern.'

'What's this?' Basil enquired, and was shown the invitations, which made him look thoughtful and pull at his gingerish side-whiskers. 'I'd expected to be away that week.'

'That's a shame,' I said. 'Then we shall have to refuse.'

'Oh, but we must go to the ball!' Mama cried. 'We've waited so long. Grace will be so excited...' She paused, puzzling over the tricks her memory played her. 'Grace *was* so excited. Oh, do you suppose...? Could we somehow arrange for her to have an invitation, too? If we were to contact your uncle Henry...'

'In her delicate condition,' I said, 'Grace won't want to be travelling, not even to a Birthday Ball.'

'Oh... no, of course not. I'd quite forgotten.' She passed a hand over her brow as if to straighten her thoughts, then looked from one to the other of us hopefully, like a child eager for treats. 'But *we* shall go, shall we not?'

'Not if Basil has to be away. We can't go without an escort.'

'Perhaps I could rearrange my meeting,' he offered.

'Oh, please do! Please do!' Mama begged.

Later, in the privacy of our room, Basil asked me why I didn't want to go to the ball. He himself was not especially keen on 'do's' of that kind, but he was surprised to find that I felt the same. Surely I didn't want to disappoint Mama when she was so looking forward to it?

My reasons were many and confused. I could not easily bring myself to socialise with people who had reviled me. Besides, I was so habituated to wearing working boots and heavy serge that an evening dress and dancing slippers would feel very strange. No longer the young girl eager for a party, I was a married woman, a working woman.

'That's excuses,' Basil said, watching me narrowly. 'What are you afraid of? You've been up to the big house before. You went to a dinner party there once.'

'Yes, that's so, but...'

'You never talk about it, though. Most women'd be dining out on that tale for years to come.'

'It was a very long time ago,' I said, beginning to unpin my hair as I sat before the dresser mirror.

Basil came to stand behind me, watching me through the mirror. 'Did something bad happen?'

'Bad?' I watched my own reflection, unable to meet his eyes. 'In what way?'

'I heard what happened – it was a rowdy night. Someone got thrown in the lake. Who brought you home?'

An awkward pin had got tangled in my hair. Its extrication enabled me to lift my arms, hiding my face and the flush that was too revealing. 'Why... you know who took me – my uncle Henry.'

'Your uncle Henry was too busy to drive you home. He was occupied with Kitty Hambledown.'

A nervous pulse beat visibly in my throat. 'Who told you that?'

'Kitty Hambledown did.'

'I had no idea you were on such intimate terms with the miller's daughter,' I retorted.

'Blast it, Rose!' He leaned over me, catching my wrists and forcing my arms down in front of me, so that his arms circled me and his face was next to mine, blue eyes glaring at me through the mirror. 'I want to know! What happened that night?'

Hoping he couldn't see the vein in my throat which, to my eyes, was throbbing like a telegraph key, proclaiming my guilt, I said, 'The prince sent for me. I... I'd rather not recount what happened. Suffice to say I repulsed him. That made him angry. And I was afraid. I fled, and… and one of the other gentlemen rescued me and brought me home. I don't speak of it because I don't care to remember it. I have no wish to go back. We shan't be missed.'

'We shall! They say he has a memory like an elephant. Do you want to offend him again? What was it like, that night? I've a right to know. What did he do? What did he say?'

The idea of the prince making advances to me both annoyed and excited him. Disturbed by the prurient light in his eyes, I leapt up and moved away. If he probed into detail of that night he might start to wonder exactly which gentleman had gallantly rescued me. Thank God no one had seen me leave with Geoffrey!

'I do have another reason for not wanting to go,' I said.

'Indeed? What can that be?' He started languidly towards me, with a purpose I recognised.

'The same reason as Grace.'

That stopped him. He stared at me in disbelief, then in a growing wonder that was awful to see. 'You're going to have a child? You're having *my child*?'

'I am.'

'But… That's wonderful!' Laughing, he came and clasped me in his arms, kissing me, then touching my waist with gentle, wondering fingers. 'When?'

'Early summer. Probably May.'

'Oh, Rosie…' As he looked at me, his eyes misted. 'Rosie, that makes me so proud… But May…' He did quick calculations in his head. 'You'll only be four months on by the time of the ball. Of course we must go. I'll buy you such a gown as you never saw. Yes! We'll go to London to buy it. And Mother H, too. You must have everything just right.'

His unfeigned joy was a relief. If he was pleased then I could be pleased. No one would take this baby from me. It would be something of my own – something to love and care for. I began to look forward to the spring.

–

The evening of the ball was an evening of bright moonlight, with frost sparkling along the edges of Commodore Wood. Our invitations saw

263

us safely past the police guard at the gate and then we were heading down the drive among other conveyances all queuing for their turn by the red and white porch.

And then the house… Light and noise and gaiety. Brilliant light, night turned to day by gas lighting which flooded the scene. And the noise – the orchestra playing in the gallery while in the Great Saloon below politicians and princes chatted amiably with Norfolk neighbours. A flurry of silks and tulles, a glitter of gold and jewels… Three hundred guests came to help celebrate the twenty-sixth birthday of the Princess of Wales.

We stood in line to be announced and to be greeted by our hosts. Here was the princess, stunning in pink despite being five months pregnant, despite her limp – the 'Alexandra limp' they called it, and some idiot women copied it to be like her, perhaps thinking to flatter her. She had become a leader of fashion. Around her slender throat she often wore a jewelled ribbon, and many of the ladies present had taken up that charming idea, including myself – my ribbon was dark green velvet, matching the trimmings of my gown. Pinned to the ribbon I wore the locket brooch that carried Geoffrey's likeness.

My hand sought the locket and, as if my thought had summoned him, in that same moment I saw him.

Our eyes met across the room with a force that robbed me of breath. I hadn't expected him, had thought he was still in Italy, but he had been watching me, waiting for me to notice him. I felt as though I had been punched, somewhere in my middle, and I was conscious of the child nestling there. My hand went instinctively to protect it – or perhaps to conceal it. Nausea stirred in me. Perspiration pricked out from every pore. A slow smile curved Geoffrey's lips as the crowd closed between us. But from then on I covertly watched for him.

Lucy was never far from his side, delicate in a froth of blue silk. She still habitually shielded her mouth, but she no longer hung back, seeking shadows; instead she clung close to Geoffrey, clutching his arm, seeming to be drawing comfort and strength from his nearness. There seemed to be a new serenity about her. Their stay in Italy must have wrought some change. I was glad for them. Yes, of course I was.

Princess Alexandra greeted us gaily and graciously, and introduced us to the handsome young equerry who accompanied her – Oliver Montagu, an officer in the Royal Horse Guards, son of the Earl of Sandwich. One of the most eligible bachelors in the kingdom, he was her devoted friend, her perfect knight and champion. His feelings showed clear in the way he looked at her. I pitied him as he stood beside her while she made sure all her guests were equally welcomed.

And then we were being greeted by the prince himself, his smiling glance assessing my figure as he bent to kiss my hand.

'Mrs Pooley. Delighted to see you. And Mrs Hamilton – a pleasure, ma'am. Well, Pooley, you should think yourself a lucky man. Not every pretty girl comes complete with a farm, what?' He laughed heartily at that. 'Knew she'd be snapped up. Told her – you ought to be married, my girl. Keep you out of mischief, eh? Good to see you all. Good to see you.' And we moved on.

We mingled, making conversation, finding old friends, dancing… I was honoured to be engaged by, among others, the Earl of Leicester, Lord Coke, by the Duke of Cambridge, and by one of the younger brothers of the Prince of Wales, Prince Alfred, who was the same age as I. Nervous, I regaled him with the story of my first fox-cubs, named Bertie, Affie and Vicky after himself and his older brother and sister; he was kind enough to be amused.

I danced with my uncle Henry, now promoted to major and one of the prince's most trusted equerries, and then my husband led me through the paces of a polka which, for other dancers, became so energetic that one gentleman crashed to the floor and brought his partner down with him, to general astonishment. The Prince of Wales proved equally lively and had his pretty partner sliding about the polished floor.

When, later, he approached and asked for the pleasure of a dance with me, Basil requested that I be treated with care, 'Because of her condition, sir.'

The prince's interest quickened, blue eyes bright above his beard. 'Ah, so that's the way of it, eh? Trust me, Pooley.'

Somewhere in the middle of the dance, he murmured, 'Glad to see you took my advice. Glad we're friends again. I'll be round to see you. Talk about the farm, eh? After you've had the child, maybe.'

Was that a proposition? Though my heart felt unsteady, I said demurely, 'You'll always be welcome at Orchards, sir.'

The elderly General Hall escorted Mama as we went in to the supper room, where we found ourselves near Geoffrey and his wife and, as neighbours will, we fell into conversation. Geoffrey said that his parents had been forced to decline the invitation to the ball; Sir

Arthur was suffering badly with gout, which was why Geoffrey had come home from Italy to take over the management of the estate.

'Otherwise, we might have stayed longer. My wife adores Italy. Isn't that so, Lucinda?'

A wistful look misted her eyes as she glanced up at him. 'Yes.'

'Well, it's a beautiful country,' Basil said. 'I was in Naples once. Do you know it?'

Lucinda turned great eyes on him. 'Oh, yes!'

She was almost animated as they discussed the city of Naples, leaving Mama and me astounded; neither of us had had any notion that Basil had been abroad. Mama demanded to know when, and why hadn't he said, to which he replied that he hadn't got round to telling us his whole life story but perhaps if we lived long enough he might.

And while this went on Geoffrey and I shared social smiles that covered the private messages we exchanged with our eyes. Undercurrents of longing flowed strong between us. Nothing had changed. Nothing ever would, not for us.

Dancing began again. We all wandered back to the saloon where Coots' band was launching into a Viennese melody.

'Do you waltz, Mrs Devlin?' Basil asked of Lucinda, who cast a horrified look at Geoffrey and said, 'Oh, no. No. I'm afraid...'

'Of course you do,' her husband encouraged.

Her hand was hovering near her mouth, but with both of the men determined to cajole her she gave in and allowed herself to be led away, glancing over her shoulder appealingly at Geoffrey.

Behind me, General Hall harrumphed: 'Looks as if she's being taken to the scaffold! Come, ma'am, shall we find a seat and watch the fun?' He was past dancing, but Mama happily went with him to a couch backed by potted palms and the wooden statue of a Red Indian chief.

After that it was unremarkable that Geoffrey should ask me to share the waltz with him.

Though I stared over his shoulder, not daring to meet his eyes, we communicated by touch and by the easy way we moved together, as if we had been doing it all our lives. How right it felt to be in his arms, to feel his love enfold me...

'You're the loveliest woman in the room,' he said softly.

Though pleasure flushed through me, I laughed, 'That I am not.'

'To me you are.' His voice dropped to a vibrant undertone, 'I've missed you. Have you been well?'

'Quite well. And you?'

'Easier in body than in mind and heart.' His arm at my waist drew me closer as he spoke, his muscles tightening as he felt me stiffen and try to keep away. 'We're doing nothing wrong,' he muttered close to my ear. 'Is it a sin to enjoy a few moments together, in full public view? The princess doesn't think so.'

Her Royal Highness was passing nearby, dancing lightly, despite her stiff leg, in the arms of Oliver Montagu, and on her face as she smiled at her partner was such a look of adoration that I turned my eyes away, feeling that I was intruding.

'If she can steal a little oasis of happiness in the desert of her marriage,' Geoffrey said, 'why can't we?'

I did look at him then. 'She wouldn't do anything wrong! I won't believe that of her.'

'Nor I. Nor I! But she finds comfort with Montagu, and how can we blame her? God knows the provocation is there. Her husband makes no secret of his own wanderings.'

As we whirled in the dance, I caught sight of Basil, gamely trying to entertain a blushing Lucinda. He was never a graceful dancer. He must have stepped on her gown, or her toe – something made them falter and stop and I saw him apologising, reddening to the roots of his hair. A wave of sickening guilt caught at me.

'But *my* husband isn't unfaithful,' I said. 'He tries his best to please me. If he can't be everything I wanted, then… then the fault is mine, not his. My dreams were always too high and wild. I should be grateful for his protection. He's a good man, by his lights.'

'You care for him?'

I thought about that, wanting to be honest, watching the room pass behind his shoulder. 'I wouldn't want to hurt him. I owe him a great deal. I think you should know… I'm carrying his child.' I looked up as I spoke, so I saw the shadow that crossed his eyes at the news.

He regarded me steadily, sadly, while our feet continued to move in sweeping rhythm. 'He's a f-fortunate man,' he said. And he drew me in closer, his cheek a breath away from my brow, his hand enfolding mine, our bodies swaying in unison as the music carried us round. 'I wish you both joy.'

I glimpsed the conductor's baton up on the curtained gallery, marking off time, marking off the last moments of my last dance with

Geoffrey. Though we hadn't said it out loud, I had a feeling we had just said goodbye.

He and Lucinda left soon afterwards. I didn't see them go but the crowded room was suddenly empty. My head was heavy with tears. My heart ached.

'Damn it, where's Devlin gone?' The prince strode up, in a temper caused by the defection of Geoffrey and his wife. 'Sneaked off, eh?'

'I think his wife was feeling unwell, sir,' I said.

'Well, it's too bad. It's really too bad of them! I won't have people leaving early, spoiling the fun. You can tell him, when next you see him, that I'm most displeased. I don't care what the excuse is. Pregnant, is she?'

All around us people looked askance at the free use of such an indelicate word in company.

'I really don't know, sir.'

'Well, if she's not, she ought to be. Only way to keep a woman in her place, eh, Pooley? Keep her busy. Keep her out of mischief. No, damme, I'm annoyed. Really annoyed.'

One of his beautiful partners slid up, her white hand insinuating itself under his arm as she pouted up at him. 'But *I* haven't deserted you, Bertie. Is little Mrs Devlin prettier than I?'

His brow drew down momentarily, then he gave a shout of laughter. 'No, by George! Not by a long chalk. Let them go. What do we care? Come on – another jig. Another jig!'

Everyone joined in the merriment – even the princess, standing close beside Oliver Montagu.

–

Hypocrite that I was, I kept Geoffrey's likeness in my locket, though now I put the locket away, wrapped in a square of black velvet in a corner of my jewel case. I took it out now and then, when the longing got too unbearable. Perhaps one day my daughter or granddaughter would wear it, and find the picture and wonder. As for jewellery, I had other pieces in plenty, some from Great-grandmama and Aunt Agnes, some beautiful items which had belonged to my mother, and some bought for me by my husband. Though most of these last were too gaudy for my taste, I wore them to please him. Those months when I was breeding were the happiest Basil and I ever shared.

Fecundity was in the air. My sister Grace produced her daughter, Mary Anne, in January, and then in April Princess Alexandra, who was in residence at Sandringham, went unexpectedly into labour. Despite the fact that all her children had been born prematurely, nothing was ready for her confinement. Essentials were hurriedly sent for, local shops plundered; the villages were alive with gossip.

Poor princess. Her little Alexander lived only a matter of hours. She was obliged to watch from her bedroom window as the tiny coffin was borne across the park, followed by her husband and her two small sons. Mama and I, with Narnie, attended the service.

We laid a posy of spring flowers among the grander wreaths on the sad little grave beside the path. My heart went out to the princess. I wept for her sorrow and prayed with all my soul that my own child should be safe.

Basil, who had been away for several days, was angry to discover that I had been to the funeral. He forbade me to go out again before our child was born. And I, touched by his concern for me, obeyed him, though the incarceration was a trial of my patience – I was never good at sitting idle.

Our son, George Victor, was born at noon on Thursday 11 May, 1871. He emerged yelling thinly, a wrinkled, red little gnome of a child with a funny tuft of yellow hair and his father's big hands and feet. In response to the child's wailing, I heard my husband shout aloud for sheer joy. His boots pounded on the stairs and, despite the doctor's protests, he erupted into the room, shouting, 'A boy? Is it a boy? Let me see!' Shown his son, he burst into tears and came to kneel by the bloody bed sobbing hoarsely, muttering incoherently, 'Blast! Blast!' He lifted his face – drowned blue eyes, flushed skin, yellow hair – so like the baby it made me laugh and cry all at once.

'A son,' he croaked. 'Blast, Rose, you've given me a son!'

Biting my lip to stop the crazy laughter that welled up in me, I said through my tears, 'Are you pleased?'

'Pleased? Why... I could fly!'

He leapt up and in a whirl of motion ran from the room. I heard him thudding down the stairs and out by the front door, where he could be heard yelling, 'It's a boy! A boy!' to the gardeners and then to the yardman – and to Ben Chilvers, who happened to be passing by and took the news back with him to Dersingham.

Basil's undisguised delight touched me and deepened my fondness for him. This was something we truly shared, our love for our son.

'Let me hold him,' I begged the midwife as she cleaned the baby's face. 'Please… just let me hold him.' I wanted him now, before someone could snatch him away from me.

Though she would have preferred to wash him properly, and me too, before she let me handle him, she swathed his naked body in a blanket and placed him in my arms.

Great bewildered eyes stared at me from that little wizened face. He was a tiny, warm bundle, weighing scarcely anything but oh so alive, so very dear. My son. Such a flood of feeling welled inside me that it rose and swamped me from toes to scalp, waves of emotion, fierce protective love and a sweet, sweet fulfilment. This tiny scrap of a person looked at me and laid claim to my aching heart.

'Hello, monkey,' I murmured, awarding him the pet name which Mama thought disgraceful but which, to him and me, was a secret way of saying that I loved him utterly.

-

During my lying-in I was touched to receive a visit from the Princess of Wales and her three older children. Though still pale and sad after the recent loss of her own baby, she smiled on me and admired Georgie, and even held him in her arms, while the young princes, Eddy and George, and four-year-old Princess Louise, wandered curiously about, peering in cupboards and wardrobes, clambering on the furniture and generally behaving 'like a band of wild Indians' as Mama complained later. I have to admit that I wouldn't have allowed children of mine to behave in that way, but Princess Alix was so gracious and indulgent, laughing at them even as she chided them, and kissing Georgie's little hands, that I lay marvelling at her presence in my humble bedroom.

-

My little monkey occupied me almost exclusively during that summer. He was not a big, lusty child, but he grew fair and healthy as any mother could wish. I delighted in watching him develop. The times when we were alone together while he fed at my breast were so sweet that I often sat on, holding his small, tender warmth and watching him breathe, long after he was replete and snoozing.

Basil took an equal delight in the child. He never thought it unmanly to bounce his son on his arm or play, 'Piggy went to market', to make Georgie give the funny little giggle that we all adored. I began to understand why people said that a child could cement a marriage. Certainly Georgie brought Basil and me closer.

'One would think he had fathered half a dozen children already,' Felicity Wyatt remarked with amusement. 'He handles Georgie so capably. My own papa never had anything to do with any of us until we were of an age to hold a rational discussion.'

She and her mother and sisters called frequently, drawn by the magnet of the baby, over whom they all cooed and sighed. Kitty was especially fond of him and never minded if he was sick all over her skirts.

My mind being fully occupied with my son, I was for the first time grateful to have McDowall as a farm manager. Everything seemed to be going well with the farm. I took Georgie out to show him the fields and the orchards, the barns and the yards, the docile cows and the woolly sheep, the baby pheasants parading after their mother, the rooks flying, and the hares... the hares, of course! I could laugh even at them now, seeing Georgie's delight in them.

Mama seemed happier than she had been for years, with three grandchildren to cosset. She divided her time between Orchards and Thetford. When she was with us, Narnie frequently came to visit – so frequently that she all but lived with us, but I was too content to object. Life had settled into a calm pool and I was reluctant to stir the mud that waited below the unrippled surface.

–

Johnny's presence caused the only unease in those halcyon days. During his first summer vacation from university, he came home out of curiosity to see his young nephew, for whom he stood godfather. He went out a good deal, off to see the Esham people, or to spend days with George Pooley, but he was with us more than he had been since Father died. He remained a difficult, withdrawn young man, and to Basil he was cold and often deliberately rude.

One evening at supper, Johnny regaled us with accounts of loose talk he had heard in the backrooms of Cambridge – treacherous, anti-royalist talk, grievances against the Queen but mostly against her oldest son, his wild lifestyle, his sexual adventures, his gambling 'with *our* money, granted out of the nation's coffers'. The mutters had even repeated the calumny that the death of the infant prince had been a 'wretched abortion'.

'Don't you dare repeat such lies at my table!' I exclaimed.

My brother flashed me an angry look. 'I didn't say I believed it, I said it's what people are saying. Lots of people. Sequestered here in Norfolk you don't hear the half of it. Mr Dilke even stands up in Parliament and makes republican speeches. People are starting to hate the whole royal family. They call them "a bunch of Germans". They'd like to see 'em all hanged.'

At this Mama cried out in horror, her hands to her throat.

Basil leaned to lay a comforting hand on her arm. 'Don't worry, Mother H. It'll all pass over. It's a storm in a tea-cup.'

'Oh, is it?' Johnny retorted. 'What do you know about it?'

'I get about. I know what goes on.'

'You wouldn't know a republican from a rhinoceros! You can't even read without a finger on the page to guide you.'

Throwing aside his napkin, Basil got to his feet, his face flushed. 'I won't be spoken to like that in my own house!'

'Whose house?' Johnny too leapt up, sending his chair to crash against the sideboard. Mama was in tears, biting her knuckle.

'It's me that's the legal tenant here!' Basil shouted.

'Only while my trustees let you stay!'

'Then perhaps you'd like us to go? I don't need this place, you know. I can be gone tomorrow. Rose and I—'

'Oh, please!' I jumped up in alarm. 'Stop this arguing. You're upsetting Mama. This is your home, Johnny. Of course it is. No one disputes that your rightful place is here. Please stop and take a deep breath before one of you says something he'll regret.'

They glowered at each other, dislike and distrust singeing the air between them. In the end, it was the more mature Basil who sighed, 'She's right. Like it or not, boy, we're family. We can't fall out over this.'

'And don't call me "boy",' Johnny said bitterly. 'I wish you'd all stop treating me like a child!'

My brother proved to be right about the unrest that was growing under the banner of republicanism. Newspapers and magazines told of crowded meetings, vitriolic speeches, violent demonstrations... The danger came fully home to us when we were offered police protection, a guard at our door in case anti-royal agitators took it into their heads to strike at the prince through his Sandringham properties. We ourselves refused the offer, but Basil slept with a shot-gun at hand. After Georgie was born, he didn't spend a night away from home. Not for months. We were more harmonious than I had ever dared to hope.

–

Since my father died, with Sir Arthur Devlin increasingly eccentric, hostilities between Orchards and Ambleford had dwindled into a lingering rivalry between the Devlin men and ours. This culminated, in the summer of 1871, in a fist fight at one of the local inns, followed by a court case in which four men were fined – two of ours and two of theirs. As a result, Geoffrey Devlin wrote to Basil to suggest that each of them should pay his own workers' fines and that any remaining ill-feeling might be dissipated by a cricket match.

Basil, being an excellent bowler, welcomed the challenge, and the match was organised for September. Johnny was still with us and, despite disagreements with Basil, was eager to play his part in defeating the detested Sir Arthur's men. Sir Arthur himself was by that time out of reach, growing ever more eccentric and confined indoors because of ill-health.

I didn't attend the cricket match, my excuse being breast-feeding Georgie, but I heard all about it later when Basil and Johnny came rolling in hilarious with ale and victory. The match had been going to Ambleford until Ben Chilvers, called in to bat for our team, came out to face his father's bowling. Arms flailing like a windmill, Amos had thundered down the pitch, bowled – and Ben cracked it for six. He had continued to score heavily, while Amos grew angrier and angrier, ball after ball scorching down the wicket to be sent sky-rocketing, for sixes and fours, until the match was well won.

The Ambleford team's disappointment had been drowned in Mr Geoffrey Devlin's hospitality, though during the celebrations Ben Chilvers had had to leave – one of his children had been taken ill.

'Which one?' I asked in sudden unease.

'Alice,' Basil said. 'But it's just some childish ailment. Probably a cold. You know how Chilvers dotes on all his three.'

That was true enough, but even so I was concerned for little Alice.

As an afterword to the cricket match, that evening a drunken Amos Chilvers came shouting up to the house, accusing us of turning his son against him. He threw a half-brick through our conservatory window with a great shattering of glass and, when Basil went out with a shotgun, Chilvers offered to fight him hand to hand. He swung one wild punch and fell down, too drunk to stand up. Basil and Johnny dragged him to one of the outhouses, locked the door and left him.

'You remember all that trouble there used to be between us and Ambleford,' Johnny said later. 'And that fire that was started and blamed on me. I often wondered if Amos Chilvers was behind it. Victor used to tell me how Chilvers hated Father. And the troubles did stop after Father died. Don't you think we ought to tell the Devlins what sort of man they're employing?'

'You can't blacken a man's name without proof,' Basil said.

'We've got proof! He was here tonight, shouting threats and abuse. He broke a window.'

'He was drunk,' I said. 'He was upset. Besides, if he was the one who caused the trouble I'd rather not give him cause to start it again. Let him sober up and then let him go. He's an old man, eaten up with ancient grievances, but he's still Ben Chilvers' father.'

'I'll talk to him,' Basil decided. 'When he's sober, I'll let him know what we suspect. And I'll tell him if he doesn't leave us be he'll be for the high jump next time.'

Amos Chilvers was let go next day, still truculent, but silenced by whatever Basil had had to say. After that I forgot him; more important worries arose when it became evident that little Alice was sickening for something a lot worse than a childish cold.

It was the beginning of the terrible '71 epidemic of low fever.

Four

The source of the typhus was thought to be a drain near Wolferton Creek, where the chapel folk had had their Sunday school outing and some of the children had been found playing in the dirty water. But whatever the source, its effects were all too evident: throughout the local villages, men, women and children took sick. In the heat of late summer the disease spread like gossip.

With harvest being brought in at the same time, every able-bodied person was needed either in the fields or nursing the sick. As I went about my tasks I saw young Reverend Lancaster fumblingly binding sheaves, and old Billy Morton, who was eighty, driving a laden wagon; Milky Mickleborough, though nearly blind, climbed up to thatch my stacks when Benstead fell sick. Everybody helped.

The Wyatts lent their aid in nursing, too; we went from house to house about the villages as need arose. The beautiful Chloe, bent over a steaming tub, possing bed linen, was something to see, as was young Verity spooning medicine into Bessie Rudd, who had run her farm single-handed for as long as I could remember, and Felicity weeping over a dying child. So many pictures in my memory. So much sorrow.

Young Alice Chilvers recovered. We rejoiced at that, but her father and little brother had fallen sick, too. Benjie threw off the illness, but his father lay near to death for days until the crisis passed and his mind cleared again. I shared Pam's relief that her family had been spared.

Between working in the fields and tending the sick to all hours, to my sorrow I lost my milk and was forced to begin feeding Georgie with cow's milk. But that did mean I could leave him more in Narnie's care and not have to keep hurrying home every few hours.

'It's not right!' Basil ranted at me. 'Your place is here with your son! If you bring the fever home to him—'

'I shan't!' I cried, though that was my deepest fear and I watched Georgie constantly for any sign of fretfulness. I was careful always to

275

change my clothes when I came in hot and dishevelled from a house of sickness, and to wash all my exposed skin, and keep our room well aired. Miss Florence Nightingale's ideas about hygiene and cleanliness had been instilled in me by my aunt Agnes.

We lost Bessie Rudd, and Annie Mickleborough the laundry-woman. We lost several old friends and some younger ones. Someone mentioned that one of the McDowall children was down with the disease, too, but when I called at the house on the corner of the lane Mrs McDowall would hardly open the door.

'Yes, it's our Stella,' she informed me through a two-inch gap. 'But it's all right, Mrs Pooley, I'm nursing her. She's doing all right. You've enough to worry about without concerning yourself with us.' Somewhere in the house a child cried out for her and she glanced round, clutching a shawl round her throat. 'I'm coming, love!' she called and looked again at me. 'Thank you for calling, Mrs Pooley, but if we need you we'll send. I can look after my own.' And she closed the door in my face.

Had I imagined it, or had she been bruised around the eye and on her throat – bruises she had held the shawl to hide? Had she suffered an accident, or was she sickening, too?

'She's fine,' McDowall said when I asked him. 'Och, she had a wee bit of a fall, that's all. Rushing to attend the child. It's always happenin'. She worries too much, does Mary. Makes a real martyr of hersel'. Take it slow, says I, but she willna'. You know what some females are like.'

Partridge shooting continued, though in the heat of that autumn the sport was thin, the birds scarce and wild. Nevertheless there were volleys off in the woods as I drove back from Dersingham one October day and was accosted by Amos Chilvers. He stepped out of a hedge and grabbed the pony's bridle, stroking its nose and murmuring to it in a way that calmed it – I had forgotten his reputation as a Whisperer, master of the old horse magic.

'What is it you want?' I asked, keeping my head up and looking him straight in the eye.

'Just a word, that's all.'

'A word about what?'

Taking off the round-crowned hat he habitually wore, he reached inside his fustian jacket and brought out a carving – a fine carving of a horse standing alert with ears pricked. This he presented to me, eyes bright and watchful over a rough moustache now wholly grey. 'It's for the boy.'

'Why...' I was so astounded that I found myself accepting the gift. 'Thank you. It... it's quite beautiful. Georgie will love it.'

'It's nothin'.' He stepped away, unable to look at me for embarrassment. 'For a Hamilton, yore not so bad. Well, don't let me hold you up. Go you on!' This last was for the pony as he clapped his hat on its rump and it set out again, barely giving me time to gather the reins.

The incident caused me a deal of puzzlement. Was the gift a way of apologising, or of saying thanks because I had helped to nurse Ben and the children? I should never fathom Amos Chilvers.

The wooden horse stood on a corner of the dressing-table, where Georgie could see it from his cot. He lay smiling at it, talking gurgling baby talk, his little dimpled hands working as if he would like to grab it if only he knew how.

October became November. The last of the funerals was held; the last invalid began to regain strength. As the days went by without new fever cases, Mr Lancaster held a special service of thanksgiving that the toll had not been worse.

But the typhus had not done with us yet. When the Prince of Wales came to Sandringham for the shooting, he was already sickening with the disease. Within days he was desperately ill. His groom, who had also fallen prey to the illness, died of it. The prince looked likely to follow him. The news was grave.

After the warm autumn, winter arrived fierce and early, with heavy snows that froze solid, forming a thick white icing over the land. Amid those snows, the royal family gathered – brothers, sisters, cousins and spouses crammed into Sandringham House and spilled over as house-guests at other villas on the estate. The impending drama drew journalists, too, and crowds of ordinary folk from near and far to wait in apprehension by the gate for the bulletins which, during days of highest crisis, were issued every few hours.

And then Kitty Wyatt also became ill. She was with us at Orchards, nursing Georgie, when she first complained of feeling unwell, so Felicity took her home. By the evening, Kitty was feverish, her skin erupting in red spots. When I called the following morning to see what news there was, Mrs Wyatt wept silent, helpless tears. Was her darling Kitty to be the last, belated victim of the low fever?

However, the doctor diagnosed not typhus but measles. Kitty had suffered that illness in childhood and this, it appeared, was a mild recurrence, no doubt brought about by debility following her recent exertions during the epidemic. How we teased her for alarming us all.

For my little monkey, though, measles was no teasing matter. His body broke out in the scarlet rash; he was feverish and fretful; he cried constantly and pitifully. And then he was quiet, suffering, burning up with the disease in a way that not all the doctor's potions, nor all the cool water, nor all the love in the world could halt.

While I nursed my son, news from Sandringham filtered through to me, often via Reverend Lancaster, who was attending the big house regularly to offer comfort. His Royal Highness's condition was grave – so grave that the Queen herself journeyed to West Norfolk by rail and joined the anxious party at the big house. When the prince rallied, Her Majesty left, only to be summoned again within days because his doctors thought the end was near. Mr Lancaster said that Her Majesty was distraught; she was prey to a superstitious terror that her oldest son was doomed to die on 14 December, ten years to the day after his father passed on.

'So what if he dies?' Basil said bitterly. 'The Queen's got plenty of other children. I've only got one boy. If he dies, what'll I do, eh, Reverend? Shall you be able to explain it to me?'

'I suggest you should put it in God's hands, Mr Pooley,' the rector replied.

Basil sat by the cradle day after day, watching our son grow weaker. And in between whiles he raved at me: 'You should have stayed with him! He needed his mother's milk. You were off nursing other folks' children when you should have been at home with your own. If he dies, Rose, I'll never forgive you. Never!'

Narnie too held me responsible. Whenever she came to the house she would stand over Georgie, her eyes dark with doom. 'You should never have brought that horse into the house,' she pronounced one day, nodding at the carved toy. 'That's what's doing it.'

'The horse?' Basil repeated. 'Why, what—'

'He's a witch, that man Chilvers.'

Denying my own sudden terror, I gasped, 'That's superstition!'

But Basil's eyes were on the horse, his mind working, remembering things he had heard about Chilvers. He grabbed the toy.

'Basil, no!' My cry hung in the quiet room as he flung the horse on to the fire.

I watched it burn, feeling sick. Remembering Victor dying amid the fire of an explosion... myself as a child, trapped in a stable, with hooves trampling near me... nightmare memories mixed up with formless, primeval fears about witchcraft and vengeance, about carven images imbued with spells...

'You've killed him,' I choked.

'What?' Basil glared at me. 'It's wood! You can't kill wood. What's the matter with you, Rose? Are you mad?'

I said nothing. I couldn't. I sank down beside the cradle where my son lay burning up with fever. In some dark, pagan part of my mind, I was sure that by destroying the horse Basil had destroyed our baby.

A pall seemed to hang over not only the farm but the whole county, amid clouds laden with snow. Though it was bitterly cold, with hard snow lying frozen inches thick along the lanes, every day crowds gathered by the Norwich gates at Sandringham House to wait for news of the prince. Her Majesty's terror, reported by the press, infected many people as 14 December approached.

That fatal Thursday seemed to promise a crisis for both the prince and Georgie. I felt that their fate was linked somehow. If one survived, then both would. If not...

The day came. Long minutes dragged into hours and still both patients battled their illness. The day passed, and an endless night.

In the morning someone came running with news of the latest cautious bulletin from the big house: '*His Royal Highness has rallied a little*', it said. For Prince Albert Edward, the crisis was past, the long recovery begun.

The crisis passed for Georgie, too. He died that night, 15 December 1871. He was seven months and four days old.

–

After we buried our darling my husband found business that kept him out of the house. He blamed me for everything.

Left alone, I too blamed myself, for neglect and for accepting a gift from Amos Chilvers, and for having let my first baby be taken from me. Perhaps this was a punishment. Perhaps I was fated never to raise a child. I believe I came near madness. I sat in my room, wanting no food, nor company, assailed by black headaches that made me want nothing but to sleep, my mind shutting out a truth it could not bear. When Pam Chilvers came to visit me I refused to see her – I couldn't have borne her sympathy when a part of me blamed her father-in-law for ill-wishing my baby.

Reverend Lancaster helped me. He came and sat with me, talking of courage and strength, and listening as I poured out my grief, reliving memories of those few short months when my little monkey was my whole life. I also blurted out my superstitious fears about the wooden horse, and he helped me see how irrational such thoughts were. Why should Amos Chilvers wish to harm an innocent child?

Grace brought her children to stay, to offer what comfort she could. I was grateful, but in the night, if Tommy or Mary Anne cried, I often found myself out of bed, imagining it was Georgie needing me.

–

Before Christmas, I was touched by another personal visit from the princess, driving herself in a pretty little horse-drawn sleigh jingling with silver bells. Pale from her recent worries, but with a new light of contentment in her eyes, she came to me without words and embraced me warmly before drawing back to look at me.

'I too have lost a child,' she reminded me. 'I know how it feels. Oh, my dear, I feel so sad for you. Forgive me. I would have come to see you before, but, as you know, I have had other things on my mind.'

'You're too kind, ma'am,' I managed. 'Thank you. And the prince – how is His Royal Highness now?'

'He is recovering, thank God. Still weak, but recovering. It's good to be needed, don't you agree? I can't tell you how happy we are, here in our beloved Sandringham.' She sighed, with a little wistful smile. 'If only we could stay for ever how happy I should be.'

She wouldn't stay. She had to get back to Bertie. But she promised she would visit me often. She loved the homely farm. And she had always known, from the moment we met, that she and I would be friends.

When it was sure that the prince was out of danger, so great was the relief that the whole nation joined in the celebrations. If His Royal Highness had planned it, it could not have worked out better. His illness had brought the Queen out of her incarceration at Windsor; her people had been vouchsafed a sight of her and they had shared her deep anxiety over her son; but most of all they had been privileged a glimpse into the abiding love that Princess Alexandra had for her husband. The story of her vigil by his bedside, her patience and fortitude through all manner of stresses, and now the way she stood beside him, radiant in the new togetherness they shared, touched all our hearts. In a brief few weeks, the spectre of republicanism withered.

For the princess, a semblance of happiness had come at last. For me, it remained ever more elusive.

Basil and I remained apart in spirit. He was out most days, when the weather allowed, and when it did not he shut himself in the farm office, writing painstaking letters or poring over newspapers. Outwardly, nothing appeared to have changed between us. Only he and I knew that when we were alone he hardly looked at me, hardly spoke to me, never touched me. Often in our room he would sit by the empty cradle, looking down into it, rocking it. Remembering…

It hurt me to watch him, and to know that he still blamed me. We might have comforted each other, but between us now the chasms opened wider and deeper than ever.

'Perhaps we should put the cradle away,' I said one night when the house was still, with a silence that told of more snow falling. 'It only reminds us—'

He looked up, so that I saw the tears in his eyes. 'Oh, yes, you'd like that! You'd like to put that right away out of sight, the way you've put him.'

'Basil… Please don't. I know you miss him. I miss him, too. Don't you know that?'

He dashed a hand across his eyes, watching the cradle again. 'You never wanted him.'

'Don't say that!'

'You never wanted me – why should you want my child?'

'Oh, my dear…' Drawn by the pain in him, I went to stand by him, a hand kneading his shoulder. 'I do care for you. There has been fond feeling between us. And you must believe… Georgie… my little monkey…' Tears had got into my voice. 'You will never know how much he meant to me. Or how much I grieve for him. And blame myself. Though I don't know what I could have done differently.'

Shaking away from my touch, he got up and turned burning eyes on me. 'You could have stayed with him. You could have been a proper mother. Your place was *here*, not roaming around after Chilvers and his brood, and all the rest of them. They're not *your* people, Rose. You don't own them.'

'An employer has certain duties,' I said stiffly. 'While I keep the farm—'

'Oh, the farm. The bloody farm!' He thrust his face near to mine, making me step away from the hatred I sensed in him. 'That's all you ever cared about. What will you do when Johnny comes home and wants to take over? I shan't stop him, you know. I'll give up the tenancy. Gladly. God knows I never wanted it.'

The chill of the room was reaching me. I huddled into my shawl for comfort, saying, 'We can put this behind us. We can begin again. We won't forget Georgie, but—'

'If you tell me there'll be other children,' he raged, 'I'll hit you.'

Feeling my eyes sting with distress, I shook my head. 'What do you want me to say? Shall we go on like this – like strangers? Basil... it's cold. Come to bed.'

After the candles were extinguished, in the cocoon of a bed warmed by stone bottles, he lay with his back to me. I wished to sleep, except that too many nights had passed with only cold silence between us and if we were to mend our marriage we had to re-find some sort of sharing. So I stretched out my hand and touched him. He felt warm beneath the flannel nightshirt.

'Basil... Won't you hold me? I'm cold.'

I played the coquette, against both nature and inclination. In truth I felt no desire for him at all, but duty and fondness drove me to caress him, until I felt the undeniable stirring in him. With little preamble and no finesse he threw himself upon me, and forced his way into me.

I lay beneath him feeling cold, letting him ride it out. His body battered me, tearing at me, hurting me. Using me. That was all it was.

At last he fell away, panting, lying for a while on his back before his breathing quietened and he turned away from me, tucking the blankets round him. He had never been quite so brutal before, never taken me without at least a show of consideration. Was this how it was to be? For the rest of our lives?

–

On a February day when the air held hints of coming spring, when the birds were active, the bees busy in their hives, two cultivators and a drill out, and the first crocus peeping through beside the drive, I came in from the lambing pens to be met by a distraught Mama.

'Ellen has given in her notice! She wants to leave immediately! She says her family needs her.'

The lady's maid herself, when called to explain the suddenness of her defection, looked pale and peaky, her eyes reddened from weeping.

'Is there illness in your family?' I asked.

She hung her head and looked at the floor. 'Yes, madam.'

'Then of course you must go. But there's no need to hand in your notice. When the situation improves...'

'No, madam. I shan't come back.'

She had never been the most communicative of persons. I could extract no more from her, nor did I have time or energy to try. She left that same day; Benstead drove her to the station.

Kitchen gossip, naturally, found more diverting reasons to explain Ellen's sudden departure. I was in the passageway, sorting linen in one of the airing cupboards, when I heard Mrs Benstead and Swift discussing the matter. The cook averred that Ellen had received no letter or telegram to inform her of illness in her family, and the maid said that a message could have come to the post office, where Ellen had been only two days before, 'on errands for the missus'.

'Then why,' said Mrs Benstead, 'have she been all red-eyed and sniffly this past two week, heh? And why, if she was on her way to Lancashire, did she buy a ticket for Huns'ton?'

'Is that right?'

'So my Herbert say, and he know the station master well.'

'Then what d'you reckon is the answer?' Swift asked.

'If you want my opinion, there's a man in the case.'

'A man?' The maid was aghast. 'But she seem such a quiet sort o' mawther.'

'Them's the sort you have to watch.'

'Lor'... But who...'

'Ah, well, that's the question.'

At that point I closed the airing cupboard door with a bang and the discussion ended abruptly.

Whatever the truth of Ellen's leaving, in her absence Mama grew more demanding of my time and attention. She had become used to having someone with her all the time, tending her and fussing her. We immediately advertised for another maid, but then Mama complained that she didn't want a stranger, she wanted Ellen, she didn't understand why Ellen had had to go, and if she couldn't have Ellen then she wanted Narnie, it wasn't fair that… and so on.

Basil, who until then had been remarkably tolerant with her, took to losing his temper. 'You're always whining! Nothing's ever right for you. It's time you realised you're a grown woman, not a silly spoiled brat.'

His unkindness made Mama weep. I remonstrated with him, but that only made him angrier, and our quarrels further upset Mama. We were all on edge. Since Georgie died nothing had been right.

And so, because I simply hadn't the energy to cope with Mama as well as all the rest, I drove over to Willow Cottage and asked Narnie if she would come back to the farm.

Narnie blew down her nose and folded her arms over her ample bosom. 'Oh, yes, you'll come and ask for me when you're in trouble. That's all very fine and grand when you need me. But what happens when you find a new maid? Will you send me back to be on my own again? I'm not so sure I want to be back and forth, forever packing and unpacking, at my age. I'm near seventy years old, you know.'

She had never complained about being back and forth between the cottage and Grace's house in Thetford, but I let it go. My strength was at too low an ebb for arguments; I agreed that, if she came, she could stay for as long as Mama wanted her.

'Even when you get a new lady's maid? You'll have to get one. I can't cope with everything my Miss Flora needs, not at my age.'

'Yes, we'll have a new maid as soon as we can.'

'Well now.' Smug satisfaction shone from her. 'Well now. At last you're considering others beside yourself. A pity you didn't turn that way before. For it's my opinion that if I'd been there at the farm, nursing him, that sweet little boy of yours would still be here.'

She might as well have driven a knitting needle into me. 'Narnie…' I said in a low, trembling voice. 'You are the most evil old besom I've ever known, and if Mama didn't need you I wouldn't let you over my threshold, not ever again. If you come to Orchards and make trouble…'

She stared me in the eye, her own gaze cold and unwavering. 'What troubles you have, you brought on yourself, Miss Rose. Still, if it comforts you to blame me instead… my shoulders are broad. But you remember something, too – I know your secret. I've kept it all these years. A word from me would've destroyed your reputation, ruined your marriage. It still could. Force me to it, Miss Rose, and...'

I felt sick as I left the cottage. Though the day was bright with spring, for me it was shadowed with bitter menace, clouds of despair dimming the sun and muffling the birdsong. I never wept easily, but on that day the tears rolled down my face, cooling in the breeze, and I whipped up the pony until the trap jumped and bounced along the lane, tossing me half out of my seat at every rut.

I didn't see the horses until we were almost on them, and then I had only a glimpse of a gleaming chestnut flank and mane, both riders hauling their mounts aside, the man shouting out in protest. We treated them to a shower of dust and stones, driving furiously on before I fully registered the identity of the couple – Geoffrey and his wife. That knowledge made me apply the whip with even more force.

We flew into the yard scattering chickens, going at such a pace that I was forced to swerve to avoid the barn. The trap teetered on one wheel, then settled with a jolt, and the frightened pony reared, getting its legs tangled in the harness. A couple of men stared from the barn, Benstead looked his astonishment from a pigsty, and the boy Jack came running to my aid.

'You all right, Miss Rose?'

'Yes.' I leapt down, tossing him the reins. 'Yes, see to it, will you?' Ashamed of myself – ashamed for risking the horse, and the trap, and ashamed for not being able to hide my distress, I half ran up to the house and to my room, where I threw myself down and wept – really wept – for the first time since Georgie died.

So Narnie returned to the farm to be companion to Mama, and we acquired a new lady's maid. There were new faces in the kitchen, too: Howlett left – she went to a new position in Lynn and her place was taken by two young girls from village families, Starling and Finch. Since we already had the faithful Swift, Narnie remarked sourly that it was becoming a proper aviary, and sounded like one when the lady's maid joined in the kitchen gossip.

The lady's maid, a pert dumpling incongruously named Violet, was a busy little body, always chattering about nothing in particular, though she learned to hold her tongue in Narnie's presence. Mama didn't seem to mind the chatter; Mama's world was becoming more confused with every day.

If emotions at the house were fraught, there was an undercurrent of unrest about the farm too, which at first I put down to my own lack of tolerance. The men seemed to move more slowly; they obeyed orders, but only after a pause; frowns and black looks followed me, and under-breath mutterings, and when two or three were gathered together their conversation would stop as I went by.

Nor was the discontent only at Orchards. Many farms around the district were plagued with petty mischiefs. One of the sail reapers at Ambleford was damaged while left overnight in a field during haying, and even dear old Farmer Pooley found slogans daubed on his barn calling him a 'slave-driver'.

In June, when the shearing gang arrived, the trouble escalated. One of the shearers was a pro-union man who had been working in the south the previous year and now came to spread his doctrine of discontent in Norfolk. Low pay was one of the unionists' main grievances, and bad housing, and the old, old complaint of being robbed of common lands during enclosures. Or so McDowall told me.

'The pay's nowhere near as low as it is in the south,' I argued. 'I agreed to raise it again only last season. The men know the trouble I'm having with damaged crops and increased costs and all the rest.'

'Aye, well,' McDowall rubbed his bony nose. 'Trouble is, they don't always believe it. They can see the signs – ye've acquired an engine and a carriage. There's more servants in the house. Ye can always find the money for fine clothes and jewels and—'

'That's enough!' I would not lower myself to remind him that the things he mentioned came from my husband's generosity, not from the farm's profits.

He spread his hands in a shrug. 'Ye asked me what they were sayin'. If ye don't like it, that's nae fault o' mine.'

'I expect you to stamp out this talk, not agree with it,' I returned. 'I won't condone rabble-rousing at Orchards. You can tell this – this trouble-maker to pack his bags and get off my land.'

I should have known better. The shearers worked as a unit, and if one went, all went. If McDowall had been the kind of steward I needed, he would have reminded me of that; instead he carried out my orders to the letter. By morning, with only half the sheep shorn, the shearers were on strike, though still camping in my barn. They weren't due at their next place for a week, the foreman told me; they had to have somewhere to stay until then.

McDowall proved no help at all: he didn't see what he could do about it; he'd only been following orders. Damning the man in my mind, out of exasperation I decided they could sit it out and whistle for their pay. I sent Benstead in pursuit of all the other gangs in the area, begging them to fit us in. They refused.

Basil, arriving home in the middle of this upheaval, went down to the yard and negotiated a settlement, which involved a promise of extra pay.

'Better that than let the sheep suffer,' Basil said when he returned. 'I've told them there's to be no more union talk while they're here. Why you had to let it get this far, you stupid hen—'

'Don't speak to me like that!'

'I'll speak to you any way I like!' he returned. 'Women shouldn't be allowed in business. You let your emotions get in the way. You lost your silly temper and look what happened. If I hadn't been here—'

'It's McDowall's job to sort these things out, not mine! If he'd handled it differently—'

'Don't blame McDowall. Fact is, a woman isn't suited to this life. The sooner Johnny comes home the better, or this farm'll go to ruin.'

It wasn't true, I thought fiercely. I could manage the farm perfectly well, given proper support from my workers. McDowall had failed in his duty of backing me up. I suspected he had actively encouraged the trouble. Like the affair of the hay, which rotted because McDowall ordered it cut too soon, the incident of the shearers stayed in my mind, niggling, like grit in a shoe.

—

Johnny came home only briefly that year. He accompanied Mama and Narnie on a visit to Thetford and then he went off to spend some weeks with friends in the West Country. Letters told of his enjoyment of Devon, his eager studying of farming methods in that county, and there was mention of a young lady named Clara, sister of a friend he had made at Cambridge.

'Sounds as though he's mashed on the girl,' Narnie snorted.

'Oh, surely not!' Mama replied. 'Why, Johnny's only twenty years old. He can't possibly be thinking of marriage yet.'

Nevertheless, my brother was growing up. In another year he would be leaving university.

–

The newly-formed Farm Labourers' Union spread unrest across the west and south of England. Sporadic strikes broke out; farmers retaliated with lock-outs, some as near to us as Suffolk. The news was reported in the papers and we heard more about it from George Pooley, who was a member of the local Farmers' Club where such news was discussed; like so many institutions, the club was a male-only preserve and therefore, to my annoyance, barred to me.

The Farmers' Club had word that a unionist speaker was coming to Dersingham and that a meeting was being called on the common for a Sunday night in July. George Pooley and some of the other farmers planned to go along to hear what was said.

One evening, in the week before the meeting, I walked the fields alone with my secret thoughts, sending hares starting, hearing pheasants cry, breathing in the scent of bean flowers and ripening grain. How peaceful it was when work was stilled for the day, when evening shadows lengthened and swallows swooped. As I walked, I assessed the crops – oats nearly ready, given another week or two of good weather; barley golden, too; wheat needing longer, ears still tinged with green and grain oozing milky juice under a probing thumbnail. Once I had dreamed of teaching Georgie such things.

'Miss Rose!' The hiss brought me round, startled, to see Jack Huggins roll out from under a hedgerow where he had been hiding so quietly that I had passed him unseen.

'Jack, you rapscallion! What are you doing there?'

His grin split his dirty face, showing the gap where he had lost a front tooth in some brawl. He still looked an urchin, slight for his fourteen years, though he was better dressed and better fed now. He had a roguish gleam in his eye, and his silky golden locks curled down his neck from under a battered old peaked cap he kept from his days in London. He sported a couple of pheasant-tail feathers in it – moulted ones, I hoped. 'Been waitin' for you, Miss Rose.'

'Oh, yes? Is that all you were doing?'

"Course!' His bright eyes and innocent expression demanded what on earth else he might have been up to there in the hedge. Poaching? Heaven forfend!

Yes, I thought, poaching it was without a doubt; if I probed I might find a wire noose not far away, probably more than one, with a garrotted hare waiting to be collected. 'Jack—'

'Got this for you, miss,' he broke in, and with the air of a conjuror in a sideshow he produced a piece of paper from his pocket. 'I'd've brought it before, on'y Mr Benstead's been on me tail all day and I hen't had the chance to git away.'

'What is it?'

'Gentleman give it to me. Met 'im in the lane this mornin'.'

'What gentleman?'

'Just a gentleman. Wouldn't know 'im again if I saw 'im.' He pushed the note into my hand and winked. 'Not when he give me a whole shilling. Don't know nothin' about it, me. Note? What note? G'night, miss.' Doffing his feathered cap as if he were a courtier, he turned and went leaping away. A piercing whistle brought a little terrier barking after him.

I knew who the note was from, even before the handwriting confirmed it. It was simply a folded piece of paper written on one side. Not very discreet, except that Jack Huggins had had no schooling and couldn't read, besides which I had a feeling I could trust the young rogue not to betray me. Presumably 'the gentleman' had guessed the same. He had written:

Meet me – PLEASE – at the cottage where we met before. This afternoon, 2 p.m.

This afternoon.

The message had come too late.

-

That evening, by candle-light, I studied my reflection critically for the first time in months. Outwardly I was a mature woman of twenty-eight, with careworn hands and marks of sorrow on my face. It was a thin face, freckled from the sunlight, haloed by unkempt red hair that would never stay in a tidy bun. Beneath its dusty black my figure was thin, too, angular and bony. Youth was passing, along with hopes and dreams. I stared into the mirror, into my own empty eyes, and I knew that if I had had the note in time I would have gone to meet Geoffrey, and be damned to the consequences. Because inside me I was still the young girl with impossible dreams.

Having undressed, I turned down the lamp and lay awake in the darkness thinking of Geoffrey. I tried to picture him but the picture wouldn't hold steady, only fragments glimpsed as if through water. I almost got out of bed to look at the likeness hidden in my locket, but if Basil came and discovered me...

Even as I thought of him I heard his step in the hall. He was coming up early. Oh, God... not tonight, please. As the door opened, light misted in from the lamp he was carrying. I feigned sleep, hearing the familiar sounds as he began to undress; the creak of springs as the bed sank under his weight; his boots thumping to the floor. After a while the light went out, the covers lifted and he climbed in beside me, propped on one elbow, saying, 'I'm off to Norwich tomorrow. Taking the first train. I'll be gone a week. Right?'

'Aren't you going to this unionist meeting?' I asked. 'I thought you told your uncle George...'

'So I did, but something more important's come up. What do I care about a farm labourers' meeting? My uncle'll tell you what goes on.' He waited a few seconds, then: 'Right,' and he lay down, turned away from me.

Silently I lay listening, waiting, until his breathing told me he was asleep, and then, released from fear of my husband's attentions, I called up the shimmering fragments of my lover's image. I could no longer pretend to myself that Basil cared for me, or I for him. Any chance of happiness between us had died with Georgie. And so I sought consolation in dreams and fancies, assuring myself that thoughts could not be sinful. The sin would occur only if I allowed my dreams to become tangible. And that I would never do.

–

With Basil away and Mama and Narnie again in Thetford, Uncle Jonathan and Aunt Beatrice drove over in time to attend church. Beatrice wanted to see the Prince and Princess of Wales and their five offspring. The prince, who had been convalescing abroad, had returned for a brief stay at Sandringham before resuming his court duties.

I had no opportunity to converse with either the prince or the princess, but His Royal Highness doffed his hat and called, 'Good morning, Mrs Pooley!' across the crowd, and Princess Alix acknowledged me with a smile and a gracious nod of her head.

'How proud you must be to know them!' Aunt Beatrice said.

'Indeed I am.' After all the months of disgrace it was an undeniable pleasure to bask in royal approval.

My aunt and uncle remained with me for lunch and afterwards took a walk about the farm, though neither of them was as spry as in former days. Aunt Beatrice, troubled by rheumatics, walked with the aid of a stick, coming behind while her husband walked with me and talked of what might happen the following year when Johnny came of age.

'I imagine he'll be glad of your services as housekeeper,' Uncle Jonathan said. 'Shall you and your husband plan to stay?'

'I think not. Not for long. Once Johnny is settled, we shall probably move away.' Basil had spoken of moving to Norwich, though I couldn't imagine what I should find to do with myself in a city, without the demands of the seasons and the crops.

'And your Mama?'

'I imagine she will go on as she does now, dividing her time between Orchards and Thetford.' So long as William Turnbull will stand for it, I added ruefully to myself.

'And will Miss Narborough continue to be her companion? The reason I ask, Rose, is Willow Cottage. I know you wished to continue renting it, in case Miss Narborough decided to go back, but it doesn't do to let a property stand empty, especially with the winter in prospect. And we need a place for our old butler, Marshall, for his retirement.'

Silently, I gave best to Narnie, saying aloud, 'Then by all means let him have it. I can't imagine Narnie ever being persuaded to leave Mama – or Mama to allow it.'

My aunt and uncle left after taking afternoon tea; Beatrice wanted to attend evening service at her chapel.

–

All day, behind the quietness and the usual Sunday routine of milking and horses being tended, I had sensed an air of anticipation about the farm. I had let it be known that the men were free to attend the union meeting if they wished, but I had also asked McDowall to go and bring back news. However, as the lonely evening dragged on, my own curiosity drove me down to the yards to harness up the pony and trap. I didn't trust McDowall; George Pooley would bring back a more reliable report, but it might be days before he had the time to come to Orchards… so I rationalised, giving myself excuses to go when actually it was my own curiosity that drove me.

The sun was low, a few men making purposefully along the lanes in twos and threes. The meeting was to be held in an area between the common and the Sandringham Warrens, among gorse bushes and heather. Going round by a devious route, I left the trap in a clearing in the plantations and stayed discreetly among young pine trees on the hill, from where I saw that several hundred men had gathered – so many that some of them must have walked miles.

As the light faded, lanterns were lit, raised on beanpoles. Someone started to sing a hymn unfamiliar to me, though many of the men took it up and soon the warm twilight was loud with male voices raised in fervent chorus. The sound sent shivers down my spine. It was a 'ranter's' hymn, I guessed, with a chorus that spoke of conflict and marching with banners.

Given the distance, and the growing twilight, I couldn't see much of the speaker. He stood raised on an improvised dais, with a phalanx of supporters around him. He appeared to be dressed much as his audience was dressed, in Sunday best of dark suit and white shirt, but when he began to speak his voice carried with clarity and passion. I didn't catch every word, but I heard the gist.

He preached the evils of low pay and bad conditions; he called the squires 'land-stealers', the farmers 'slave-drivers'; he railed against the injustices of a law that allowed a gamekeeper the right to search a man at any hour of the day or night. 'The game laws are unjust! They should be abolished. Shooting should be stopped. It's a privilege of the rich, and makes temptation for the poor.'

At this point a voice intervened, complaining that the union was trying to set class against class. The lone voice belonged to Reverend Lancaster.

'Priest of Baal!' the answer boomed from among the crowd. 'Friend to the tyrants!'

'Yes. Yes!' cries came. 'Throw him out. No room for enemies here.'

A flurry in the throng said that moves had been made to carry out this order, but the speaker raised his voice, appealing for calm. 'We're not here to do violence. Not yet! We're here to tell you how strong we can be if we stand together. Let him stay. Let him listen and take heed.'

He cited the example of the French Revolution. Carried away by his own rhetoric he even hinted at the efficacy of arson and murder, and he raised the old republican complaints against the royal family.

A few bully boys were moving among the crowd. There was a commotion on the periphery, where I now saw a knot of men standing together in the shade of a patch of gorse. I guessed they were members of the Farmers' Club. Their presence had been discovered; the bullies were moving in on them, jostling them.

My attention was so fixed on that spot that I was late in seeing another couple of shadows detach themselves from cover and make sidling way towards me. One of the men was slight, the other as tall and thin as the bean-pole he carried, a lantern swinging from it sending slants of light across his scarred, ravaged face.

Davy Timms.

The smaller man looked like my old enemy, the ex-gamekeeper, Pyke.

As I turned to look for a way of escape, another figure loomed up behind me, tall in the shadows, wearing a wide-brimmed hat pulled low over his face. His hand fell heavily on my arm as he nodded to the others, 'That's all right, bor, I'll tek care on 'er. Come you on, Miss Rose, ma'am. This is no place for you.'

Despite the country accent, the labourer's clothes, and the hat that disguised his face, I knew the timbre of Geoffrey Devlin's voice when I heard it. I also knew well enough not to argue, not then.

The two men stopped. The light swung, and by its gleam I saw Timms's eyes, cold and watchful in his ruined face.

Half leading, half pushing me, his fingers biting into my upper arm, Geoffrey hustled me back down the slope towards the place where I had left the trap. When I glanced back I saw that we were well out of sight of the meeting, though the glow of its lanterns still showed on the rise, behind dark sentinel tree trunks, and occasionally a shout of agreement could be heard as the speaker raised some point.

'You're hurting me,' I complained.

The pressure eased, but only a little. He said furiously, 'Why in heaven's name did you take the risk of coming here tonight?'

'I might ask you the same! Dressed like that… Who do you think you are – Sidney Carton?'

'At least I wasn't fool enough to come alone.'

'Oh?' I glanced round, but in the shadows among the young pines I could see no one else.

'Your uncle, Henry Hamilton, is with me,' Geoffrey said irritably. 'The entire purpose of our being here was to discover what was said. Now, thanks to you, I shall have to rely on Major Hamilton's memory. We both agreed it was imperative that you be got away.'

If Uncle Henry was here, then the prince too had sent his spy. None of us could afford to be complacent.

'I have as much reason to be here as you do!' I retorted.

'You should have sent your steward.'

'I don't trust my steward.'

'Why not?'

'Because I don't! He's probably there cheering with the rest of them, if he's not in the inn pretending it's a fuss about nothing. Besides, *I* run Orchards Farm, not him. If my men are being talked into treachery—'

'You shouldn't have come alone! Where's your husband?'

'Away, as usual. I don't know where he is or what he's doing half the time – but that seems to be the way with modern marriage, thanks to the example of His Royal Highness. Companionship is as outmoded as fidelity.'

Muttering an oath, Geoffrey swung me round against the wheel of the trap. 'If that's a jibe at me,' he said fiercely, 'the only reason I sent that note was because I wanted to warn you to keep away from this meeting! Go home. If there's g-going to be trouble, I want you well out of it.'

'Why should there be trouble?'

'It's brewing. Can't you feel it? Someone disabled our reaper, and last night an attempt was made to fire one of our barns.'

'What?'

'The attempt was unsuccessful. The dogs disturbed him in time, thank God, but—'

My throat felt clogged with fear. If there was an arsonist on the loose, none of us was safe. 'Do you know who it was?'

'No. The dogs roused us, but he got away.'

'Have you ever suspected… the man Chilvers – Amos Chilvers?'

'Our teamsman?' Geoffrey considered, then admitted, 'I've heard the stories they tell about him. He's a surly devil, it's true. And he seems to have had some personal grudge against your father. But he's a fine man with horses. I've no reason to suspect him of doing harm at Ambleford.'

'Even though he's a close associate of Davy Timms?'

'Who?'

'One of the men who accosted me just now – the one with the scarred face, on account of which he bears a weighty chip on his shoulder. His sister is married to Chilvers's son. They go drinking together, so I've heard.'

'Well, there's no crime in that, surely. What are you implying – that Chilvers is part of a conspiracy?'

'I only meant...' What had I meant, except that I was worried for him? In little more than a whisper, I begged him, 'Be careful. Please be careful.'

The night came alive with awareness, unspoken messages sparking between us.

When at last he spoke, his voice was low and taut. 'I waited an hour at the cottage on Friday. Why didn't you come?'

'The boy didn't give me your note until too late.'

In the silence I heard the faint sound of the unionist's voice, and a murmur of approval from the men. The earth was dark, the sky still streaked with light.

Geoffrey swept off his ridiculous hat and came nearer. In the darkness his face was just a pale blur marked by the thick line of his moustache. 'D-do you know what day it was on Friday?'

My heart seemed to lurch. I turned my head away, looking off into the dark woods, moistening my dry lips. 'The nineteenth of July.'

'Ten years to the day.'

'Yes.'

'You remember?'

I closed my eyes tightly, feeling my throat choked with anguish. How could I forget the date we first met – really met – in the old hut in the woods? What made me want to weep was the fact that he remembered it, too.

'Rose...' His hand touched my shoulder, tentatively, pleading. I covered it with my own hand, feeling his fingers link urgently with mine. Love and longing fought a silent battle with conscience. And then, helplessly, I lifted a trembling hand to touch him, and in the same moment he reached for me.

As our lips met an explosion of emotion blinded me, searing my brain and setting my flesh alight. It came so suddenly I had no defence. We had waited too long. Desire like madness raged through me as we kissed and pressed together, both of us caught up in a wild need of each other.

Then a sudden, louder roar from the meeting reminded us of where we were. Geoffrey lifted his head, glanced back up the hill. Feeling the night air about me, I came awake as if from deep dreams, shivering a little.

'I must go.'

'Forgive me,' he said anxiously. 'The fault was mine – all mine.'

Loving him for wishing to spare me the guilt, I laid my hand against his cheek. 'If there was fault, it was mine too.'

'I love you. I always have. I always shall.'

'And I you.'

'Then… will you meet me again? At the cottage. Tomorrow?'

I meant to say no. But as I stood there looking up at him a long, long breath sighed quietly out of me. What use to deny fate?

'Yes. Tomorrow.'

I hardly slept that night for thinking of Geoffrey being in disguise at that unionist meeting. What if he were discovered? The men would be angry to think that he was spying on them. Some of them were known trouble-makers. Was he in danger? When I did drift off it was into muddled, disturbing dreams from which I woke with a jerk, wide awake again before cockcrow. For a moment I had fancied I heard Georgie crying.

By the time the men started arriving I was down in the stables with young Jack, petting the saddle-horses and giving them sugar. Ned Plant came first, as always, leading his cart-teams in from the meadow where they ran free on summer nights, and behind him tramped the others in ones and twos. Those I encountered greeted me civilly, doffing their caps with a, 'Mornin', Miss Rose. Bootiful day that be, fare to be fine for harvest.' At least they all turned up, despite unionist speeches.

McDowall, arriving late, seemed flustered to see me there. He gave out the day's orders and at Plant's call of, 'Collars on', the horses were equipped with suitable harness for that day's work. I took McDowall aside and asked him about the meeting. He said it had gone much as expected – a deal of hot air, some feelings relieved, but no sign of any real trouble. I guessed he hadn't even been there. Still, I thought with a chirrup of heady, guilty excitement lightening my spirits, I should hear the truth of it soon enough – from Geoffrey.

–

The garden at Willow Cottage was lush with summer, rampant now in Narnie's absence. The guardian willows at the gate stirred in the breeze and lavender spread half across the path, with bees loud in the sunny air. Just visible over the ivy-clad wall and the towering yews, the church clock showed the hour of two. I thought of Cassie, lying behind that wall with a white marble angel to guard her. What would she say if she could see me now?

The key fitted the lock, the door opened under my hand. The living-room beyond was starkly tidy, emptied of all personal touches, dimly lit behind closed curtains, and smelling faintly of camphorated oil.

'Hello?' There was no reply. The place felt empty. Not even the cat was here – Narnie had brought her to Orchards but she kept running away and we heard that someone in Feltham had taken to feeding her.

Taking off my hat and shawl, I went into the bedroom. It was dim and warm, curtains drawn against the light. A swivel looking-glass stood on the dressing-table, so low that I was forced to bend to see myself, patting my hair into place, biting my lips, pinching my cheeks. Vanity...

Then I froze as I heard the front door softly open. My heart stopped, then began to race, while colour rushed to my face.

'Rose!' a voice called. A woman's voice. 'Rose, are you there?'

It was Felicity Wyatt.

'Rose!' she exclaimed with pleasure as she saw me. 'I thought that was your pony trap by the gate. Why... what's wrong, my dear?'

'You startled me, that's all,' I said with a breathy laugh. 'I was thinking of something quite other and suddenly there you were.'

Felicity peered at me. 'You look flushed. Have you been crying? Oh, my dear... I've been shedding a few quiet tears myself. I came to put some roses on Cassie's grave. They're almost over, but you know

297

how she admired those big pink roses with their lovely scent. And I went into church – to say a prayer or two for Geoffrey Devlin.'

'For Geoffrey?'

'Why, yes. Hadn't you heard?' Her eyes were wide as she came closer and laid a hand on my arm. 'My dear, it's terrible. He was attacked last night. Stabbed. With a knife. They fear he may not live.'

Dear God. Cataracts roared in my ears and the cottage dimmed as I fought a wave of faintness. Through clouds of fog, Felicity's voice: 'Why, Rose, you're ill! Whatever is it?'

'It's nothing. It's nothing!' Brushing her aside, I made my way to an armchair and sat down with my head bent to my knees. 'I didn't sleep very well, for worrying about that meeting.' I looked up, my head reeling, nausea stirring inside me. 'Is that where it happened? Where is he now?'

'My dear…' Felicity looked perplexed. 'You're not making much sense. What meeting?'

She knew very little. What she had heard was servants' gossip, repeated at third or fourth hand, via the local carter, that Geoffrey Devlin had been attacked by a man with a knife, and that he was badly injured. 'Mama sent to Ambleford for news, but all the man brought back was that Mr Devlin is being attended by the doctor. His life is hanging by a thread. It *is* terrible, isn't it? He's such a dear. And poor Lucy! She must be worried out of her mind.'

'Yes. Yes, indeed.' I thanked providence that this was the ingenuous Felicity. If the perspicacious Cassie had been there she would have guessed my secrets at once.

Five

My life was suspended as I waited for news of Geoffrey, wanting to go to him, yet forbidden by all the laws of sense and society from doing so. Somehow I managed to put on a show of normality about the farm and in the house, and with so much to do there were moments when I forgot. Then I would find myself alone, temporarily unoccupied, and back rushed the fear and the awful, awful not knowing. The pictures built by my imagination were a torture and a punishment.

Since I did have one ally, in the shape of Jack Huggins, I charged him with the task of bringing me news. He went over to Ambleford two or three times: 'Oh, don't worry, miss, on'y the stablelad saw me. I cracked on as how I was skivin' off, over there for a chat.'

The attack had not happened at the unionist meeting. According to servants' gossip, Geoffrey had returned home late that Sunday evening after dining with friends. He had been preparing for bed when, seeing a shadowy figure in the garden, he had gone out to investigate and had been attacked. Though terribly wounded, he had managed to get back to his room before collapsing. His terrified wife had raised the alarm.

'Dunno what happened to the dogs, though,' said Jack, taking off his hat to scratch his fair curls.

'Dogs?' I repeated.

'They've got three great wolfhounds keep guard after dark. Had 'em a couple of months now. But not a peep out of 'em that night.'

Belatedly I recalled Geoffrey saying something about dogs – dogs which had frightened off a would-be arsonist. Why hadn't they raised the alarm over this new intruder?

The answer came with a blow like iced lightning – a man who could 'witch' horses might also have power over dogs. Was Amos Chilvers involved in this, too?

The police, investigating the stabbing, came to Orchards asking about troubles we might have had, and I mentioned Amos Chilvers.

Yes, they said, someone else had raised that name, but Chilvers had been at a meeting on the heath and afterwards at the inn in Dersingham; he had spent the night at his son's house, snoring off the beer. I was relieved about that, for Ben's sake.

It seemed that the unionist meeting had been called at the wrong time and in the wrong place. Harvest was imminent, promising bonuses which the men needed to clothe and shoe their families for the winter, and the republican talk had not impressed the men of Sandringham; they owed their livelihood to the Prince of Wales and they were still loyally thankful that he had survived his illness. However, some slight dissension continued to simmer, especially as the weather worsened and less work was available, so that casual labourers were thrown back on the parish. Some went north where the pay was better, where there were mines and factories; others migrated to the colonies. The shooting offered some of them employment as beaters now and then, but many of them would perforce be out of proper work until spring.

–

To my intense relief, word came that Geoffrey was beginning to recover. Within a month he was reported, via a friend of Felicity's who lived at Ambleford, as having been well enough to attend Ambleford church with his wife and mother. 'Though he still looked pale and was evidently weak,' Felicity informed me. 'Thora Thomas said it was quite touching to see how solicitous Lucy was, and how concerned she looked. Perhaps this will bring them together.'

'Perhaps.' So long as he was recovering, nothing else mattered.

'Anyway, it appears they're all going to Italy for the winter. Lady Ophelia thinks the warmer climate will be good for Sir Arthur's gout, and it will certainly be better for Geoffrey to convalesce in the sunlight.'

'Yes. Yes, it will.'

The story never changed. Geoffrey was going to Italy with his wife, and I must remain at Orchards with my husband.

–

The shooting season brought the Prince of Wales and his family back to Sandringham, where that winter they remained in residence from

October to February with only the occasional excursion elsewhere to open a building or an exhibition, make a speech, or attend a special dinner. The big house was filled with a succession of illustrious guests for whose enjoyment shooting parties were organised, and days out hunting, walks about the estate, trips to the coast to watch the sea on wild, windy days, and of course dinners, soirées and balls…

Whenever they shot over Orchards' land, Basil and I were invited to join the parties, Basil with his gun and I to add my company to the ladies' at luncheon. The shoots were getting bigger, great *battues* with a score of Guns and dozens of beaters, so that birds and hares fell by the hundred. I still objected to the way my land and my crops were despoiled for His Royal Highness's pleasure. But I had learned not to say so, not out loud.

During those months, Princess Alexandra often visited me at the farm, bringing her children to scramble in my parlour, rush up and down my stairs, play with my dogs and explore the barns along with Jack Huggins. The small princes loved to be out with stable-boys and grooms – their language was a disgrace. They also loved their homely home at Sandringham. What they dreaded was being obliged to visit Windsor and to cower under the stern, repressive gaze of their grandmother, the Queen.

It saddened me that I had no child of my own to join their romps.

'Perhaps one day soon,' the princess comforted me. 'Only God can decide such things. For me…' a shrug, a smile, 'well, Mrs Pooley, for me he was perhaps a little too generous. Oh, I love my children dearly. I would not be without any one of them, and if only my baby Alexander had lived I would have loved him too, but alas my strength is not what it was. I do not think there will be more.'

We talked of farming, of our families, and of our grief for children lost to us. She spoke, too, about her friend Oliver Montagu, whose deep affection was a comfort at times of stress; from the things she said I guessed the affection was returned, though in a purely platonic way. She never said a word amiss about the prince, never complained, nor blamed, nor criticised. She was always true to him, in word and deed. Except, I gathered, that she no longer shared his bed.

I almost wished the same could be said of me. Though I longed for another child I dreaded the nights when Basil came early to our room and subjected me to attentions which, at best, were brusque, designed only to quiet his own frustration. I was happier when he departed, leaving me free to lie and dream about Geoffrey, far away in Italy. Was he fully recovered? Part of me hoped he would stay away, well out of danger, for the police had never discovered the attacker. But most of me yearned for him to come home. Even if I didn't see him, it would be a comfort just to know he was nearby.

—

Basil and I attended the informal tenants' dinner, held in November at Sandringham House, a merry occasion when the prince danced with most of the ladies. When he sought me out a second time I was conscious of jealous stares and whispers as we whirled about the floor. He was testing my mettle, taking me headlong through a jig, and I, feeling reckless, matched him step for step, skirts billowing behind me. When the dance ended with us both breathless, His Royal Highness bellowed with laughter and declared that I had quite worn him out. But his eyes conveyed other messages. I interested him. My very coolness was a challenge.

A few days later, the prince called on me at the farm. He came alone and unheralded on a frosted, foggy day when he knew my husband was away. Fortunately Mama and Narnie were with me and I kept them close, despite hints that His Royal Highness would have preferred to see me alone. The visit was brief – merely a neighbourly call as he happened to be passing, so he claimed.

As I saw him to the door, he leaned close to me, almost touching me – he was much too fat for a man just turned thirty-one – and his pale blue eyes shone as they studied my face.

'We shall expect to see a good deal of you this winter, Mrs Pooley. Be sure you remain available to accept invitations.'

'Your Royal Highness is most kind,' I murmured. 'So long as my husband is here to escort me...'

A smile twitched in the shadow of his neat beard. He understood me very well. 'Oh, with or without. With or without. We can always find someone to escort you. But *you* must come. That's the thing. My wife's concerned about you. Says you need to get out more. Get some colour in those pale cheeks, what?' He put out a gloved fist and raised my chin, forcing me to meet his sparkling eyes. 'Well, what do you say?'

What could I say? 'I shall do my best, sir.'

Though Basil affected not to like 'fancy do's' he contrived to be available for the princess's Birthday Ball in early December – the most glamorous occasion on Norfolk's social calendar. He provided me with another new gown of the latest style, and when he saw me fully dressed he told me I was 'still a very handsome woman'. I fancied there was pride in him as he led me under the brilliance of gas lamps, into the great saloon.

Once again the prince paid me embarrassing attentions, to the seeming amusement of his wife. Her faithful Oliver Montagu was never far from her side, and among the crowd my uncle Henry engaged himself with various lovely ladies. Most of the company seemed occupied in flirting with people other than their partners. It was modern manners, fashionable in all the best circles, thanks to the Prince of Wales, every shade of human relationship from platonic love to downright adultery, practised with only a modicum of discretion. But that discretion was still necessary; anyone who ignored it was soon cast out from the charmed circle.

That night, as if the prince's interest in me had restirred his own desire, my husband made love to me almost gently. He told me again that I was beautiful, and he took pains to rouse me to readiness before he came to me. In the darkness I tried to picture Geoffrey, light shining on his soft dark hair, smiling…

When it was over and my husband had turned away, snoring as soon as he flopped down, I felt the tears on my face. As always I was left with a gnawing hunger for physical release. No mental illusion could dispel the truth of my unhappiness. Where was Geoffrey? *How* was Geoffrey? Oh, dear God, keep him well for me. Keep him safe.

–

Over Christmas, Grace and her family came to stay, filling the farm with noise and chatter, and the running, shouting and crying of children – three of them now, the youngest just nine months old. Johnny came home too. He, Turnbull and Basil had some fine after-dinner arguments about politics and business, which my sister and I were glad to escape.

After the Turnbulls had departed, the weather clamped down. Deep snows fell. The temperature dropped below freezing and stayed there for weeks; work on the land was impossible. With wages rising, costs increasing, and hares nibbling away at my meagre profits, I couldn't afford to pay men for nothing. I had to lay off some of our regular hands, since there was no work to be found for them, though I did my best to choose only the young, single men with no families to support. Every farmer was doing the same – which meant that the pool of discontents was enlarged and men without work gathered on village greens and at lane ends, stamping their feet, rubbing their hands and muttering with iced breath about injustice.

It was so cold, and the snow so deep in the woods, that even the shooting had to be abandoned; the Prince of Wales and his guests found amusement in tobogganing and snowball fights, and in skating on the lake.

However, it wasn't cold enough to deter Basil from his business. As soon as the railway was cleared for traffic he set out for Wolferton through crusted snow, bound for Norwich and then for Leeds. He expected to be gone for two weeks or more.

It was said that the prince had informants everywhere. I can only assume that he must have had one at the railway station; on the day Basil left, a message came from Sandringham House to remind me that ice-skating was available on the lake every night; I was welcome to go whenever I wished.

Mama thought I would be mad to turn down such an invitation – Mama never did comprehend the subtler ramifications of such things – but Narnie had deeper thoughts and suspicions. And I, too, thought it more prudent to stay away from the ice-skating.

Then one evening my uncle Henry arrived – in the princess's own dainty sleigh, with silver bells jingling on it, silver trimmings on the ponies' harness, and silver lamps gleaming.

'My dear, your pumpkin awaits!' Henry exclaimed as he stood in our hallway in winter uniform, whiskers bristling. He was almost as plump as his master. 'Do be a good girl, go and change into something a little prettier, find your skates and come along. Their Royal Highnesses won't take no for an answer.'

'Oh do, Rose!' Mama cried, clasping her hands. 'Oh, how exciting! What an adventure.'

Given no choice, unless I wished mortally to offend my royal landlord, I did as I was bidden, though my thoughts were dark with misgivings. I wore my green velvet with Russian frogging, and its matching hood to keep me warm, and a fox-fur muff for my hands. Swift, despite my protests, produced a pair of Johnny's skates for me, and Violet insisted on helping me dress, tidying my hair and draping the hood just so.

Cinderella had had her fairy godmother to protect her. All I had was my uncle, who had once before proven himself no white knight. He whipped up the ponies and we went jingling off through a clear night shining with stars. As the icy air rushed past my face I huddled deeper into my hood and muff. 'I hope I shan't regret this.'

'Regret it? My dear girl – a party at Sandringham...'

'The last time you took me to a party at Sandringham—'

Henry cut me off: 'Don't be so damned provincial, Rose. You're a married woman. You know what's what. Nobody's going to force you into doing something you don't want to do. Enjoy yourself, for goodness' sake! Many a young woman would give her eye-teeth for the chance.'

We skimmed through deep snow across Sandringham Park, seeing the lake in its hollow surrounded by a ring of lights, and the tall-chimneyed roofs of the house black against the sky beyond. With stars thick overhead and snow underfoot, with great trees studding the park and hanging over the frozen lake, the place was turned into fairyland by the light of coloured lanterns strung in trees. Flaring torches ringed the lake and marked paths across the ice, and fires blazed here and there with groups of spectators huddled round them.

Uncle Henry stopped the sleigh and bade me alight, then he drove off into the darkness to see the ponies safely tended.

Music flowed from the island in the lake, where a band was playing. A crowd of villagers, graciously allowed to come and witness the spectacle, gathered around fires at the far end, while the prince's guests dotted the slopes below the house. Figures appeared and vanished in the torchlight as they moved across the ice, their voices calling, laughter breaking out as someone fell. Two ladies were being pushed in chairs fastened to slides. A string of six or seven people went whirling by, the last in the chain being whipped at alarming speed round a bend, to disappear behind the shrubberied island, where firelight glinted on brass instruments as the band played waltzes. From the shrieks that followed, I guessed that the last man in the chain had come to grief, shot off the ice into deep drifts of snow.

Keeping on the periphery, among the shadows, I made out a few familiar faces of people I had met on previous occasions. There was a tent set up below the terrace with tables beside it, and a brazier or two – roasting chestnuts, I guessed. Then I heard the princess's laugh and saw her swirling on the ice, arm in arm with one of her ladies-in-waiting. I was standing near a flare when she picked me out and came skimming towards me, calling, 'Welcome, Mrs Pooley. Put on your skates. The ice is wonderful!' Laughing, she moved on, her weak side supported by her companion.

It was only then that I realised I had left my skates in the sleigh, but on reflection, seeing the grace of some of the skaters, I would not have cared to display my lack of practice.

The chain of skaters appeared again, going a little more sedately. It passed a young woman in a dark blue outfit trimmed with white, and the last man in the chain grabbed her hand, making her squeal. But she could match any of them. Rather than being dragged behind, she skated more quickly, so that the chain formed a U as they came speeding past me, skates whispering like bird-wings.

The net of skaters almost scooped up another couple, who struggled to clear the way and just escaped, the man supporting the woman. But he was unsteady. His feet went from under him and he fell flat on his behind, much to the amusement of his companion.

Light illuminated the lady's face briefly and, to my astonishment, I saw that it was Felicity Wyatt. As to the man with her... as far as I could make out he was a stranger, a big man, dressed in a thick top coat and flat-crowned hat.

'My dear Mrs Pooley.' The prince's voice broke across my thoughts and I spun round to find him smiling at me. 'Aren't you frozen stiff standing there? Why don't you join them?'

'Oh, I... I'm afraid I don't skate, sir.'

'What, never? Then let someone take you in a chair.'

'Oh, no! No, thank you, sir. I'm happy just to watch. It's a wonderful sight.'

'It is indeed,' he said, but his eyes were on my face. 'Come, let's go and get some negus to warm us.'

He tramped off through the trodden snow, leaving me to follow more slowly. I glanced at the lake, figures swishing and gliding, in and out of the flaring light. There was no sign of Felicity and her intriguing escort, not on the ice nor on the banks, where spectators were dark shapes against flares and firelight.

The prince was returning to find me, bringing two steaming tumblers of watered wine mixed with sugar and spices. The hot drink was welcome, warming both my hands and my insides as I replied to the prince's light conversation. But when someone else came up to speak to him, I edged away and lost myself in the shadows.

Making my way up the slope to leave my empty tumbler on one of the tables, I saw Felicity again, standing by one of the braziers enjoying roasted chestnuts which her sturdy escort held in his gloved hand. Her plain face was alight as she looked up at him; she was chattering breathlessly, recounting some family incident.

'Felicity,' I broke in, touching her arm. 'Hello. Whatever are you doing here?'

'Rose!' she beamed. 'Oh… we were invited to come at any time, whenever we pleased, so long as the ice lasts. Christiana and Kitty and Verity have all been on other evenings, so tonight I let myself be persuaded.' She slanted a mischievous glance at her companion. 'I had a good excuse, as you can see.'

Beneath the brim of his hat an edge of red firelight shone on the side of his face, gleaming in soft fair hair growing long to the collar of his coat. A slow smile spread, showing his teeth and lighting his eyes. Just for an instant – of absolute sheer panic – I fancied it might be Hal Wyatt. But no, this man was more relaxed, more amenable.

My expression as I peered at him made Felicity laugh. 'You don't remember him, do you?'

'I'm afraid…'

'It's Robert. It's my brother Robert.'

'Good heavens!' The exclamation was out before I could stop it. The sickly boy, rumoured to be afflicted with consumption, had turned into a well-built, attractive man of apparent robust health.

He offered me chestnuts, which I ate with relish, and then he fetched more cups of hot negus that spread a warm glow while we talked. New Zealand had worked wonders for him, he said, given him health, strength and confidence. He had his own sheep farm now – hundreds of broad rolling acres of grass and forest. He described it with wide gestures, building pictures that made me feel I could see the green landscape with its mountains and spouting geysers. Robert loved it, that was clear. However, he had thought it time that he paid his family a visit. He intended to stay a while, maybe six months or more, and then – who knew? – he might try to persuade one or more of his sisters to go back with him. Single young ladies were in short supply in the colony.

'That's not for me,' Felicity sighed. 'But Kitty, or Verity...'

'You could all come,' Robert said, so earnestly that I had to laugh. 'No doubt he would welcome three or four young ladies to keep house for him.'

His grin told me he didn't mind my teasing, though he said, 'Oh, I've a Maori woman does that, and very efficiently, too. But I won't deny it's lonely at times. That's another reason I came home. Do either of you ladies have a friend in need of a husband?'

Felicity and I shared a look. She said, 'We shall have to put on our thinking caps. I'm sure we can find you someone. What do you say, Rose?'

At that point, His Royal Highness came up, chided me for 'disappearing' and rather pointedly drew me away from my friends. I saw them return to the ice, making off into the darkness. The prince led me down to the lake, where he tried to borrow some skates for me, so that he might judge my skill for himself. As I demurred and protested, Duke Francis of Teck gallantly came to my aid by suggesting that the prince might strap on some skates and show his own prowess. Others, overhearing, joined in the fun. Joking attempts were made to impel His Royal Highness on to the ice, while he spluttered with laughter and loudly objected.

Under cover of the jollity, I made my escape. Risky as it was to keep evading the prince and thus chance his anger, it would be riskier still to stay within his orbit. The last thing I wanted, largely because of my friendship with the princess, was to have my name scandalously linked with that of His Royal Highness.

On cold feet, I slipped and slithered across the slope, skirting a naphtha flare – and stopped, disconcerted, as a man turned to face me.

In the bright yellow light of the flare Geoffrey and I stared at each other, both of us startled, both of us uncertain. Was he thinner than I remembered? Were those fresh hollows under his cheekbones, or was the firelight throwing shadows, aided by my own anxiety? I remembered another night, another meeting, and in his face I read an unguarded longing that said he remembered too. I was aware of a strong force between us, trying to draw us together. It took all my will to step backwards, away from him. As I turned blindly away, I heard him say my name, and in the same moment a clear voice cried, 'Geoffrey!' Not far away, out on the ice, stood the expert skater in her dark outfit trimmed with white. I recognised her now: Lucinda, Geoffrey's wife. Not waiting to see what happened between them, I hurried away into the night.

All I wanted was to escape. I hoped to find Uncle Henry, who might take me home. But Henry, as always when I needed him, was nowhere to be seen. There was only one thing to do, and that was walk home.

In an attempt to keep myself completely hidden, I picked my way up to a knoll overlooking the lake, where chestnut trees spread bare branches. It was dark there, apart from the starlight on the snow, and in the shadows of the trees I doubted I could be seen by anyone within the gleam of light. The night was still, and though my face and hands were cold the rest of me was tolerably warm as I looked back on the scene – watchers by the fires, skaters flitting into light and melting into shadow. From that distance they were just moving shapes, touched by light. I didn't know where Geoffrey was, or Lucy. Probably away beyond the island, hidden by the bulk of trees and shrubs where firelight played on the men in the band. I was nearer to the far end of the lake, where two fires warmed the knots of villagers who had been allowed to come and watch the gentry at play.

To complete the spectacle, a sparkle of fireworks exploded in the sky, sending yellow flickers trailing in an arc across the stars. 'Ooh's' and 'Aah's' arose. A rocket sprang up, shedding streamers of silver fire, to blossom in great red globes that faded and died; then a shower of golden rain erupted, lighting up the house on its rise above the lake.

Half blinded by the brilliance, I fancied I saw someone moving towards me in the deep shade. I blinked to clear the illusion, but the shadow was still there and as he came into the faint starshine between two trees a burst of green light told me he was no phantom. Then he was beside me, reaching for me, saying, 'Oh, my dear darling…'

The sound of it pierced all my defences. I found myself moving into his arms, lifting my cold lips to meet his, melting against him. Like coming home after a long and weary journey.

'Oh, love,' I breathed, laying my head against his coat while he wrapped me more closely, his face bent near mine. 'Are you safe? Are you well? When I heard you were hurt…'

'I know. I know. I wanted to write to you. I planned to get a note to you, through our young go-between, but they allowed me no time alone. We were away to Italy before I gathered my wits. Dear love, if you knew how desperately I missed you…'

His mouth enveloped mine again, sweet savage kisses telling our mutual feeling.

'I missed you, too,' I whispered when I could. 'I was so afraid… To know you were hurt… Not to be able to see you… Do you know who did it? Was it Amos Chilvers?'

He didn't answer me. 'Rose,' he muttered against my brow, holding me painfully tight. 'Oh, my darling Rose, when may I see you? I must see you soon. I need to be with you. I know you don't care for Pooley, and Lucy…' he paused, adding in a rush, 'God help me, but I no longer care what Lucy thinks. She's forfeited all right to my loyalty. It's you I love. Come to me. Is the cottage still empty?'

'No. No, it's been taken.'

'Blast!' he muttered. 'I was afraid of that.'

'Geoffrey…' Easing a little away, I looked up at him, though in the darkness he was only a black shape. 'What is it you're asking of me – to become your mistress?'

'Yes.' Blunt and honest – disconcertingly so.

'I see.'

'Only until I f-find some other solution,' he said.

He hadn't changed – he still sought to sweeten the bitter pill with promises half-meant. There was no 'other solution', not for us. Divorce was unthinkable. The scandal would drive us into social exile: his father would probably cut him off from his inheritance, and I would bear the label of 'scarlet woman' for the rest of my life.

'It will be all right,' he promised. 'Nobody cares about such things any more. Everyone does it. We can be discreet. No one will ever know.'

'Except us.'

'And we…' he murmured, 'we shall be happy at last.'

Wanting to believe it possible, I gave him my mouth again, driving my hands into his hair to hold him down to me. Maybe he was right. Maybe we should take our chance of happiness before age and duty separated us for ever.

'I love you,' he murmured.

'And I you,' I replied, burrowing against him.

We stood together simply holding each other, enjoying being close and warm in the winter night.

On the periphery of my vision, down at the end of the lake, villagers clustered in laughing groups about their kindling fires, supping on beakers of hot-pokered beer supplied from a small stand under the trees, where a barrel had been set up. Beyond them, across the snow-covered park, under the flare of colour from the fireworks, more people were coming. Coming purposefully. A whole crowd of them.

'Geoffrey... look – those people...'

Pale starlight on snow showed up the dark figures – a score of men, maybe more. A sudden burst of red light from the sky lent them menace, showing us the placards they carried, with slogans unreadable from this distance. A voice bellowed above the faint strains of the band and the laughter from the skaters: 'Down with all tyrants! Down with injustice! Down with privilege! Give us work!'

They came on, striding through the snow, all of them beginning to shout out their grievances and their hatred of the prince. The villagers were milling in alarm, cries of, 'Shame!' and 'No!' coming clear on the night air.

'My God!' Geoffrey released me and turned away. 'I must go and warn the prince. Stay here, Rose. Stay out of sight!'

I watched him go, wondering if there would ever come a time when – or a place where – we could be together without the world intruding.

'They skate while we starve!' the bellow came. 'Down with privilege. Justice for the people!'

They were among the villagers now. Some scuffling broke out. The beer barrel went flying, rolling and bumping, and I heard a woman scream. The shouts became less coherent, imbued with hate and anger.

The prince's guests became aware of the trouble. Voices cried alarm and a surge for the safety of the house began. From elsewhere, men started toward the intruders, who were staking their placards in the ground. A little knot of them grouped under a tree, struggling to hang something from a branch. One man brought a burning brand from a fire and set light to the object they had hung – a crude dummy, perhaps an old scarecrow.

The skaters were fleeing the lake. Guards came running from their posts, hastening to protect the prince. The trouble-makers scattered, some going back the way they had come, others making off towards the trees that bounded the church, two or three making up the slope towards me where shadows lay deep. One man, labouring in the snow, with a scarf coming adrift around his head, almost ran into me before he saw me, baulked, and dodged past. But not before I had recognised him. Another, a few feet away, deliberately changed course and charged into me, knocking me flat. He was disguised, wearing a knitted helmet that left only his eyes exposed. But I knew his tall thin shape – that balaclava hid a hideously scarred face.

The first man was Amos Chilvers. The second was Davy Timms.

Some of the folk from West Newton came to my aid and helped me up, leading me to where their fires still burned. The protesters' placards, now stuck in the snow at drunken angles, carried various hastily-scrawled devices: 'Game for all', 'Repeal the game laws', 'Their pleasures, our poverty'. The scarecrow, hanging with legs charred and smouldering, had round its neck a label on which was scrawled 'HRH Fat Berty'.

–

The incident at the lake left a shadow of uneasiness over us all. If the agitators had dared to challenge the prince himself in the grounds of his own house, none of us was safe. When, a few days later, men came to enquire if I knew anything that would help them find the perpetrators of this outrage, I named Amos Chilvers and Davy Timms. This time I had seen them. There was no mistake.

A few of the malcontents had been apprehended at the scene. Half a dozen or so, including Amos Chilvers, were arrested later, making all of us feel safer. They were sent to Norwich prison to await trial, while enquiries went on and the newspapers speculated whether this was a new upsurge of republicanism or just another outbreak of unionism. Village opinion turned against the radicals, though there remained a core of bitterness in some minds and hearts.

Because of my friendship with the Chilverses, I felt badly about my part in Amos's arrest, but when I saw Ben and Pam they reassured me.

'I'd've done the same, had I seen 'im,' Ben said. 'Crazy old fool. Led astray by Davy Timms, that's the trouble.'

'Our Davy have never been the same since he came back from India,' Pam argued, with tears in her eyes. 'Don't you lay all the blame on him. Your father never took much pushin'.'

Davy Timms remained at liberty, though in hiding. His sister Pam had no word of him, so she maintained, but from that time on there was awkwardness between us. It saddened me to feel a rift widening between me and a couple I had come to regard as good friends.

--

The incident at the lake caused a great deal of talk in the villages, and King's Lynn too was buzzing with it. Basil heard some of the gossip on his way home; it caused him to arrive in a foul temper.

Hardly was he inside the door than I heard him shouting for me. I chanced to be upstairs and went to the landing, where I saw poor young Finch struggling up carrying Basil's heavy valise. In the hall below, Basil was shouting, 'And tell her to come at once! I'll be waiting in the parlour.'

The maid looked at me unhappily, 'Master says—'

'Yes, I heard.'

He was pacing the room, hands deep in his coat pockets, his face red with both cold and anger. I wondered how I could ever have thought him good-looking; the years were coarsening him in many ways. When he saw me, his chin thrust out belligerently. 'I won't have this, Rose! Blast, that I won't! Do you know what they're saying?'

'About what?'

'About you and that... you and His Almighty Royal Highness the Prince of Wales, God rot him!'

'No. What are they saying?'

'That he's got his eye on you – and I know that's true, I've seen it for myself. I also hear you've been entertaining him here while I was away.'

'He came once!' I defended myself indignantly. 'He stayed no more than fifteen minutes. Mama and Narnie were with us the entire time.'

He threw his hands in the air, 'Well, it's got to stop!'

'And how do I stop it?'

'You can stop encouraging him!'

That made me angry. 'I've never encouraged him!'

'No? Do you deny going there, all by yourself? Going to an ice party on the lake with all those fine fancy folk. Flaunting yourself. You think that's where you belong, don't you? Among the gentry. Oh, I heard all about it. I heard it from old Sam Rudd. "There's me and my missus drinkin' beer down one end," he tells me, "and *your* missus up by the big house drinkin' negus with the prince." How do you think that makes me look? Like a prize fool, that's what!'

'Oh… don't be so provincial, Basil!' I snapped. But he was right: what might be all very well for an actress in London was scandalous behaviour in a respectable married lady from Norfolk. 'If it bothers you so much, another time I won't go unless you're there.'

This mollified him, though he remained irritable with me. I had a feeling that he had been spoiling for a real fight. But I was in no mood for fighting with him. He didn't really care what I did, so long as folk didn't gossip about it. It was his good name he was worried about, not me.

—

When the boy Jack covertly passed me a note from Geoffrey asking me to be at the Tuesday market in Lynn the following week, I knew it would be wiser not to go. I decided not to reply to the note. Nevertheless, I found myself working out reasons why my presence at the market was vital, and when the morning came I set out in the trap. Benstead and the boy had gone ahead with the bullock cart, taking a few of our beasts to the cattle fair.

The pens were noisy, cattle lowing and jostling on straw-covered cobbles, the warm stench of ordure filling the air. I encountered George Pooley and asked his advice over prices, then I instructed Benstead what rate to haggle for, promised him a bonus if he exceeded it, and left him to handle the business. Making my way through the throng, I came to an area where eggs, pickles, jams and winter greens were being sold by farmers' wives and village women, from stalls or from the backs of carts. When I spied Geoffrey watching for me, I wove a discreet path among the market-goers, looking at the goods on display as if I were thinking of buying, though beneath my outward composure my heart was thudding, and perspiration prickled under my stays despite the cold wind.

'Mrs Pooley,' Geoffrey greeted me with a formal doffing of his hat and a slight bow. He enquired after my health, and that of my family, and I replied in kind, both of us playing a part for the benefit of any witness who might know us. Slowly we drew a little away from the crowds, where a railing surrounded a stand of young trees, and after some more inconsequential small-talk he leaned closer to murmur,

'We can't talk here. Come to Greyfriars Gate. I know a place there. I'll go ahead and wait for you.'

Before I could answer, he was gone.

Six

Greyfriars Gate was a narrow thoroughfare between tall tenements on whose ground-floor shops – an ironmonger, a butcher, a haberdasher – stood shoulder to shoulder with dwelling houses. It was in a mean area of alleyways and yards near the docks, and there was a beer shop whose garish sign claimed it to be the Jolly Tar Inn. Children played whip and top, or sat in the gutters, unkempt and dirty, and the people I passed cast sidelong looks at my clothes, as if such finery was unusual among them.

Geoffrey was waiting in a narrow, badly-lit passageway down which he led me to a door. Beyond it lay a dark lobby, barely large enough for two of us, with a closed door either side of a flight of steep, uncarpeted stairs. We climbed the stairs, coming into a room whose single sash window looked out on the backs of other similar houses. It smelled of neglect and stale sweat. Some attempt had been made to make the room welcoming: there was a fire in the grate, a few cheap fairings for ornament, bright knitted covers on cushions and bed.

The bed – a single brass bedstead with a sagging mattress...

Seeing my feelings written on my face, Geoffrey said, 'It was all I could find. I know it's not...' He glanced round the room, his lips twisting as if he was noticing its condition for the first time – the spotted mirror above the chipped mantelpiece, the stained, threadbare carpet. 'I'll understand if you prefer not to stay.'

It was a shabby room, used for shabby purposes. I knew I had made a mistake in coming. 'I'm not this sort of woman, Geoffrey.'

'I know that.'

'Then why did you bring me here?'

'Why did you come?'

I glanced at him, but couldn't bear to meet his eyes fully. 'I don't know.'

'Ten years ago you knew.'

'Ten years ago it was different. Ten years ago I was a child. I hardly understood what was happening. Now, I know all too clearly. I'm risking everything.'

'I know that,' he said again.

'I'm ashamed of myself. I know I shouldn't be here.' I let myself meet his gaze as I admitted, 'And I'm afraid.'

He watched me for a silent moment. 'Of what?'

'Of myself, I think. I know I shouldn't be here, but here I am.'

'Here we both are.' Stepping closer, he let his hand brush my cheek before, tentatively, he bent and kissed me, very softly, his lips lingering, not demanding but warmly clinging. When he lifted his head I saw the dark blue eyes smoky with desire. 'The place isn't important. We can be ourselves here. We're together. That's what matters.'

Disturbed by feelings that made my heart beat so fast I was breathless, I turned away and went to take off my hat, watching my reflection in the spotted mirror. I was aware in every nerve of being alone with him at last, and of the bed lying there waiting. I thought of making love with him, and the picture made my head spin so that I shut my eyes tightly, trying to blot it out, while hot blood flooded every vein, rippling across my skin, making my cheeks burn. I cooled them with my hands, and saw Geoffrey still watching me.

'So...' he said. 'What do you suggest we do?'

I had to clear my throat before I could say, 'We could talk. It's been a long time since we were able to do that freely.'

'Talk.' His mouth quirked ruefully. 'Yes, we could do that.' He laid his hat on top of some old books on a shelf, tossed his coat aside too and settled himself in a sagging armchair. 'What shall we talk about?'

My mind was empty of ideas. Searching for a coherent subject, I grasped at something that had been puzzling me. 'That night at the lake... What did you mean about Lucinda?'

Geoffrey's face went still. He didn't reply.

'You said she had forfeited your loyalty,' I reminded him. 'You said—'

'I know what I said.' He got to his feet and brushed past me, going to the window, his back turned to me. 'I'm sorry, I'd prefer not to discuss Lucinda.' When I didn't respond, he looked over his shoulder, challenging, 'Do you want to talk about Pooley?'

'No.'

He turned away again, tense in every muscle, then, sighing heavily, he came and laid his hands on my shoulders, studying my every feature. 'Perhaps this was a mistake, Rose. I should never have asked you to come. I thought you were ready, but if you expect me to make polite conversation...' His glance settled on my mouth, striking sparks of response in me as he went on in a low, vibrant voice, 'All I can think of is how much I want to make love to you.'

As I looked into his eyes the cold knot inside me came undone, melting into frank desire. My whole being was alive with need of him. Having come this far, how could I hold back? Unable to speak, I lifted my hands to lock them about his neck and draw his mouth down to mine.

As we kissed with aching tenderness, the room faded into insignificance. He had been right – surroundings didn't matter. The only reality was Geoffrey, holding me, touching me, unpinning my hair to let it fall in crisp waves that played through his fingers. I felt myself trembling. The need in me was overwhelming. We had waited too long. Too long.

We said very little. Between us words had often been superfluous. Now we spoke with our eyes and with our hands, touching and holding and clinging, and with burning, aching lips that drank deep of forbidden wine and came back ever more thirsty.

He was warm and tender, gentle with me. The trembling became shivers of unbearable desire as, impatiently, we tore free of the final barriers of clothing. When we stood naked before each other I saw that in his eyes I was beautiful, as he was for me, all mature man now, tall and lean – with a new, hateful scar jagged on his chest. How near his heart! Seeing it, I let my shaking fingers trace its shape.

'You might have died.'

'But I did not. I'm alive. I'm here. With you. At last.' As he spoke, he folded me in his arms and bore me to the bed. That sagging, squeaking bed with its thick feather mattress, rough blankets, knitted patchwork coverlet... It might have been a couch of softest pink cloud.

My senses were filled – the touch of him, the sight of him, the sound, the scent, the taste... He taught me the difference love could make. With him every part of me was stirred – heart, mind, soul... Such a sweet soaring need, such a blending, and then a raging torrent of feeling that blinded and deafened me to everything but my love and my need, lifting me ever higher.

A wave of delight overflowed through all my being, spilling out in a flood so swift and complete that I heard myself moan aloud in despair that it was over.

Against my ear, Geoffrey breathed a shaky laugh and withdrew from me, expending himself with a groan into the sheet. Even in his extremity, he thought of me.

We lay entwined, sated with lovemaking, holding each other, lips meeting and sweetly clinging, flesh against flesh speaking eloquently. Comfort, such as I had never had from Basil. Comfort such as I needed most desperately. I felt like a desert plant, denied water for years, flowering in bright profusion at the magical touch of rain.

Slowly, slowly, the world re-formed itself around us. Somewhere a child was crying. A church clock struck the hour. I counted the chimes. Eleven o'clock.

I kissed his hot skin, letting my fingers enjoy the feel of flowing muscle. 'I love you.'

'And I you.' He raised himself to look at me and stroke the hair from my face. 'I worry about you. I know you're unhappy, love.'

Watching him, loving him, I traced the dark line of his moustache. 'Not now. Not here, with you.'

Dark eyes heavy with sadness stared at me as he smoothed my cheek, stroked my hair. 'I'm sorry about the child.'

'Child?' I felt stricken. How did he know?

'Your son.'

Georgie – how could I have forgotten my little monkey? Memory caught at me, cobwebbing my throat. 'Yes.'

'And Pooley?'

'We live like strangers. We—'

His fingers stopped the words. 'No, don't. Don't speak of him. I don't want to know.' He laid his head against mine and was silent, as if trying to master some strong emotion. After a while a heavy sigh escaped him and he rolled over to lie flat on his back staring at the ceiling. 'What are we doing, Rose? There's no future for us. There never was. Except for the intervention of death—'

'Don't!' I twisted to look at him. 'No, don't think it. We mustn't wish them dead.'

He gave me an odd, sardonic smile. 'It wasn't them I was thinking of. Oh...' at my look of horror he took my face between his hands and kissed me hard, leaving my mouth bruised. 'Don't look like that.

I don't mean it. Just sometimes, when my life seems to have lost all meaning...' With one finger he traced the line of my brows, the shape of my nose, a tender light growing in his eyes. 'Do you know how expressive your face is? I could never tire of watching your face, love. I felt that when I first knew you. If I hadn't been such a young fool... I should have defied my parents. I should have made you my wife. If only I had had the courage...'

'Hush.' I stopped the words with my fingers across his lips. 'We can't change what is, Geoffrey.'

Our love found expression in physical closeness, until once again desire blotted out all else. He loved me sweetly, leading me to my fulfilment while himself holding back.

Again he left me in time, his body rigid until he let out a long, long breath and a shudder ran through him. His arms tightened, until I almost cried out for the pain of it, as he kissed me fiercely. Then he turned away and sat up, stretching himself like a cat.

I laid a hand on his back, spreading my fingers against the play of warm muscle under his skin. 'There was a time you were not so careful.'

'I know.' He glanced down at me, sadly and tenderly. 'Thank God nothing came of my stupidity.' Nothing – only a child lost for ever, and three years of exile for me. But now was not the time. When I told him, everything must be right. I managed to return his look steadily, and even to smile a little. 'You should have a child, love. You should have an heir. Is Lucinda...' But before I could frame the question properly he abruptly got up and began to dress.

'It's late. We must go.'

And so I knew that he did not wish to talk about his wife, any more than he wished to talk about my husband. In this private world, Lucinda and Basil had no place.

–

As I walked away down the narrow street, my lips still bruised from his kisses, every step brought me nearer to reality – nearer to the guilt that waited, driving away the warm glow that was on me. I had planned to visit Aunt Beatrice but I was afraid she would see the truth written on my face. Everyone I encountered seemed to look at me with knowing eyes.

My way led down St James Street, where the sign on a window still read 'J. Stead, Seamstress'. I sometimes saw Mrs Stead about the town, grown older, greyer, thinner... still alone. Was that the fate of mistresses?

Adultery. It was an ugly word.

–

Despite my misgivings, and my frequent vows to end the affair, Geoffrey and I continued to meet as often as we could. For a few hours on each occasion the sordid room on Greyfriars Gate was transformed into an arbour of love, where heaven was briefly ours.

What harm were we doing? Basil no longer wanted me, and Geoffrey's marriage was not happy – he never talked about Lucy but that in itself seemed to indicate how little he cared for her. But each time I left him my conscience told me I should not see him again. If we continued in that way, we should be discovered sooner or later. Or perhaps our love would become as unclean as the room where we met. We might come to blame and hate each other for the squalor of it.

Despite all my rationalising, the meetings continued. Each time, I promised myself, would be the last. But each time, when it came to it, I had to see him just once more. And once more. And once more.

The cold weather held into March. We suffered a minor disaster when the shepherd's hut went up in flames during lambing. It took with it the orphan lambs that Taggart had been rearing by hand, though the shepherd himself was unharmed – the fire started during the day when he was at the far side of the lambing pens. But it upset him. I can see him now, almost in tears, wearing the clothes he had worn for weeks, with a thick growth of beard – during lambing he never left his post or shaved. He swore that he had left his stove safe. He couldn't think how it could have happened. It didn't make sense.

We put it down to a freak accident. But it did mean that Taggart had to sleep in the barn, away from his flock for a few hours every night, and a few nights later something got in among the lambs and killed a dozen of them, and two ewes, mangling their throats. The vet said it looked like the work of dogs.

'Ye shouldna have peached on the man Chilvers,' was McDowall's opinion. 'He has friends hereabouts. Yon Davy Timms is still at large.

And there'll be others who'll no' be pleased that you turned their friend in to the Peelers. If ye ask me, this is their revenge.'

It was not a comfortable thought.

Nor was that an end to it. When it seemed that the thaw was coming, the men set to work readying the farm equipment. Only then did we discover that two of the ploughs had been damaged: one had a handle sawn half through, on the other the links and chains that held the whipple-trees had been loosened. Along with the trouble in the lambing field it left suspicions hanging. Were there militant unionists among my own men? McDowall denied it, and so did Plant – Orchards' men were all loyal; it had to be outsiders.

We informed the police, with little hope of their catching the culprits; many petty crimes were being perpetrated against farmers by unionists and other malcontents. This month it was Orchards, next month it would be somewhere else.

Basil too seemed to think that Amos Chilvers's accomplices must be behind the troubles, but he became impatient when I wanted to discuss it. Any small interest he had taken in the farm seemed to have evaporated, along with any tender feelings he had once had for me.

Since I could hardly share my worries with Mama, who would have fretted herself into hysterics, or with Geoffrey – those precious hours when we met were too brief to waste them in discussing farm business – I found myself confiding in Robert Wyatt. Now that he was back staying with his family at the Grange, Robert frequently accompanied Felicity on her visits.

'It's a bad time for farming in England,' he agreed. 'Everything's changing. And I wouldn't be a tenant to the prince, not at any price. Have you ever thought of emigrating? Maybe you should come out and see how we do things in New Zealand.'

He had been so successful himself that he saw emigration as the answer to everyone's ills. However, when I mentioned this conversation to Basil he said that Robert Wyatt should 'keep his blasted advice for those that need it. We're doing fine here, without his interference.'

Basil did not take to Robert, not at all.

But Felicity and her sisters enjoyed being squired by their handsome brother. He was certainly of a more pleasant disposition than Hal, and better looking, too, with much of the open air about him, in brown skin, fair hair streaked with sunlight, broad smile, ready laugh, and merry hazel eyes.

On 7 March, that year of 1873, my brother Johnny gained his majority and came home to claim his inheritance. The formalities were completed at the solicitor's office in Lynn, where the uncles, as trustees for Father's estate, handed over responsibility to Johnny. They would continue to stand by as advisers, naturally, but he was now master of his own fate. The fact seemed to bemuse him.

We celebrated with a family dinner at Weal House, to which everyone came, including Uncle Henry. I overheard him telling Johnny about some of his foreign trips with the prince, to which Johnny replied, 'Yes, that's what I want to do – travel. One can get tied down too soon, don't you think?'

Uncle Henry, nearing forty and still a merry bachelor, heartily concurred.

Next day we held a feast for our workers, who cleared one of the biggest barns and decked it out with bunting and lanterns, celebrating the coming of age of their new master with dancing and an impromptu variety show, with everyone giving his party piece. Benstead recited a droll monologue; Ned Plant revealed a magnificent bass singing voice; Taggart played the fiddle, accompanied by his wife on a penny whistle, and young Jack Huggins amazed us all with a juggling act in which he kept a ball, a stick, and a milking stool all spinning in the air together. When McDowall's children, Stella and Donald, appeared in Scottish dress to perform a sword dance, it seemed to point to a happy future of contentment for us all, working together as one unit.

The only shadow over the evening was my concern about Johnny, who despite his smiles remained grave and somehow apart.

It was a day or two before I had the chance to tackle my brother about his intentions. On an afternoon when at last freezing winds gave way to milder breezes, he and I rode out to see the farm and I pointed out the various fields, the merits and drawbacks of certain areas of clay or gravelly sand; I told him about the current stage of ploughing and harrowing, of our problems with the freezing weather, foot-rot among the sheep, blight in the beet, and of course the game that caused so many headaches both with its rearing and its destruction.

Johnny listened, nodded, said, 'Yes' and 'No' and 'I see.'

Having had enough of it, I drew rein and looked directly at him. 'Well, are you going to take it on, or not?' I hadn't meant to sound so aggressive but I was tired of his attitude. I had worked for over four years in order to keep the farm for him; I had married Basil in order to keep the farm for him; I had sublimated my life, my hopes…

Johnny slid me a sidelong look. 'Take it on? How do you mean?'

'Don't you know what I mean? The farm's yours now. Are you coming home to take over?'

He blinked at me. 'Hasn't Basil talked to you about it? I told him – at the party in the barn – I asked him if he'd be willing to stay on for a while. He said he would.'

That surprised me into silence – I had thought Basil was only waiting his chance to be gone.

'There's so much I want to do before I settle down,' Johnny said. 'So much more I have to learn. Farming's not what it was in Father's time. The great plains of America are opening up, and they're vast. Grain, and cattle – when the new refrigerator ships get going they'll be sending us beef, too. With steam ships moving cargoes that much faster there'll be more and more produce coming from abroad. Not only from the Americas but Australia and New Zealand. We're going to have to think differently, work differently, to face that challenge.'

He reminded me of Victor, enthusing about steam-engines. He also reminded me of Robert Wyatt, with whom he had had at least one long, intense discussion.

'Since you say "we",' I remarked, 'am I to assume that you do intend to be involved?'

'Of course! Of course I do. I regard it as a sacred trust, left to me by Father. But…' He frowned, trying to find the right words. 'But first I want to finish my education, and see something of the world.'

A sigh eased out of me, barely audible in the breeze, and I turned my eyes to the rolling horizon where young winter wheat was showing green. Along the headland a boy ran with a clapper, crow-scaring. 'Robert Wyatt's persuaded you to try New Zealand, I suppose?'

'No. I'm going to America.'

I looked at him along my shoulder. 'You have it all planned?'

A slight flush burnished his pale cheek as he admitted, 'A friend of mine… well, he has an uncle – Sir Youngman Houser – who owns a spread out there – a cattle ranch, that is. I'm going out there for a year, to work with him and travel about a bit.'

'I see. And what will happen when that year is over?'

'Then… then I'm not sure. Look, I know you love the farm. The thing is… when I do take it on, you'll have to leave. I couldn't live in the same house as Basil, and besides… besides, I shall want to do things my own way, without you for ever at my elbow watching me. This way, it means you can stay here for a bit longer.' He searched my face for a moment before saying again, 'I thought you'd be pleased.'

Odd how the human mind works, how we can delude ourselves. In all the time I had striven, both while Father was alive and since he died, the farm had been all-important to me. Yet now that I was expected to stay on, to keep fighting against impossible odds, I realised that I had actually been looking forward to relinquishing the burden.

'Basil thought so, too,' Johnny said. 'He agreed to stay on as nominal tenant because he thought it was what you wanted.'

'Well, it is, of course,' I said, and – perversely enough – in part it was true.

Because that was what he wanted to hear, Johnny didn't probe further. 'Then what are we arguing about? Come on, I'll race you back for tea.'

He won the race. I let him. I hung behind and eventually let the horse slow to a walk, my thoughts in turmoil. I loved the farm; it was my home and I wanted to stay, but at the same time I had dreamed of letting go the work and the worry, of turning to my own life. In some vague subconscious I had looked forward to having time for myself – time, perhaps, to mend my marriage, to plan on raising a family.

As for my other, wilder dreams about Geoffrey Devlin… they would always be with me, no doubt. But they were unattainable. If I were sensible I would pack them away and look to making something of the reality that was my lot.

I asked my husband why he hadn't told me about his conversation with Johnny. 'I thought you hated the farm. You've often said—'

'Maybe I've changed my mind. You're happy here. I'll stay for your sake.' But he wouldn't meet my eye.

Baffled by his sudden consideration, I said, 'I could be happy elsewhere, if it was what you wanted. I shall soon be thirty. If we don't have another child soon it may be too late.'

'No good either of us pinning our hopes on that. Look at your aunt and uncle at Weal House, wed for nigh on forty year and no child to show for it. Best have something else to keep you occupied.'

Once he had been eager for us to have a family, but since Georgie died he seemed to have lost his appetite for fatherhood. Indeed, he so seldom turned to me in the night that there was little likelihood of my conceiving from him.

My life was in flux. My destiny lay somewhere away from Orchards Farm, but the shape and manner of it were hazed in uncertainty.

–

At last the weather gave, the ploughs, harrows and seed drills went out. I hired a team of local men to pick stones; it was back-breaking work, but most of the men seemed glad to be earning. However, there was still some discontented muttering, especially when March Manyweathers brought storms of hail, high winds and driving rain.

On a brighter day, when the young crop was springing green and the hedgerows budding with hawthorn blossom, I walked out to Batty's Bottom, our lowest field, to assure myself its heavy clay soil was ready for harrowing; I didn't entirely trust McDowall's judgement on the matter. As I came out of the gate in my working clothes, boots heavy with clotted mud, serge skirts ragged and filthy at the hems, I saw in the lane a young woman, seated side-saddle on a lovely chestnut gelding, her head and shoulders framed against the brightness of the sky behind her.

She might have been a model for a fashionplate, wearing a grey velvet habit trimmed with black. Black feathers bobbed in a matching cap, with a thick, spotted veil drawn over her face.

She had been waiting for me.

Lucinda Devlin. Geoffrey's wife.

'Mrs Pooley,' she greeted me.

Though my palms pricked with apprehension, I managed to reply calmly, 'Mrs Devlin. Good morning.'

'I've been wanting to speak with you.'

'Indeed? Will you come up to the farm? My stepmother—'

'I should like to know what's going on between you and my husband.'

I stared up at her, at the feathers describing a graceful curve against the cloud-scudding April sky, at the pale face with its cruel disfigurement half concealed behind the veil. Through a throat that was suddenly dry, I said, 'Going on? I'm sorry, I don't—'

'Please don't trouble to lie. I know what's between you.' A tear trickled down her cheek and tangled in the veil, and when she spoke I heard the catch in her voice. 'Oh, don't worry, he hasn't betrayed you. He never would. Not Geoffrey. It's just that I know him so well. I always knew there was someone. I've often suspected it might be you. But I was never sure, not until that night at the lake. It was written on both your faces. He came after you, didn't he? You were together, in the darkness. You've been seeing him ever since then.'

'Mrs Devlin…'

'No, don't.' She put out a hand, palm forward, as if to bar the sound of my voice. 'Don't deny it. I'm not angry. I'm almost glad, in a strange way, that I know who you are. It means I can appeal to you, woman to woman. The others… well, the others were just passing fancies. I didn't care who they were, so long as—'

I found my voice, though it sounded unfamiliar even to me. 'Others?'

'Did you think you were the only one?' She shook her head, pitying me. 'Oh, no, Mrs Pooley, there have been others. Many others. Here and in Italy. In London, too. Men…' Her mouth twisted on the words, 'Men will take their pleasure, no matter who suffers for it.'

Other women. Shock held me cocooned, unable to think.

'I have tried not to mind it,' Lucinda was saying. 'I knew he would always come back to me. But you… there's something different about you. I know it from the way he speaks of you, and from the way he looks at you. The way he acts when he's been with you. And it frightens me. Oh, please, I beg you…' She was almost strangling on her tears, her voice growing thick and faint as she pleaded, 'Don't let him leave me. I don't care if you sleep with him. I don't care about that. Be his mistress if it makes him happy – and it does, I can see that. I won't try to stop you. I won't make trouble. But… don't let him leave me. That's all I ask of you. Please… don't take him away from me! If he sends me back to Italy, I… I'll kill myself. I will, I'll kill myself!'

She slapped her riding crop hard across her mount's rump. It reared, its eyes wild, forelegs flailing, then thudded to earth and set off at a gallop, its rider urging it to greater effort.

Around me the birds sang, building nests. The hedge was thick with bursting buds, the breeze spoke of milder days to come. I loved the spring, but at that moment I was cold as winter.

The following Tuesday I drove to my rendezvous with Geoffrey with his wife's words echoing in my mind. *'The others… just passing fancies. Men will take their pleasure…'* I wanted to trust Geoffrey. I did believe in him. And yet… and yet I was tormented by the insecurity that is the lot of all mistresses. How could I be sure of him? If I were just one of many… I couldn't bear the thought.

'Be his mistress if it makes him happy…' By giving me her permission, she had made it impossible for me to go on.

Leaving my trap outside a hotel on the square, I made my way through the town to Greyfriars Gate like one sleep-walking. Yet I was seeing clearly for the first time in weeks. I hated all this deceit and subterfuge. Once, when I was an innocent of eighteen, deception had been an excitement, a giddy game with love as the prize. Now my adult-self saw the tawdriness of it: my adult-self was tormented by self-disgust. This would be the last time. That I promised myself.

On that day the room seemed all the more threadbare, its furnishings mean and worn, its adornments cheap gloss on dross. Someone had been cooking cabbage nearby; the smell had permeated the room, adding to the musty, stale-sweat odour. I had time to savour it, for Geoffrey was late. Waiting, I sat in the sagging armchair, whose bright cushion covers could not disguise the worn places where horsehair poked through, coarse and black.

Hearing the passage door close, and eager footsteps on the bare stairs, I got to my feet and stood tensely facing the door as Geoffrey came in. He tossed his hat aside and started towards me, saying, 'Forgive me, love, I was detained by some fool of a—' and then he saw my face and stopped. 'What's wrong?'

I had intended to be cool and dignified, but my plans went awry as I threw out my hands in a gesture of anger and futility. 'What could be wrong? Except that I had a visit from your wife.'

His arms, held out to hold me, fell to his sides, and it was as though a light went out behind his eyes. 'Ah,' was all he said, but the syllable held a world of meaning. It seemed to declare his guilt.

'Is that all you have to say?' I cried. 'You let me believe I was the only one. You let me come here to this awful place, and all the time…' A shudder ran through me. 'I feel dirty. Soiled. Used! How many other women have you brought here?'

Unable to bear the pain I saw in his face I turned away, going to the window, where down in the yard a thin dog was tied, and next to it a crawling baby, also tethered as it played in the dirt under a line of listless, discoloured washing. I felt sick with self-loathing.

'None,' he said in a strange, soft voice that made me look sharply round.

'Don't lie to me!'

'I've never lied to you! How many times must I say…?' His anger died as swiftly as it had come. 'I suppose I haven't been completely honest, either. But I promise you, I've brought no other woman here. N-not *here*.'

Not here. The implications resounded between us like the echo of hammer on anvil.

'Then where?' I choked. 'Have you found more salubrious quarters for your other doxies?'

His face twisted in a grimace that may have been meant as wry humour but looked more like pain. 'Just what did Lucy say, Rose, that made you hate me so? D–did she tell you that I'm a lecher? A wretched seducer?'

'She told me there had been other women. Many other women.'

For a moment he stood there, watching me, eyes bright, with both irony and despair.

'Do you deny it?' I cried.

'No.' He threw himself down in the lumpy armchair, sighing heavily, saying wretchedly, 'No, Rose, I don't deny it. Yes, there have been other women. But not here. Not since you and I have…'

Turning away, I stared unseeingly at the smeared window, fiercely denying the tears that came crowding in my head.

'For most of them it was their t-trade,' Geoffrey said.

I spun round, crying, 'What?'

'Well, what did you think?' he asked, eyes sparking in a face pale with anger. 'Of course there have been other women – enough to keep me sane. I took my comfort where I could, from women who were willing to give, if only in return for money. I'm a man, not a celibate monk!'

'You have a wife!'

He leapt up, throwing out his arms. 'A wife who is no wife!'

I stared at him, uncomprehending.

'I see she forgot to tell you that!'

Feeling myself tremble, I managed, 'I don't understand.'

'No? Nor I!' He swept a hand through his hair, staring at me with hard bright eyes. 'But the fact is she can't bear to be touched. N–not in that way. Not as a wife should. What was I supposed to do, Rose? Comfort myself with c–c–c–cold baths?'

In a passion of despair he pushed past me and stood staring down at the fire, his hands raking again and again in his hair, combing it back and back and back. 'It was not my choice. Not my choice. I would have been faithful to her, if only...'

Chills of horror ran through me. Hurting for him, I went to him, reaching to his shoulder. 'Geoffrey...'

He snapped his arm down so suddenly that his elbow caught me in the face. I reeled away, yelping with pain, a hand to my eye, as with an exclamation of dismay Geoffrey turned and grabbed me, saving me from falling, saying anxiously, 'I'm sorry. Oh, love, I'm sorry. I had no idea you were so close. Have I hurt you? Let me see...'

The heat of the bruise was high on my cheekbone, just under my left eye, but it was nothing compared to the fire that sprang into life between us as we looked into each other's eyes and I saw his anguished tears.

'I have never loved any woman but you,' he vowed hoarsely. 'Do you believe me?'

Feeling the immediate response in my womb, I could only obey the dictates of my heart. I wanted to believe him. I wanted to hold on to the one dream that had endured for me. Even his wife had said that he cared for me in a special way.

How does one explain the mindless madness of desire? It comes without warning, without bidding. As one, we reached for each other like starving beasts, made more eager by our brief misunderstanding. For a while we had feared that we were losing each other. Now we pressed together, unable to be close enough, hating the thickness of winter clothes between us. Our hands tore and fumbled with buttons and fastenings and flowing skirts. Still dressed, too impatient to wait, we fell together on to the sagging bed, our bodies seeking, finding, joining... This time the ecstasy swept both of us up and carried us on together, to a peak where a cry escaped me as I felt his climax catch him unawares and my own delight overflowed in a rush of fulfilment.

Afterwards we lay together, holding tightly to each other until our breathing quieted and the beat of our blood calmed to a normal rate.

'I'm sorry,' he kept muttering. 'I'm sorry, I didn't intend…'

'It doesn't matter,' I whispered recklessly. 'It doesn't matter. What will be, will be. Let fate decide.'

'I love you.' Then he lifted himself to look at me, and what he saw made his eyes fill with rueful laughter. 'Oh, love… You're still wearing your hat!'

He was still reluctant to speak of his marriage; he felt it was disloyal, that the problem was his and Lucy's, not mine.

'You've said too much to stop now,' I reasoned. 'I want to know, Geoffrey. When she agreed to be your wife she surely knew what marriage meant. Are you saying she refuses to—'

'It's not like that.' Wearily he rolled on to his back and lay staring at the damp patch on the ceiling. 'She doesn't refuse. She doesn't have to. Seeing her go pale, staring at me, shrinking from me, near fainting with fear, shaking so violently she might have fever… God knows I'm no saint, but neither am I a ravisher of terrified virgins.'

'You mean… you've never made love to her at all?'

'No, never.'

The idea was inconceivable. 'But… is she ill?'

'Perhaps. In her mind, anyway. Don't ask me to explain it, for I can't. She's a confused child.'

'Then why did you marry her?'

Sighing, he shook his head, rubbing his face as if he were tired. 'It seemed to be my duty.'

The match had been planned for years. Their mothers, Lady Devlin and Lady Elston, were second cousins; Sir Arthur Devlin and Lord Elston had long engaged in joint business ventures. Both families having only one child, they had decided to merge their fortunes in the marriage of their offspring.

'I knew that there was an agreement of sorts,' Geoffrey told me. 'But Lucy is eight years younger than I. She was little more than a thin, shy, nervous babe when I first knew her. The idea of our marriage was far off in a future that might never arrive. The reality of it didn't impinge on my life. I was fond of her, as I might have been fond of a younger sister. And I was sorry for her. I pitied her.'

'Because of the scar on her lip?'

'That happened when she was twelve – she fell down some marble stairs. It made her even more timid and afraid, and it made *me* most reluctant to hurt her further. As she grew up, she talked about our being married as if it were a means of escape from her life in Italy. She clung to my hand and spoke of her longing to be transported away from "this dreadful place".'

'But she loves Italy.'

'I know.' He sighed. 'I know. It makes no sense. Now that she's away from it, she pines for her home. But then… then she could hardly wait for her eighteenth birthday, when our formal engagement would begin.

'I was not so sure, especially after I met you. I was hoping to find a way to escape the agreement. But when I returned from Italy and found you were gone away I told myself it was meant to be. I wrote that letter, believing it was the honourable thing. I tried to forget you. Then you came home again and I knew my feelings had never really changed. But you appeared to want nothing more to do with me. And anyway, by then I had committed myself irrevocably to Lucy.'

The delay over their wedding had suited them both. Lucy had been nervous and Geoffrey had hoped that time together might deepen his feelings for a girl who was still emotionally immature.

'I suggested that, if she wished to change her mind, she should not feel bound by the promises our parents had made, but she wept and begged me not to desert her…' The memories made his eyes bleak. 'I had no choice but to honour the obligation. Perhaps I should have been stronger, but I simply could not bring myself to abandon her.'

On their wedding night, sensitive to what he understood to be the normal fears of a young virgin, he had respected her wish that he should wait, but as the weeks passed he grew impatient, until finally he had tried to make love to her only to have her turn into a frightened animal, huddled in a corner, shuddering and shaking. Despite all his patience she had remained terrified of the physical act of love. She was a damaged child.

She was also, when roused, possessed of a violent temper, usually directed against herself.

Recounting this part of it, Geoffrey's face was troubled. 'She blames herself for her inability to be a proper wife. She threatens to injure or kill herself. She rides like a madwoman, and if I try to stop her she turns on me. I must tread warily.' He lifted heavy eyes to meet mine. 'I'm afraid she may end up in Bedlam.'

'You mean…' I could hardly say the words, 'she's mad?'

He watched me for long moments in which I heard my own heart beat louder and louder with apprehension, until at last he said quietly, 'It was Lucy who stabbed me.'

Seven

I stared at him, a sick trembling starting inside me as I looked at the jagged scar that marred his chest. 'Dear God…'

'She has fits of jealousy. She accuses me of unfaithfulness.' He grimaced and threw out a hand. 'Sometimes she has cause.'

'She told me she didn't care.'

'Nor does she, most of the time. Only when she fears I may leave her. That night, after the unionist meeting… You were much on my mind. I kept thinking of being with you at the cottage the next day. Perhaps she smelled the desire on me – she has such instincts, like a wild animal. She had the knife. She threatened to kill herself if I left her. When I tried to stop her, she turned the knife on me. It was so quick. So quick I didn't feel the wound. I could hardly believe it when the blood started to pour from me. And then she screamed, and kept on screaming…'

Knowing how dreadful it must have been for him, I laid my head on his chest, huddling close to him. 'There was no shadow in the garden? No intruder?'

'I invented that story to shield Lucy. What else could I say – that my wife had tried to kill me? Was I to stand by and watch her imprisoned? Or be the cause of sending her to a lunatic asylum? She is my wife. She relies on me to protect her. That's all she asks of me – to stay with her and keep her safe from all the monsters in her mind. I can't leave her. You must understand that.'

'I do,' I said sadly. 'Yes, I do.'

Geoffrey lifted my head and regarded me with sadly tender eyes, scanning my face as if he would memorise every pore. 'I love you.'

For answer, because no words could express my feelings, I leaned and kissed him softly. His response was warm and immediate, rousing unbearable longings in both of us.

At Orchards, I encountered Narnie in the front hall. 'What have you done to your face?' she demanded.

'Face?' The mirror told me I had a red weal under my eye, where Geoffrey's elbow had caught me. 'I bumped it on the edge of a stall in the market – I was too busy watching the bullocks. How is Mama?'

'She's as well as usual. Got herself all excited on account of Billy Boy's birthday. You know how she is. I'll be glad when I get her safely to Thetford.'

I had forgotten they were off to Grace's again, for the baby's first birthday.

Narnie said, 'Why don't you come with us?'

'I can't. There's all the spring work to think of, and Basil may be home any day. He'll expect me to be here.'

'Him!' she snorted. 'Fine sort of husband he is. Never at home.'

'He comes when he can,' I said. 'He's a busy man.'

She paused a moment, studying me with narrowed eyes. If I had been Grace, or Mama, she might have enquired into the reasons for my pale face and hollowed eyes, but I had long ago forfeited any place in her affections. She just grunted, 'Then you'd better stay and wait for him,' and went on her way.

Going into the drawing-room, I stood gazing at my mother's portrait, wondering if she would have understood the passions that drove me. What if a child were to come of this day's indiscretion?

I should welcome it, I thought recklessly. Geoffrey's child.

Yet the thought was as bitter as it was sweet. He already had a child. He had a daughter, and I had allowed her to be taken from me.

–

Geoffrey and I did not meet for a week or two – he had other pressing commitments which kept him from being in Lynn on market days; but messages exchanged via Jack Huggins told of his continued affection and his longing to be with me again. I missed him, too. Without him I was lonely. Without him my misgivings loomed ever larger.

I was a married woman and he a married man. We were both doing wrong. My conscience whispered with my doubts and my doubts worked on my guilt. I counted the days to my menstruation.

Meanwhile petty annoyances continued to plague the farm. Someone cleared all the tarred brambles out of the hare runs, leaving them open for the animals to get at our young corn; replacing them took several days' work. Then an old and valued hedge burst into flame and scorched the blossom from several trees in the orchard. Basil happened to be at home at the time and he helped put out the fire.

'This was no accident,' he said, coming in with black smears on his face. 'You should have kept your mouth shut about Chilvers and Timms. And that man Pyke's still about – he's now working in the quarry at Snet'sham, so I hear.'

One evening we attended a dinner party at the Grange, but Basil was in a bad mood and didn't try to conceal his unreasoning dislike of Robert Wyatt. When the gentlemen emerged from their conversation over brandy and cigars, my husband made excuses and hustled me away. He complained that Robert was, 'Too inquisitive for his own good. Nothing but questions, questions...'

'Only because he's interested.'

'He's too interested – in you!'

'Oh, don't be absurd,' I sighed. 'He's a friend. I've known him all my life. And I like him.'

'Well, I don't.'

I didn't argue. I felt irritable myself, and I had stomach cramps and other sensations which told me my fears of pregnancy were unfounded. Illogically, the knowledge made me want to weep with disappointment: this time I wasn't going to have Geoffrey's child – I wasn't going to have any child. Perhaps God was punishing me.

Or was it a blessing? Was it a final chance for me to put things right? In my heart I knew I couldn't go on as I was.

Feeling in need of a change, I gladly accepted Aunt Beatrice's invitation to spend a few days at Weal House and attend with her a reading from the late Mr Dickens's works. She invited Basil, too, but he claimed other things to do – he was never happy at Weal House.

On a warm and sunny Saturday afternoon, Beatrice and I took a stroll through town to the Walks, where we remarked on the activities of the birds and the tender young greenery in the trees and bushes. 'Spring is really here,' my aunt smiled, her arm through mine as she walked with the aid of her stick.

Other people had had the same urge to be out, boys and girls, lads and lasses let free from work, nursemaids with prams, mothers and matrons, artisans and gentry, strolling under limes and chestnuts where a thick haze of spring was spreading. Music floated from the bandstand, and a Punch and Judy man had set up his tent under a tree, the performance watched by a small crowd of children and adults. We paused to watch, laughing at the puppets' antics.

Then fingers fastened briefly on my wrist. 'Rose...' a vibrant voice breathed low, and as I turned Geoffrey tipped his hat to my aunt. 'Ah – g-good afternoon, Mrs Hamilton. Please excuse me. I need to have a word with Mrs Pooley. About that hedge,' he told me, though his eyes held other messages. 'I thought we should sort the trouble out before it goes much further. If I may...'

He moved away, obliging me to follow him. I saw Aunt Beatrice frown as she stared after us. Geoffrey headed away from the crowd, to a slope of grassed hill dotted with japonica bushes bright with waxy pink flowers. He kept slightly ahead of me, walking briskly until we were clear of any possible listeners.

'You shouldn't—' I began, but he cut me off.

'I know I shouldn't, but what choice had I? I tried to get a message to you but the boy said you were with your aunt. The maid at Weal House told me where I might find you.'

'You went to Weal House? Geoffrey—'

'I know!' He stopped and turned to me. 'I know it was an indiscretion but I didn't know how else to manage it. Forgive me, please. I had to see you today. I didn't want a hasty note to tell you I had gone.'

'Gone?' The word echoed hollowly inside me.

'Lucinda's father has been taken ill. She wants to go home to Italy to be with her mother. I tried to persuade her to go alone, but she became hysterical. She won't go without me.'

I seemed to have played this scene before. The first time we parted he had been going to Italy. I had known that it was an ending. I knew it now. I knew what I ought to do – I ought to say that we could not go on, that I must make my life with my husband. Much as I loved Geoffrey, there were times when love was not enough. Other things had equal importance – reputation, family, peace of mind...

All of that was in my mind. And there it remained. I couldn't bring myself to speak it aloud.

'It may be for only a week or two,' Geoffrey said.

'Rose...' Aunt Beatrice called from a few yards down the hill. 'Rose, dear, is everything all right?'

Fumbling in my reticule for a handkerchief, I called back, 'Yes, Aunt, I'm just coming.'

'I won't embarrass you further, love,' Geoffrey murmured. 'We'll meet again when I come home. Please God it won't be long. I shall miss you.' With which he doffed his hat, sketched me a formal bow and added more loudly, 'Good afternoon, ma'am,' as he set off down the hill, passing Aunt Beatrice with a 'Good afternoon, Mrs Hamilton.'

'Rose!' Aunt Beatrice struggled on stiff knees to my side. 'Wasn't that young Mr Devlin from Ambleford? But you're weeping! What did he say? Has he upset you?'

'It's nothing. Only...' I cast about for some explanation. 'Oh, some problem over our boundary hedges. You know the trouble Father always had with Ambleford. I just... I just didn't seem able to—'

'Well, really!' She was indignant on my behalf. 'And I always thought Mr Devlin such a pleasant young gentleman. That he should accost you like this, and leave you in tears, why, it's... it's a disgrace, that's what it is. Come, my dear, let's go home. We'll have some tea. That will make you feel better. I always say a good cup of tea is nearly as refreshing as an hour of prayer.'

I don't remember which extracts from Mr Dickens's novels we heard at the reading that evening, but I do remember weeping profusely over most of them. I soaked three handkerchiefs.

—

The following week, on a day when the April sun had the strength of summer, the Wyatt girls and Robert called in at the farm on their way to stroll round Sandringham Park and admire the new house. They persuaded me to go with them. As we walked, we observed the site where a new water tower was being built on the hill behind Orchards Farm. After his illness, and the typhoid outbreak in the villages, His Royal Highness was taking pains to ensure the purity of his water supply.

I found myself telling Robert about the nuisance the building of the water tower was causing me. Since the spring that fed the supply was in Poacher's Wood, contractors came and went across my land, chewing up the paths with their heavy wagons, spilling bricks and leaving mess. At least the problem was finite; once the tower was complete the men would go away.

'And are your other problems as easily resolved?' Robert asked.

'Other problems?'

'Whatever it is that's troubling you.'

Robert was almost as perceptive as Cassie had been.

'Most of my troubles are so totally beyond solution that I have abandoned even thinking about them,' I said lightly. 'Every farmer has worries. The weather, the work-force, the bills to be paid… Let's talk about something more amusing. Ladies, do step out a little more or we shall never get there.'

I drew Felicity and her sisters round me, and laughed and joked to dispel any hint of unease. Perhaps Basil had been right to sense danger from Robert. He was an attractive man, physically strong yet kind and gentle. I found his company disturbing.

Next day he came again to the farm, without any of his sisters, and he found me equally alone – I had let Violet have an afternoon free; she was walking out with the grocer from Dersingham and he had taken her to the beach. I believed I had mentioned this possibility to Robert the previous day.

'Yes, that's right,' he agreed with a grin that dimpled one brown cheek. He stood in my hallway, hat in hand, broad and smiling, long fair hair touched with sunlight. His voice was light tenor, with a touch of a drawl that he had picked up while abroad. 'I also know your husband's away. That's why I came – to see you alone. But I promise you, cross my heart and hope to die, I have no evil intent. In which case, may I come in? I'd like to talk to you.'

'About what?'

'Oh, this and that, you know. This and that.'

I sent Swift to fetch some apple wine, while I led the way into the conservatory. Outside, thick pink and white blossom decked the apple trees. The sun felt hot through the windows; potted plants made drifts of condensation on the glass. The patchwork cushions adorning the wicker armchairs had been made by Grace – a Christmas gift.

'Would you care to sit down?'

'Thanks.' He sank down into one of the chairs, stretching out his long legs, lacing his fingers across his waistcoat and regarding me with his head on one side. 'Well… so, what shall we talk about? Oh – Felicity said to tell you she had a letter from Chloe, who sends her kindest regards and hopes you're well.'

339

Chloe, married now for a year or so, lived with her doctor husband along the coast at Cromer. 'That's sweet of her. Ask Felicity to send the same in return.'

We chatted idly for a while, about his sisters, about the farm…

'You know,' he said at length. 'If you need someone to talk to, I've a willing ear and a strong shoulder.'

'What makes you think I'm in need of a confidant?'

A slow smile warmed his eyes. 'Well, are you?'

'Certainly not. And if I were… I do have friends. Felicity in particular. Reverend Lancaster calls quite regularly. And there's always Mama, and Narnie.'

'When they're here. Which isn't often, so it appears. Strikes me they could be staying away to avoid that husband of yours. What's wrong with the fellow? He's jumpy as a hare in March. You know, I never thought you'd marry someone like him.'

'Then who had you in mind?'

His grin turned wry. 'Me, mostly.' And then he laughed. 'Well, a boy can have dreams. To me you were special. I'd have killed for you.'

'What nonsense,' I chided. 'Blatant flattery.'

'It's simple truth. I did once come to blows over you. Got my nose bloodied.'

'By whom?'

'My brother. Hal.'

A pulsating silence spread between us. All trace of humour had gone from his face. He was trying to tell me something – something I had no wish to hear.

Then the door slammed open, startling us both. Basil was there, his face dark with anger, his presence like a draught of cold air. 'I knew it,' he snarled. 'I knew it! Can't leave you alone five minutes, can I? Every time I go out of this house, there's some man waiting to sneak in behind my back.'

Robert shot to his feet, outraged. 'Now look here, Pooley—'

My husband stepped away from the door. 'Out. Out! And don't come back. You're not welcome here.'

'He's entirely welcome!' I exclaimed, getting up from the chair.

'Not to me, he's not. And I'm the master here, remember? Remember?'

Robert looked at me, frowned, and decided not to interfere between us. But he left without hurry, coming to where I stood, taking my hand in farewell.

340

'Out!' Basil said.

With a final worried look, to which I replied with a little shrug – 'don't concern yourself, it will pass' – Robert left.

Shaking my head, I let go of a weary sigh. 'He was only paying a neighbourly call. He's a friend – a very old friend. There was no harm in my entertaining him alone for five minutes.' The only reply was a black frown. 'I'm tired of this, Basil. So very tired. It's not as if you really care. You're just looking for a quarrel. Please… Can't we find some way to—'

Glowering at me, he thrust the door closed and said in a low voice filled with hate, 'I always knew you were a whore!'

The charge made me flinch as though he had hit me.

'Don't deny it!' he roared, making a vicious, chopping gesture. 'That's why you went to Brighton. You were sent away for whoring.'

Dismay sent my thoughts scattering. 'Basil…'

'Everybody knew it. Everybody! Except me. I didn't let myself believe it. I worshipped you. You…' He looked me up and down, a sneer contorting his features. 'You with your high and mighty ways. Miss Rose Hamilton. Viscount Colworth's granddaughter. Too good for me, weren't you? Wouldn't look twice at Basil Pooley, except to make use of me. No, you had your sights set a lot higher. As high as the throne of England.'

Not that again. 'You're mad,' I said tiredly.

'Then what about Devlin?'

That name came like a slap. Guilt wrapped its coils about my vocal chords and threatened to strangle me, but Basil was too caught up in his own temper to notice my reaction.

'I've not forgotten how he stood up for you that time – in front of the prince and all,' he raged. 'I always thought it was queer. Well, this time you were seen, blast you! Strolling on his arm in the Walks, for all the world to see. People couldn't wait to tell me. Couldn't wait!'

In the Walks… Thank God that was all. 'I was not on his arm,' I denied hoarsely. 'We were talking. As neighbours will. How people do twist things. Didn't your informant tell you that Aunt Beatrice was there, too?'

But he wasn't interested in facts. What scorched him was not that I might have been unfaithful, but that people were talking.

He struck out at a plant pot on a ledge, pushing it to topple and fall with a crash that made me cover my ears. Shards of earthenware scattered, soil spilled and rolled. Basil walked through it, coming for me, saying through his teeth, 'Blast you, Rose! You've made me look a proper fool!'

I didn't see the blow coming. I just felt the force of his fist against the side of my face. It sent me reeling. A slap jerked my head the other way. My foot caught in the chair leg. I toppled and, trying to save myself, brought down another plant. Dazed, I lay amid the crushed foliage.

'Get up!' he commanded. 'What would your father say if he could see you? Rose Mary Hester Hamilton. Look at you, lying in the dirt.'

'Down at your level,' I muttered. Hating him with a soul-deep loathing, I got to my knees and, with the help of a chair, started to pull myself up.

'Nobody would blame me if I divorced you,' he said. 'Then we'd find out the truth once and for all. How would you like to have your history examined in court, eh?'

Dizziness swirled round me as I gained my feet. All too clearly I could see myself in court, having my past recounted in lurid detail: the rumours about Hal Wyatt, my recent association with Geoffrey... it would all be uncovered. Disgrace for Geoffrey, misery for Lucy – and ruination for me. Any jury of decent, God-fearing citizens would damn me to a living hell. For I was the woman taken in adultery.

'You wouldn't dare!'

'Wouldn't I, though?'

'I'd fight you all the way. And all your own skeletons would come rattling into the open. Are you so lily-white that you'll risk that, Basil?'

It was pure bravado, firing arrows into mist, but something struck home with greater severity than I had expected. His ruddy face went sickly pale, then flushed scarlet as the blood came rushing back and his eyes bulged with fury. Muttering obscenities, he turned and stamped away, slamming the door behind him. I heard the front door slam violently, too. Basil was gone.

Trembling, I sank into a chair, my head in my hands until the tremors passed and my head cleared. Basil, too, had things to hide, it seemed. I suppose I had suspected it. Whatever the truth, neither of us dared risk the exposure of a divorce court. So we must remain bound together: stalemated, and stale-mated. Until death...

Thank God for the farm, and practical problems. Hard as it was to keep going, the work kept me sane.

When Basil came home after three days, we went about our lives in separate silences. In bed at night he lay so that he didn't have to touch me. I couldn't sleep. I lay awake hour upon hour, drained to exhaustion for fear of what he might be planning.

I began to think that the only answer was to leave him, once the farm was safe in Johnny's hands. With my responsibility for Orchards dispensed with, I would be free to go where I pleased – even if it meant leaving with my reputation in permanent ruins, going into exile and disgrace again, this time for ever.

Of one thing I was sure – rather than risk dragging him, and Lucy, down into the mire with me, I must never see Geoffrey again.

–

Mama and Narnie returned to Orchards briefly but, sensing the sour atmosphere, took the first opportunity to return to Thetford. Their excuse was to be present for Tommy's fourth birthday. It had, however, become obvious that Mama much preferred to be with Grace. Since Father died, the farm was full of hurtful memories for her. But she also enjoyed life in town, and the social status which the Turnbull name ensured was more to her taste than the workaday farm.

I felt ever more isolated.

It seemed almost the final straw when His Royal Highness, chancing to pass me in the lane during one of his brief respites at his country home, rather than cheerily greeting me with a smile and a flirtatious remark, glowered, grunted and rode by.

I was soon informed by my friends in the villages that the prince had been heard to cut dead someone who mentioned my name. 'He say, "I prefer not to be reminded of *that* there lady," he say.'

What had I done now?

It was Mr Lancaster who told me that the Waleses' heir, young Prince Albert Victor, had developed a fever after a weekend at Sandringham. Tainted drinking water was held to be the cause. Someone had sought to ingratiate himself with the Prince of Wales by inferring that, the spring supplying his water being on my land, I must be responsible for contaminating it.

The agent, Mr Beck, called at the farm in a hopping rage. He had discovered a manure heap seeping only yards away from the spring in Poacher's Wood. Knowing nothing about this, I was horrified. But

McDowall, called to answer to the land agent, claimed that he had specifically asked me if I was sure I wanted the manure dumped there.

'Ye told me it was all right. I don't recall ye mentioning the spring. Maybe ye forgot it was there.'

'Then it was up to you to remind me – if you told me at all.'

He looked the picture of injured loyalty. 'I did so tell ye! Och, but ye've not been yersel' lately, one way and another. I blame mysel'. I should've realised ye weren't thinkin' clearly. Aye, it's my fault, Mr Beck. I'll get the heap moved right away.'

Somehow, while gallantly taking the blame, he managed to make me look like a muddle-headed, incompetent, emotional female, if not a downright liar. I knew Mr Beck had taken the point. Word would go back to the prince – yes, Mrs Pooley had been up to her tricks again.

'That chap Beck want shootin',' George Pooley commiserated when I told him. 'He have it in for you and no mistake. Me too I shouldn't wonder. Got a big black mark across my name – in the prince's book, any road.'

'Why, what have you done?' I asked.

It appeared that His Royal Highness had sent his agent to make an offer for Mr Pooley's best game coverts in Blackthorn Wood, which adjoined a part of the Sandringham estate. But Pooley was an old-fashioned sportsman. He liked to go out with a few friends, a few good dogs, and enjoy a day's sport in leisurely, gentlemanly fashion, giving the game a fair chance to hide. He shared my revulsion for the great *battues* favoured by the prince. Shoots at Sandringham were more like wholesale butchery. So he had refused the royal offer.

'I say no. "Not at any price," I say. So he want to lease the wood, and I say "No" again. So he say, "All right, Pooley, we'll rent that off of you by the season," he say. "That you will not," say I. "That's not for sale, nor lease, nor lend. Not for love nor money." "Well, His Royal Highness won't be best pleased to hear that," he say, and I say, "I don't care whether he's pleased or not, that wood have been in my family for nigh on five hundred year and in my family that will stay." And so it will, least while I'm here to see to it.'

'Three cheers for you,' I replied, heartened to think that there was someone who actually dared stand up to the prince.

As haysel ended, when long hours in the fields were sapping my resources, I had word that the Prince of Wales was out inspecting our coverts with Mr Jackson, his head keeper. I set out to find him, thinking to explain to him that I was his most loyal subject, and that I would be the last person to wish harm to him or his in any way. If he cared to check, he would find that his spring water was now as sweet as he could wish and I would personally ensure that it stayed that way.

If I had been less tired I might have realised the futility of such a quest. I had been working in the sun all day; I felt out of sorts, irritable and uneasy, with a headache behind my eyes – I often had such symptoms at a certain time of the month. In that mood, it seemed to me that a confrontation was the only answer.

I found His Royal Highness strolling among hazel thickets, with Mr Jackson in his green velvet coat beside him, a following of equerries and underkeepers, and two or three dogs wagging around. As I sank into a curtsey I saw the prince's scowl. He didn't greet me, or smilingly chide me for being so formal, as once he might have done.

'So, Jackson,' he said loudly, 'you'll be sure to provide good sport for my birthday shoot this year. I've plans for the biggest *battue* ever seen in England. I'm inviting all the best Guns. I'll expect a good bag. A thousand brace, eh? See if Orchards Farm can provide us with a thousand brace.'

'Why…' Mr Jackson slid a glance at me, seeing my horror. 'I'll do my best, sir.'

A *thousand* brace! If it was to be even half possible it would mean extra vigilance all summer, work and nuisance and headaches for me and my men, with the keepers constantly on watch to make sure we harmed not the smallest partridge or the weakest leveret. And after six months of that we would face the upheaval of the shoot itself, hundreds of beaters tramping over the land, noise, havoc, slaughter… all for the sake of a tally in a game book. The biggest *battue* ever seen. One thousand brace. An impossible order.

The prince was looking at me, his eyes narrowed and mean in his fleshy, bearded face. 'You won't have any objections to that, will you, Mrs Pooley?'

'No, sir.'

'No. I should hope not. This is my land, after all. Since you've prevented me from giving my guests the chance to shoot across the best coverts in Norfolk, I choose to do it on Orchards Farm instead. Good day to you.'

He strode past me, calling the dogs to follow.

'*The best coverts in Norfolk*'? Blackthorn Wood, of course. Once out of favour, any calumny would be believed against me. Now the prince thought I had colluded with Pooley, solely to thwart his desire for Blackthorn Wood! I didn't think I could bear any more.

–

Since it was midsummer the evenings remained light. It felt humid, too, as if a storm were threatening. The haying was done, the hands all having an evening's rest, so the farm was quiet. But the house seemed airless, its silence confining as a prison. I was hot and restless, suffering from a headache, longing for someone to talk to.

Going down to the yards, where the hayricks smelled sweet in the warm evening, I encountered Plant heading home, and with him old Milky Mickleborough, who had once worked for my father as cowman. Now he was nearly blind, looked after by his unmarried daughter, who took in washing and sewing to support herself and her father.

The old man was always scavenging after bits and pieces, making and mending in order to earn a copper or two to fend off the threat of the workhouse. Plant had found him examining an old cart of ours which, after years of wear, was all but falling to pieces.

'He want to know how much you want for it,' my teamsman said. 'That, and a few other odds and ends as we've got together. I was a-goin' to ask Mr McDowall in the morning, but...'

I asked to see the 'odds and ends', which were mainly rubbish we would probably have thrown away. The cart might have been worth a pound or two, but seeing the old man's rags and evident ill-health, I said he could take it.

'I don't want no charity, Miss Rose,' Milky objected, peering at me closely in an effort to see my face.

'It's not charity,' I said. 'If you get that cart fixed I'll expect you to run a few errands for me. Come back and see me when you're ready to go to work.'

Satisfied with that, he went on his way. He took the cart with him, loaded with his other acquisitions, himself between the shafts like an old shambling rickshaw man. Plant walked beside him, while I stood at the gate and watched. Seeing the way the wheels wobbled out of true, I wondered if the cart would last as far as the village.

Their going made the place seem even quieter. And I was in need of company. Even Basil would be better than no one.

I found myself in the stables, stroking the horses, talking to them, even telling them some of my thoughts. 'Why is Basil never here when I really need him?'

'Miss?'

The small voice made me turn to see Jack Huggins peering out of the hayloft where he slept.

'I thought you'd be out rabbiting,' I said.

'No, not tonight, miss.' For once he didn't cheekily deny any criminal intent. His small face looked intense, his eyes bright. 'Maybe you ought to try the old cockler's cottage.'

I frowned at him, my aching brain trying to make sense of what he had said. 'What?'

'Old Fenny's place. Out near Onion Corner. Mr Pooley goes there sometimes.'

'Does he? How do you…?' I stopped myself. Who knew how Jack knew what he knew, except that he slipped about, here and there, watching and listening? It was an instinct with him, to know everything and to be ready for anything. 'I thought Old Fenny Jakes was dead.'

'So he is, miss. Took by pneumony, last winter. Nice old bloke, too.' He swung down from the loft and dropped lightly to the ground. 'Shall I harness the trap for you?'

He knew more than he was saying – more than I cared to ask. It would be undignified of me to question a stable boy about my own husband. But what was Basil doing at Fenny's cottage? My mind couldn't grapple with the problem. Best go there and find out for sure.

The decision to go to the cottage seemed to have been made for me.

As he handed me the reins, the boy said, 'D'you want me to come with you, miss? It's late. It'll soon be dark.'

'Not so dark that I can't get there and back on my own.' I didn't want him along with his sharp eyes and ears. I had to travel this road alone, wherever it might lead.

The evening was glorious, a mackerel sky painted in shades of grey and blue, with the sun sinking in clear yellow light. Over the marshes, clusters of swifts whirled and screamed, after flies, and beyond them flocks of gulls wheeled in the evening light. A jay went hastening by, showing off its blue rump, and a family of tiny pheasant chicks scampered ahead of me, frantically searching for a gap in tall grasses while their mother cried out to them anxiously.

But behind me, in the south west, black clouds were rolling up. Distant thunder muttered along the horizon and the wind began to rise. I wished I had brought a shawl; the air had turned cold. My head was pounding spitefully, laying a cloud on my brain that made it difficult to think. Where was I going? Oh, yes…

A red squirrel darted from the centre of the lane, vanished into undergrowth and appeared again darting up a tree-trunk. The sky ahead was turning pink and gold, the sun a bright ball low down, hiding itself behind a tangle of trees. Behind me the storm clouds moved closer, blotting out the brightness.

With the scent of wild garlic strong in my nostrils, I left the trap at the entry to the lane. I couldn't have said why, not for sure. But a part of me – the instinctive part that had sensed what the boy Jack hadn't told me – said that I should go warily, keep watch, look sharp.

Beyond the cottage, a rough paddock had been fenced off among the trees, and in it grazed the grey gelding hack that Basil often rode on local journeys. The horse looked at home there. It snorted softly and came over to stand by its fence as I approached.

A child's crying came from the cottage, whose windows were open to the air. It looked tidier than when I had last seen it, when Basil brought me here to meet Old Fenny seven years ago. In that time the thatch had faded from gold to grey. The fence was mended, the path had been cleared, the old nets and lobster pots taken away, the garden weeded. Fresh brown paint gleamed on window-frames and door, and the windows shone, backed by lace curtains that billowed in the rising breeze.

I heard a woman's voice, crooning a lullaby. The sound made me stop, listening to her song. I didn't want to go on. I didn't want to know.

But curiosity drew me, dreamlike, to the open door, where I saw the room beyond, the fire burning, the lamps already alight. Inside the cottage, twilight had come. The woman sat in Old Fenny's rocking chair with the child against her shoulder. It looked to be about a year old. She had been feeding it; her bodice was still undone, exposing the pale roundness of a heavy, blue-veined breast. As I watched, she seemed to become aware of the cooling draught. She shivered and got up, starting towards the door.

The woman... I knew her now, knew her as she stopped dead, seeing me there, her mouth opening, her eyes staring. Ellen Earley. Ellen Earley, once our lady's maid.

'Miss Rose!' She clutched the baby to her, grasping the edges of her bodice. Over the child's small squirming body she gaped at me in fright. Her tongue came out to moisten her lips. She said, 'What...?' and then, frantically, 'It wasn't *my* fault. I swear it wasn't. He made me. I was a good girl before I met him.'

My brain laboured, trying to make sense of what I had found. I suppose I knew what it was; I just couldn't believe it all at once.

'I *told* him he should have let me stay further away,' she cried. 'I *knew* you'd find out if I came to live so close. But he wouldn't *let* me stay in Hunst'on, *nor* go to my folks in Lancashire. He wanted me *near*, where he could see me and the bairn.' My silence seemed to frighten her more. She blurted, 'Anyway, *I'm* not the only one. Not by a long chalk. *Ask* him. Ask him about that Mrs Longville. She *calls* herself Mrs Longville, but—'

'Shut your row, Ellen!'

The snarl came from behind me. Basil stood there, trees tossing behind him against a sky gone ink-black shot through with swirling grey, as if the clouds were boiling. The gusting wind brought the sharp damp scent of rain, through which my husband's face was set, with glinting eyes. He looked like a stranger.

'Is this true?' I said stupidly.

'I *told* you should let me go home!' Ellen cried.

Basil ignored her. He set down the creel of fish he was carrying and caught my arm. 'This is no place for you. Come, I'll take you back to the farm. There's a storm brewing.'

'I can drive myself,' I said, and tried to shake free.

His hand tightened cruelly, his fingers biting into my arm. Eyes hard as sapphires, he said, '*I'll* drive you.'

He was far stronger than I. Though not tall he was broad and muscular – and besides, he was my husband: I had vowed to obey him. And so, like one trapped in a nightmare without will of my own, I let him propel me back to the lane. Behind us Ellen wept, clutching her baby to her and shouting, 'Pooley, no! Don't! Pooley...'

'What about your horse?' I asked.

'I'll come back for it.'

My arm was starting to tingle, the blood flow restricted. 'Basil, you're hurting me!'

He only pushed the harder, herding me ahead of him down the lane while behind us Ellen Earley cried, 'Don't do it, Pooley! It's not worth it.'

We had reached the trap. 'Get in,' my husband ordered. 'I'll take you home.'

'I don't need you to take me home,' I retorted through gritted teeth, climbing up to the trap. 'I don't want you at Orchards any more. Stay here with them. This is where you prefer to be, isn't it?'

I meant to drive off and leave him, but as I reached to untie the reins Basil leapt up beside me. His body thrust at mine, sending me sprawling as he forced himself into the seat.

Face grim, he gathered the reins, letting off the brake. He lashed at the pony, startling it. 'Go on. Go on!! Giddup!'

The jerk of the trap over-balanced me further and I found myself clinging on desperately, trying to regain the seat while the vehicle bucked and swayed beneath me.

Storm clouds had brought an angry purple twilight full of gusting wind, flying leaves and heavy spots of rain. As we left the wood a small branch fell across the track behind us. The trap lurched round the corner, into the wider lane. All the time Basil urged the horse faster, using the long end of the reins as a lash. Beside me, the drainage ditch glinted in the livid light from the sky. Thunder ran muttering along the horizon.

Still holding on for dear life, at an ungainly angle in the corner of the seat, I looked at the man beside me. This man with whom I had lived for four years. This stranger. I kept seeing the cottage, and Ellen so peaceful with her baby. The baby – that was why she had left the farm. Mrs Benstead had been right to guess at 'a man in the case'. The man in this case had been my own husband.

Had I ever known him at all? His face was contorted, dark with blood, eyes glinting cold as lightning flared, teeth bared in a rictus of fury as he whipped at the horse, shouting at it to 'Giddup! Faster! Go on, giddup!'

Up ahead, the ditch met a deeper dyke that ran at right-angles to it, so that the lane took a sharp right-hand bend. Basil knew that as well as I, yet he didn't attempt to slow down.

Among the confusion of doubt, anger and unease that filled me, fear raised a tendril that grew swiftly, blotting out all else. 'What are you doing?' I managed. 'Are you trying to kill us both? Basil...'

He was driving too fast. Much too fast. The reins slapped, the trap jumped and jolted. Lightning seared the sky, terrifying the pony. The sharp right-hand bend lay not far ahead. The strong onion scent of wild garlic filled my nostrils.

'Slow down!' I begged, grasping my husband's arm. 'Slow down!'

He shook me off, so violently that his flailing hand cracked numbingly across my nose. The blow sent me back into the corner, sideways across the hard leather cushions, my hands grasping for a hold. Pain blinded me momentarily.

We were at the corner.

At the last minute, he dragged the pony to the right. The trap lurched like a live thing, trying to toss me out. A cry snatched from me, shredding in the wind. But my hands held firm. The trap settled back to a level. I found myself kneeling on the footboard, clinging to the back and side of the seat. We were past the corner, charging on down the twisting lane.

'Basil!' I gasped. 'Stop! Don't do this. Let's talk about it. Please stop and let's talk about it.'

He only whipped the pony harder. Flecks of her sweat flew back like spume. The storm was coming nearer, thunder crashing and then rolling, like a drum thrown to bounce down stairs. Out of the purple twilight a flight of duck came low, wings whirring as they called their alarm. I wished I could fly.

'Basil!' I clutched at his arm, fastening my hand in his sleeve. 'You'll kill us both! Is that what you want?'

He flashed me a look like demons, his eyes seeming luminous in a face that was near black in that strange light, running with sweat. 'I shall jump free. You're the one who will drown.'

Drown?

The bridge. The little narrow wooden bridge over the little narrow Babingley river. The river was in flood after spring rains, running full and deep.

I lunged for the reins, thinking to halt the pony. Basil fended me off. In desperation I threw myself at him, grasping for the reins. We struggled fiercely. Close as lovers. Deadly as enemies. I clawed for his face. I remember his breath on my cheek, the feel of his clothing, the odour of his skin.

The rest is only impressions. The bridge racing closer. The river, glinting dark. Bushes tangled thickly along the banks. Out of these bushes, something white, startling in the darkness. Huge wings flapping. A swan! The pony screaming, hooves pawing the air. The trap, slewing round, bucking under me. Tossing me free. The sky revolving around me. The swan flapping away. Thunder cracking. Wood splintering. Basil's cry.

And then nothing.

Nothing.

Part Four

Hester's Girl

One

Voices came as if through water, blurred and distant. Faces swam through mists. In my half-conscious moments the voices spoke to me and I answered. Then the mists claimed me again.

When I woke it was evening. I knew that from the angle of the light. My head ached. I felt weak and thirsty. But at least the woolly feeling had left me.

A woman stood by the window, staring out over the garden and the woods, watching colours change in the sunset sky that framed her.

Moistening parched lips, I managed, 'Please... a drink?'

With a little gasp the woman turned and came hurrying to me. It was Felicity, her face radiant with relief, though behind it I could see the strain she had been enduring. 'Rose! You're awake! Oh, my dear... Yes, a drink. Some cordial. I'll water it down a little.'

Only when I tried to sit up did I realise just how weak I was. My muscles wouldn't work. Felicity had to sit beside me and support my head while she helped me sip the cordial. Blackberry cordial, from brambles in Poacher's Wood.

'Have I been ill?' I asked.

She made me comfortable against the pillows and sat beside me, holding my hand. 'Yes, my dear.'

'How long?'

'Five days now. You've had concussion. A nasty blow on the head, and a little fever. I can't tell you how glad I am to have you back in your right mind. I must go and tell the others.'

The others' were Narnie and Aunt Beatrice. They came hurrying, as best they could with their rheumaticky legs, and wept over me. Grace had wanted to come, Narnie told me, but they had thought it best that she stay where she was, with her children and with Mama.

'You know how illness upsets your poor mama,' she added. 'So I came in her stead to be with you. And I shan't leave until you're fit and well again, my lamb.'

My illness had brought her from Thetford, made me once again her 'lamb'. In her own strange way she did still care for me.

'God has answered our prayers,' Aunt Beatrice cried, tears of joy in her eyes. 'I've prayed for you constantly, my love.'

'As have all of your friends,' Felicity added. 'We've had so many anxious enquiries.' She smiled as she recalled, 'Mrs Benstead said we ought to put a bulletin board at the gate – as they did at Sandringham when His Royal Highness was ill. Now, I think we should let you lie quietly a while. Mrs Hamilton, Miss Narborough… it's your turn to rest. Why don't you have Mrs Benstead make us all some tea? I'll sit with Rose.'

At the door, as they left, there was some whispered conversation of which I made out only Felicity saying, 'Yes, yes. I'll do it.'

She seemed reluctant now to look at me. She paused to rearrange the set of hairbrushes I kept on a tallboy, then went to straighten the curtains and look out on a sky that had turned to ink and flame. The blackbird that nested every year in the berberis under my window was singing tunefully, and I saw the martins swoop – or was it bats? How I loved the farm. How glad I was to have been allowed to survive to enjoy it once more.

'Thank God you were strong,' Felicity said. 'But then you have always been a fighter.'

'Have I?'

'Far stronger than I. I've marvelled at you sometimes. You remind me of a saying my father has – "It's not the beaten man who fails; it's the one who lies down." You never have lain down. You've been knocked off your feet, but you've always jumped up and carried on fighting.'

'That's not strength,' I denied ruefully, 'that's stubbornness. And impetuosity. Hamilton failings, I fear.'

She turned and moved softly back to stand by the bed watching me with soft, sad eyes. 'Whatever you may call it, you're going to need all your courage now, my dear. There's something I have to tell you. You… you haven't asked about your husband.'

Basil. My mind panicked, my thoughts fragmented. I didn't want to think about Basil.

'Do you remember anything about the accident?' she asked.

The storm. The trap, jolting. Flying leaves on the wind. The smell of wild garlic. The bridge. Basil saying, 'It's you who'll drown…' He had tried to kill me.

'No.'

'You were out on the Babingley marshes in the trap – you and your husband. There was a thunderstorm. The horse must have bolted. The trap overturned – at the bridge near Onion Corner. Fortunately you were thrown clear, into the bushes.'

I felt numb. 'And he?'

'I'm sorry to have to tell you, but… he's dead, Rose. His neck was broken.'

Though I heard the words, they didn't seem to have any meaning, not then. Shock had cushioned me. 'What about the pony?'

'She's all right. She had a bad fright, but your man Plant's taking good care of her.'

My lovely Beauty. I thought of her high-stepping along the lanes. I thought of her whipped to terror as lightning flared…

Felicity said, 'Mr Pooley – Farmer Pooley – has made arrangements for the burial to take place at East Esham, next Friday afternoon.'

'What day is it today?'

'It's Monday. The last day of June.'

Apart from concussion, shock and bruises, I sustained a black eye and innumerable small cuts and abrasions. My nails were broken, too – from clawing at the trap, and at my husband, in a frenzy of fear.

Determined to be well enough to attend the funeral despite the doctor's remonstrances, I lay in bed listening to the sounds of nature and the farm, letting my thoughts drift. I slept long hours every night and more hours in the day, often prey to strange dreams but otherwise more peaceful than I had been in all of the four years I had been married. I was not sorry that Basil had gone – I should be a hypocrite to claim otherwise, though I had never wished him dead.

About the rest – about that last night – I tried not to think. But there were times when I imagined his step on the stair and a shudder of horror raised the hairs along my spine.

My recovery was unhelped by the descent of Grace, with all her children, and Mama, who couldn't take in what had happened. I blessed my dear Felicity, who shielded me from the worst of it. Nevertheless, when the appointed day came I was still shaky, glad of the support of my friend and my sister, one on each side of me.

The storm had brought with it a cold front whose showers still persisted, so we walked beneath umbrellas. There were few mourners – just those of us from Orchards, with Felicity; George and Eliza Pooley, with their daughters and sons-in-law; Aunt Beatrice and Uncle Jonathan; and Mr and Mrs Wyatt with Robert.

I don't remember thinking or feeling anything.

Vaguely aware of other presences in the background, I thought little of them until, as we left the graveside, Grace on my right and Felicity on my left, my sister hissed, 'Who *are* those people?' She indicated the woman who stood at the far side of the churchyard, with beside her a young girl perhaps sixteen years old, both of them attired in full mourning.

'I don't know.' As far as I could remember, I had never seen either the woman or the girl before.

'Then what are they doing here? They were at the back of the church during the service, and now they stand there watching...'

'I believe it's Mrs Longville and her daughter,' Felicity said.

'Who?' Grace demanded.

'Mrs Linnet Longville. Have you never met her, Rose? She used to be acquainted with your husband. Surely you remember. It was she who arranged for Victor and me to meet.'

Threads of memory gathered like fronds of mist. Mrs Linnet Longville, who kept bees. 'I do seem to recall your saying something of the kind. Her husband's a sea captain, is he not?'

'He was,' Felicity replied. 'I think he must be dead now. I've heard her referred to as 'the Widow Longville'. Shall I go and speak to her?'

'No!' The word escaped sharply as I clutched at her arm. 'No, leave her to grieve in her own way.'

It was only later that I understood myself, when I finally remembered where I had heard the name 'Mrs Longville' quite recently.

–

In order to save me the trouble when I was unwell, the Pooleys had arranged the funeral repast at their farm. Mrs Pooley had put on a generous spread of pork pies and hams, pickles and crusty loaves, cakes and jellies, all home-made from home-grown ingredients. Half a dozen grandchildren raced in and out – the oldest boy was destined to inherit the farm some day – and on the surface the mood was light, as if everyone were anxious to forget our reasons for gathering.

Farmer Pooley seemed especially jovial, playing the host with such hearty verve that I guessed it was a cover for his real emotions. But after a while he asked me to attend him in the front parlour, and there he set aside his mask: his smiles died, his whole body drooped. He became suddenly tired and old, a man turned seventy and feeling every year of it.

'There's business has to be seen to,' he said, closing the door so that we were shut together in a brooding silence emphasised by the slow, ponderous ticking of a huge, ornately-carved clock on the wall.

The front parlour was seldom used. Light came dimly through thick lace curtains and potted plants. In one corner a piano stood silent, as it had done for years; neither of the Pooley daughters had displayed any talent for music. Grass-green velveteen draped across piano, tables and sideboards; even the mantel was swathed and bobbled. On top of the draping, decorated boxes of all sizes stood among dozens of silver-framed photographs depicting the family at various stages, along with glass domes which kept the dust from stuffed birds, paper flowers, shells…

Pooley walked heavily across the room, favouring his arthritic hip, feeling in his waistcoat pocket for a key, his air that of one who has an unpleasant duty to discharge. In a corner, another velveteen-draped piece of furniture proved to be a bureau, which the farmer unlocked, taking out a legal document tied with red ribbon.

'It's the will,' he said, keeping his back turned to me. 'His solicitor sent it me from London.'

'Have you read it?'

'Yes.' Suddenly agitated, he turned to look at me, waving the will in the air. 'The latest codicils were added last September. But that's been changed over and over. Basil kept changing his mind. If he'd a lived, he'd probably have changed it all again. He can't have meant… I don't understand it. That's wholly 'mazed me. I know things weren't all honey 'tween you two, but… Well, that don't fare to be my business, but if I'd a known, I'd a given him a piece of my mind. Still, that's too late now. That seem to be all legal and proper.'

'Are you trying to tell me he's cut me out?' I asked.

'No. Not entirely. He's left you… this.'

'This' was a painting which lay face down on a sofa. Pooley turned it over, showing me the picture contained by an ornate gilt frame. Done in oils, it was a study of Orchards in springtime, a fine painting evoking the atmosphere of a working farm.

'He commissioned it, special,' Farmer Pooley said, fixing his eyes on the painting to avoid looking at me. 'Then he gave it to me for safe-keeping. Two year ago. About the time the little 'un passed on.'

'Ah,' I breathed, comprehending. At a time when things were well between us, Basil had planned a surprise to please me. But by the time the picture was complete he had changed his mind, because Georgie had died and he blamed me for it. So he had bequeathed it to me as a reminder, meant to wound me. Which it did. '*The only thing you care about's the bloody farm,*' he had said.

'Who has he named as his main heir?' I asked. 'You?'

Carefully, Pooley laid the painting down, saying, 'Well now, as to that, Miss Rose… He left me and Eliza some personal bits and pieces – mementoes, so to speak. The girls, too.'

'And the rest?' Seeing him hang his head, staring down at the will which he still held tight in a big, horny hand, I felt both sorry for him and impatient with him. 'Mr Pooley, I think I'm entitled to know how he's disposed of his estate.'

'He's left it…' he said slowly, 'to the children of two friends of his.' He looked up, inspired with an answer to the mystery: 'Children. See – he always liked children. Always wanted some of his own. If only you'd had another child—'

'What friends?' I broke in.

He stared at me unhappily. 'Nobody you'd know, Miss Rose.'

'You think not?' Wanting to release him from his torture, I held out my hand, 'Let me see the will, if you please, Mr Pooley. Let me read it for myself.' While I did so, he stood over me, restlessly shifting from foot to foot. The will was a morass of legal jargon, written in neat copperplate.

'I don't understand whatever made him do it,' Pooley said. 'You could contest it, you know. You're his legal widow. You're entitled to at least a third—'

But I wasn't listening. I had just found the details of how Basil had disposed of his main estate: it was somewhat complicated, but the gist of it – the names of his two 'friends' whose children would be beneficiaries – stood out in letters that burned into my mind: 'Ellen Earley', and a certain 'Linnet Longville'.

Pooley and I agreed not to mention it to anyone else, not yet. We both needed time to think.

–

Solicitous over my welfare and determined that I should convalesce in peace, Felicity was instrumental in seeing that Mama and Grace, with the children and sundry' nursemaids, including Narnie, all went off again to Thetford only a few days later. Felicity herself planned to stay at the farm: 'For as long as you need me, my dear. I somehow feel it's my place. We might have been sisters if Victor had lived.'

'If Victor had lived,' I said, 'so many things would have been different. Felicity, where exactly does Mrs Longville live? I think I might pay her a call.'

'What a good idea. I'll come with you.'

'There's no need for you to trouble yourself.' What Mrs Longville and I must say to one another might be better said in private.

But Felicity would not be dissuaded. 'It won't be any trouble to me, my dear. I certainly don't intend to let you go out alone – you're not at all well yet. Besides, I've sadly neglected Mrs Longville in recent years. After Victor died I couldn't bear the thought of going back to Drayton. I really should go and pay my respects. I don't even know how long it has been since she lost her husband.'

Since my trap was in Ben Chilvers's workshop, undergoing repair, Felicity organised a carriage and coachman from the Grange and we set out on our visit one afternoon in mid-July.

Drayton village lay a few miles south of Feltham, its church, inn and cottages centred around a broad green in a hollow where three lanes met, shaded with copses, gardens brilliant with summer flowers, vegetable patches neatly hoed. Mrs Longville's cottage lay apart, down a narrow lane sheltered by tall hedges. A white gate led to gardens lush with roses and hollyhocks, alive with bees hunting in a patch of lavender, and butterflies congregating in the blossoms of the buddleia. The cottage itself was thatched, beetling eaves over small leaded windows, backed by an orchard of apples and pears, and on a lawn to one side a small girl, perhaps four years old, romped with a clutch of kittens while a couple of dogs lazed yawning nearby.

'It looks as though she has acquired yet another daughter,' Felicity said with a fond look for the child. 'Poor Mrs Longville. She always said her husband yearned for a son.'

As we walked down the path, barking sounded and another dog dashed into sight, leaping round the pinafores of two brown-haired girls aged about thirteen and ten. They stopped when they saw us, blushing and giggling, before darting back out of sight.

'That must be Clara and Beth,' Felicity said. 'My goodness, how they've grown since I saw them. And… ah, yes, here's Amy.'

At the corner of the house now appeared the oldest sister, who had been with her mother in the churchyard. She was the fairest of the four, her hair hanging loose about her shoulders, her pinafore neat over a short black dress that showed black stockings and button boots.

Regarding us warily, she called, 'Mother!'

A moment later the door opened wider, disclosing the figure of a neat little body of middle years – about forty, I guessed – dressed in full mourning, tastefully though not expensively, as if she tried hard to keep up appearances on a small income. Seeing us, she began nervously to pat her tidy hair.

'My dear Mrs Longville,' Felicity greeted, her hand extended. 'Forgive us for calling unexpectedly. I don't believe you know Mrs Pooley.'

Mrs Longville ignored the proffered hand; she had not taken her eyes from my face. She said, 'We haven't been introduced, but I know her. I've been expecting you. Perhaps you'd like to come in, Mrs Pooley. No – just Mrs Pooley, Miss Wyatt – would you keep an eye on the children for me, please?'

Disconcerted by being consigned to the role of nursemaid, Felicity looked askance at the child on the lawn. Then, realising that Mrs Longville wished to speak to me privately, she nodded. 'Yes, of course,' though she gave me a puzzled glance.

'Amy will make you some tea. Won't you, Amy?'

Amy, with a speaking look for her mother, hurried away, while Mrs Longville gestured me inside and closed the door, pointedly shutting Felicity out.

The cottage was homely, clean but slightly shabby, with evidence of make-do and mend. Signs of children and animals lay everywhere, toys on the floor, a ball of wool unravelled across a peg rug, a chewed bone in the hearth. Evidently Mrs Longville liked animals – her ornaments included many pottery representations of cats, dogs, rabbits and birds, in various sorts and sizes, mostly mass-produced fairings. The room was also enlivened by large vases crammed with flowers. I caught myself wondering how familiar it had been to Basil. Had he felt more at home here than he had felt at Orchards?

Having straightened the cushions on a couch, Mrs Longville gestured me towards it. 'Have a seat.' She herself chose a straight-backed chair by a table littered with scrap-book cuttings. She sat erect, hands folded in her lap, waiting.

Now that I was there, I hardly knew how to begin. 'I understand you knew my brother, Victor Hamilton.'

'I knew Basil Pooley better.'

'Ah. Yes.' Her bluntness dispensed with any need for polite prevarication. I was glad of it. All I wanted was the truth. Once that was clear, I intended to put it behind me and go on. 'That's what I thought. Are you aware that he made your children his main heirs?'

'He always said we'd be all right if anything happened.'

'And to me – his wife – he left almost nothing. Perhaps you can explain that to me, Mrs Longville.'

She looked down at her hands, lacing her fingers, rubbing her thumbs. 'I can and I will, if you really want me to, but I warn you… you won't like it.'

'I'm quite sure of that.'

Her head came up and she regarded me in speculative silence for a moment, as if I were not what she had expected. 'I've had his uncle here, you know, asking the same questions. Not that I told him anything. I thought that ought to be between me and you. Not that I want to cause you grief. If you hadn't come I'd never have said a word. But, since you're here…'

'Be so good as to tell me the truth, whatever it may be.'

'Very well.' She considered a moment before beginning. 'I knew Basil Pooley for a long time. Nearly twenty years. I knew him better than anyone. Used to work for him at one time.'

That surprised me. 'In what way?'

'I ran one of his houses. The one in Norwich.'

Puzzled, I leaned towards her. 'I'm not sure I understand. You mean, you were his housekeeper?'

'I mean, I kept a bawdy house for him.'

The phrase made me sit back, stunned – this was certainly *not* what I had expected. 'A what?'

'A house of pleasure – a house of ill-repute, you'd probably call it.'

Her flat, emotionless voice went on, telling me more about the 'businesses' my husband had conducted. Prostitution, locally and later in London, and on to gambling, and the fringes of crime... His various properties about the country all had some hidden connection with the illicit. He had made his money out of vice.

It was so unexpected that I couldn't find words; I simply sat there letting her assault my ears with facts that destroyed every illusion I had ever nurtured about Basil.

'He just got deeper and deeper once he'd started. He was good at it, you see. It made him a lot of money. But he didn't like me being involved. He was fond of me, in his way. So he got me out of it. Set me up in a place of my own. And came and stayed with me. Often.'

She watched with bright, narrowed eyes as this news percolated through my numb brain.

'I see,' I said. 'And did your husband know about this?'

A sharp, impatient laugh escaped her. 'There wasn't any Captain Longville. I invented him for the sake of propriety when Amy came along. The only man I've ever been married to – married in all but legal name, for sixteen years – is Basil Pooley.'

Before I could begin to frame a response, she went on, 'We even lived together once, like a regular married pair, for about a year and a half. We let this cottage out to a tenant, and had a house in London. In Camden Town.'

I must have made some exclamation, for she nodded, 'That's right – the same house where he took you for your honeymoon. But he couldn't settle in town. His heart was always in Norfolk – especially this last few years, after you came home. When he heard you were in bad trouble because you'd upset the prince, back he came. The girls and me stayed in London for a bit. I'd have been better off staying there for good. But when this cottage fell vacant again, back I came too, like the fool I am. I came to be near Basil. And Basil, he came to be near you. He was obsessed with you.

'You were miles above him – that's what he always thought. He couldn't believe his luck when you asked him to marry you. He thought he'd got the prize. The fairy princess. Forbidden fruit.' Her mouth twisted. 'Of course, he had to marry you to get what he wanted, while I gave him everything without any ties. I made it too easy for him – that was my mistake. Basil Pooley always wanted what was out of reach. But when he got it he soon got tired of it. It was the game he liked best – the chase. He soon came back to me. I knew he would. I was always more his sort. I understood him. We had more in common. And we had the girls – his daughters. Look at them out there, bless their hearts. Basil Pooley's daughters.'

Like one bewitched, I did as I was bid and looked out of the window. Amy was bringing a tray of tea; the two middle girls came running to join the party; the smallest one sat on Felicity's knee as she read a story.

Basil's daughters.

'How old is she?' I croaked. 'The baby – how old is she?'

'She's four. She was born in December '68, just before he married you. Perhaps if she'd been a boy things might have been different. But I can't rear boys. We had three, but they all died before they were two years old. That hurt him bad. He always wanted a son and heir.'

Oh, dear God. I closed my eyes, but inexorable memory presented me with the sight of Basil rushing into the room where I lay in childbed, almost beside himself because I had given birth to a boy.

'Well,' Mrs Longville said flatly, 'at least he got one before he died.'

My eyes snapped open. 'My son is dead!'

'Not yours. The other one.'

My mind went blank. 'Other one?'

'Well, you do know about that, don't you? That woman Earley told me you turned up at the cottage. It was because of her he changed his will. That's why the girls and me'll only get half – because that bitch gave Basil the boy he so dearly wanted!'

The cottage seemed suddenly airless. I remember clawing for the door, gulping in the fresh air as I ran down the path and out to the lane, where I stopped in confusion, wondering where I was. Felicity came flying after me, all concern, got me into the carriage with the coachman's help and sat beside me holding my hand, anxiously asking what was wrong.

'Don't ask,' I told her. 'Don't ever ask. I never want to think of it again.'

I couldn't help but think of it though. Inexorably the thoughts went on, round and round until my brain hurt. My hands clenched so tight in anger that my gloves cut off the blood and made my fingers go dead.

All Basil had ever wanted was a son. So when had he turned to Ellen Earley – as soon as Georgie died? That had been December. Ellen had left the farm in February. Had Basil seduced her while he claimed to be grieving for our son? Would he have married Ellen if I had died that night at Onion Corner? Would he have stayed with me if Georgie had lived? And still kept going back to Mrs Longville and their daughters when it suited him, as he had throughout our marriage?

The thought caused a hiccup of wild laughter to erupt in my throat. I let it out, the sound tearing at my ears and my aching head, laughter turning to cries, cries to sobs, and then tears of both fury and pain. Even his kindnesses to me seemed suspect now. Our marriage had been a sham, a deceit, a falsehood.

Oh, Georgie, my darling monkey!

Felicity held me, soothing me, saying, 'Yes, cry, my dear. Cry it all out. You'll feel better for it.'

At Orchards a letter awaited me. It bore the royal crest and it came from Mr Beck, an official and officious communication pointing out that, with my husband dead, the farm no longer had a legal tenant. The agent wished to know what I and my brother intended to do. He had several eager applicants waiting to take on the farm. Did we not think it might be best for us to sell up and move on? He wanted my answer by Michaelmas.

Evidently the prince was grasping his chance to get rid of me. He couldn't even wait a decent interval before trying to throw me out.

Watching me, Felicity said, 'What is it, my dear?'

'Read it for yourself. Excuse me.'

In a turmoil of anger and distress, I sought the solitude of my room. I stood at my window for an age, staring unseeingly at the garden and the apple trees beyond, one glove half off. In my head the years unrolled – the years of my life at Orchards; the years of my marriage to Basil.

Had it all been for nothing? Was I to lose the farm at last?

I was still standing there, lost in mists of memory, when Felicity came knocking softly on the door. Her face was a study of concern when she saw me.

'My dear… Are you intending to go out again? You haven't even taken off your hat and coat. Come, let me help you.'

'No!' I flinched away from her, then saw her face. 'Oh, forgive me, Felicity. I'm out of sorts. It's not necessary for you to help me. You're not my lady's maid.'

'But I am your friend,' she answered softly.

'My very best of friends,' I assured her, laying my gloves aside as I reached to the enamelled pin that held my hat.

'Shall you employ another lady's maid?' she asked. 'Now that Violet's to be married, you really need—'

'I really need to live according to my income,' I replied with a wry smile. 'It won't stretch to lady's maids.'

'Won't it? But I thought…'

'You thought I would be a rich widow? Not so, I fear. Basil left only debts.'

Her open face plainly showed her concern. 'Oh, my dear…'

'I shall manage very well,' I assured her. 'I have a little money that Father left for me. And there's my jewellery, which I can sell if need be.'

'Oh, my dear…' she said again, lost for words.

'I shall manage,' I repeated, and sat down at the dressing-table.

As I tidied my hair at the mirror, she stood behind me, watching me in the glass. 'We must talk about the future, Rose. There's something I'd like… But not now. I came to say, you have a visitor. I told the girl to say you weren't at home today, but he insisted you be told he was here, so I asked him to wait.' She leaned past me, picking up a tail comb which she used to tuck some stray ends of my hair into its bun. 'There, that's better,' she approved, 'though you're still too pale for my liking. It might do you good to have some different company. He brought some lovely yellow roses which I told Swift to put in water. Yellow roses are your favourite, are they not? Mr Devlin always did have a charming knack of choosing… Why, Rose, what's wrong?'

I had got up, almost thrusting her aside as I went to the window. But it was too late. Not even Felicity could have failed to see the hectic colour that had flooded my neck and face at the sound of his name. I cooled my cheeks with my palms, feeling giddy as the blood receded, leaving my head and heart pounding.

Geoffrey was here. How I longed to see him. I had only to walk down the stairs and—

'I don't want to see him.'

'Why not? Surely an old friend…' She stopped herself, evidently not wishing to pry. 'But I expect our visit to Drayton was enough for one day. I'll ask him to come back in a few days, shall I? You should be well enough to receive callers by—'

I swung round. 'I don't want to see him!'

Felicity blinked at me in astonishment. 'But why ever not? I thought you liked him. He certainly seems very concerned about you.'

Knowing only that if I saw Geoffrey at this juncture something disastrous would happen, I turned away, moving across the room. 'Then tell him I'm well enough, considering the circumstances. But don't let him come again. Tell him not to concern himself about me. He's not to come back, Felicity. Make him understand that.'

She said, 'Very well,' but I heard the bewilderment in her voice and I knew I should have controlled myself rather than give her cause to wonder. It was all too much. I could almost feel myself being torn apart by all the pressures on me.

But even then I had an insane desire to rush after her, to stop her, to see Geoffrey and throw myself into his arms where I so dearly wanted to be.

Instead I sat down and wrote to Johnny, asking him to come home as soon as he could, or risk losing the farm. The last of my strength was rapidly draining away and all I wanted to do was to turn over responsibility to someone else and go away, somewhere peaceful and quiet – somewhere I might gather the pieces of my life and build them into a new shape. There had to be a better life waiting somewhere.

—

The only person I took fully into my confidence at that time was Farmer Pooley, because he wanted me to contest the will and I had to explain my reasons for not doing so: if we went to litigation a whole horde of skeletons would come clanking out of their hiding holes for the edification of the gossips. Besides, I wanted none of that ill-gotten wealth. It was best left as it was. At least the innocents – Basil's children – would not suffer.

Since I had already told the lie to Felicity, Pooley and I agreed that we should let it be believed that Basil had been living beyond his means and had left nothing but debts. The rest was handled discreetly by the London solicitor.

Before the summer ended Mrs Longville and her four daughters left Drayton village. I heard that Fenny's cottage was also empty – Ellen Earley and her son were gone. It was all over. Except for memories.

In a long letter, Geoffrey assured me that he understood my reluctance to see him at that time. It was perhaps best that he should stay away until my husband's death was no longer the cause of speculation and rumour. He did not want to put extra pressure on me, but neither did he intend to stay away for ever. Too much remained to be said between us.

He had come home from Italy in haste as soon as he heard what had happened.

> *I have been desperately worried about you. How did the accident happen? Was it truly an accident? You see how my fear for you plays on my imagination. I must know everything before I am satisfied. I regret his death, as I regret the untimely death of any man, but since my main concern is for you I can only be glad that you are free from an unfortunate marriage which you should never have been obliged to contract. If only I had had the courage to trust in my feelings for you all those years ago, then perhaps we should be together now.*
>
> *I long to see you, even in other company. Are you really well? Please be sure to take care of your health. I know Miss Wyatt will look after you. If only I could share her task, how happy I should be. I shall not be content until I see you for myself.*
>
> *As to Lucy, she remains in Italy. Her father's illness is terminal. When I left he was in a deep coma from which he was not expected to awaken. His death will be a release for us all, especially Lucy. She has hinted at some things which I do not care to commit to paper. Suffice to say, if what I suspect is true, the man richly deserves the hell that awaits him. I shall return to Italy within the next few days, and I expect to stay until all is over. By the time I come home I trust you will be as eager to see me as I to see you. I may bring happy news.*

Happy news? How could there ever be happy news for us? He had a habit of trying to quiet my fears with hopeful promises, but all we had given each other was guilt and loneliness. It couldn't go on.

My reply, which I penned in haste, was brief – a jumble of conventional condolences and wishes for both his journey and the impending dramas which both he and Lucy must endure. 'But pray do not do anything rash on my account,' I added, reminding him of the promises he had made to poor Lucy. We could not take our happiness at her expense. I told him that I needed considerable time to think and re-evaluate, that nothing seemed certain any more.

Thus I rebuffed him, anxious to be rid of extra complications. My life seemed fraught enough already – questions about Basil, gossip and speculation, condolences and commiserations; however kindly meant, even the curiosity of those closest to me seemed an intrusion at that time, on top of which there was the prospect of raising crops amid the welter of hares and pheasants and partridges which must be preserved in readiness for the great slaughter in November, and all the time the threat of possible eviction...

I sometimes thought that if I didn't escape for a while I would run mad. Consequently, when some friends of the Wyatts offered us the use of their villa in the south of France for as long as we wished to have it, I let Felicity persuade me to take a holiday. I felt like a traitor to the farm and my labourers, but when Robert Wyatt agreed to keep a general overseeing eye on things, I laid aside my final doubts. My reserves needed recharging. Besides, McDowall would cope.

–

We crossed the Channel by steam-packet in mid-August.

The villa proved to be a charming little hideaway on the edge of a village not far from Nice, among craggy hills and white houses drifted with bougainvillaea. It was wonderfully peaceful there.

As my physical strength returned, Felicity and I went walking further and further, to favourite spots in the woods and a particular cove with steep steps leading down to a rocky beach. Felicity amused herself by sketching, and I kept notes of our exploits, the different flora and fauna we found, and the methods of cultivation and husbandry which, in the hills among the vines and goats, were so different from our Norfolk ways.

The local people regarded us as typically eccentric English ladies. From the woman who cooked and cleaned for us, we learned that we were known as 'the ancient virgin' and 'the skinny widow'.

Letters from Robert Wyatt reported a few arguments with the gamekeepers when their interests conflicted with those of the farm;

there was also a storm which slightly delayed the start of harvest, but all in all Orchards was managing well enough without me. That was good to know, though I still felt I should not have deserted my post.

One day, Felicity having gone off with her watercolours to catch the bay in a particular light, and our daily woman being engaged about some family concern, I occupied myself in preparing a meal. Fresh vegetables lay about the kitchen, waiting their turn for attention, while I tried my hand at pastry for an apple pie.

The day was warm, the sun bright with that quality of light one finds only in the south of France. Light poured in through the open doorway, bringing the sound of singing birds and the distant sea, while a cat which had adopted us lay stretched indolently along the window-sill, ignoring the colourful goldfinch that had so far escaped the cage-bird trappers and hopped outside the door after crumbs. I was aware of all these things, and of the peace of the place, but while my hands rubbed butter into flour my mind was divided, part of it in Norfolk with the farm, part in Italy with Geoffrey.

With a flurry of wings and an anxious call, the goldfinch fled. The cat, too, stirred itself and leapt from the window-sill to the high garden wall, where it poised watching as a step sounded in the yard and a shadow fell across the sunlight. I thought the arrival must be Felicity, then I saw that it was a man. He halted on the doorstep and removed his hat, but even then, with the light behind him, it took a moment for my brain to register what my startled eyes were telling me. I had never expected to see Geoffrey here – and I in an apron!

'May I?' he enquired.

I jerked myself back to some semblance of sanity. 'Oh – yes. Yes, please do come in. I just… I didn't…'

He smiled a slow smile that made my heart twist painfully in my breast. 'I'm glad to see you, too.'

'May I offer you a drink?' I sounded like poor dear Mama, grasping at trivialities.

'Thank you, no. I had a late luncheon at the inn in the village. The *patron* told me where I might find you. Is Miss Wyatt with you?'

'No, she's out at present.'

'Good.'

As he made a move towards me, I added, 'But she may be back at any moment. Geoffrey, you—'

'Don't tell me I shouldn't have come. I had to. I agonised about it but in the end it was as simple as that – I had to see you, and nothing else mattered. I had to know how you are, and whether... whether you still care for me.'

How was I to answer that? I stood like a fool, wrist-deep in a bowl of pastry, staring at him across the littered table. 'I shall always care for you. You know that. But still...'

'But still there are proprieties and conventions and all the other t-trammels that society puts upon us – yes, I know!' Agitated, he spun to look out at the yard, thumping the side of his fist against the jamb. He was silent for a while, breathing deeply to calm himself, eventually glancing round to say, 'Forgive me. I'm on edge. I've hardly slept for days, thinking what I should say to you and wondering how you would respond. Your letter... it seemed to imply that you had doubts about your feelings for me.'

For that I was sorry. I was aware of the trouble he must have gone to in order to make the journey, just to see me, and there was a part of me that, watching him, wept with loneliness and need. But I was no longer eighteen. I knew too well the consequences we were courting.

'I seem to have doubts about everything,' I said.

He turned his head to look at me across his shoulder, frowning as he sought to read my mind. 'You should know, before we go further, that my marriage to Lucinda is ended. I have applied to the courts for an annulment.'

Annulment? My heart seemed to rise into my throat and stop both my breath and my larynx, and then it beat on, fast and unsettling, as my rational mind reviewed all the consequences that must crowd in the train of this news. The case would be a sensation. It would destroy poor Lucy. And what of Lady Devlin? – that haughty, frosty matron. What of Norfolk society, and all the avid tongues that loved to wrap themselves about such luscious scandal?

Unerringly answering the most clamorous of my questions, Geoffrey added, 'I have done it with Lucy's full and free consent.'

Laying the back of my hand to a head that was spinning, I said, 'I don't understand. She was terrified of your leaving her. She begged me not to take you from her.'

'But then her father was alive.'

Seeing me still baffled, he slowly closed the door, giving us more privacy, and then he came to sit on a corner of the table, watching me with sombre eyes, while quietly and steadily he told me the dreadful story.

I can never think of Lucy without remembering that day. It comes back in vivid colour, sight, sound and scent – the small kitchen with the sun slanting in through the window, the cat prowling outside, the smell of meat cooking in the oven beside the fire, herbs hanging from the ceiling, apples in a colander by the sink waiting to be peeled, and my fingers clotted with sticky pastry. These impressions, along with my awareness of Geoffrey, all mingle inextricably with the story of tragic Lucinda de Crecy, only child of the wealthy Lord Elston – wealthy and, so Geoffrey now knew, perverted beyond all pity.

The noble lord's excesses as a young man had caused him to be banished by his family to Italy, where his depravity could be better concealed. His sexual tastes ran to children, both girls and boys. No child had been safe with him. He had even used his own daughter.

'He – and his friends,' Geoffrey said, his eyes sparking as he thought of it, 'abused her, beat her, defiled and raped her – from the time she was three years old. Three years old, Rose! That scar on her face... When she was twelve her father threw her down some stone stairs because she refused to perform an act too hideous for me to describe to you. And her mother... her mother knew what was happening, but she never raised a finger to interfere.'

'Dear God!' I remembered Lucy – that dreadful blemish on her lip, the fear that constantly shadowed her eyes, her preference for muted colours, and her bursts of wildness. Poor child. Poor, helpless, frightened child.

Much as she had loved the warmth of southern Italy, she had grasped at the chance of escaping into Geoffrey's protection. She had come to England as soon as the engagement became official on her eighteenth birthday. But she had found every reason to delay the wedding. She wanted a perfect knight – a protector, not a lusty, flesh and blood husband.

Her father had found excuses not to attend the wedding, perhaps because of his guilt, and fear of being unmasked. But Lucy had remained terrified of him; she had always refused to go back to visit her parents without Geoffrey beside her. Her greatest terror had been that Geoffrey would desert her and leave her prey again to her father's demands. But she didn't blame her father. Tragically, she blamed herself for what had happened, wished herself dead, and had even tried to kill herself – by riding too hard, and then by the knife which in her madness she had turned on Geoffrey.

'She's scarred more deeply than any of us can guess,' Geoffrey said. 'Scarred both in body and in mind.'

As a child, Lucy had taken music lessons at a convent near her home, a place where she had found solace and comfort. It was here that she had at last felt free, after her father's death, to speak of his abuse of her, and the nuns had advised her to share the truth with her husband. Piece by sordid piece she had opened her heart and faced her fearful memories. It had sickened Geoffrey; he was still angry for her sake, and felt even more protective of her.

But Lucy no longer needed his physical protection. With her father dead she was free.

'Her dearest wish is to retreat to the safety of the convent,' he told me. 'She talks of taking the Catholic faith, and perhaps joining the order. One thing is beyond question – our marriage is over. Lucy will never be able to fulfil a proper wifely role, not for me or any other man. The scars cut too deep for that.

'And so, when I asked that she consider an annulment, she agreed. It may take a few months and, undoubtedly, there will be gossip when the case comes to court. But, when it's over, I shall be free to marry again.'

There. We came back to the nub of it. Unable to meet his eyes, I worked my pastry, pushing it from my fingers in sticky lumps. 'What do your parents say to this?'

'I've yet to tell them. I imagine my mother will blame Lady Elston for misleading her. But with my father becoming more senile every day, my mother has plenty to occupy her.'

Concerned, I glanced up at him. 'I'm sorry to hear that.'

'Thank you.'

Deep, strong undercurrents ran between us, unspoken but evident to us both. His eyes probed and questioned. I could read the pain and puzzlement in him, but I couldn't bring myself to confront it.

Instead I toyed with the pastry, saying, 'There were people who said you married Lucy because of her inheritance.'

'I know.' He let the silence lengthen, then, 'Were you among them?'

'There were times when I wondered,' I admitted, and lifted my eyes again to see his reaction.

A corner of his mouth tucked in wryly as he stood up, easing an aching shoulder muscle. 'Such brutal honesty, Rose. No, the prospect of Lucy's money may have been part of my parents' reason for wanting the match, but it wasn't mine. Ambleford has its share of troubles. The cost of upkeep of the estate, and the house, grows all the time, and we have the same problems as you have at Orchards – increasing wages, the expense of improvements, the threat of drought. Storm, disease, unionists—'

'At least you don't have someone else's hares eating all your profits!'

His eyes glimmered. 'No, indeed. The game – and the debts – are all our own. Though despite the debts we're quite comfortably situated. We shall manage well enough.' Holding me with a level gaze, he added, 'We shall manage *without* Lucy's dowry. I want no part of it. No part of her.' His voice dropped to a vibrant undertone. 'It's you I want beside me.'

The pulse in my throat was pounding. The kitchen seemed airless. I couldn't speak.

He watched me with dark, searching eyes. 'I'm tired of doing what's expected of me. It's time I became my own man. I want you to be my wife, Rose. I want you to share with me whatever I have – to be, in time, Lady Devlin, mistress of Ambleford. Not now, not at once, but in a year or so, when the dust has settled and we are both decently free… I don't promise it will be easy. There'll be raised eyebrows. There'll be rumour and innuendo. But if we stand and face it together…' He stepped towards me, saying urgently, 'Rose! Answer me! We can be together at last. I thought you wanted that as much as I do. Why do you hesitate?'

'It's too soon!' I managed, the words coming out cracked through a throat that ached with unshed tears.

'Too soon? You've known for years that if the chance came—'

'I mean it's too soon after Basil… Too soon for me to make such momentous decisions.'

Once it had been he who prevaricated, now it was I who faltered at the brink. I couldn't have explained why, only that I could hardly bear the thought of facing all the gossip, of confronting his mother and my family, and all our friends – and our enemies… I was still under the displeasure of the Prince of Wales, under threat of losing Orchards; I had barely recovered from a murderous attack by a man I had called husband… It was too much to contemplate all at once. I hadn't the strength, or the courage.

'Don't you want to be my wife?' he said.

'If only it were that simple! I've so many other things to settle first. Other responsibilities. The farm. And Mama. And Johnny. And…' Despair caught in my throat as I bit my lip hard. How could I explain what I didn't understand myself?

'Very well.' A shutter had come down behind his eyes. He didn't move, except to stand straighter, but he withdrew himself from me emotionally and I knew I had wounded him deeply. 'Very well, I'll not press you further. Perhaps, when you're ready, you'll let me know when it might be c-convenient for me to call.'

I couldn't let him go like that. 'Geoffrey!' As he turned to the door, I begged him, 'Wait. Please.'

He must have heard the catch in my voice for he stopped and looked back at me. 'Well?'

I drew a long, painful breath. 'We've always been honest with each other. Tried to be. As honest as we could. Before we think of planning a future, there's something… something of the past that you should know. I should have told you before, but I was afraid of what might happen. I was afraid that…' I couldn't find the right words.

He came closer, laying a hand on my shoulder, his other hand under my chin making me look at him. 'What is it? Just tell me. Simply.'

Watching him through a blur of hot tears I pressed my lips together. There was no easy way of saying it. 'I had a child. Ten years ago. In Brighton. I had your child.'

For a moment he didn't move. He searched my eyes, his own face still. 'A child,' he said flatly.

'It was a girl. They… they took her away, as soon as she was born. I never saw her again.'

'A child.' His voice was quiet but there was a kindling in his eyes and I could see his thoughts busy behind it as he stepped away from me. 'Good God… Why didn't you tell me? If I'd known—'

Frightened by the way he was looking at me, I broke in, 'What would you have done? You were obligated to Lucy. You wouldn't have been allowed to marry me. Your parents would have seen to that. Would you have defied them, at risk of being sued for breach of promise, disgraced, talked about – and probably cut off from your inheritance?'

'You should at least have given me the choice!' he said hoarsely.

'How could I? You had left me. Used me, misled me, and then abandoned me – that was how it seemed to me.'

'I had a right to know!' he insisted. 'I trusted you. I knew there'd been rumours of a child, but I was sure you would have let me know had it been true. Did you even try to contact me?'

'I didn't know how! You had gone to Italy. They watched me every minute. I was eighteen years old, Geoffrey.'

'And you believed me inconstant. Is that how much our love meant to you?'

'I was frightened. Confused. Alone. I was a farmer's daughter, and you…' I shook my head, using my wrist to wipe away a tear. 'I'm sorry, I should never have told you. It's much too late. She's gone. I don't know where she is. She might be dead. We shall never know—'

'We could at least try! Tell me about it. Who was the midwife? Did you have a doctor?' He was feeling in his pockets, bringing out a notebook and a pencil.

Dismay flushed through me. 'You'll never find her. No one will remember. No one ever knew the whole truth. Except maybe my aunt Agnes.'

'Even so – tell me! Damnation… don't you realise she may be the only child I shall ever have?'

He questioned me closely and I, despairingly, recounted all I could remember, watching him write it down.

Often though I had imagined this moment, I had never thought it would be like this. Why hadn't I realised how much it might mean to him?

'Suppose you do find her?' I asked. 'What will you do?'

Eyes afire with determination, he said, 'I shall bring her home with me, of course.'

For the merest moment my heart leapt with joy. And then reality sobered me. Would he burden our child with the knowledge of her origins, with the label of bastard, and make her live amid gossip and scorn for the rest of her life?

The thought made me feel faint. 'But you can't! Imagine what dreadful scandal it would cause! Your mother will never accept her. Your mother has always hated me. She'll never forgive me for—'

'My mother will have no choice,' he said flatly, making for the door. 'If I have a daughter alive somewhere then she belongs with me – she belongs at Ambleford. I suggest you decide whether or not you wish to join us there. Let me know when you do.' He opened the door, then turned to add, 'But make it soon, Rose. I shan't wait for ever.'

And he left me staring at the sunlight pouring through a doorway that was suddenly empty again.

Two

A day or two later, a letter from Johnny reached us, terse with fury at the prince's attempts to pry us out of our home; of course he intended to take on the tenancy, which was his by legal right. He had written to Mr Beck confirming this and he intended to be home 'before Christmas'.

The end of my quest was, suddenly, in sight.

'Shall you stay and be your brother's housekeeper?' Felicity asked as we sat in late September sunlight, with trees moving softly in a breeze from which the wall of our small garden sheltered us.

'No, I don't think so.'

'But he'll need someone.'

'Mrs Benstead will manage admirably.'

'And you?'

'I shall go away.'

'Away? But, Rose, you love Norfolk.'

'Do I?'

'Of course you do! It's your home. You've fought so hard to stay there.'

'Well, now I've had enough. I'm feeling my age.'

'How absurd!' she scoffed. 'You're not thirty yet.'

'Even so, I'm tired. Tired of struggling against impossible odds.'

'You're only saying that because you're still not strong. When you feel better—'

'When I feel better, I shall still know that I have to leave Orchards. If I stayed I wouldn't be able to keep myself from watching the fields and checking the stock – and criticising. Johnny's task will be difficult enough without that. No, when he takes over the tenancy, I shall have kept the promise I made to Father. That's all I ever wanted.'

'Is it?' Her expression intrigued me. From under the brim of a straw hat she was watching me with troubled, almost frightened eyes.

'There's more to it than that, Rose. It's because of Geoffrey Devlin, isn't it?'

The charge caught me off guard. Before I could find a reply she went on: 'I saw him the other day. Someone told me a gentleman had been asking for us and as I came up the cliff path I saw Geoffrey leaving. Striding away as if you'd had a quarrel. He didn't see me — he was too intent on his thoughts. I wanted to ask you about it, but when you didn't mention it I thought it best to be discreet. You were in a terrible mood, Rose. Besides, there have been other hints of an attachment between you. After your accident, when he wanted so badly to see you and you became so upset… And while you were ill… you were delirious one evening. You spoke his name. You seemed to think he was there.'

Having long been needing to confide in someone, I let out a long, long, almost peaceful breath. 'Did anyone else hear?'

'Just Miss Narborough. We agreed that you were talking nonsense. Perhaps an old dream, a young girl's fantasy…'

But Narnie was no fool. Perhaps she had guessed the answer to the old mystery. Not that I cared – so long as she didn't threaten harm to Geoffrey.

'Cassie always used to say that Geoffrey Devlin was your secret hero,' Felicity recalled.

'Cassie saw too much. I could never hide anything from her.'

'And you still think of him in that way? Oh, my dear, that's a dangerous road. It was wrong of him to come here. Everyone knows that he and Lucy are not happy. Even so, they're married and…'

Wanting to comfort her, I reached to touch her hand. 'Don't concern yourself, Felicity. I promise you I shall do nothing rash.' The true state of Geoffrey's marriage would be revealed soon enough, but not through me.

'Well, if you really mean to leave Norfolk…' she said. 'It has been in my mind to ask you whether you think it might be an idea for us to… to find somewhere we might live together.'

I looked up, surprised. 'You – and I?'

'We've been so comfortable this last few months, haven't we? Papa would find us a little house, wherever we choose. I know we could be pleasant together, Rose. You don't have to give me an answer at once, but do at least think about it. We could be companions for each other in our old age. Sisters – sisters in sorrow.'

Phrased like that, it sounded less than appealing.

–

All the time we had been away, I had not been able to rid myself of thoughts of the great shoot that the prince planned for his birthday. It was like a storm hovering on the horizon, drawing steadily nearer. One thousand brace. Orchards would never stand it. I knew I had to go home, to be there, to stand in defence of my land and my people, whatever the result.

There was another reason, too – I wanted to be nearer to Geoffrey. There had been no word from him. Not that I expected to hear. He had made it clear that I must make the next move. Going home was a start.

Felicity and I returned to find autumn colouring the Norfolk land-scape with scarlet and gold, flame and rust. Mrs Benstead and the maids had the farmhouse sparkling, the larder overflowing with good food, the air redolent of baking and pickle-making and plenty. Haystacks loomed tall about the yards; pigs were fattening in their styes, sheep in the pasture, bullocks coming home from the marshes; shelves in the fruit store groaned under their burden of apples and pears. And – what both pleased and saddened me – my trap was repaired good as new, thanks to Ben Chilvers, with a fresh coat of red paint and black and white curlicues done by the local sign-writer. The trap would always be a reminder of Basil.

McDowall and I walked the farm, under a sky of scudding clouds whipped up on a wind that tossed bright leaves through the air and had gulls and rooks struggling. As we talked, I learned of arguments with gamekeepers over nests and young birds that had had to be left undisturbed, so that weeds choked the fields and some areas could not be harvested; and I saw for myself the presence of hares so numerous that a field of mangold tops was a solid mass of heaving brown bodies.

'The keepers deny it,' McDowall said, 'but they're importing hares by the hundred. We'll have nae beet tops nor green crops left by the ninth o' November.'

'Why didn't you let me know?' I demanded.

'What could you have done to stop them? What can anybody do?'

The keepers' only concern was to provide ample game to make the prince's birthday *battue* the brilliant success he so confidently anticipated. The ninth of November was a scant two weeks away.

The prospect depressed me. I foresaw only more of the same, on and on for ever – bigger and bigger shoots, more and more Guns, huge numbers in the game record books. His Royal Highness refused to understand that a farmer had to make a living. If farming interfered with his sport then farming must give way. How could one fight that kind of arrogant, selfish blindness?

On a fine afternoon, out walking with Felicity and me and his three younger sisters, Robert Wyatt let the others get ahead while he recounted one or two things that McDowall had omitted to tell me. The men had been grumbling, essential work had been neglected, and Ned Plant was once again threatening to leave. Robert hadn't informed me of these things because, as he said, he hadn't wanted to worry me unnecessarily while I was trying to recoup my strength.

'It's not my place to say it,' he added, 'but your McDowall is a poor sort of steward. To begin with, he's never where he should be. Once he knew you were gone, he started taking time off, vanishing for hours or days, leaving everything to poor old Ned Plant – without whom you'd be in sorry straits, I'd have you know. It's him that has kept this place going. McDowall's just plain lazy. And he's undermining morale with his lackadaisical attitude, putting things off, letting things slide. If he'd been my man, I'd have sacked him long ago.'

'And who might I get in his place?' I sighed. 'Better the devil you know… Anyway, Johnny will be home soon. He'll deal with it.'

'Let's hope he hurries, or he may be too late. If Beck has his way you won't need a steward. For you won't have a farm.'

'What?' My scalp felt tight with alarm. 'What do you mean?'

'I mean that Beck's planning to put one of his cronies in at Orchards. I met the man – not more than a week ago. He was riding the lanes, viewing the farm, bold as you please. He'd even been up to the house and asked to be shown round, though apparently Mrs Benstead soon saw him off.'

'She hasn't mentioned it to me!'

'I told her not to bother you with it. I said the man had misunderstood. I didn't want the servants fretting.'

'And where did *you* meet him?'

'I happened to be riding by when I saw him examining the soil in that lower field of yours – the one with the heavy soil and the willow copse. Batty's Bottom, isn't it? Anyway, when I asked him what his interest was, he said he was to be the next tenant. He even hinted that he'd come to some financial arrangement with Beck – bribed him, not to put too fine a point upon it – to get the Hamiltons out and himself installed.'

I could only stare at him, shivers parading up and down my spine. 'Oh, Robert…'

'He said his name was Towers – Sebastian Towers, if that means anything to you. I didn't reveal who *I* was, except that I said I was from New Zealand. So he talked quite freely. Seems his wife and daughters are looking forward to having their social prospects advanced by the connection with the prince.'

'Oh, dear heaven,' I sighed. 'That man Beck has done nothing but work against me ever since I faced up to him at the audit. Maybe we should let this Towers person have the place. He may not think it such a bargain when he knows what living with the prince and his shooting really means.'

'You're just weary,' Robert said with a smile.

'I've only recently returned from a long holiday.'

'Not long enough. It can take years to recover from the sort of blows you've had lately. Years, and maybe a whole change of scene. Felicity tells me you and she may think of setting up home together.'

'It has been mooted.'

'But you're not ready to give up on life, I'd guess.'

I sighed, shaking my head. 'I don't know.'

'You'll never give up, Rose. It's not in your nature. You're a fighter.'

'I used to be.'

'A leopard can't change its spots.' He turned aside to lean on a field gate, beyond which the root tops were thick with brown bodies, all chewing merrily. When we shouted, the nearest ones started up and ran a few yards, only to settle down to feed again.

'Hopeless,' I sighed. 'They'll ruin us, but what does the prince care? Mr Towers should see this.'

Squinting against the low sun, Robert pulled his hat brim down, not looking at me. Nor answering me. What he said was, 'How would the prospect of New Zealand appeal to you?'

The idea was so unexpected that I couldn't think how to reply. I watched his averted profile, taking refuge in misunderstanding. 'I thought you already had a housekeeper.'

'So I have.' He turned his head to look at me with steady hazel eyes. 'You know very well what I'm saying, Rose. I'm asking you to be my wife. I think we could do well together. I've always been fond of you, you know. Since we were children.'

'Robert…'

'Think about it,' he advised. 'Wouldn't it be better to come away with me rather than stay here pining for Geoffrey Devlin?'

The blood drained from me with a chill, the surge of it sounding in my ears like the sound of the sea in a shell. Had Felicity betrayed my confidence? Hardly able to think, I breathed, 'Who told you that?'

'Hal did,' Robert said quietly.

'Hal?'

'After you went away to Brighton, he told me what had happened. He laughed about it – how he caught you running to the woods and made a wild guess about Devlin, and saw the truth from your face.'

Dear heaven… Hal had *guessed* the truth? Then Geoffrey hadn't told him about us. Geoffrey hadn't lied to me.

'We had a terrible fight about it,' Robert said. 'I told you he gave me a bloody nose, didn't I? It amused him that everyone thought *he* was the man in the case. It added to his reputation.'

'Then why…' I managed, licking dry lips, 'why did he tell *you* the truth?'

'Because he knew it would hurt me.'

He didn't need to say more. One of Hal's main talents had been for inflicting pain on those weaker than himself.

'It doesn't matter, though,' Robert said, laying a hand on my arm. 'It's all past and done with. Come with me to New Zealand, Rose. A wife like you would be an asset. You're a lady. You have breeding. But you don't mind hard work. You know about the land – about sheep. I don't want a milk-and-water girl who'll sit on a cushion and sew a fine seam. I need a partner. A helpmeet. There are precious few comforts out there, but it's a good, healthy life for a strong woman. Think about it, won't you? I plan to go back early next year. We could get married quietly, just before the ship sails. Lord knows you're no grieving widow. Why be hypocritical about it? It would surely save you from being haunted by the past. Out there nobody cares about that. You can make a fresh start.'

It was not the most romantic proposal a woman ever had, but at least it was honest. I asked him to give me time to consider.

Feeling less at ease with him, and needing time by myself, I made my excuses and turned aside to walk through the fields alone, leaving the Wyatts to go on to the Grange for tea. My talk with Robert had only presented me with more problems. Did I want to remove myself to the other side of the world with a man for whom I felt nothing more than friendship? Wasn't one loveless marriage enough for any woman?

There was also the new threat to our tenure of Orchards. What hope had I of outwitting Beck if he had set himself to get rid of me at last? He had the prince's ear, the prince's approval, while I was still out of favour. Damn the man!

For the first time in months a surge of real emotion set my blood drumming – a surge of anger. How dared Beck plot to take Orchards away from me? Had he really promised the tenancy of Orchards to someone else? How *dared* he?

I found myself emerging from the fields into the narrow hilltop lane where the new water tower stood tall among trees, a magnificent erection of gothic red brick. A hare scurried away from me, startling two more that bobbed up among the grasses and loped away down the lane, only to veer aside as horses came trotting, a pair of fine bays drawing a closed carriage. Its passage made me draw aside to give room and I glimpsed the royal coat of arms on the carriage door.

I started to walk on after it, but a voice from the carriage bawled, 'Stop!' Someone inside thumped on its roof to signal the driver and he drew rein some yards ahead of me. The door swung open. An equerry stepped down, doffing his hat.

'Mrs Pooley,' he called. 'His Royal Highness would like to speak with you.'

Sighing to myself, for I had hoped to remain unnoticed, I trailed through the grass and directed a curtsey to the open doorway of the carriage. In the shadows, framed against the far window, I saw the top-hatted head and shoulders of the Prince of Wales.

'So you're back, Mrs Pooley,' he said shortly. 'Not before time. Been neglecting your duties, I'd say.'

'I left the farm in good hands, sir,' I replied, though the criticism stung.

'It's not the same as being here yourself. Not the same at all. It seems to me you're guilty of neglect. These lanes need making up, and the verges ought to be cut. Your fields are rough with weeds and your outhouses need a coat of paint. It's not good enough, Mrs Pooley. I expect my tenants to have a care for appearances. This is Sandringham estate, not some run-down, uncared-for open village.'

'I shall be glad to set things in order,' I said, 'but it can't be done until the shooting season is over and we are no longer hindered by the need to tread softly for sake of Your Royal Highness's game.'

The equerry beside me drew a sharp breath of reproof and I saw the prince's eyes narrow.

'I hear your brother is intending to take on the tenancy now your husband is no longer with us,' he said.

'That was my father's intention, sir.' Had he something in mind to thwart those plans?

'How soon is he expected home from his jaunt to America?'

'Quite soon, sir. Quite soon.'

'What's he doing over there when he's needed here, tell me that, eh? Gallivanting about, wasting his time like so many of the younger generation these days. Well, he had better come home soon, Mrs Pooley, or he may find that my intentions differ from those of your father. Tenancy agreements have their bounds, you know. Can't let one of my farms go to ruin for want of a proper master, can we?'

Oh, I detested him for his arrogance, for half-spoken threats that he would carry out without a second thought as to our welfare. Anger made me blurt, 'Then perhaps Mr Towers will do better, sir.'

'What?' He sat forward, so that I could see him more clearly. 'What's that? Who the devil is Mr Towers?'

'It seems he's the man your agent has chosen as the next tenant for Orchards,' I said, feeling so bitter and helpless that I no longer cared if I offended. 'Well, why not? Mr Beck has worked for years to get rid of me, it seems only right that he should have the privilege of choosing the next tenant. Especially when, as I hear, he expects to be well rewarded for his patronage.'

'Mrs Pooley!' The equerry was outraged. He tried to intervene, but the prince snapped, 'Leave it, Waterson.' Through the shadows his eyes narrowed as he perused my face. 'Is this true, Mrs Pooley?'

'It's what I've heard, sir, and I've no reason to doubt my source. But one thing I do know – your land agent hates me and has for years taken every opportunity to blacken my name. He has done his utmost to work against me – and against you, sir, for he's told you lies and twisted the truth in order to turn you against me. I am Your Royal Highness's most loyal subject, though I confess I am not the most meek and mild. And now my brother stands to lose his inheritance – everything my father worked for – because of one vindictive man who has deliberately poisoned Your Royal Highness's opinion of me. It cannot be right, sir. It cannot be right!'

The prince looked furious. I half expected to hear him order me to the Tower, echoing Mr Carroll's Queen of Hearts – '*Off with her head!*' Frowning as blackly as ever I had seen, he settled back into his seat. 'You should have been here, Mrs Pooley, not hiding away in France all summer. I only hope, for your sake, that all is ready for my birthday *battue*. I shall hold you personally responsible if anything goes wrong. Good day to you, ma'am!'

The equerry, giving me a look of deepest disgust, stepped back into the carriage, the door closed and it was away.

I stood a while sunk in depression, close to tears; thanks to my temper, I had just ensured that Johnny would be put out of Orchards.

–

Later, at the farm, Felicity commiserated and soothed me, assuring me that the prince was not so vindictive as I imagined. Little she knew, thought I. She talked encouragingly of our going away somewhere and setting up home together once Johnny was installed as tenant at Orchards – I had not told her of her brother's different proposal and neither, apparently, had he.

Everyone had ideas of what I should do with my life. Everyone except me; I was just floating, letting events sweep me along. To disaster, so it felt. To add to my torment, there had been no word from Geoffrey since I returned home. What had he discovered in Brighton? Had he found any clue to the whereabouts of our daughter? Every time I went out I half dreaded to hear some new tittle-tattle about a child brought to Ambleford, but there was only silence.

Had he grown tired of waiting for word from me? Had he turned elsewhere for comfort? How could I blame him if he had? He had been patient with me despite all the times I had doubted him, or let my fears override my love for him. And when, at last, he had been free to ask me to marry him, all I had done was prevaricate.

The days drifted away, towards the prince's birthday and the great shoot.

On the night before the shoot I couldn't sleep. Tomorrow the prince and his guests, his dogs and his guns would be taking over my farm.

The keepers, who had camped out in my coverts all summer to guard the game, had warned me that they intended to beat through Poacher's Wood, then across the meadow and the field called the Upper Half'un, to the copses on the hill behind the house. Carriages would fetch the Guns back to the big house for luncheon, and the afternoon would be spent around Five-Acre Wood. It was as if the prince, bent on vengeance, had determined to violate every part of the farm I held dearest. Pegs had already been set out to mark the positions for the Guns. Farm roads would be off-limits to everyone except those involved in the shoot. It was proof that the farm was his, not mine.

I crept downstairs in the middle of the night and huddled by the parlour fire, nurturing the embers into a small blaze. Felicity was asleep in the guest room which she had made her own since June, and the tweenies and Swift were in the attic dreaming their own kind of dreams. Shivering, I stared into the fire, remembering the times Geoffrey had been in this room. How I wished he were here now.

The noise was at first so distant that I couldn't make it out, just a commotion that resolved itself into sounds of shouting and dogs barking. I stood up, hugging my dressing gown round me, staring at the velvet-draped window. The sounds were coming from Poacher's Wood. Coming nearer. Men, and dogs.

And then there was a shot – a single blast of a shot-gun quite close at hand. The shouting came nearer, and the cacophony of dogs. Then someone hammered at my door.

I pulled back the curtain, unlatched the shutter and opened it a fraction, peering out into the night. Across my driveway one or two lanterns gleamed on a group of men with noisy, restless dogs.

'Mrs Pooley!' the shout came from the front door. 'Mrs Pooley. Get down here!'

Taking my lamp into the darkened hall, I approached the door and called, 'What do you want?'

The door reverberated under a fist. 'Open this door! Open it, in the name of the Prince of Wales!'

Carrying my lamp behind my head, I opened the door enough to see who they were. It was the keepers – an angry knot of them with equally disturbed dogs. They had been keeping watch, guarding their precious birds for tomorrow's slaughter. In the darkest hours someone had invaded the preserves, marauders with dogs bent on destruction.

'They came this way!' the keeper named Twistle said angrily, his eyes bulging in his red face. 'This way! Towards your house!'

'And what are you suggesting?' I returned. 'That they came to me for shelter? I'm here alone but for Miss Wyatt and three maids.'

'Then what about *this*?' another man put in, and as the group parted he dragged something up my steps and dropped it to lie there.

Blood and brains spilled across my porch. It was a dead dog – a Staffordshire bull terrier, one of those stocky, muscular dogs with huge jaws, bred for strength and vicious temperament. But this one would fight no more. It had been shot at close range by a gun that had torn its head apart and left one eye hanging by a thread of flesh.

The sight brought acid nausea to the back of my throat. 'How dare you bring that to my doorstep?'

'Is it yours?' Twistle demanded.

'Of course it's not mine! I never kept a dog like that, as you know very well. How dare you come to my house in the middle of the night and accuse me without evidence? The prince shall hear about this.'

'It's you that'll hear from *him*. When he finds out about this…'

But before he could complete his threats there came a shout from the drive. 'Hark! There's more dogs! In the woods. They've come back. They're after the birds! Let's go!!'

Dogs and men turned heel and merged into the night, only their voices, and the fading twinkle of lanterns, drifting back. In my porch they left the bloody obscenity that, not many minutes before, had been a powerful dog.

'Rose?' Felicity was at the head of the stairs, a pale shape on the edge of the light from my lamp. 'Whatever is it?'

I closed the door, not wanting her to see what lay outside. 'Poachers in the woods, apparently. It's nothing, Felicity. Go back to sleep.'

Never at her best in the small hours, Felicity retired, yawning.

In my own room, I leaned from the open window, feeling rain mist on my face as I watched lanterns dance in Poacher's Wood. Men shouted, dogs barked. Twice came shots. All of it interspersed with the distracted cries and flutterings of disturbed pheasants. Some of them came across the garden, half running, half flying, squawking and croaking pitifully. Frightened so badly, they would not come back, not for days, if ever. Poacher's Wood would not provide its expected tally towards the prince's 'thousand brace'.

I got dressed and went down, found a sack and wrapped it around the heavy, lifeless body of the dog before dragging it to one of the outhouses where I left it for the night. Then I got a bucket and a brush and scrubbed my porch until every trace of mud and blood was gone, all the time wishing bitter vengeance on the head of whatever enemy was doing this to me.

I should be blamed for it, I knew. Someone was determined to ruin me.

Sitting back on my heels in the porch, I admitted defeat. I couldn't go on. I couldn't face it alone. I needed someone... No, not just someone – I needed Geoffrey. 'I'm there, if you need me,' he had said. 'Just send for me.' Was that still true? Perhaps now was the moment to find out.

I wrote a note to him, asking him to come and see me; I said I was anxious to talk to him. Just before dawn I went down to the stables through seeping rain and told Jack Huggins to take the note over to Ambleford first thing in the morning.

'Get it to him as soon as you can. I've got to see him, Jack.'

-

As was usual during a shoot, all fieldwork was suspended in order to avoid hindering the sport in any way. Not that the weather was conducive to outdoor work, or to comfortable shooting; the prince's thirty-second birthday dawned dismal and wet, and as the day progressed the weather grew steadily worse.

Anyone else might have called off the shoot, but not Prince Albert Edward. Not even the weather was to be allowed to thwart his triumph.

Keepers and beaters gathered in the yard at first light. I saw them head off towards the coverts, and heard the whistles and calls that helped them communicate. And then I saw the caped figure of the head keeper, Mr Jackson, striding up the drive.

Anticipating his errand, I was at the door before he reached the porch. I said, 'If you want your evidence, it's in my outhouse. Do you know your men left it on my doorstep? A dead dog, Mr Jackson. Shot through the head. They came here in the middle of the night and...'

'Yes, Mrs Pooley, I know,' he replied with sympathy from under the brim of a deerstalker hat. 'And I'm sorry. I'll have someone collect the dog as soon as we have a spare minute. My men overstepped the mark. All the same, your name is being loudly mentioned in connection with all of this. The birds were badly disturbed. Poacher's Wood'll provide poor sport. You can't expect His Royal Highness to be happy about it.'

'But why does he always blame me?' I demanded. 'Oh… never mind, I don't expect you to answer.' With an effort I contained my temper. Mr Jackson was doing a difficult job with a difficult master behind him. 'Did they manage to catch any of the perpetrators?'

'I'm afraid not. They weren't after catching the birds, it seems, only killing or frightening them – and then they made off before my men had time to re-muster. Your man McDowall heard them go by his house. The noise disturbed him and he was up and about when we got there, so he was able to point us in the right direction. But the villains had gone. Clean away.'

'Do you think they'll be back?'

'Probably so,' he said. 'But not here. No, they'll move on to other preserves if they come at all. After today, there'll be precious little game left on Orchards. Well, good day to you, ma'am. And again – please accept my apologies for any inconvenience my men may have caused.'

At least I knew there was one member of the prince's staff who believed in my innocence.

Shortly afterwards, horses and carriages arrived, bringing the Guns to take up their first positions despite the continuing rain. Because I had no choice – and because I was too angry to stay in hiding – I went out to greet my royal landlord and his sporting gentlemen friends and offer the usual hot toddies, which my maids distributed.

The party was all excitement. Journalists asked questions and took notes, and a photographer had set up his equipment under a large umbrella to record the great event. He had the prince and his most illustrious friends pose with their guns, and Mr Jackson and a dog or two, in the lee of my barn.

There were policemen about too, patrolling and keeping watch. Some of them seemed to have orders to watch me and my house.

The prince, jovial and expansive among his companions, was evidently determined that nothing should spoil his day. He didn't speak to me, but from the way he looked at me I knew it was not over yet.

The matter of the violated preserves was simply in abeyance until the shoot was over.

Well, I too would have something to say when this day was ended. I was tired of being unjustly accused.

They did not stay long. The conventions attended to, they were anxious to get to the cover of the woods.

Trying to ignore the sound of guns, I sat in the farm office going over the accounts, which had been kept in my absence by McDowall. My thoughts distracted me and I kept making mistakes of calculation, obliging me to go over and over the same figures.

A knock on the side door startled me. What now? More trouble with the pheasants? The passage door opened and I heard Finch muttering, 'All right, all right. Give a body time to get her apron on!'

A few minutes later she was tapping on the office door, informing me that, 'Miss Mickleborough's asking for you, Miss Rose. Says she won't come in but she's got to see you. Proper state she's in, too.'

Hurrying down the passage, I found the woman waiting in the rain. She was in her thirties, thin and bedraggled. Her clothes, and the shawl drawn tightly round her head, were soaked, and water dripped down a face in which her eyes glinted with bitter fury.

'Goodness, you're wet through!' I exclaimed.

'So would you be if you'd been kept waiting in this rain for half an hour,' she said sharply. 'The marshals wouldn't let me through on account of the shoot.'

I started to ask her to come in, but she interrupted brusquely: 'No, thanks, I won't stay and hinder you. I just came to bring you this.' She thrust her hand towards me. 'Well, take it. It's all there. Five pound – wasn't that what you wanted?'

'Five pounds?' I stared blankly at the coins she held out on her wet palm. 'For what?'

'For a rotten old cart and a load of rubbish!'

I had forgotten all about the things I had let old Milky have, an age ago, last June.

'Well, take it!' she repeated, trying to force the money into my hand. 'Now that my poor old Dad's pawned every last thing he owned, take it! Count it. Five pound.'

'But I never asked him for money!' I exclaimed.

'No – you sent your steward to do that piece of dirty work. Dad paid him, eventually. Scraped all his bit of savings together, even what he'd collected towards his burial. But your man came back, demanding to be paid again. Reckoned he'd never got the first money. Huh! Forgot to give it you, more like! And Dad hadn't the sense to ask for a paper to prove it. You should be ashamed of yourself, hounding a poor old man. It's made him ill, all the worry. But between us we've managed it. See? There it is. Five pound. And this time I want a receipt. I want it from you, yourself.'

By this time I too was angry, though not with her. I asked her in and sent for towels and hot tea while I calmed her and made her repeat her story over more coherently. I had *given* her father that old cart, expecting no payment. And I had certainly not authorised McDowall to extract payment by what amounted to threats and extortion.

'Give your father his money back,' I said, going to my cash tin, taking out another five pounds. 'And this, too, since McDowall had the gall to take it. I'll stop it out of his wages if necessary.'

She gaped at me. 'But he'll not admit it, will he? Harassing a poor blind old man. Taking money off him twice… He'll say it's not true. I've got no proof. How do you know *I'm* not lying?'

'I just know,' I said. I knew McDowall. At least, I was beginning to know him at last. My instinct had been right about the man all along. 'Apologise to your father for me. Tell him I knew nothing about this but that I'll see McDowall never bothers him again. Look… come to the kitchen and have something to eat. Mrs Benstead's been stewing some mutton. You look as if you could do with some.'

She seemed grateful to accept and when she left she took a big jug full of mutton stew to share with her father.

Meanwhile, with my instincts all in full cry, I returned to my ledgers and discovered that the anomalies were not caused by my inability to concentrate: there were in fact a succession of minor adjustments, so well hidden that I might never have found them if I hadn't deliberately set myself to the task in order to forget what was going on outside. Evidently McDowall had been practising petty fraud, leeching himself extra cash here and there.

Damn the man! I should have got rid of him long ago. This was one thing that could not wait for Johnny. I had to tackle McDowall now, while I was still angry enough to say what must be said.

Donning a waterproof cape, I took my umbrella and went down to the yards through lashing rain.

A few of the men were in the barn, chopping feed for the animals and oiling tools. In the bullock pens, Benstead was mucking out soiled hay while Plant and the boy Jack were in the stables grooming the horses and cleaning tack. None of them had seen McDowall since early morning. They assumed he was with the shoot somewhere.

Or perhaps he had gone home, where he could be warm and dry, not expecting me to check on him in such weather. I wondered if I had been guilty of neglect, even before the accident, becoming ever more immersed in my personal problems and letting the farm go. If this was the way McDowall had been going on then I should have noticed it before. I should have done something.

As I went out to the streaming yard, Plant came after me. ''Scuse me, Miss Rose,' he said, tugging at the brim of his hat. 'Can I have a word?'

'Of course.'

'I'm afraid I shall have to give you my notice.'

Nothing could have dismayed me more. 'You want to leave us?'

'Not "want to", Miss Rose,' he assured me gravely. 'But it seem as how Mr McDowall en't satisfied with my work and—'

'Oh, what nonsense!' I exclaimed. 'Your work has always been exceptional. Mr McDowall has said nothing to me about this.'

'No, miss. He wouldn't.'

With a glance behind him at the stable, he moved further away from other ears, obliging me to follow him until we were under the shelter of the covered walk between the bullock pens. The beasts in their stalls looked at us curiously, blowing through their nostrils, and at the far end of the pens Benstead went on with his work.

'Truth is, Miss Rose,' said Plant in an undertone, 'Mr McDowall and me hen't seen eye to eye for long enough. It's not my place to speak ill of my betters but there's things… well, I've not been happy about things.'

'What things?'

But he was reluctant to admit what was on his mind. I could gather only that he did not approve of some of McDowall's methods and that 'things' were getting so bad that he felt he couldn't stay any longer.

'In view of what I'm discovering,' I said, 'it may be McDowall who goes. And if that happens, Plant, I shall ask *you* to take over as steward. How would you feel about that?'

His mouth dropped open. He was astounded. But as he clutched at his hat and stammered an incoherent answer I could see he was pleased.

'Did McDowall ever ask about that cart, and those oddments that we gave to old Milky?' I asked.

'Why... yes, he did. To be honest with you, Miss Rose, he wasn't best pleased to think you'd let that go for nothin'. He said he could have got a couple of quid for it at least.'

'Did he indeed? Well, thank you, Plant. That's most helpful.'

Buoyed up on a wave of righteous anger, I strode on.

'Miss Rose!' The boy Jack was coming after me, hopping from tussock to tussock among the mud. For a crazy moment I thought he was going to say that Geoffrey was coming, but, 'The gentleman wasn't there. Been away from home for a while, so they said. But they expect him back at any time.'

'Today?'

'P'raps today. P'raps not. They're not sure. Anyway, he'll get your message soon's he comes. I left the note with the scullery maid.' His cheeky grin made his face look elfin. ''S'all right, she won't tell nobody. She's good at keeping secrets is Becky. She likes me.'

Geoffrey was away – why hadn't I thought of that possibility? Why had I been so sure he would come running at my call, simply because I needed him so badly? Even when he received my note, he might choose not to come. Farmers' daughters couldn't reckon on happy endings. Farmers' daughters had to be strong in themselves.

The centre of the lane was clogged with mud churned up by wagons and horses. The verge was thick with soaking grasses. I tried to keep to the edge between, where the grass was flattened, but still my skirts brushed in mud and wet, while rain dripped through a canopy of ragged autumn leaves. By the time I reached Wood Lodge I was thoroughly damp and ill-tempered.

My knocking brought no reply. Then, as I stepped back to look at the house, I saw the lace curtain in a room above the porch drop back into place. Someone was spying, waiting for me to leave. Irritated, I knocked the harder.

Eventually I heard a bolt being drawn. The door opened a few inches, enough for Mary McDowall to peer out at me, her free hand clutching her shawl about her. She was pale, slight, her black hair already touched with grey. Brown eyes regarded me apprehensively.

'We don't often use the front door,' she said. 'I was busy. I didn't hear you at first. What can I do for you, Mrs Pooley?'

'You might let me in out of this weather,' I replied.

She hesitated, then with evident reluctance opened the door further. I shook my umbrella outside as best I could before stepping on to the doormat, but Mrs McDowall looked askance at the drips from my cape that spattered her clean linoleum. The narrow staircase hall smelled strongly of soap. Every polishable surface gleamed – mirror, banisters, brass doorknobs and fittings, even the treads of the uncarpeted stairs. Peg rugs, freshly washed, lay on scrubbed linoleum. There was nothing out of place, no hint of untidiness, no speck of dust... Yet somehow it was not a welcoming house.

Mary McDowall did not invite me further inside.

'Is your husband here?' I asked.

'My husband?' She clutched the shawl tighter, her eyes darting. 'No. No, he's not here. Isn't he at the farm?'

'I would hardly have come here in this weather if I had found him where he ought to be. Where is he, Mrs McDowall?'

'I don't know. I really don't know. He doesn't tell me anything. Please... will you excuse me a minute? I must get a cloth. Wait here.'

She hurried away, down the passage and into a room which I guessed to be a kitchen from the glimpse I had before she closed the door. All the doors in the hallway were closed, making the place gloomy; the strong scent of carbolic soap made my nose itch.

When she returned, she brought with her a cloth with which she proceeded to wipe up the water I had inadvertently dripped on to her floor. She knelt by my feet, working round me fretfully. She didn't mean to be rude; she evidently had an obsession with cleanliness and neatness.

Taken aback, I said, 'I'm sorry to have made work for you.'

'It's no bother. It's just that if McDowall comes and finds it like this, he—'

'Then you're expecting him soon?'

She stopped her wiping, becoming still for a heartbeat or two, then, keeping her head bent, she said, 'I don't know where he's gone. I don't expect him back before dark. He doesn't usually get in from work before dark.' It sounded like a lesson she had learned by rote.

'Is that what he told you to say?'

'That's all I know, Mrs Pooley.'

'Very well. Then if you see him before I do, please tell him to report to me at the farm office. At once. Whatever time it may be. I shall be at home all day.'

'Can you tell me what it's about? He's sure to ask and if I don't know…'

'Just tell him I've spent all day going over the accounts and I'd like to discuss them with him. Oh, and… tell him I had a visit from Sara Mickleborough. She brought me five pounds. I think McDowall will understand.'

When I left she was still using the cloth to wipe the floor with swift, forceful strokes, though any drops I had left were long since dried.

–

Later, at the farm, Felicity and I sat by the parlour fire enjoying a pot of tea. Outside, rain still wept from the sullen sky.

The shoot had ended some while ago, even the most enthusiastic Gun defeated by the relentless downpour. I had half expected to be favoured by an angry visitation, either from the head keeper or some other of the prince's minions, come to demand an explanation for last night's excursions, but so far all was quiet. Perhaps they were mustering their evidence.

As the day waned, early because of the heavy cloud, I rang for Swift to light the lamps.

'Why,' the maid exclaimed as she went to draw the curtains, 'en't that the McDowall boy now comin'? Soaked to the skin, poor mite. He's a-comin' to the side door, Miss Rose. 'Scuse me.'

As she left the room, I got up and went to the window, but the boy had already reached the side porch and was battering with the knocker.

'What is it?' Felicity asked. 'What can the boy want?'

'I'm not sure. Usually the McDowalls keep themselves very much to themselves.' After my earlier encounter with Mary McDowall, this visit from her son was disquieting.

Going out to the side passageway, I found young Donald gasping out his message to Swift. 'Got to get Miss Rose! He said I was to bring Miss Rose. Quick.' Seeing me, he darted past the maid, wringing a sodden cap in his hands. He was a sturdy lad, eleven years old, with an earnest freckled face, and he was wet through, his clothes sticking to him, his hair flat to his head, his eyes wide and wild as words poured out of him. 'Oh, Miss Rose, will you come? It's my mam. She's hurt bad. Very bad.'

'Hurt? How?'

'Her face, and her arm… I thought she was dead – I thought for sure this time he'd done her in.'

That gave me pause. 'Someone hurt her, you mean? Who?'

He stared at me, his face working, then burst out, 'My dad! It's my dad! Our Stella said I wasn't to tell, but I was so scared. I thought Mam was dead! I had to get help, didn't I, miss? I just ran out without thinking and…'

'Whoa,' I calmed him as I might have calmed an agitated pony. 'It's all right, Donald. You did exactly the right thing. I'll come right away.'

'Then I'll go back. I'll go back and tell them you're on your way. Thanks, Miss Rose, ma'am.'

'But Donald—' He was gone. In his wake, damp twilight lapped into the passage through the open door.

'Shall I get your cape and umbrella, miss?' Swift asked. 'They're in the laundry room. They should be about dry.'

'I'll get them. You fetch your own coat. I want you to come after me. Heaven knows what's happened, but I may need your help. Tell Miss Wyatt that I shall be back as soon as I can. Tell her to stay here. There's no point in our all getting wet.'

In the passageway, I found Mrs Benstead and the boy Jack Huggins agog with curiosity. Judging by the wing of chicken he still clutched in his fist, Jack had been partaking of the cook's benevolence, as he so often did. But I was glad to see him. I sent him to get a lantern so that he might accompany me, and when he returned he was enveloped in a weatherproof cape and broad-brimmed hat, his rapscallion's face bright with excitement.

The rain was not so heavy as it had been earlier. As Jack and I reached the gate a break in the clouds showed a streak of evening sky and the drizzle lessened to a spray borne on a brisk, drying wind. It reminded me sharply of the night I had come home after Victor died.

Outside Wood Lodge a cart waited, the horse bedraggled and sorry for itself in the damp evening. Then as we approached the house its door opened, showing us young Stella McDowall standing there with a lamp, beckoning me. She was on the edge of womanhood, tall for her age at thirteen. She flushed and bridled a little at seeing Jack Huggins.

'Come in, Miss Rose.' She glanced up the stairs, calling, 'She's here! Miss Rose is here!'

A man appeared in the shadows of the landing. For one mad, fearful moment I thought it was McDowall. But he was much bigger than McDowall, and as he came down the stairs I saw the way he limped on a twisted foot, even before lamplight showed me the grave, familiar face of Ben Chilvers.

'You alone, Miss Rose?' he asked.

'No, Jack's with me. And my maid, Swift, is on her way. Well, come in, Jack!' He had hung back, evidently wary of Stella.

'Maybe the boy can go for the doctor,' Ben Chilvers said, and asked the lad, 'can you find your way to Ders'n'ham in the dark?'

'Easy! *And* I know where the doctor lives.'

'Good. We'll need the constable, too. Send someone to tell the constable to come.'

'I'll be back afore you know it.' With which Jack was gone, away into the rainy dark, leaving Stella looking askance at the marks he had left on her mother's clean floor.

The carpenter nodded approval. 'I'm glad you brought him, Miss Rose. I didn't fancy havin' to leave you here alone. That McDowall might come back.'

'Do I understand… he hurt his wife?'

'Beat her half to death,' he said grimly. 'It appears it's a reg'lar thing with him. This time, the young 'uns thought she was dead. I was goin' by in my cart when the boy come out yellin' that his dad had killed his mam. I've got her to bed but that's all. I'm no medical man. She might have broken bones. Go up and see her, will you, Miss Rose? And you, Stella… come you and help me. Best see that back door's locked good and tight.'

As Stella looked at him the light from the lamp she held showed up the yellowing remains of a bruise under her eye. 'I don't know what will happen when my dad comes back. When he's mad… When he knows we've told on him… he'll be so mad. He'll kill us all!'

'No, he won't,' Ben Chilvers said stoutly. 'For I shan't let him.'

As they departed on their errand, I climbed the narrow stairs to where candle-light beckoned from an upper room.

Mary McDowall lay on her back on the low bed, still fully clothed, with her son keeping anxious vigil beside her. Her face was so swollen it was unrecognisable; blood smeared from her nose, from cuts about her eyes and on her mouth. Her eyes were half closed, nestling in puffed flesh of an angry scarlet and bruise-blue out of which she regarded me with despair. Her hands and arms were bruised, too, covered in weals and marks where blows had fallen as she tried to defend herself.

'I'm here to take care of you,' I told her. 'Just lie still. Don't try to talk.'

'She'll be all right, won't she, ma'am?' Donald asked, a trace of tears in the corners of his eyes.

'Of course she will.' I rumpled his hair, hoping to reassure him. 'Don't you worry. Go down and tell them I need hot water and towels.'

Donald hurried away.

The bedroom had once been as neat and shiny clean as the rest of the house, but now it showed evidence of a bitter struggle. Shards of broken ornaments littered the floor; a chair lay on its side; the tallboy was slightly displaced, as if someone might have fallen against it; a curtain hung torn and an embroidered runner, tossed on the floor, showed the black mark of a man's boot. There were spots of blood on the floorboards too, and more smeared across the hearthrug.

Footsteps sounded on the stairs. It was Swift who appeared with the steaming enamel jug.

'Oh, miss!' she breathed on seeing Mary McDowall. 'Oh, miss, the poor soul.'

Once I had reassured myself that Mrs McDowall had sustained no worse than cuts and bruising, we set about undressing her, easing her out of her blood-stained clothes so that we might bathe her sores and soothe them with balm. Her limbs and body bore the marks of many abuses both past and present. Was it any wonder she preferred to play the recluse when she had frequent bruises to hide?

I wielded a warm wet flannel while Swift held the bowl for me. My ministrations must have been painful, but Mary McDowall bore it all stoically, only wincing now and again. Presumably she had become used to enduring pain.

'He's not a bad man,' she muttered at length, her voice thickened and painful through swollen, broken lips. 'He's just got a quick temper. This was my fault.'

'It was not your fault!' I replied. 'Never in this world.'

'But it was. I shouldn't have said… I didn't mean it. I just wanted to stop him.'

'Don't try to talk.'

She ignored me. Her tongue came out to moisten her lips and she winced as she found an open sore. 'When I said you'd been here, he was angry. He thought I'd told on him. So I said if he didn't stop I *would* tell. I can't stand by and let him keep on. But he just went mad. He hit me and hit me. I thought he was going to kill me.'

'Hush,' I soothed her. 'No more talking. Not now. Lie still and rest. Where do you keep your clean nightgowns?'

She indicated the tallboy, from whose drawers Swift extracted a blue cotton nightgown.

'I just don't know what'll happen now,' Mary McDowall wept. 'There was no need for anyone to know.'

'There was every need.'

'But I feel as if I've betrayed him. He'll never forgive me. I've let him down fine and proper this time.'

She wept bitter tears as we helped her into the fresh nightgown and eased her into bed.

Stella and Donald had been waiting anxiously outside the door. Now I let them in and they sat one on either side of their mother, like chicks nestling to the comforting warmth of a hen. Mrs McDowall spoke to them softly, reassuring them, for they too were afraid of what might happen. They were terrified of their father, and of what he would do to them when he discovered himself in trouble because they had dared to ask for help.

After a while, Mary McDowall fell into a doze, and I persuaded the children to leave her. Swift took them downstairs, suggesting games that they might play.

But just as everything was settling down a loud banging sounded on the back door which lay below the bedroom window. The sound was accompanied by a fierce, deep-throated barking from more than one dog. Mary McDowall came awake with a start and a little cry.

'Damn ye, Mary!' her husband's voice yelled above the cacophony of the dogs. 'Let me in. I'll teach ye to lock my ain doors agen' me.'

Three

Hearing her husband's voice, Mary McDowall flung her hands to her face in fright, her eyes wide above spread fingers that choked a cry.

I leapt up and went to throw the window open. The scent of a rain-washed night met me, while below me faint light from the kitchen window showed the figure of McDowall and the dog he held straining on a leash – a Staffordshire bull terrier, like the one that had been shot in my garden last night. Nor was it the only one. In the shadows behind McDowall I made out at least one more figure with a dog, and there might have been two.

Had my own steward been working against me all this time?

Behind me the children pounded up the stairs, screaming, 'Mam! Mam!' They burst into the room and threw themselves at the bed, one either side of their mother, who held them to her fiercely, saying, 'Hush, he'll not hurt you again. He'll not hurt any of us any more.'

At the sound of the opening window McDowall's dog had started to rear, its great ugly head thrown back as it barked angrily, wanting to be at my throat. I was glad to be out of reach.

'You let me in, or...' McDowall began, only to stop as he realised I was not his wife.

'Or you'll do what, McDowall?' I demanded. 'Let your dogs loose in my coverts again? I warn you, we've sent for the constable.'

With that the kitchen door opened, spilling more light against which Ben Chilvers's shadow loomed large. The dogs barked even more furiously, straining their leashes to get at him with their sharp snapping teeth.

'Stay back!' McDowall shouted. 'Stay back or I loose the dog.' He and his confederates were backing away, restraining the leaping, straining dogs. 'Damn it, Chilvers, d'ye hear me? These animals'll tear ye to pieces if we let 'em. Close yon door. Close it!'

The back door closed, cloaking the garden once more in shadow.

'And stay indoors!' McDowall yelled. 'Anybody puts so much as a finger out, the dog'll have ye. D'ye hear me, Mary? I'll be back, don't you fret. I'll be back fer ye. I'll make ye sorry ye ever peached on me.'

The children wept harder, huddling to their mother, whose arms held them tight to her. Above their tousled heads she gave me a fierce, bright look that was at once courageous and afraid.

'He may try,' I said. 'But he'll have to go through me to do it. Don't worry, from now on I shall make sure you're safe from him.'

Outside, the sound of barking was now accompanied by thumps and scratchings. But it sounded as if only one dog was left. When I looked out I saw the animal loose in the yard, throwing itself at the kitchen door, snapping and snarling. McDowall and his companions, and the other two dogs, had melted into the dark night.

Behind me Swift appeared, evidently frightened by the clamour. She closed the door, giving me a wide-eyed look. 'Oh, miss!'

'Quiet down!' the sharp order came from the yard below.

Ben Chilvers had opened the kitchen door and was standing on the doorstep. The dog did not attack, but it continued to bark, making little snarling rushes towards the carpenter. 'Quiet, I say!' he ordered again. This time the animal fell silent but remained watchful, ears pricked, every muscle tensed. Ben stepped out from the house, walking softly, talking in a soothing yet authoritative voice while holding something out in his hand. The dog seemed suspicious; but after a while it ventured nearer, sniffing at whatever he held. Without haste, so as not to startle it, he grasped the ropes attached to its collar and, still talking in a sing-song mutter that seemed to mesmerise it, he led it away and tethered it safely in the garden.

Returning across the yard, he tipped back his head as he saw me at the window, saying, 'He won't bother us no more, Miss Rose.'

'How on earth did you do that?' I asked.

'That? Oh…' He shrugged. 'That weren't nothin'. I've yet to meet the dog as I can't master, given half a chance. Amos taught me that when I was a little 'un. D'you want me to go after McDowall?'

'No. No, let the law deal with him. I'd prefer that you remain here if you would. At least until more help comes.'

'Glad to, Miss Rose,' said he. 'Long as you need me.'

The dog's whole attention seemed fastened on whatever it was he had left on the ground near it. Ben told me later that it was a few pieces of meat, sprinkled with other ingredients, some from the kitchen and some which he always carried with him 'in case of need', though he refused to reveal their recipe – Ben was as close with his 'witching' secrets as ever his father had been.

As he returned to the kitchen, Mary McDowall's voice drew my attention back into the bedroom and, realising that I was letting cold air in, I closed the window.

'It's all right, McDowall's gone.'

'And the dogs?'

'Safely tied up.' No need to tell her that other dogs were still at large, along with her husband and his confederates.

'Thank God.' She closed her eyes tightly for a moment and when she looked at me again there were fresh tears on her lashes. 'I never thought he'd do it, not really. I never really thought… I should have warned you before. I know I should, only I was so afraid of him.'

Going closer to the bed, I said, 'Warned me of what?'

'Of what he was doing. What he was planning. Those dogs…'

'Yes?'

'They've been training them. To kill pheasants. To get you in more trouble. They wanted you put off the farm.'

'They?'

'McDowall and that man Pyke – the one that used to be an under-keeper. The one you got dismissed for lying about your fox-cubs.'

I had never dreamed of any such thing. My old enemy Pyke and my steward McDowall plotting against me? For how long? My mind was busy, incredulously filling out the picture. 'Was it those dogs that killed my sheep? Did McDowall set fire to my shepherd's hut, and damage my ploughs, and—'

'I don't know,' she wept, 'not for sure. He never told me half of it. But I know he got the idea because of the other troubles you'd had – with Ambleford, and the mischief that the unionist agitators were making. He said you'd think it was part of the same thing.'

'He was right. I never suspected anything like this. What can his motive be, Mrs McDowall? Why is he doing it?'

'Oh, he claims he's working for the union, but it's more for pure spite. He's eaten up with jealousy and hate.' Her fingers swept tears from her eyes, but more filled their place. 'He hates being given orders by a woman, and being beholden to you as his employer. And he hates the Prince of Wales, too. "Fat German bastard" – begging your pardon, Mrs Pooley, but that's what he calls him. "Not fit to be our king", according to McDowall. He thinks all kings and gentry ought to be shot, or have their heads chopped off, every one of them. Leeches. Lazy fat slugs and leeches, that's what he says.'

'I wish you had told me this before.'

'How could I?' she cried. 'I was afraid of what he'd do to me. And he's my husband. What's going to become of us if they put him in prison? What's going to become of the children and me? Oh, dear Lord. Oh, my dearest Lord!' She hugged her children to her and wept.

'To begin with, you can come and stay at the farm for as long as you need to. Please... don't distress yourself. I'll do everything I can. Swift, go and look down the lane. See if there's any sign of the doctor.'

'What about the dogs?' the maid fretted.

'You're safe from them.' But seeing that she was still afraid to go down, I started for the door. 'Oh, very well, I'll go myself.'

As I went down the stairs Ben Chilvers appeared from the kitchen to ask, 'Everything all right, Miss Rose?'

'She's very distressed. She says...' and I found myself repeating what Mary McDowall had told me about her husband's activities.

The news made Ben Chilvers look grave. 'I on'y wish as I'd paid more heed to my father last time I saw him – at Norwich gaol. He said as how you'd better watch out for an enemy close at hand. He said I should warn you. But I thought he was just ramblin' – I thought he prob'ly meant Davy Timms was still about. And it was about that time that Mr Basil got killed. You seemed to have troubles enough without me addin' to 'em.'

'I would never have suspected that he meant McDowall,' I sighed. 'But... it was kind of him to want to warn me.'

'He never wished you harm, Miss Rose. Not you personally. I hope you can believe that.'

As we stood there in the neat, clean hallway, hurried footsteps sounded on the path outside, ending in a heavy hammering on the door.

'Who is it?' the carpenter demanded.

'Dr Hardy,' came the reply. 'Who do you think it is, man? Didn't you send for me?'

While the doctor examined Mary McDowall, I sent the children to get ready for bed and Swift to put the kettle on. I remained in the bedroom, standing by while Doctor Hardy tested his patient, making sure she had no broken bones. He told her she was a lucky woman, and that another time she might not be so lucky. She should have gone to him before. Or did she want to end up on a mortuary slab, and maybe one or both of her children with her?

Seeing that his brusque manner was upsetting her, I attempted to divert his attention by asking, 'Did Jack Huggins come back with you, doctor? Or did you send him for the constable?'

'I sent word to the constable by a neighbour,' he replied. 'The boy rode back with me. But he slipped off when we arrived. Bound for the farm, I believe. Reckoned he could smell trouble. Odd chap, that one, Mrs Pooley. If he was in my employ, I wouldn't trust him further than I could throw him.'

Many people felt the same about Jack Huggins. For myself, I had learned to trust his instincts.

'A lad like that can find no end of excuses to slip away from his duties,' the doctor added. 'He made out he'd seen a light somewhere in the direction of your barnyard, but if he did he must have eyes like a cat, for I couldn't see a glimmer.'

Feeling uneasy, I went to the window which looked out across the back yard and vegetable patch to the part of Poacher's Wood which lay between lodge and farm. By night there was little to see, only the dark shapes of trees against a sky where clouds were shredding, letting patches of starry sky show through. A grey brightness showed where the moon rode low, veiled by racing cloud.

And then, away in the direction of my rickyards, I saw another light, flaring yellow behind black tree trunks and branches. Even as I watched, it grew and brightened, flickering from yellow to red.

There was fire at Orchards Farm.

Hurrying down the stairs, I called to Ben Chilvers, who appeared in the hall with Swift behind him.

'The farm's on fire!' I gasped. 'Swift, stay here with Mrs McDowall and the children. Keep all the doors locked and stay inside. I'm relying on you to look after them.' And I flung the door open and ran down the path, lifting my skirts clear of puddles and shrubs.

Behind me I heard Ben Chilvers breathing hard, trying to keep pace but falling behind because of his twisted foot. I didn't wait for him. My feet skidded and squelched in mud but I hardly noticed. All my mind was on the glow I had seen.

As I drew nearer the farm I saw the light again. Behind an old elm in the hedgeside, above the bulk of corn ricks, it showed me a wafting of brown smoke speckled with floating debris. The fire was in the stackyard!

Skirts flying about me, I raced through the open gate, sending sleepy geese scattering. We kept a bucket upturned on the pump. I grabbed it and plunged it into the water trough. Its weight dragged at my arm. Water slopped on to my skirts as I ran.

One of the corn ricks was well ablaze. Red flame and crackling yellow sparks licked up its sides. A second stack was beginning to roar, the fire building at one corner. Feeling the heat on my skin, I ran to throw my puny bucketful. The flames faltered and hissed, then licked out more strongly, seeking to awaken a response in a neighbouring stack. I backed away, an arm thrown up to shield my face from the blast of heat.

'Miss Rose!' The warning yell made me spin round. As I did so a gun boomed. A spatter of shot thudded into the piled sheaves behind me.

The glare showed me a man – McDowall – struggling with a slight youth – Jack – who was trying to wrest the gun from him. McDowall kicked out, loosing the lad's hold. The gun swung viciously. The lad went sprawling. The man darted away into the shadows.

'Jack!' Smoke wisped out of a third stack as I ran across to where the boy lay fallen. He tried to get up, but sank down again with a cry of pain, a hand to his ribs.

'I can't breathe, Miss Rose. He's done me ribs in. I can't breathe!'

'Breathe shallow. Breathe slow. Here, take my arm. You must move, Jack. Away from this stack.'

Fear brought a cold sweat to my brow as I helped the boy away from danger. Black smoke eddied about us, bringing the scent of heat and charring. It choked in my lungs, bit at my eyes, sent tears running down my face.

There came a shout. I paused, listening. Another shot boomed not far away. My heart thudded harder in response. Ben! I thought. Where was Ben Chilvers? But there was no time. With every second the fire was eating deeper into my precious harvest.

When Jack was safe in the lee of one of the pigsties, I went running for the bucket I had dropped and filled it again, carrying it slopping and heavy to empty it on flames that seemed to lick the harder. My efforts were hopeless.

And then I heard the commotion in the stables. Because of the chilly rain, even the carthorses had been put indoors for the night. Now they were whinnying and stamping, frightened by the smoke. If the fire spread to the stables…

Once again I picked up my skirts and ran. The stables were in darkness, full of the bitter scent of drifting smoke. Feeling my way blindly, I called out to each horse, slapping hindquarters to make it clear I was there. The horses were unsettled, stamping and shifting. More than once I found myself crushed against a partition, trapped there until by dint of cursing and pushing the great shire moved, allowing me to untie the rope. One by one I heard my old friends clatter out, hooves loud on the flagstones in the stableyard as they headed to safety. And all the time, through the windows, the glow of the fire seemed to brighten. The sound of it grew louder, crackling and roaring, spreading to devour everything we had worked for.

When at last I stumbled, coughing and tear-blinded, from the stables, I heard voices calling. People were there, running, calling instructions. I learned later that Mary McDowall had sent her son to rouse the nearest villagers. They turned out, men and women and children, all who were able.

'There are fire buckets here!' I called. They hung under the eaves of the stables, a dozen and a half black leather buckets painted with Father's initials, W. J. H. I began to take them down, handing them out to my willing helpers.

The commotion had aroused Orchards House, too. Through swirling smoke Felicity came running with the three maids – and a thin young man whom I recognised with a shock as he grabbed a bucket from me.

'Johnny!'

He stopped, looked at me, said, 'Later, Rose,' and followed the others to the pond.

Felicity would have taken the last bucket, but I wanted it for myself. I sent her to look to Jack Huggins's welfare. My task would be easier if I could be sure the boy was cared for.

More help was arriving all the time as word spread, or as people looked out and saw the glow in the sky and guessed what it meant. They came from all directions, on foot or on horseback, in traps or carts that were left haphazard about yards and lane while their occupants ran to offer whatever help was needed.

We formed a chain, swinging heavy buckets from hand to hand, passing empty buckets back. Johnny remained last in line, scooping up the water from the pond, wet to the thighs and ankle-deep in mud. The breeze that drove the fire also cleared the skies, so that stars and moon lent their pale light to the livid scene. The rickyard was alive with brilliant blazing light, with smoke that drifted and eddied in choking clouds, with a fierce noise of crackling and roaring. The stacks blazed all down one side of the yard. Dark figures of men and women moved against that awful glare, working to contain the fire.

In a burst of noise and motion, two horses raced into the yard drawing a fire appliance which bristled with men who swiftly unharnessed and dragged it into position. It came from Feltham Grange. Robert Wyatt had brought it, along with extra hands to help. A long hose was unrolled, its end thrown deep in the pond to suckle while the men began working the handles on either side, pumping up and down. Soon water spurted from the nozzle. But not enough.

'The hose is blocked!' someone yelled. 'For God's sake, men... Unblock the hose!'

Another horseman galloped into the confusion. He launched himself from the saddle and strode urgently about, grasping arms to whirl people round, demanding, 'Where's Mrs Pooley? Mrs Pooley! Where—'

My heart lurched with gladness. Geoffrey had come.

Someone pointed, and he saw me. For a split second we stared at each other through the livid shadows and I saw the relief that flooded through him. He had been afraid for me. But, seeing me safe, he turned to matters more urgent, going to help with the faulty hose. Our personal concerns could wait. For now it was enough that he had come.

Faint in the distance, I seemed to hear a bell. Others heard it, too. Someone said, 'Listen,' and for a moment we all paused with heads cocked to hear the brazen jangling that was coming closer. It passed by Wood Lodge, turning into the farm lane.

With a rumble of wheels, a clanging of bells, a furore of galloping hooves and tossing manes, four matched blacks stormed through the gateway, pulling a fire engine that gleamed with fresh paint and polished brass. I saw the royal crest on its side – it was the Sandringham fire engine, and with it ten stalwart men in black uniforms with gleaming brass helmets on their heads. An involuntary cheer went up from my weary helpers.

Soon another stream of water was pumping on to the fire, while the bucket chain resumed with an extra surge of energy. The Sandringham engine had given us hope that we might, after all, conquer the fire before it consumed all of the corn.

Streams ran down the yard where still the buckets passed. But slowly, noticeably, the fires were subsiding. Their glare was fading, leaving the glimmer of a few lanterns hazy yellow in the smoke that lingered to taint the moonlight.

I took a moment to investigate a dull pain in my forearm and found my sleeve sticky with blood. The doctor later removed three shot-gun pellets – McDowall's murderous attack, though thwarted by the boy Jack, hadn't quite missed. For the moment, realising it was not serious, I ignored it. There was too much else to occupy me.

Through blurred, aching eyes, I began to identify some of the figures working so hard to salvage what they could. There was Ned Plant rounding up the horses, and with him the current backus boy, a lad not more than nine years old; the local blacksmith lent his muscle to the fire engine team. Beside him, to my relief, was Ben Chilvers, safe and well, and not far away the gamekeeper Twistle and a couple of his lads; Reverend Lancaster, hatless, was among villagers, men and women, young and old, who formed the bucket chain; my brother Johnny was with them, too, and the maid Finch; Robert Wyatt was also in the thick of it, directing the pumping of the Feltham fire engine. And there – there! where I let my sore eyes dwell for a moment of weary content, was Geoffrey, tending Mrs Benstead, who seemed to have got a piece of chaff in her eye.

But when I looked further my mind played tricks; among familiar local faces I fancied I recognised the handsome, dark-haired Duke Francis of Teck.

Even as I blinked to clear my eyes of the illusion, someone called out, 'That's enough! Enough! It's out.'

A great sigh went up as everyone relaxed. I found myself weeping and laughing, laughing and weeping, embracing those about me and crying incoherent thanks. Part of the corn was ruined. But part was saved. That was what mattered – that, and the fact that so many people had come to help me – people I had known all my life; people I had greeted in the streets; people I had nursed, children I had dandled, mothers I had visited, fathers I had employed...

It humbled me to think they had all turned out at my need.

Now that the struggle was ended, we became aware of the wet and the cold, our clothes soaked from pond water, our muscles aching, our eyes stinging. In glimmering darkness shot through by streaks of light from a lantern or two, the scent of charred straw came dank. I daren't think what sight awaited me in the stackyard in the morning.

'You all deserve a drink,' I called to those around me. 'Come up to the house. Finch – see to it. Get some of the men to help. There's ale, or brandy. And tea if anyone wants it.'

A thin cheer went up as most of the crowd made a surge towards the house on its rise beyond the lane. The maids would see that everyone's thirst was wetted. For the moment I needed to be sure the horses and the bullocks were safe. And Jack. Of course, Jack!

'They took him up to the house,' someone said – it was Mrs Taggart, the shepherd's wife. 'Miss Wyatt went with him. Mrs Benstead, too. And the doctor.'

'Ah. Good.' If Doctor Hardy had come from the lodge then Jack was well enough cared for and I could allow myself to think of other things.

My injured arm was aching now, still seeping blood that had soaked down to my hand and made my fingers sticky.

'Well, Rose.' Johnny stood before me, dishevelled and exhausted, muddied to the knees and beyond from wading into the pond.

'Well, Johnny…' I returned with a grimace that stretched the scorched skin on my cheek. 'A fine homecoming. When did you arrive?'

'I'm not sure what time it was. I got a lift on the carrier's cart from the station. I hadn't been here long when we saw the fire. What's been happening?'

'Too much.'

Not even trying to explain, I made across the yard.

Outside the stable, where the horses had been tethered back in their stalls, a knot of men had gathered, arguing and discussing. Ned Plant held aloft a lantern whose yellow light shone on the streaked and sweating faces about him. Among them were several game-keepers – some of the ones who had so rudely roused me the previous night.

In the midst of the group, Geoffrey looked grim as he listened to what Ben Chilvers was saying. The carpenter was apparently telling him the story of the night's events. All the men were eager to have their say, to recount their own experience. I saw Johnny listening intently to it all.

At their feet, McDowall lay on his side on the ground, hands trussed behind his back, still squirming now and then as if testing the strength of his bonds. He was securely tied, both at wrists and ankles. The eye I could see was closed by a reddened swelling.

He had left his companions to go about their own work while he came to the farm and fired my stacks. In fleeing from the yards after attempting to shoot me, he had blundered into Ben Chilvers in the darkness. The second barrel of the gun had gone off – harmlessly, thank God – and a brief struggle had ensued. Bruises from that encounter still showed when the steward was arraigned before the magistrate and sent for trial on charges which included arson and attempted murder.

His confederate Pyke was arrested that same evening while trespassing with dogs in the game preserves in Commodore Wood, and with him they captured Davy Timms. Timms won leniency because of the evidence he gave, which sent Pyke and McDowall away for a long time.

But that was yet to come.

'What shall we do with him, sir?' Ned Plant was asking Geoffrey.

'If I had my way,' Geoffrey answered darkly, 'I'd string him from the nearest beam. But since we're law-abiding citizens I suggest you lock him up in a secure place and keep a guard on him until the constable arrives. The constable has been sent for, I assume?'

Several voices assured him of that.

'Let's put him in the root shed,' Benstead suggested with the belligerent air of one who sees a chance to redress old grievances. 'I'll stand guard.'

'*I'm* taking charge of him,' the keeper Twistle said, shouldering his way forward. 'Got one or two questions to ask him about some dogs. Though some of you can stand your watch if you please.'

Several of them, including Ben Chilvers, hoisted McDowall's struggling, cursing body on to their shoulders and bore him away.

A man beside me – whom I discovered to be Robert Wyatt – said, 'You should be inside, Rose. There's nothing more you can do tonight. Let me take you up to the house.'

His fingers fastened just where my arm was burning from the shotgun pellets, making me wince away from his hold. I saw Geoffrey watching, his face bathed in pale lamplight, bleak with weariness, grimed with dirt, his eyes dark expressionless pools. What had he surmised from that small intimacy of Robert's?

'Are you hurt?' Robert asked sharply.

'It's nothing.'

A flash of white drew my attention as a portly figure, until then anonymous in the darkness, stepped into the light and took out a handkerchief to wipe his brow. 'What excitement! I gather the villain has been apprehended. Not only an arsonist but a desecrator of game preserves, it seems. He'll be severely punished. Rest assured of that, Mrs Pooley.'

I peered at him, trusting neither my eyes nor my ears, but both senses continued to confirm that the Prince of Wales himself stood before me. He had been in the shadows with three other men whom I now identified. One of them, unmistakable as he stepped smiling into the light, bowing elegantly to me, was indeed the handsome Francis, Duke of Teck. The second was the Maharajah of Jaipur, and the third I did not know, except that he too had been among the Guns that morning. All of them were dressed for the evening, and even in that light I could see that their fine clothes were dishevelled, damp and smoke-smudged.

All the indications said the prince and his companions had been deeply involved in that evening's adventures. The prince was carrying one of the shiny brass helmets worn by his fire engine team, and his white gloves were smudged across the palms and fingers. Had he ridden on his own fire appliance to come to my aid?

'I'm impressed,' he informed me. 'I've witnessed a fine show of community spirit here tonight, my dear Mrs Pooley. You evidently have a great many friends on Sandringham estate. It bears out what I've been discovering – which in turn confirms all that my dear wife has so often told me. She is very fond of you, you know.'

'Sir?' I managed, a hand to my spinning head.

He came closer, taking my arm to draw me a little apart so that he might speak to me privately. 'After our little chat the other day I had someone make a few enquiries,' he informed me in an undertone. 'I learned only this evening that you were right about Beck – he's been more than zealous in his duties. If I had known what was happening I should not have allowed it to continue, but no one bothers to tell me these things.'

413

Because you generally refuse to listen, thought I.

'However,' he added, 'I intend to make amends.'

'You're very kind, sir,' I murmured, not without misgivings – his idea of 'making amends' was usually to issue invitations and order his toadies to do the same, as if his patronage could heal every slight.

'Not at all. Not at all.' He took my hand, patting it consolingly. 'Things will be different from now on. Why...' Noticing someone standing nearby, listening, he peered through the shadows, 'Who's this? Can it be your brother?'

'Yes, sir. My brother John Hamilton.'

Putting off his intimate, confiding self, the prince resumed his favourite public persona, bluff and hearty, affable man among men, greeting Johnny with a warm handshake. 'Well, now, young Hamilton, you've chosen a fine time to come home, it appears.'

'Yes, sir,' Johnny mourned. 'Just when Orchards is facing ruin.'

'Nonsense, boy! Don't be such a pessimist. You should try to cultivate some of that fine fighting spirit your sister's always shown. Damme if she hasn't had me on the hop more than once!' He laughed uproariously – his high humour said he had enjoyed his adventure of that evening. 'A fine woman. Fine blood in her veins.' Struck by a thought, he turned again to me, adding, 'Your mother was a Colworth, was she not? Yes, I thought so. Can't let that strain go to waste. You ought to be married again. We'll have to see who we can find for you. Someone with grit in his craw, eh?'

The thought of having a husband chosen by His Royal Highness was less than blissful, but another thought bothered me more. Although it was hardly the time, there might never come another moment like this; so I said, 'And what of Orchards, sir? Unless my brother retains the tenancy, everything my father worked for will—'

'Oh, pish and tush!' His Royal Highness chided, waving a hand in my face. 'What do you take me for, Mrs Pooley? Am I an ogre? Am I so high-handed? Of course your brother shall have the farm. I'm delighted to welcome him home to Sandringham. Be ready to accept invitations, both of you. As to the farm, my solicitor will draw up a new agreement – concerning future rights, and due damages and suchlike. We must have these things clearly understood. The papers will be ready for you to sign in a week or two, young Hamilton. If there's anything my chap's forgotten, have your sister go down and chivvy him, eh?'

Johnny, bemused by such largesse, stammered something.

'Oh, and – those new cottages I'm building in West Newton,' His Royal Highness went on. 'I've told Beck that two of 'em are to be allocated for use by Orchards men. You can assign them to those that best deserve them. Will that please you, Mrs Pooley?'

Such unlooked-for generosity, at such a moment, overcame me. I couldn't speak for emotion.

'Oh, come now. Come! Don't weep, my dear.' He put his handkerchief into my hands and laid his arm about my shoulders, pressing me close to his side, saying in an intimate undertone, 'Come, it's not so bad. Orchards will thrive under your brother. I'll see to that. Pray, don't distress yourself.'

The note in his voice, allied with the probing of his fingers on my flesh, made me feel hot. In another moment I might have pushed him away and undone all the benefits I had won, but—

'Excuse me, sir,' Geoffrey's voice sounded firm as he intervened, easing me away from the prince's unwelcome attentions.

'Huh?' His Royal Highness squinted up through the lantern's gleam. 'Well! Devlin! What—'

'In all the excitement, you may have forgotten that you're expected at Chelderton Manor, sir. You have an engagement to dine with Lord Endersleigh.'

'Good Lord! Hah, hah! So I have. Completely forgot.'

'And perhaps a change of clothes…' Geoffrey murmured.

The prince glanced down at himself. 'You're right, Devlin. Can't appear in public soaked to the skin and grimy with smoke, eh? Though it would put some pep into the party, damned if it wouldn't. Stir 'em up a bit. D'you think old Endersleigh will believe our excuse for being late? He knows I find him a pompous old bore. Still,' with a sly grin for me, 'he won't dare sit down to dine without us.'

Laughing, he and his party departed, brushing off the thanks I belatedly called after them.

His going made the few who remained as spectators start to move away, heading for the house and the promised refreshment. Johnny went with them, surrounded by a group of delighted men who suddenly saw their future secured. The new master was home; the prince was smiling again. It augured well.

I found myself standing between Robert and Geoffrey, aware of the animosity tingling in the silence between them.

'Well, if you'll excuse me...' Geoffrey began.

Was he leaving? I turned to him in dismay, and saw him give me a tight little smile.

'I too am expected at Lord Endersleigh's for dinner. I was about to dress for the evening when I saw the fire from my window. Perhaps we can talk tomorrow.'

'Yes. Yes, come tomorrow. Please.'

He gave me a grave, intimate look. 'I shall be here. Good night, Mrs Pooley,' and, with a nod for Robert, 'Good night, Wyatt.'

As he strode away I suddenly wanted to weep and I realised how tired I was – physically tired, emotionally wrung. My body ached and my arm was throbbing. I daren't even think what the morrow's dawn would reveal.

'You're a damn fool, Rose,' Robert said roughly. 'How long can you go on playing with fire? I thought you were going to come away with me and forget him.'

'That's one thing I shall never do,' I replied.

'What – come with me?'

'Forget him.' Shivering a little in the cold and damp, I looked up into his face. 'Knowing that, Robert, would you still want me?'

–

Another sleepless night followed. Though the doctor had removed the shot-gun pellets and dressed the wound with a bandage, it remained painful.

At first light I went down to the yards to see what awaited me. The men were gathering, wandering curiously about and discussing the fire. Perhaps a third of the stackyard was a sodden, blackened mess. Some of the other corn was soaked through and might have to be written off. Clearing up would be no easy task.

'Well, what about it?' I asked Ned Plant. 'Heaven knows our new steward will have his work cut out, but the job's yours, if you'll take it.'

Yesterday he had glowed at the suggestion, today he only looked glum. 'I'm not sure as I warrant the honour, Miss Rose.'

'Why not?'

'Well... I blame myself for all o' this trouble. I knew he was a wrong 'un. But – blast if I thought he'd a gone this far. I never dreamed as how he'd wholly turn against you, Miss Rose.'

'Don't blame yourself,' I sighed. 'None of us guessed it would come to this.'

'Still, I should've known.' He shuffled his feet, looked at me askance.

'Beating our breasts and apportioning blame isn't going to get this farm back to rights! I need you, Plant. The farm needs you. What do you say?'

He drew himself up, taking a long breath. 'That'll be a privilege, Miss Rose. Thank you, Miss Rose.'

'Don't thank me,' I said ruefully. 'I'll expect you to earn your pay. Gentlemen!' The call drew the men towards me. 'From now on you'll take your orders from your new steward – Mr Plant. I know I can count on all of you to give him your best support. Very well, Mr Plant, take over. I leave you in charge.'

'Right, then.' Wearing his new authority with pride and assurance, Plant began to assign the men to their morning tasks. I had a feeling he would do well.

As I moved away, Johnny came striding across the yard, pale and bleary-eyed, looking as if he had leapt straight out of a deep sleep, dragged his clothes on and come out. He stopped beside me, staring at the state of the rickyard, shaking his head and sighing. 'It's even worse than I feared. What are we going to do?'

'What we always do in such cases. We lick our wounds, count our losses, thank God it wasn't worse – and carry on. It's a challenge for you. But it's not total disaster.'

A shudder ran through him. He folded his arms, hugging himself for warmth, his eyes on the activity in the rickyard. 'You know I said that… that you'd have to leave when I came home?'

'Yes?'

His face twisted as he glanced at me sidelong. 'Miss Wyatt thinks you're going to set up home with her. And last night her brother hinted that you might be thinking of emigrating with him.'

'Those are two of my choices.'

'Then you haven't decided yet?'

'Not entirely.'

Squinting against the growing light in the sky, he huddled closer into himself and looked up at the barn, where a cock was crowing as if trying to rouse the entire county. Whatever Johnny was trying to say was evidently difficult for him; his Hamilton pride was squirming.

'One reason I didn't want to come back…' he said eventually. 'I think I was afraid. Father assumed I could do it, but I wasn't so sure, and last night when I finally realised what a responsibility it all is… I don't think I can do it without help, Rose.'

Knowing what it had cost for him to make that admission, I tucked my hand under his arm and regarded him fondly. Despite the scent of burning that still haunted the yards, despite the ruined cornstacks and the mess everywhere, I felt a spring of optimism rise in me. 'Whatever made you think you had to?'

'I wanted to be like Father.'

'Father didn't start out alone! He had Farmer Pooley as his mentor. And he made mistakes. We all do.'

'Then… will you stay, at least until I get settled? Without even a steward…'

'We have a steward,' I informed him, a little wryly. 'I'm afraid I appointed Ned Plant, just this morning. I should have consulted with you first, I suppose. You'll have to bear with me, I've become too used to making decisions on my own.'

A trace of a smile lightened his gloom. 'He's a good man.'

'You'll not find a better. We're fortunate to have him. In fact… I think we can count ourselves fortunate in many ways.'

'Fortunate? We've just lost half our harvest!'

'We might have lost it all,' I reminded him. 'But it had been raining heavily, so everything was damp. And Jack Huggins had his wits about him, so we discovered the fire sooner rather than later. We might have lost lives, too, if McDowall had had his way. So, yes, I'd say we were lucky.'

'Even though we'll make a financial loss this year?'

'There are more important things. Anyway, Uncle Jonathan may be more willing to talk about a loan now you're here – especially while we're in favour with the big house. If we get that new agreement the prince promised… You know, I've a feeling he's under pressure – from his mother and his wife – to be more reasonable over the game. Oh, it will never be easy, playing tenant to His Royal Highness, but let's make the most of it, while he's smiling on us.'

Walking beside him, my hand under his arm – in the way I once walked with Victor – we returned to the house for breakfast.

Orchards House was busier than it had been for years. In one room Mary McDowall rested, with her children not far away. In another Jack Huggins lay with his ribs tightly strapped, being looked after as if he were a lordling because – as he himself immodestly claimed – 'It was me what saved Miss Rose's life. That villain would've shot her, if it hadn't been for me.' Well, it was true, so how could I begrudge him his glory? Felicity had taken charge of both invalids and was happily busy with so much caring to do, while in the kitchen Mrs Benstead planned menus and the maids came and went about their chores.

In a quiet moment before breakfast, I went into the drawing-room, where a newly-built fire was licking its yellow flames round the coals, making them start to glow and send out heat. From above the mantel, Mother's portrait gazed out, her eyes seeming to meet mine levelly, gently... expectantly?

She didn't belong here any more, I realised. She was *my* mother, but not Johnny's. This was his place now, and when he felt more secure he wouldn't need me any more. When I left, I would remove Hester from Orchards and leave Johnny free to replace her with a portrait of Mama, his own mother, if he so wished. When I left...

It struck me that I didn't belong at Orchards any more, either. My task was done, my quest fulfilled, the promise kept that had been made to Father. In a short while, when Johnny was settled, I would be free to leave.

And go where? So many options lay open to me. The childless Aunt Beatrice would welcome me at Weal House as a companion for her old age; Felicity offered a place as *her* companion. Or I could become a governess, or a schoolteacher, as Aunt Agnes had planned.

Should I choose to remarry? Should I go to New Zealand with Robert Wyatt? Or should I risk the gossip – and the formidable Lady Devlin - assuming that Geoffrey still wanted me?

So many roads... But I already knew which one I most wanted to take.

As I stood there, communing with my mother's ghost, I realised that for the first time in my life I was free to make my own choice, for my own reasons. No constraints remained – no father, no husband; no farm to make demands, not even convention or the possible disapproval of society – or even of the Hamiltons – for I had been through that fire and it no longer held terrors for me. For the first time in my life I was myself: not a daughter needing approval, not a niece to be moulded by a maiden aunt, not a child to be chastised or a wife unwanted. I was a woman in my own right, tempered by fire – Rose Mary Hester Hamilton Pooley.

'Hester's girl,' I murmured to myself, believing I saw an answering gleam in my mother's eye. Perhaps at last I had become the woman she had wanted me to be – the daughter she had given her life for. I had a feeling that she – and Father – would have been proud to see me now, despite my imperfections.

''Scuse me, Miss Rose.' A flustered Swift dipped a curtsey from the doorway. 'I said you hadn't had breakfast yet but he—'

'I couldn't wait,' Geoffrey finished for her as he pushed the door wider and stepped past her. He was still wearing evening clothes; he was unshaven and he looked tired, but there was determination in his eyes and the set of his mouth. 'I know it's early. Or perhaps it's late. I haven't slept. I was at Chelderton Manor until after three. Talking with the prince. And now I want to talk to you. And I want you to t-talk to me. Once and for all, Rose—'

'Thank you, Swift. That will be all,' I said, nodding at the goggling maid. 'Close the door behind you. And make sure we're not disturbed.'

Let the kitchen make of that what it would.

When she had gone, Geoffrey threw off his cloak and came to crouch by the fire, holding his hands to the growing blaze. 'It's chilly this morning.'

'Yes, I noticed.' Unable to resist some small contact, I touched his hair, feeling the silky strands against my fingers. 'You should have had some rest. Though I'm glad you came.'

He didn't answer me at once. He seemed to be lost in his own thoughts, staring at the fire; then all at once he turned to kneel at my feet and fasten his arms about my waist, burying his face against me. 'I didn't get your message until this morning. When I got home from Chelderton the girl gave me your note. I didn't even wait to get changed. Rose, my love… You did need me, after all.'

'Of course I needed you,' I responded, holding him to me. 'I have always needed you.'

He looked up at me, a new light of hope in his eyes. 'Then are you ready to give me your promise? You'll marry me, when the time is right?'

'If you will have me.'

In a rush of motion he got to his feet and reached for me, but stopped himself and, sobering, let his hands fall. 'First... First I should tell you something. I've been to Canterbury.'

'Canterbury?' My heart hesitated and then beat on swifter and swifter – my heart understood, even if my head didn't.

Reaching into an inside pocket, he took out a slim leather wallet. Inside it, he had a photograph which he gave to me. It showed a pretty young girl with long curling hair. She was wearing an apron over a neat tartan dress, and in her hands she held a whip and top. She was, I knew, ten years old.

As I stared down at it, the picture blurred through a haze of tears. 'Is this...?'

'Her name's Annabel,' he said.

I couldn't have spoken, even if I had known what to say. Annabel? I would never have called her, that!

'I employed a detective to find her,' Geoffrey said. 'It took a long time, but in the end, with the help of Doctor Proudfoot, the man obtained the information which led him to Canterbury. When he told me what he'd found, I decided to travel down there myself.'

Again I waited, my finger stroking the smooth surface of the picture, touching the image of my lost child.

'Her adopted father's a sub-dean at the cathedral,' he said. 'His wife was once a nurse. She served in the Crimea with Miss Nightingale. She knew your aunt, Miss Agnes Hamilton.'

I could only nod. Yes. Yes, go on.

'They're good people, I can assure you of that. Annabel is their only child, and very dear to them. She's a beautiful child, happy and unafraid. She has your eyes, your smile...' He took a long breath, adding more quietly, 'She put me in mind of Lucy. That was how Lucy should have been – untouched, innocent, her young life unmarred by adult vices...

'I couldn't bring myself to harm that innocence. To have wrenched her away, brought her here... it would not have been fair to her. Or to you.'

Lifting drowned eyes, I found him watching me sadly.

'You understand, don't you?' he asked. 'They let me meet her and talk with her, but I didn't tell her who I was. They've promised to keep us informed of her welfare. I'll settle some money on her, and

perhaps when she comes of age we'll tell her who she really is. But…
Much as I wanted to, I couldn't bring her back with me. Not now.
Not yet. To her, you and I are strangers.'

'I know that,' I managed hoarsely. 'I'm just… I'm so glad to know
she's well, and happy.' I looked down at the picture, knowing it would
be etched on my heart for ever. So long I had waited, yearned, and
wondered. To have this much of her was more than I had ever hoped
for. It would be enough. 'May I keep this?'

'Of course. I brought it for you. Oh, my love…' Gathering me to
him, he held me close and I let my arms slip round him, leaning on
him, comforted by his nearness.

There was so much I wanted to share with him – the truth about
the accident at Onion Corner; the truth about my marriage; my hopes
and fears and despairs through all the long years we had been apart.
But that would come later, at leisure. We had all the time in the world.
For now it was enough that we were together, with the rest of our lives
still to come.

'Why have you kept me waiting for so long?' he asked. 'I hoped
you would write to me from France, but no letter came. And then I
heard you were back in Norfolk and I looked in vain for a message.
Many an evening I've driven by and watched the house – watched the
lamp glow in your room – sat at your gate and willed you to look out,
or even to spare me a thought.'

I lifted my head, saying, 'I've thought of you constantly.'

His arms loosened their hold on me. 'That wasn't the impression
I had last night. You appeared to have a whole c-covey of admirers
running to your aid.'

Knowing jealousy when I heard it, I refused to give it credence by
denying it, even if he wasn't entirely serious. 'I needed them all.'

'Then perhaps I was superfluous.'

'What nonsense! You know that's not true! I wanted you above all.
Oh, love… until now I wasn't free to think of my own future. I've
been too busy. Fighting to keep the farm; battling with the prince;
having my steward turn against me, my harvest destroyed, being shot
at… But I've thought of you all the time, and missed you, and wanted
you—'

As I spoke of being shot at, I instinctively cradled my arm, drawing
his attention to it, and then to the bandage that showed beneath my
sleeve.

'Were you hurt? No one told me!' Frowning with concern, he laid his hands on my shoulders. 'Shot? By whom?'

'By McDowall. Oh, it's nothing. Just a flesh wound. It bled a little, that's all. I was lucky. Young Jack was there. He shouted to warn me, and then he went for McDowall. Got a rib or two cracked for his pains, but he's bearing up bravely.'

He didn't answer for a moment, he just watched me with a fierce, possessive set to his mouth. 'Did you really miss me?'

'How can you ask that? Yes! Yes, I missed you so much I hurt. Lying awake these long dark nights… If I'd known you were at my gate…'

'Oh, my love!' he muttered hoarsely, reaching for me, his mouth taking possession of mine and his arms closing about me to hold me achingly close, confirming all that lay between us, making promises for the future…

When at length we broke apart, he touched my face, tracing the line of my cheek as he surveyed me with tender eyes.

'Will you marry me?'

'I've said so.'

'I want to hear you say it again,' he informed me. 'I need to be thoroughly convinced that it's true.' A little smile curved his mouth and made his eyes gleam. 'Not that you have a deal of choice in the matter. You may not know it, but you're obliged to marry me now, whether you like it or not. It's by way of being a royal command.'

'Indeed?' I felt dizzy with happiness. 'And how could that be?'

He was watching my mouth hungrily. 'I told you I spent half the night talking to the prince. I told him everything. He understands, love. We have his blessing. With his approval, and his friendship, the gossips won't dare speak against us. After he has been so kind as to offer his patronage, you wouldn't dare offend him by refusing me, would you?'

It would not be as easy as he foresaw, but it didn't matter. Whatever lay ahead, Geoffrey and I would face it, together. For now I was content. For now a bubble of joy was waiting to burst inside me. 'Blackmail, Mr Devlin?'

'Blackmail, coercion… kidnap, if I have to.' Fierce passion burned in his eyes as he swept me more tightly against him, adding, 'I shall never risk losing you again. Not for a day. Not for a minute. You're mine, Rose Hamilton. Now and for ever. You're mine!'